Joss Wood loves books and traveling—especially to the wild places of Southern Africa and, well, anywhere. She's a wife, a mum to two teenagers and slave to two cats. After a career in local economic development, she now writes full-time. Joss is a member of Romance Writers of America and Romance Writers of South Africa.

When **Lauren Canan** began writing, stories of romance and unbridled passion flowed through her fingers onto the page. Today she is a multi-award-winning author, including the prestigious Romance Writers of America Golden Heart® Award. She lives in Texas with her own real-life hero, two chaotic dogs and a mouthy parrot named Bird. Find her on Facebook or visit her website, laurencanan.com

THAT NIGHT
IN TEXAS

JOSS WOOD

MARRIAGE
AT ANY PRICE

LAUREN CANAN

MILLS & BOON

First Published in Great Britain 2019
by Mills & Boon, an imprint of HarperCollinsPublishers,
1 London Bridge Street, London, SE1 9GF

That Night in Texas © 2019 by Harlequin Books S.A.
Marriage at Any Price © 2019 Sarah Cannon

Special thanks and acknowledgement are given to Joss Wood for
her contribution to the Texas Cattleman's Club: Houston series.

ISBN: 978-0-263-27179-9

0519

MIX
Paper from
responsible sources
FSC® C007454

This book is produced from independently certified FSC™
paper to ensure responsible forest management.

For more information visit: www.harpercollins.co.uk/green

Printed and bound in Spain
by CPI, Barcelona

THAT NIGHT
IN TEXAS

JOSS WOOD

Rebecca Crowley—amazing writer and Jozi survivor—
thanks for sharing Houston with me.
And for introducing me to Mexican beer,
Colombian food and pumping your own gas.
It'll be a trip I'll always remember.

Nkosi Sikelel' iAfrika

One

Vivi Donner gripped her steering wheel and leaned forward, hoping that the extra couple of inches would help her see better through the gray, dense fog. It was another awful day after a string of terrible days, and like the rest of the residents of Houston, Texas, she felt both battered and shattered. After the storm that had led to devastating flooding, a blast of sunshine would help. But a clear day would also force Houston to face the destruction that had been caused and to take stock of the extensive damage to homes and buildings. Vivi jerked her eyes off to the side and the fog cleared just enough for her to see the piles of debris, broken branches and ruined furniture on the sidewalks.

Thank God her house, and that of Clem's sitter, Charlie, was undamaged. The same couldn't be said for The Rollin' Smoke, the famed barbecue restaurant where she worked as head chef.

According to Joe, the owner and her mentor, her beautiful, newly updated kitchen was ruined. The renovations to the restaurant had been finished just six weeks ago, and the new floor, booths, tables and chairs were all wrecked, as well. Garbage and debris still covered the floor, and all hands, including hers, were needed on deck.

As the head chef who answered only to Joe, she could wait until her staff did the heavy lifting and cleaning before she returned, but she wasn't a prima donna. How could she be? She'd worked her way up the ladder at the restaurant—albeit in record time—from dishwasher to head chef, but she still knew how to get her hands dirty.

Joe's name might be on the deeds to the eatery but The Rollin' Smoke was hers, dammit, and Vivi wanted to be there to pick it up and dry it off.

Seeing that the road ahead was closed, Vivi turned down a side road. The fog was thicker here, and her visibility was rapidly decreasing. If it got much worse, she'd have to stop and wait it out, but that could take hours. Where was that damn sun? She lifted one hand from the steering wheel and rubbed her hand on her soft denims, trying to wipe away the perspiration. God, this was scary.

The ringing of her phone had her butt lifting two inches off her seat. Fumbling, she hit the screen to answer the call. "God, Joe, you scared me!"

"Are you in the car? Please tell me you're not driving!" Joe's voice rose in panic.

"Actually, I'm crawling along." That way, nothing bad could happen.

"Turn around, go back home."

Vivi fought the urge to do exactly that. She wanted to pick up Clem and take her back to their house, climb into bed and pull the covers over their heads and hide out from the world. But she'd done that for the first quarter century of her life and she refused to live like that again. Life was for living, dammit, and part of that living was accepting the good with the bad.

Having Clem and being her mom was not just good but stupendously awesome. On the flip side, a devastating storm and the resulting flood was bad—*terrible*—but it had happened, and she had to deal with it.

"I have a job to do and a restaurant to clean up so that our lives can return to normal as soon as possible. A little destruction won't stop the ravenous appetites of Houston meat eaters," Vivi told Joe, ignoring the sense that she was standing on a precipice. She had a feeling that nothing would ever be the same again.

Vivi shivered as a cold chill ran up and down her spine. Her mom would've said that a devil was dancing on her spine, but Vivi shook that thought away. Her mom's superstitions and beliefs, a curious mix of religion and craziness, no longer had a place in her life.

She was just freaked out by the fog, the lack of streetlights, the whistling wind and the piles of debris she occasionally caught a glimpse of in her weak headlights. They all contributed to the spooky atmosphere.

"Just be careful, please," Joe begged her before disconnecting the call.

Another shiver raised the hair on her arms and Vivi swore. Dropping her eyes, she looked down and located the temperature controls. She punched the button to warm the interior of the car. It was hot and humid outside, but her body had other ideas.

Grateful for the blast of warm air, Vivi checked her rearview mirror and saw a cop car on her tail, blue lights flashing. Vivi scanned the road ahead of her, cursing when she realized there was nowhere to pull over. He was close to her tail and she saw, in her rearview mirror, big hands fly up in obvious frustration. He needed to be somewhere else and she was in his way. Her only option was to speed up and hope a spot would soon appear where she could pull over.

Vivi flexed her fingers and took a deep breath. And as soon as she accelerated she saw the spooky outline of a tree in her path. She slammed the brakes, felt her car slide, then fishtail. She spun her wheel and tapped her accelerator to pull her out of the slide.

Her engine roared and her lungs constricted as the car scrambled for purchase on the slick surface. She heard the ping of gravel hitting her paint. Gravel was better than slick asphalt, she decided. She'd be out of this mess in a minute. Then she'd stop, restart her heart and go home and cuddle Clem.

She might even pull those blankets up around her head, just for a little while.

But those thoughts were short-lived when she felt the car bounce over some uneven ground right before she felt the nose of the car dipping. Her vehicle slid down an embankment, its underside scraping over rocks and debris, and she looked out her window onto a gully containing swiftly running, black water. Her veins iced up and panic closed her throat. She was heading for that cold, foul water. God, there had to be something she could do to save herself, but her brain refused to engage.

Clem's beautiful face, those bright blue eyes and impish smile, swam across her vision as water covered her feet and soaked her jeans. As it crawled up her thighs, she felt Clem's arms around her neck, her gentle breath on her face.

Open the damn window, woman.

The voice in her head was from the past, but his tone was hard and demanding. Vivi slapped her hand on the button and the window slid down. A hard wave of water rocked her sideways, but she felt a strong hand on her shoulder and a comforting presence.

You can do this. Just keep calm.

Why was she hearing Camden McNeal's voice in her head? She looked to the passenger seat, almost expecting to see the sexy ex-oil rigger there, tall and broad and so damn sexy. Clem's eyes in a masculine, tough face.

Take a deep breath...and another...

The water hit her chin and drops of dirt smacked her lips. Vivi took in another deep breath as water covered her head.

Hold on to the wheel and release your seat belt...

She pushed the lever and felt the seat belt drift away. Without it anchoring her to her seat, she felt buffeted by the water. Panic clawed at her stomach, twisting her brain. A twig scraped over her eyebrow and Vivi closed her eyes. What was the point of keeping them open? She couldn't see a damn thing as it was.

Survival instinct kicked in and she banged the frame of the open window, fighting the urge to haul in a breath.

She had to live. She had a little girl to raise. Grabbing the frame, she fought the water, scrabbling as she placed her feet against the console and tried to push herself through the open window. But she felt like she was trying to push through a concrete wall.

Wait five seconds and try again...

I don't have five damn seconds, Vivi mentally screamed.

Sure you do.

Vivi cursed him, her hands gripping the door frame.

Five thousand one, five thousand two—God, she needed air—five thousand—

She couldn't wait any longer. Completely convinced that she was about to die, Vivi pushed against the console, pulled against the window frame and shot out of the car. It was dark and cold and scary, but there was light above her. She'd head for that. Light was good, light was safety…

Light meant Clem.

She was so close—her fingers were an inch from the surface—but her lungs were about to burst. Another kick, another pull…

Vivi's head broke the surface and she pulled in one life-affirming breath before darkness hauled her away.

Camden McNeal placed his palm on the window of his home office and looked out at the disappearing fog. He rolled his shoulders, trying to ease the tension in his shoulders and his back. He'd swallowed some painkillers a half hour ago, but the vise squeezing his brain had yet to release its claws. He felt like he was about to jump out of his skin.

Lifting his coffee mug to his lips, he took a large sip, enjoying the smooth taste of the expensive imported roast. He waited for the warmth to hit his stomach, but when it did, it burned rather than comforted. What the hell was wrong with him?

Yeah, the past few days hadn't been fun. Houston had been slapped senseless by a devastating storm and there were many people out there who were in dire straits, although he wasn't one of them. Not this time.

Count your blessings, McNeal…

Punching a number on his phone, he waited impatiently for Ryder to answer his call. "Cam, everything okay with you?"

His old boss and mentor had a way of making Cam feel steadier. Ryder was rock solid, as a colleague and a friend, and it never hurt to have someone like him standing in your corner. "My office is still under water and mud. All my computers are fried."

"Nasty. Hope you backed up," Ryder said.

All the time. "Yep, to a cloud server, so no information has been lost. But two of my guys have lost their houses and possessions." He already had plans in place to get them back on their feet.

"I've closed the office and told my people to care for their homes and families," Cam added.

"Yeah, I think that's standard procedure at the moment. Money and business can wait. There's more important work to do," Ryder agreed. "I spent yesterday working at a shelter. Did you go out last night?"

"Yeah, I was in one of the worst affected areas of the city—and one of the poorest. It was a community search effort to find some missing children. Two of them were found, but the third, a teenage boy, is still missing," Cam told Ryder.

Was that why he was so tense, so worried? He knew what it was like to feel abandoned, to be scared. Sure, he'd never been swept away in a flood, but he did have an idea how it felt to be poor, to live within a world that didn't seem to give a damn about people at the bottom of the pile.

He understood what it felt like to have poverty as your constant companion and hope an emotion you no longer believed in.

Cam's thoughts were pulled up short when Ryder spoke.

"Did you hear that a body was found at the construction site?"

Cam pushed his shoulders back, intrigued by Ryder's statement. "Are you talking about the TCC construction site? Sterling Perry's land?"

"Yes."

The establishment of a Houston branch of the Texas Cattleman's Club and control of it was Ryder and Sterling Perry's latest battle in a decades-old war. Both Stirling and Ryder believed that they were best suited to be the inaugural president of the new club, both wanted to be the first to create the vision of the first TCC in Houston. Neither suffered from a lack of self-confidence.

Cam knew that he'd be one of the first to be invited to join the exclusive club and the opportunity to do business with the other members, both in Houston and in Royal would be worth putting up with the politics and drama. And there seemed to be a lot of drama.

"What caused the accident?" Cam asked.

"A couple of bullets to the chest and a crushed skull."

So, not an accident then.

After discussing the murder and more TCC business, Cam disconnected the call. Walking away from the window and the view of his foggy gardens, he slumped into his butter-soft leather office chair. He tipped his head back and closed his eyes, the photograph of the missing kid flashing on the big screen behind his eyes. Dark hair, dark eyes, a sullen smile. Yeah, he recognized the look of despair in Rick Gaines's eyes, the belief that life was constantly looking for a way to slap him sideways.

It was possible that within a year or two, without help or intervention, Rick would be breaking into cars, dealing, or perhaps even be in a gang. He'd be another lost boy, flirting with jail or addiction. Cam recognized him instantly. After all, wasn't that exactly who he'd been?

Lost, lonely, confused. And Cam couldn't help wondering if Rick was even missing. Nobody had seen him fall into the water; he was simply unaccounted for. There was always the possibility that he'd used the flood as an opportunity to run away from his crappy life. Cam understood. When you were struggling to survive, you used the breaks you received...

Your childhood is behind you. That isn't your life anymore. You are now, and have been for a while, the master of your own destiny.

Cam swallowed the rest of his coffee, annoyed with himself. He didn't have time to wallow around in the cesspool of his past. He still had a massive company to run. Pulling his keyboard toward him, Cam opened his email program and grimaced at the flood of messages. Yep, as he'd expected, the financial world hadn't stopped turning. A couple of clients of his venture capital firm expressed their sympathy about the situation in Houston, but most didn't bother. It didn't affect them, so why waste the energy?

Cam was midway through typing a response to a Singaporean client when his ringing phone broke his concentration. He glanced at the display, didn't recognize the number and considered ignoring the call. Then he remembered that he'd asked the search coordinator to inform him if they located Rick. This could be an update, so he needed to take the call. He hit the speaker button with an impatient finger. "McNeal."

"Camden McNeal?"

"That's me."

"Excellent. You have been listed as the emergency

contact number of a Vivianne Donner. I regret to inform you that Ms. Donner was admitted into the ER this morning after a car accident. When can we expect you?"

Cam pushed a hand through his hair, confused. "I think you have the wrong person. I don't know anyone by that name."

"I have your cell number, sir. You are Camden McNeal, owner of McNeal, Inc., and you live in River Oaks?"

"Yeah, that's correct—"

"You might not know her, but she sure knows you. So, my question remains, how soon can we expect you?"

Cam paced into the lobby of the hospital, his long stride eating up the distance between the doors and the nurses station. He dodged a nurse pushing a pregnant woman in a wheelchair and noticed that the dad-to-be was on the verge of panic. *Rather him than me*, Cam thought. He was the product of two of the most dysfunctional people in the world and what he knew about parenting would fit on a pinhead.

His father had taught him how to steal, to hustle, to slip and slide through life, but mostly his parents had taught him that he could only ever rely on, and take care of, himself. He didn't think he had it in him to put someone else's needs and wants above his own. It wasn't something he'd been shown how to do.

And the one time he'd tried, the only time he'd laid his heart at someone's feet, ring in his hand, Emma had stomped all over it with her three-inch stilettos, her expression a mixture of genuine disbelief and pity.

Darling, you're great in bed, but you're not exactly someone to take into a ballroom. Or into a boardroom, or home to Daddy. You're someone to screw, to keep in the shadows. Marry you? You're ambitious, Cam, I'll give you that, but I'm out of your league.

It had been ten years ago, but, despite her recently making it clear that she'd made a mistake by walking out on him, her little speech was imprinted on his brain, possibly because it closely resembled his father's words of non-encouragement. *"You're a McNeal, you'll never amount to much. None of us ever have and you won't be the first."*

His bank statement and long lists of assets refuted that statement. But Cam was a realist: he might be good at business, but he'd make a lousy father and husband. Hell, judging by how fast that nameless girl in Tarrin left his bed three years ago, he wasn't even that great at one-night stands. Sex, he was good at that, but not so much at the touchy feely stuff woman liked.

Cam slapped his hands on the counter and met the weary eyes of the nurse behind it. "I got a call about a woman who put my name down as an emergency contact. I'm Camden McNeal."

"Patient name?"

Cam tried to recall his earlier conversation. "Dunbar? Dun…something?"

"Donner? Vivianne Donner?"

Cam shrugged. The name didn't mean any more to him now than it had earlier. The nurse tapped her keyboard and nodded. "Room 302. She has severe concussion and she needs a ride home, and someone to take care of her when she gets there. Down the hall, turn right and she'll be on your left."

Cam looked at the long hallway and sighed. Well, it looked like he was about to meet Ms. Donner and maybe he'd find out why he was listed as her emergency contact. Come to think of it, who was listed as *his* emergency contact? Had he ever listed anyone? Not that he could recall.

Reaching the closed door to room 302, Cam knocked gently. And when he received no reply, he eased open the door. He glanced toward the bed and waited for his eyes to adjust to the dim light.

His first impressions were of a long, slim body topped by a cloud of curls the color of lightly toasted caramel. His stomach rumbled at the thought of food. He couldn't remember when he'd last eaten, as it had been a busy, physically draining twenty-four hours. He needed to talk to the woman, get her to take his name off her papers and get some food. Maybe then his headache would finally start to dissipate.

Cam flipped on the overhead light and it took a minute, maybe more, to realize that his eyes weren't playing tricks on him, that his imagination wasn't running riot. He rested his hands on the bed next to her thigh and ordered his racing heart to slow down, his lungs to pull in air. He closed his eyes, re-centered himself and then forced them open again.

Yep, she was still there.

Cam stared down at that stunning face, his heart pounding against his chest in a fight-or-flight reaction. It had been three years, give or take, since he'd seen her last, and damn, she looked, well, *amazing*. Sure, she had three stitches holding a cut together on a finely arched eyebrow, a bruise on her cheek and a scrape across her jaw, and a deep cut on her bottom lip, but her injuries didn't take away from her drop-him-to-his-knees beauty. She'd lost weight and looked like a puff of wind would blow her away.

Turning, Cam saw the chair next to the bed. He hooked his foot around its legs and dragged it toward him. He dropped down into it and placed his forearms on his thighs, resisting the urge to shake her awake. What the hell game was she playing? She had to be playing one, because, let's be honest, everyone did.

He wasn't sure if she'd played him then, but he was certain she was playing him now. Cam stared at her as memories of that dive bar rolled over him. It had been a crap hole, little more than a shack serving watered-down drinks to the ranch hands and the refinery crews working in the area.

He'd been aware of her—Vivianne, he now had a name to go with the stunning face—the moment she stepped into the dive bar, as had every other man in the place. She'd looked so damn young and so very vulnerable with the shot glass in her hand, her eyes on the fiery liquid. He expected her to push it away, to turn tail and run, but she'd squared her shoulders and tossed the liquor back, blinking furiously as she swallowed. She'd banged her glass down, ordered another and slowly, oh so slowly, turned those brown-black eyes in his direction.

"One down, two more experiments to go."

He'd lifted his beer bottle in her direction, noting her long legs in tight, faded denim and the way her white T-shirt hugged the curves of her breasts and skimmed a board-flat stomach.

She was older than he initially thought, somewhere in her midtwenties, yet while they might be close in age, he'd figured he'd lived a thousand more lifetimes—all of them harder and rougher than hers.

He should've ignored her, finished his beer and left, but he'd turned to face her and cocked his head. "You a scientist, sweetheart?"

She'd ignored him at first, taken the second shot and

tossed it down her throat. He'd never managed to forget her answer. She'd wrinkled her nose as she decided how to answer. "Nope. Tonight I'm going to see what being normal feels like."

"There are better bars in better places," Cam had told her, hoping that she'd walk out and leave him to his beer and his loneliness. He knew how to handle his liquor and his solitude, but she had him wanting to drink less and talk more.

She'd plopped that spectacular butt down on the seat next to him, her knee brushing against the outside of his thigh. He'd felt a bolt of desire skitter up his thigh and lodge in his balls. He'd swelled and groaned. He wasn't a kid, so why was he getting turned on by a light touch and a woman who looked like the girl next door and smelled like wildflowers?

"But I can't get to those places and you look like fun."

Cam had almost smiled at that. Him fun? She couldn't be more wrong. He'd thought about leaving her there in the bar, about going back to his motel room with a six-pack, but he couldn't leave her there alone. So he'd bought her a beer and then they'd moved on to a diner for burgers and ended the evening with fantastic sex in a motel room. No names, no expectations and, yeah, he'd had fun.

He'd liked her.

And now, after three years, she was back in his life, lying in a hospital room, dressed in a hospital gown, banged up and bruised. With his name as her emergency contact number. And like back then, his mouth was dry, his heart was thumping and his pants were tight against his crotch. *Peachy.*

What the hell was going on here?

Cam felt her leg jerk and his eyes shot to her face. Her eyelids flickered, and he waited for that burst of brown, braced himself for the sexual punch that was sure to follow. She groaned, half lifted her hand and then dropped it to the bed, as if the action required more energy than she was capable of. Those long eyelashes lifted and he watched as she took a moment to focus. Her mouth tilted at the corners and her expression softened.

"Camden?"

So she knew him, recognized him. Cam frowned when her eyes drifted closed again. Oh, no, he wasn't going to sit next to her bed like a lovelorn admirer waiting for her to wake up. He was exhausted and hungry, dammit. Cam tapped her hand with his finger and slowly her eyelids lifted.

The tip of a pink tongue darted across her top lip and Cam ignored the bolt of lust as he remembered that tongue on his abs, going lower. She'd been inexperienced in that department but very enthusiastic…

Down, boy.

He rubbed his hand over his face, and when he dropped his hand again, the confusion in her eyes was replaced by panic. "Where am I? Where's Clem? Is she okay?"

She started to push herself up, groaning as she sat up. She pushed the covers away and swung those sexy, bare legs to the side. Cam immediately realized that she was trying to climb out of bed. He shot up and placed a hand on her shoulder, pinning her to the pillow. She slapped his hand away and went for the IV, trying to pull the needle from her arm.

"I've got to get to Clem. Let me go, dammit!" Her

breath hitched and panic made her words run together. "What's the time? How late is it? Where's my phone?"

Cam looked at his watch. "It's shortly past eleven."

"It's still Friday morning?"

At his nod, her shoulders dropped three inches and the cords in her neck loosened. She slumped back against her pillow and closed her eyes. "Thank God." She gripped the sheet and twisted the fabric between her fingers. When she spoke again, her voice was thin with pain and exhaustion. "I need to make a call. Can I borrow your phone?"

"Not until I get some answers," Cam told her, stepping back and folding his arms against his chest.

Vivianne released a frustrated sigh. In her eyes he saw a solid streak of stubborn under the obvious exhaustion. "I understand that. But you're not going to get another word out of me until I make a call."

It wasn't worth arguing about. Reaching into the back pocket of his jeans, he pulled out his phone, tapped in the code and handed it to her.

She shook her head. "Sorry, the world is still a bit fuzzy. Can you dial for me?"

Cam punched in the number she gave him, and when it started to ring, he handed the phone over. Vivianne placed her fingers on her forehead before speaking. "Charlie? Is Clem okay?"

Evidently the response reassured her. Those sexy shoulders dropped and the hand gripping the sheet relaxed. Cam tipped his head to the side, thinking that watching her was like witnessing a balloon losing its air. Suddenly she looked paler, more fragile, ten times smaller. And a hundred times more vulnerable.

He stepped forward, realized he was about to pull her into his arms, to offer what comfort he could, and immediately stepped back. What the hell? He didn't do comfort; he wasn't the type.

Vivianne gnawed at her bottom lip, wincing when she encountered the cut she'd made earlier. "Thanks, Charlie. I'll see you later this afternoon, maybe a little earlier if I can."

As if. According to the nurse, she had a concussion and that normally meant an overnight stay. He'd be happy to watch her all night. But only because he wanted to know what she was up to. Not because she was freakin' gorgeous. And not because he found her fascinating, or because he couldn't imagine walking out of this room without knowing when he was going to see her again.

He was just tired. And hungry. That was why he was acting so out of character. *Had to be.*

"Thanks, Charlie."

Cam jammed his hands into the front pockets of his jeans and glowered at her. "Ready to start talking?"

Vivianne sighed. "I don't suppose I have much of a choice."

"Not really, no."

"I'm Vivi Donner, by the way."

Vivi suited her better than *Vivianne.* He rolled the name around his mind and could easily imagine himself whispering it as he kissed her, painting it on her skin as he tongued her. Sighing it as he slid into her hot, wet warmth. Cam gave himself a mental punch to the temple.

Yeah, he was still attracted to her but so what? He was frequently attracted to women. He was a guy and that was what guys did. It was simple biology. It didn't *mean* anything.

"Let's start off with you telling me how you ended up

in a hospital with stitches and scrapes and more bruises than an MMA fighter."

Vivi pushed back that heavy hair and he caught a whiff of citrus and dank water. "According to the nurse, who spoke to the responding EMT, I was driving and it was really foggy. I slid off the road into a gully filled with fast-moving water. I remember going into the water and nothing much after that. The next time I came around, I was in this bed."

Every cell in his body iced over. Few people knew how to escape a car filled with water, yet she had. Thank God.

"A policeman saw me go off the road. The working theory is that I pushed myself out the window and swam to the surface. The cop saw me come up, but then I was hit by a branch and swept away. Luckily a rescue boat was downstream from me and they hauled me out. I don't remember anything after my car hit the water."

God, she'd been fantastically, ridiculously lucky. She obviously had a dozen angels sitting on her shoulder.

He desperately wanted to find out why she'd run out on him that night, why she'd insinuated herself back into his life now. She'd known him as a greasy rigger, solidly blue collar. He'd been good for a night, a roll in the sheets, and he hadn't really been surprised when he'd turned over and she wasn't there.

He was a ship in the night, here today and gone to-morrow, He only ever indulged in fun that lasted a few hours, max. He was not a guy someone like her—classy and warm—wanted to face over coffee in the morning.

Was she back only because his bank accounts were fat and his social standing solid? Because he was now apparently acceptable?

Cam felt the sharp burn beneath his rib cage and

cursed. He cursed himself for caring what she thought and he cursed her for dropping back into his comfortable, and predictable, life. He'd never forgotten her and he hated her for that. He didn't like connections, ties, memories.

Cam walked over to the window and stared out into the hospital parking lot. There, close to the entrance, was his luxury SUV, top of the line, ridiculously expensive. He lived in a big-ass house, had numerous, hefty bank accounts. He had, he reluctantly admitted, everything he'd ever wanted, yet this brown-eyed woman made him feel like his world was shifting, that something was changing.

Vivi's reappearance in his life was going to rock him to the soles of his feet.

Cam sighed before turning around. "Why am I your emergency contact person, Vivianne?"

This time Vivi gripped the sheets with both hands, and whatever color was left in her face drained away. She stared at him, licking her lips, and he could see the turmoil in those eyes, the trembling of her bottom lip. "I have a daughter, Clementine. I call her Clem. She's two years old and you are her father."

Two

Telling a guy he had a child was a hell of a way to clear a room.

Vivi looked at the door Camden had slammed closed, half expecting him to reappear and start yelling. When twenty seconds passed, then thirty, then a minute, she finally released the breath she was holding. While she was better at confrontation now than she'd been years ago, she still didn't like to argue. The same, so she'd heard, couldn't be said for Camden McNeal. All her research—and she'd researched him to death—pointed to the fact that Cam McNeal, oil rigger turned venture capitalist, treated business like a boxing ring and went in swinging. He was tough, demanding and controlling, and he didn't take any prisoners, ever.

Neither, it was reported, did he suffer fools. The business press called him a blizzard, cool and deadly, but Vivi thought they'd mischaracterized him. He wasn't cold. Beneath that icy facade resided a passionate man. A man fully in control of his volatile emotions. But cold and unfeeling? Oh, hell, no.

Vivi pulled her knees up and groaned as every muscle in her body protested. She was exhausted both mentally and physically, but she was sure there was no chance of sleep anytime soon, since she knew she hadn't seen the last of Cam this morning. Instinctively she understood that Cam had only left the room so that she wouldn't witness his anger, disappointment or shock. Or all three. He obviously needed some time to regain his famous control. That was okay; she needed to regain hers, too.

Three years and he was still earth-shatteringly sexy.

Vivi heard the ding of an incoming message and looked at Cam's smartphone, which she still held in her hand. Swiping her thumb across the screen, she saw the dial pad and impulsively dialed Joe's number, needing to connect with the only person she considered family.

After a brief explanation to Joe about the accident, Vivi told him that she was fine and that he didn't need to rush across town.

"But how are you going to get home? Pick up Clem?" Joe demanded.

"I have someone here," Vivi admitted. When she'd made Camden Clem's guardian and her emergency contact she'd never considered that he might actually need to be called. "Camden McNeal."

Joe waited a beat before snapping out his question. "And why is Cam McNeal with you, Vivianne?"

Here came the hard part.

He'd been the first man she'd noticed on entering that hole-in-the-wall bar three blocks down from her mom's house in Tarrin, a small town west of Houston. He was lounging on a bar stool, watching her with bright blue eyes. His light brown hair had been longer then, touching the collar, though now it was expensively cut. His tall, muscular body seemed harder now, as was his attitude.

"So, I've told you a little of my history with my parents," she began.

"A little, mostly that you were fed a steady diet of anti-government and end-of-the-world BS from your father and you're-going-to-fry-if-you-don't-listen propaganda from your mother," Joe said, always impatient with intolerance.

"I was an only child with ridiculously overprotective parents, so college was out of the question. Dating—unless it was arranged through my mother—was frowned upon, and socializing outside of their tight social circle was not acceptable. Drinking and dancing and sex? Hell, no."

"And hell, as you were frequently told, was where you'd end up if you flirted with those vices."

"I told you that my dad died and that the family money was placed into a trust, controlled by lawyers who were my dad's friends, and every decision we made had to go through the lawyers. I was so angry."

"I'm still not seeing the connection to Camden McNeal."

"After leaving the lawyers and my mother after the funeral, I ended up in a bar, and later, in Cam McNeal's bed. And with his baby in my belly.

"My mother was angry with me for embarrassing her on the day they buried my father, but she was incandescently furious when I told her I was pregnant. Basically, she disowned me," Vivi explained.

"Can I track her down and give her a piece of my mind?"

Vivi smiled at Joe's outrage. God, she loved this man.

"You must've been so scared, Viv."

"I was, but I also felt empowered. And free."

She'd faced a tough, uncertain future, but it was *her* future, one she'd created. "I thought about contacting Clem's father but I didn't know his surname and had no idea where he worked."

But more than that, she hadn't wanted to put herself under anyone's control again. This was her life and she was responsible for herself and her baby. She'd made this bed and she was determined to show herself that she could sleep in it.

"I relied on public assistance and bounced from job to job, first juggling pregnancy and then a tiny baby as I tried to earn enough to support us both. Then I found work with you."

Those first few months after Clem's birth had been super tough, but life had improved when she found steady work as a dishwasher at The Rollin' Smoke. She'd met Charlie, the widowed mother of one of the servers, who ran a childcare service from home. Finally, after placing Clem with someone who was both affordable and loving, her confidence had grown. She'd pestered Joe to both teach and promote her, and the result was that she'd risen through the ranks at a record pace. Line chef in three months, sous chef in six, head chef within the next year.

"And sometime, I'm guessing recently, you bumped into Cam again. Probably at the restaurant, since Ryder Currin introduced him to my place."

Nail on head. "Three months ago, I was off duty but I went into Rollin' with Clem at lunchtime to check on my kitchen. You grabbed Clem and took her into the restaurant to meet the customers."

"She is the grandchild of my heart."

Vivi felt the hard ball of emotion clog her throat. "I looked through the kitchen window and saw two men sitting at the coveted VIP table." And just like earlier, she'd found her head swimming and her throat constricting. She'd looked into that hard, sexy face and realized that her baby's dad was eating at her restaurant.

"I asked Gemma who he was."

She still remembered the words from the waitress. "The younger hottie is Camden McNeal, venture capitalist. He's one of those guys who went from rags to fabulous riches in a heartbeat." Gemma had added, grinning, "So sexy."

He was. And his sexiness was the reason for the little girl she loved more than life itself.

"Since then I've wrestled with whether to contact McNeal, whether he had the right to know that he had a daughter," she told Joe. "One day I'd decide it was the right thing to do, and the next I was convinced that it was better to leave him in the dark."

They'd met when they were both poor, both in different places in their lives. They'd moved on from the people they were then, thank goodness, and while she was proud of her achievements, his rise to success had been stratospheric. According to her research—Google, mostly—he routinely refused personal interviews; it was reported that he was cynical, controlling and suspicious, not one for making friends easily.

"I kept thinking that if I showed up on his doorstep with Clementine, he'd accuse me of being a gold digger trying to cash in on his wealth. Or he'd want to take control of the situation. And of Clementine."

"Well, that's a moot point now, isn't it?" Joe said, as blunt as always.

Maybe, but neither option was remotely acceptable.

She didn't want his money. Nothing was more important to her than making it on her own, and she certainly
wouldn't give Camden McNeal any say over her or her
daughter's life. She'd lived under her parents' control,
and she wasn't ever going back to that.

And then there was the little problem of her still
being utterly, completely, ridiculously attracted to him.
As much, or more, than she was three years ago. She
just needed to see a photo of him online and her lungs
constricted and heat rushed between her legs.

Not something she wanted to think about when
she was having a conversation with the person who'd
stepped into her father's shoes.

"But at the end of the day, Camden is, apart from my
mother, Clem's only biological relative. I was so worried that, if something happened to me, Margaret would
petition the courts for custody of Clem."

"I'd would've fought her," Joe assured her.

He would and she loved him for it. "But, because you
are close to seventy, Joe, and my mom is only in her
early fifties, and a woman, she would've won. Even if I
gave Clem to you, and I wanted to do that, I was told it
would be easily challenged given your age and the fact
that we're not related. On legal advice, I updated my
will to give Cam custody and put him as my emergency
contact number in case something bad happened."

And it so very nearly had.

And now, Camden McNeal, that gorgeous, billionaire badass, was back in her life.

He was the one thing he'd never thought he'd be.

In the hallway outside Vivi's room, Cam lifted his
hand and saw his shakes. As a young kid, six or seven
years old, when his dad left him alone, for days on end,

his hand had never shaken. When he'd scaled buildings and crept past sleeping couples to steal wallets and jewelry, he'd shrugged off the nerves and kept his cool. The day he was arrested and heard that his father wouldn't bail him out, his hands hadn't trembled.

He was a dad, he had a kid...

Life had finally found the one thing, the only thing, that terrified him. Cam rested his head on the wall and fought the urge to slide down its smooth surface. Slapping his palms on the cool surface, he locked his knees and pulled in rhythmic breaths, desperately looking for control, for a measure of calm.

He had no idea how to be a father, a parent responsible for someone else. His father had only occasionally remembered to feed and clothe him. He'd taught him how to roll a cigarette, to spot a mark, to lift a wallet. He'd taught him to fight dirty, to run from cops and social workers, to distrust the system. He'd been more like a delinquent older brother than a father, and consequently all Cam knew about fatherhood was how *not* to be one. Had Vivi recognized that in him? Was that why she never informed him of his daughter? Clementine. Clem.

He had a daughter. Cam blinked furiously, annoyed at his moist eyes. Okay, she was only two, but he was no longer completely alone. There was another person in the world he was linked to. She was young and defenseless, but that link existed, it meant *something*.

Cam rubbed his hands over his face and pushed his fingers through his hair. What now? He couldn't prop up this wall for the rest of the day. At some point he'd have to go in and face Vivi, deal with the situation he found himself in. Cam glanced at Vivi's closed door and sighed. He also needed to deal with his instant, hot-as-hell attraction that was arcing between him and the mother of his child. *Supposed* mother of her child. Cam grabbed on to that cynical thought and held on with every fiber of his being. He just had her word that he was her kid's dad. She could be scamming him, running a con. If he was sensible, he'd walk out of here right now and demand a paternity test. He should wait for scientific proof...

No, that wasn't going to happen. He was upset, confused, utterly side-slapped by this news, but his gut instinct told him that she was telling the truth. He was a daddy.

God.

Cam watched a doctor and nurse walk toward him. They stopped at Vivi's door and handed him a harried greeting. They entered her room and he followed them in, standing at the back of the room out of their way as they approached the bed. Over their heads he saw her resigned expression.

"I'm fine," Vivi firmly stated, but Cam heard the tremor in her voice. "I need sleep and a couple of painkillers and I'll be fine."

"I went to med school and studied for a dozen years. Do you not think I should make that call?" the female doctor replied, amused. She jerked her head in his direction. "Someone you know?"

Vivi's eyes collided with his and Cam felt the air leave his lungs. God, she was so damn beautiful. He'd thought so three years ago but there was a strength to her now, a maturity that had been missing in that girl he'd slept with so long ago. Back then she'd been a fun night, a diversion, a break from a hard job and constant loneliness. Lying in that hospital bed, she was now... what? He didn't know.

"I know him," Vivi said, resigned. "When can I get discharged?"

The doctor examined her eyes as the nurse wound a blood pressure cuff around her arm. The doctor pushed and prodded Vivi's slim body before stepping back and folding her arms. "I will only discharge you if you promise not to drive."

Frustration flashed in Vivi's eyes. "My car is, I presume, waterlogged and at the bottom of a gully, so I won't be driving anywhere. I'll catch a cab or Uber."

The thought of her being trapped in that car iced his veins and Cam placed his palm on the wall to anchor him. He couldn't imagine a world, didn't want to imagine a world, that didn't have Vivi Donner in it. A surprising thought, given that he'd never expected to see her again.

Vivi released a small moan and Cam's eyes flew back to her distressed face. He quickly moved to her side, placing his hand on her thigh. "What is it? What's wrong?"

"No car, no money, no phone." Vivi bit her bottom lip and he saw fine dots of blood appear there because she'd reopened her cut.

"Stop biting your lip." Her eyes flashed at his order and he noticed irritation replacing fear. Good, he could work with anger; he'd couldn't cope with tears. "I have a car and money. I'll get you home." He ignored Vivi's annoyed squawk and looked at the doctor. "Since she has a concussion, must I wake her up every couple of hours?"

The doctor shook her head. "Not necessary. I'd suggest rest and lots of it." She directed a stern glance at Vivi. "You had a nasty experience, Miss Donner, but

I also suspect that you've been burning the candle at both ends lately."

Vivi wouldn't meet her eyes, so Cam asked for an explanation.

"Ms. Donner is a bit thinner than I'd like, and those blue stripes under her eyes aren't the result of the accident but nights without sleep. She's also slightly anemic."

Vivi looked like she wanted to roll her eyes. "I am the single mother of an energetic toddler who isn't fond of sleep."

And just like that, both the nurse and doctor turned sympathetic. The nurse rested a hand on Vivi's shoulder and sighed. "Oh, honey." Without doubt, she was a mother, too, Cam thought.

The doctor shook her head. "I have a three-year-old and a six-year-old and a husband, and all three exhaust me. I feel your pain."

Cam thought they were laying it a little thick. How difficult could a two-year-old be? But Cam was bright enough to realize that if he disagreed, he might be verbally skewered by three mothers. Better to keep quiet. Safer, too.

"The point is," he said, pulling them back to the matter at hand, "I will take Vivi home."

Vivi looked mutinous. "That's not going to work for me."

"Well, it's the only way you're going to get discharged," the doctor told her. "No driving for twenty-four hours, plenty of rest and no physical activity."

Cam's eyes met Vivi's; her eyes widened and her cheeks turned a pretty pink. Sure, his thoughts kept wandering to the sex they'd shared, but because she'd suffered a smack to her head, he hadn't figured hers had, too. But that blush, spreading down her neck and disappearing under her hospital gown, told him a completely different story. Well, good.

No! *Hell*. They didn't need the complication of still being ridiculously attracted to each other. And acting on that attraction, which he really wanted to do, would just be stupid.

He'd made a point of not acting stupid, but damn, this time it was hard.

He saw confusion in her eyes, noticed her embarrassment. Cam hauled in a breath, saw that they were alone—when had the medical staff left?—and sat down on the edge of her bed. Unable to resist touching her, he allowed the tips of his fingers to trace the fine line of her jaw. "Hell of a day, huh?"

Vivi nodded. She started to pull her bottom lip between her teeth, but he tapped her lip and she let go. "You've really got to stop doing that."

"I know."

"I've got a better idea." He shouldn't be doing this, but he needed just one taste, one kiss. He needed to know whether she tasted as good as he remembered, or whether his imagination had played tricks on him for the past three years. One kiss couldn't hurt…

Could it?

Under his lips, hers were soft and silky. Holding her jaw, Cam moved his lips across hers, breathing in her scent, sweet flowers touched by dark waters. Keeping his kiss gentle because of the cut on her lip, he inhaled her breath and tasted her essence. He remembered her as being hot and sexy, but this woman, this new version of the girl he'd met, held more depth, was a hundred times more interesting. Her lips parted, and his tongue slid past her teeth and he tasted sweetness and sin, vulnerability and strength. Determination and independence masking a ribbon of fear.

Fear? What was she scared of?

He pulled back, looked into her eyes and saw that same emotion reflected in her eyes. A second later it was gone, shut up and put away. Vivi Donner was almost as good at masking her emotions as he was. The realization both intrigued and fascinated him, and the fact that he was both intrigued and fascinated worried him.

Complications weren't his thing.

Vivi swallowed and looked toward the door. "So, I guess if I want to get out of here, you're my ride."

Okay, she was ignoring the kiss, their crazy attraction. Maybe he should do the same. Yet his heart thumped when she picked up his wrist so that she could look at his watch. "If I can get home, I'd be able to sleep for a few hours before I need to collect Clem. Do you want to meet her?"

His heart bounced off his chest. He'd just found Vivi again and didn't know if he was up to meeting his daughter today. He hadn't had time to process any of this, and didn't think he even could.

"It was just a suggestion, Cam. You don't have to meet her if you don't want to. I'm not asking anything from you...not your time or money or input. So, really, no hard feelings if you say no."

Except that she would think that he was a wuss, that he wasn't man enough to acknowledge his child. If he walked away and ignored the situation, Vivi would think he was weak and selfish and a bit of a man-child. And she'd be right.

Suck it up, McNeal. She's had a near-death experience, escaped from a sinking car, got smacked around

*by river detritus and ended up in a hospital. If she can
cope with all that, you can meet a two-year-old.*

An ordinary two-year-old, maybe. His daughter?
He wasn't so sure.

Vivi tipped her head to the side. "Getting a bit too
real, huh?"

He thought about laughing her statement away—he
could be charming when he chose to be—but decided
to tell the truth. "Too real. Utterly surreal."

She twisted her lips and then her hands. "I suppose
you want an explanation."

"Do you not think I deserve one?"

Vivi lifted one shoulder, as if silently admitting that
she had her doubts. Dammit, what did she want from
him? He dealt in black-and-white; gray was his least
favorite color in the world. Cam was about to demand
that she start explaining, when he caught her touching
the back of her head, trying hard to contain her wince.
He skimmed his eyes over the bruises on her arms and
stood up, gripping the edge of the sheet.

He looked at Vivi. "I just want to see what we're
dealing with. May I?"

At her nod, he pulled down the sheet. Her gown
ended midthigh and she had a scrape on her thigh, a
bruised knee and another bruise on her shin. God, she
looked like she'd been hit by a tank.

Instead of protesting his examination of her body,
Vivi just put her head against the pillow and closed her
eyes. "I fell pregnant, but I didn't know your name—"

She didn't need to do this now. She shouldn't *have* to
do this now. Feeling suddenly protective of her, he realized her explanations could wait until she felt stronger.
Or when she was, at the very least, pain free.

He bent down and surprised himself by placing his

lips on her forehead. This crazy situation would still be there. "Not now, Viv. Let's get you home."

Vivi forced her eyes open. "I'd like to be home, clean and be cuddling with Clem."

Cam nodded. "Lie there and rest and let me see if I can make that happen."

He wanted to take her home to his place, not hers, a place where he knew he could protect her.

Cam rolled his shoulders, irritated with himself. The worst was over, what more could happen to her? Why was he so reluctant to leave her alone?

Press Release.
For Immediate Release.
Body Discovered at Texas Cattleman's Club, Houston Construction Site.

Yesterday, at 7:40 a.m., members of the Houston Police Department and emergency medical responders responded to a report of a male victim found at the west Houston construction site of the Texas Cattleman's Club, about two miles west of Highway 10. Upon the arrival of first responders, the male was pronounced deceased at the scene.

At this time the identity of the male is unknown. According to the medical examiner, the cause of death is due to a gunshot wounds to the chest. Houston Police Department detectives are investigating with the assistance of the district attorney's office. Identification of the victim and an accurate time of death are still to come. A case of homicide has been opened and no further information is currently available.

If anyone has information regarding this incident they are asked to contact…

Glass-wall offices meant eyes were on me, so I skimmed over the media release. Nothing in my face or my demeanor reflected my inner turmoil or hinted at my racing heart. I looked at my fingers, pleased to see that they weren't shaking. I pushed the paper to one side. Reading media releases has been a long-standing habit and one I am grateful for.

Reading the morning papers is another habit I've cultivated, and I pulled the pile toward me, and skimmed their pages for more information. Speculation was rampant but there was not much more to be gleaned. It was the same information, padded and puffed, but nothing new and nothing to link me to the murder at the Texas Cattleman's Club building site.

Thank God.

Determined not to miss anything—the smallest bit of knowledge might be the difference between me meeting a needle while wearing prison orange or not—I skimmed the short article buried on page 3 of a local newspaper and frowned. Taking a breath, I read it again, slower this time.

The victim has not been identified and the time of death is unknown. Like so many other properties in the city, the construction site experienced extensive flooding thanks to the once-in-a-generation storm, making identification of the victim or forensics difficult.

That statement wasn't accurate. I thought back to that morning, remembering the sharp snap of the pistol firing, the blood on a white shirt, his wide, terrified eyes as I stood over him, his life draining away. For insurance, I stared into his eyes and pulled the trigger again, sending another bullet into his already mutilated chest cavity. Fighting my panic, I acted fast and removed his wallet, his distinctive watch, the bracelets on his thick wrist, anything that might make identifying him easier. Dropping the concrete slab on his face had been added insurance, because the more time I put between his death and his identification, the better. I never imagined that I would get a helping hand from Mother Nature. The recent flood was a blessing in disguise. For me, at least.

I hid my smile and power-read through the rest of the article. Nobody working on the Perry Construction crew is talking; one worker hinted at a company gag order being in place.

At my suggestion, Sterling Perry sent an email to the construction foreman, telling him in no uncertain terms that any worker caught talking to the press would be summarily dismissed, and it pleased me that his orders were being obeyed. Excellent, since I wasn't in the mood to follow up on the issue, mostly because my interest might raise suspicion and I needed to fly under the radar. Becoming a suspect would be intolerable and jail simply wouldn't suit me.

After folding the newspaper into a perfect rectangle, I placed it on top of the pile of other precisely folded papers and leaned back in my chair. So far, so good. Nobody suspected me, nobody ever will. Thank God, because I still have a score, or three or four, to settle with Sterling Perry and his family. And with his archenemy Ryder Currin...

In my case, the enemy of my enemy was not my friend...

Three

In the hospital parking lot, Cam opened the passenger door of his SUV and gestured Vivi inside. Vivi inhaled that new-car smell and looked at the expensive seats, the massive dashboard. This was a $300,000 car, and, because she couldn't leave the hospital in a flimsy gown, her filthy, still-wet sneakers were about to touch the spotless carpet, her mud-streaked jeans were going to make contact with his butter-soft leather seats.

Nope, she couldn't. She'd take a cab home.

"Problem?" Cam asked, his voice brushing her ear. Vivi felt the heat of his body behind her and saw his big hand grip the car frame above her head, his expensive watch glinting in the sunlight. He'd come a long way in three years. A beat-up truck to this beauty, work boots to $300 cowboy boots, functional denim to designer labels. She'd come a long way, too, and she was proud of herself, but man, Cam had her beat.

It wasn't a competition, Donner, and Cam didn't have a child to deal with. You've done okay, you know you have.

Clem was safe and happy and lacked for nothing. Sure, it would be nice to have a little more stashed away for a rainy day, to have a place of her own, but it could be worse. She could still be back at her mother's, going to her church, living a small life in a small community. *Count your blessings, dammit. You have everything you need...*

"Can I help you up?"

Vivi half turned and lifted her hands. "I can't get in there, Cam."

Cam frowned. "And why not?"

"This car is brand new. I am filthy. My clothes are still damp and muddy, and I reek of ditchwater."

Spreading his legs, Cam folded his arms across his chest, and Vivi appreciated the bulge of his biceps straining the band of his T-shirt. He shook his head. "Get in the car, Vivianne."

"I can't!"

Muttering a curse, Cam moved quickly. He gripped her waist, lifted her and easily deposited her into the soft leather chair. He placed a hand on her thigh and one on her shoulder and glared at her. "It's a *car*. I don't give a damn whether it gets dirty or not. Carpets can get cleaned, leather seats can be wiped down." He leaned forward and sniffed; amusement jumped into his eyes. "Though you could do with a shower."

Vivi blushed. "I know, I'm really sorry."

Cam's thumb found the rip on the knee of her jeans and caressed that small patch of bare skin. Vivi watched his eyes darken, and emotion she couldn't identify flashed in his eyes. "You nearly died, Vivi. I'd rather have you here, dirty and a little smelly, than dead and gone."

He was so direct, so damn to the point, and Vivi liked it. She liked the way he said what he meant, whether she wanted to hear it or not. Her parents had been so passive-aggressive, so manipulative that she'd spent most of her life trying to decipher what they meant, second-guessing her responses and reactions, never quite sure if she was doing or saying the right thing. She liked direct people; she always knew where she stood with them.

"We done with this conversation?" Cam asked her.

Vivi sighed. "Yeah."

The corners of his mouth lifted. "'Bout time."

He slammed the car door shut and Vivi pulled the seat belt down as she watched him walk around the hood of the SUV to the driver's door. Long strides, messy hair, stubble on his strong jaw. He was such a man, an alpha male in his prime.

Cam pulled open his door, settled into his seat and reached for a pair of expensive sunglasses resting in the console. He half lifted them to his face when he stopped to look at her. He held out the sunglasses to her. "How's your head? Do you want to use these?"

Vivi was touched by his casual offer. Her head was pounding, and she couldn't look out of the windshield without feeling like the sun was piercing her eyes with thousand-degree needles. Her fingers brushed Cam's as she took the glasses from him and she felt another shiver of awareness. God, he was hot. And under that gruff, sweet.

"Thank you." Vivi placed the too-big sunglasses on her face and sighed with relief. The lenses cut the glare and her headache retreated from excruciating to simply horrible.

Heading toward the exit of the parking lot, Cam sent her a glance. "Where to?"

"Are you sure you don't mind driving me?" Vivi asked, half turning in her seat so that she could rest her pounding head on the soft seat. "It might be a bit out of your way."

"The address, Vivi."

Vivi recited her address and Cam activated the onboard GPS.

At the first red light, Cam turned his head to look at her. "You up to some conversation?"

"About Clem?"

"She's the most important part of what I want to talk about," Cam replied, accelerating across the intersection. He shifted, picked up speed and shifted again. He drove like he made love, with complete confidence and self-assurance. Was there anything about this man she didn't find sexy?

"I'm impatient by nature," he said, "but if you can't talk now, I will wait. Reluctantly."

Vivi pulled her eyes off his hands and sat up, stretching out her legs. She stifled a groan, her muscles screaming, volubly reminding her that she'd been in an accident, that she'd narrowly escaped drowning in a car.

Cam's hand tightened on the steering wheel. "Now that I know about Clem, what are you expecting from me? Child support is a given. Give me a number and I'll set up a recurring monthly payment."

Cam had gone from zero to sixty and she was trailing far, far behind. "But what about proof? Paternity test? Don't you want some sort of guarantee that she's yours?"

Cam's brief look was arrow sharp and laser intense. "Is she mine?"

"Yes."

"Okay, then. Let's move on."

Vivi stared at him, shocked. How could he just take what she was saying at face value? How could he trust her? She didn't trust anybody, especially when it came to Clem.

"Vivianne, thanks to my past, I've got a near infallible BS detector. I can spot a lie from fifty paces. If you want to go through the whole dog and pony show of paternity tests, we can do that, but it's not necessary. You say she's mine, I believe you. The end."

What kind of past gave a person the ability to read people, to spot lies? Vivi really wanted to know. She opened her mouth to ask, saw Cam's don't-go-there expression and backed off. Okay, message received.

Going back to his previous statement, she said, "I don't need anything from you."

She didn't. She and Clem were fine. She had a good job—the restaurant would reopen soon, any other option would not be tolerated!—and a great support system, and she was, finally, happy, dammit. She was the master of her destiny, the captain of her ship. She would not allow some rich guy, no matter how sexy and how much she wanted to kiss him, to walk into her life and rearrange it. She'd cried and fought and hustled and worked her butt off to be independent. She would never allow anyone to control her actions again.

Vivi placed her hand on her stomach and hauled in a deep breath. "We don't need you, Camden."

She heard his swift intake of breath and her eyes flew up to his. For a moment, for a split second, she suspected that she'd hurt him, that her words were like arrows hitting his soul. Then he turned those cool, mocking eyes on hers and sent her a cold smile. "Well, then, if that was the way you wanted to play it, then you shouldn't have put my name as your emergency contact." He gestured to her muddy clothing. "Because, you know, sometimes emergencies happen."

Crap. He had her there. Folding her arms across her chest, Vivi stared straight ahead, feeling like her head was about to split open. She'd made the choice to list Cam as her emergency contact, to give him custody of Clem in case of an unfortunate event.

What she'd never expected to happen actually had. And that meant dealing with Cam, working her way through this quagmire. As much as she wanted to, she simply couldn't wish him away. And even if she could, she doubted that she would. He was so compelling, utterly mesmerizing. His charisma hadn't dimmed, and he was, if possible, even more attractive than he'd been years ago. He was one of those men people paid attention to, possibly because he didn't give a damn whether you did or not.

He wasn't an easy man, nor was he comfortable, but, hell, he was interesting.

Cam reached down, flipped open the lid to the console between them and pulled out a bottle of aspirin. He tossed it into her lap and, reaching behind her seat, pulled a bottle of water from a pack on the floor. "Take a couple and then start talking."

It was one command she was prepared to obey. Five minutes later, after swallowing most of the bottle of water, she felt a little stronger. "What do you want to discuss?"

Cam's took a moment to reply. "That night…why did you leave?"

Because it was late, and she knew that her mom would be frantic. Because if she wasn't home by dawn, there was a strong possibility that her mom would call the church prayer line and every male member of the church would scour Tarrin for her. She'd known that she was in for a verbal thrashing for leaving the funeral and will reading, but if her mother found out she'd visited a bar and slept with a stranger... Well, hell, Satan would've taken cover.

But nothing compared to the meltdown her mom had descended into when she heard about her pregnancy. Hell, she was certain, was still in recovery mode.

"I didn't think that we had much more to say to one another. We drank, we danced, we slept together. We were done." Hooking up with Cam had been an act of defiance, of rebellion, and she'd never, not for one minute, thought that it could last beyond dawn. That was why they hadn't bothered with names, why they hadn't shared anything personal. They had been two people who were attracted to each other, using each other to alleviate their loneliness and have a brief physical connection. Had she read the evening wrong? Had he wanted more? Vivi frowned. "Did you want to see me again?"

Cam's jaw hardened, and he stared straight ahead. "It ended how it was expected to end."

Vivi couldn't help noticing that he didn't answer her question. She debated what to say next. She certainly wasn't going to tell him how her mother had reacted when she finally faced the fact that Vivi was pregnant, how she had screamed at Vivi for two days straight before tossing her out of the only home she'd ever known, into a strange and scary world.

Vivi tasted the same panic at the back of her throat and reminded herself that she'd survived, then she'd flourished. She was okay, Clem was okay, life was good.

"I moved away from Tarrin and came to Houston."

"Why?"

Dammit, she didn't want to answer that question. She wondered how to respond without telling him too much and decided to keep it simple. "I wasn't welcome there anymore." She saw him open his mouth and began to speak again before he could lob another question her way. "I found a place to stay, had a couple of jobs and then I found work at The Rollin' Smoke."

"Joe Cabron's place?" Cam asked.

"Yeah. I started off at the bottom of the ladder and worked my way up." Vivi heard the note of pride in her voice and didn't give a damn. She'd badgered Joe to give her more work, more responsibility, a higher wage, and every task he gave her, she'd excelled at. And when she got to food preparation, they'd both realized with equal surprise that she had a natural affinity for flavors and a great cook's instinct. Together they'd played with recipes and food combinations, and when Joe decided to semi-retire, Vivi had gotten her chance at running his famous kitchen. Her appointment had sent shock waves through Houston's culinary circles, but she'd proved her worth—taking online courses to improve herself—and was now considered to be one of the best chefs in the city.

"I'm Joe's head chef."

Cam turned his head to look at her, his eyebrows raised. "You're kiddin'."

Vivi narrowed her eyes at him. "Please tell me that you aren't another Neanderthal man who thinks that only men should barbecue."

Cam's lips twitched. "Hell, I don't care who prepares my barbecue as long as it's done right. And at The Rollin' Smoke, it's done right."

Vivi nodded. "Damn straight." She started to pull

her bottom lip between her teeth and remembered that she had a cut that needed healing. "I saw you there, at the restaurant, about three months back. You were eating lunch with Ryder Currin."

Cam nodded. "I eat with Ryder quite often and your place is one of our favorite places."

"I was in the kitchen and I saw you." She didn't tell him she'd felt like she'd been hit by a two-by-four, that her baby girl had been in the restaurant that day and he'd actually laid eyes on her before. Why complicate the story? "I asked who you were and then I did some research."

"What did you find out?"

"You're rich. You're successful. Along with Ryder Currin and Sterling Perry, you're considered to be one of the most influential businesspeople in Houston." Vivi picked at the rip in her jeans and stared out the window, idly noticing that they were just five minutes from her house. "It always worried me that Clem had no one, and if I died, she would become a ward of the state or, possibly worse, end up with my mother. I didn't know you, but I presumed that you would be a better option if something happened to me. So I listed you as my emergency contact, gave you custody of her in my will."

"And you didn't think that it might a good idea to tell me that I had a kid?"

She had, occasionally. But then she'd wavered, scared of the consequences. Because, while researching Cam, she'd discovered that the man was a control freak, a lone wolf, and that he rarely, if ever, sought business advice. It was his way, colleagues and associates were often quoted as saying, or the highway.

And that didn't work for her.

Cam pulled up to her sidewalk, parked and switched

off the growly engine. Silence filled the car and Vivi slowly removed his sunglasses and carefully folded the arms.

"So why didn't you contact me when you found out who I was?" Cam asked.

Vivi placed the sunglasses on the lid of the console and met his eyes. She decided to tell him the truth, or some of the truth. "Because I knew that your coming into our lives would change it. And I like our life, I like what I've done with it."

Can rested his wrist on the steering wheel. "Change isn't always bad, Vivi."

Vivi opened the door, and when her feet touched the sidewalk, she looked back at him through the open car door. "No, it's not always bad but it's frequently hard. And messy."

Vivi's house was a small bungalow in a solidly middle-class area. Cam slammed his car door closed and looked up and down the empty street. It was early afternoon and the streets were deserted, with most people at work. But up and down the street, he could see signs that families lived here. A tricycle lay on the postage-stamp lawn belonging to Vivi's neighbor, a soccer ball rested against a rock next to the front door of the house opposite. Cam followed Vivi up the path to her front door and wondered how she was going to break into her own house, seeing that her house keys were probably somewhere in the Gulf of Mexico by now.

Vivi didn't miss a beat. She just lifted her mat, removed a brass key and inserted it into the flimsy lock on the front door. Seriously? Who did that anymore? In his previous life that would be the first place he'd look. "You have got to be kiddin' me."

Vivi frowned at him as she pushed open the front door and stepped inside the cool interior. "Problem?"

"I cannot believe you keep a front-door key under your mat. Have you heard about these characters called burglars? Rapists? Serial killers?" Cam demanded, shutting the door behind him and flipping the dead bolt. He saw her surprise and threw up his hands. "Please, please tell me that you lock your doors when you are here alone."

"It's a safe neighborhood."

Oh, God, that meant she didn't. Cam slapped his hands on his hips and closed his eyes, striving for calm. He knew it was a long shot, but it was worth a try, if only to get his blood pressure to drop. "You do have an alarm?"

"Nope."

"Mace? Pepper spray? A baseball bat?"

Vivi toed off her ruined sneakers and left them next to the door. Her feet were grubby, but he could still see the pale pink shade of polish on her toes. Sexy feet, he thought. He now remembered nibbling the arch of that elegant foot, and the way she'd shivered when he scraped his teeth against her skin.

Not important, he told himself, especially when she was living in a house a ten-year-old could break into. He'd need to get his security guy out here, to put a decent lock on all the doors and install an alarm. If he didn't, he'd never sleep again. Or he'd be bunking down on her couch every night.

Cam followed Vivi into a small living room containing two brightly covered sofas. A small TV sat on a wooden box and a bunch of bright flowers stood on a small table next to a bookcase. Cam narrowed his eyes and read the titles: a little romance, a lot of cookbooks, some true crime. He turned around slowly, saw the small dining table and, beyond it, a galley kitchen. A tiny pink handprint on a sheet of white paper was attached to the door of the fridge with a daisy magnet. He looked but he couldn't find any photos of her daughter—his daughter—anywhere.

"I was hoping to see a photo of Clementine."

"I normally have a bunch out but I'm having them reframed." Vivi's deep brown eyes, exhausted and full of pain, met his. "I have some on my phone." Then Cam caught the sheen of tears and watched as she swiped angrily at them. "Crap, no phone! My life is on my phone. My banking apps, my photos, my contacts, recipes… Everything."

Cam knew that the experiences of the day were coming back to pummel her, and she was fast running out of steam. She needed to shower and get some rest. He couldn't help but wonder if she'd ask him to buy her another phone, to lend her money to tide her over until she managed to get new bank cards. He wouldn't be surprised if she asked him to rent her a car or, hell, buy her one. He'd had girlfriends who thought sex gave them immediate access to his credit cards, so Vivi asking him for help wouldn't surprise him. But in this case, he'd give it. Clem was his daughter and there was no way he'd watch Vivi struggle when he could make her life easier.

And if he were the oil rigger he'd been years ago, if he'd been eating at The Rollin' Smoke as a normal guy at a normal table, drinking water instead of craft beer, would she still have tracked him down, found out who he was? How much of a factor was his money in Vivi's decision to name him as Clem's father, to list him as her go-to person? Would he be half so attractive without his money?

He didn't think so.

But instead of making demands, asking for help, Vivi walked into the kitchen and filled a glass with tap water. After drinking it down, she gripped the sink and gazed at the wall of her neighbor's house with a thousand-yard stare and panic-filled eyes.

To hell with it. She ought to be done with this day, with trying to remain strong, with attempting to keep it all together. He was taking over. Cam dumped his phone and wallet on the dining table and walked toward her. When he reached her, he bent his knees and scooped her up against his chest.

"What the hell, McNeal?"

Cam glared down at her. "Just for a second, stop thinking. Is Clem safe for a few hours?"

Vivi nodded. "Yes."

"Okay then." He walked into the hallway and nudged open the first door with his foot. A small bed, stuffed toys on the pillow, little girl shoes on the floor. Clementine's room and not what he was looking for.

"What are you doing?" Vivi demanded, her body stiff in his arms.

The bathroom was the next room and Cam walked inside and dropped Vivi onto the toilet seat. Ignoring her squawk, he flipped on the taps to the shower and met her angry glare. "Again, what the hell are you doing?" she demanded.

Cam squatted down in front of her, balancing on his toes. He rested his arm on his knee and met her eyes. "Vivianne, you've had a hell of a day. You had a close call, you are banged up and bruised. You're dealing with me, the father of your child, someone you didn't expect in your life. You have things to do and are facing a few uncomfortable days."

Vivi stared down at her hands and he saw her shoulders shake. Dammit, he was saying this wrong. He placed his hands on her thighs and tapped her thigh with his index finger.

"Look at me, Viv."

He waited until all that brown met his blue. "I'm here and as much as you want me to, I'm not going away. Not today."

Vivi stared at a point past his shoulder. "I can't... I'm not good at accepting help."

"I don't care. Today you're going to." Cam stood up and flipped the shower taps to maximum. "So, here's what's going to happen. You're going to shower and while you wash that river off you, I'll make you some tea, maybe something to eat. Then you're going to climb into bed."

Vivi shook her head. "I can't, Cam. I need to collect Clem, I need to find a phone, make arrangements for a car."

Stubborn had a new name and it was Vivi. "Yeah, you're not hearing me, Viv. I'm not going anywhere. For today, I'm your phone, I'm your lift, I'm the barrier standing between you and the outside world. I'm going to do whatever you need to do because you need to rest."

Vivi opened her mouth to argue, took a breath and slowly nodded. "I'll take two hours from you. Two hours and a cup of tea."

"Three hours, a cup of tea and a grilled cheese sandwich. And we'll pick up Clementine together."

Vivi shook her head. "I don't think I'm ready for that, Cam."

Cam lifted one shoulder and let it fall. "I don't think I am, either, but that's what's going to happen." He nodded at the shower before taking a step toward the door.

Because the room was so damn small, one step was all it took to put him by the door. "Call if you need help."

"I won't."

Cam closed the door behind him and rested his forehead on the thin door. She acted so independent and determined, but was she really? Despite his so-called infallible BS detector, he had to wonder if he was reading her wrong. Was she just lulling him into a false sense of security, acting independent so that when she finally stung him, when she finally asked something of him, he wouldn't mind? Could she be that manipulative, that wily?

Yeah, he was cynical but he hadn't become that way by fluke and coincidence. And what was the point of worrying? He'd wait and see. Vivi would either disappoint him as so many had before her, or she'd surprise him. He'd expect the first and not hope for the second. That way he wouldn't feel let down.

Again.

Four

Three hours later, Vivi staggered out of her bed, thoroughly disoriented. Standing by the side of her bed, she stared out her window, surprised to see that the sun was still shining. She looked down at the pair of men's boxer shorts she'd pulled on and the thin tank top and wondered why she was dressed in her pj's in the middle of the afternoon. And why was it so quiet?

She had a toddler. Quiet was not good.

"Clem is safe, you're safe. Take a breath."

Vivi spun around and saw Camden McNeal standing in the doorway to her room, wearing designer jeans and a dark green T-shirt. His hair was shorter, there were fine lines around his eyes that hadn't been three years ago. And what was he doing in her house on a— God, what was today?

And where the hell was Clem?

Vivi lifted her hand to her throat, panic closing her throat.

"You had an accident. Clementine is fine. She's at the sitters. Charlie?"

Vivi sat down on the edge of the bed and dropped her head down, waiting for her dizziness to pass. Memories pieced themselves together. Near drowning, Cam as emergency contact, hospital, concussion. It was all coming back to her now. Blowing air out of her cheeks, she slowly lifted her head. "How long did I sleep for?"

"About three hours. I was just coming to wake you."

Vivi nodded her head and caught a glimpse of her reflection in the freestanding, secondhand mirror in the corner. She'd fallen asleep with wet hair and it was a mass of tangled, frizzy curls. She had a pillow crease on her left cheek, a bruise forming on her eyebrow, cheek and jaw. She was almost scared to look down, but she did. Black and blue with a few wonderful scrapes to break the monotony.

Because she wanted to cry—partly because she looked like hell in front of the ever-delicious-looking Camden McNeal—Vivi tried humor. "Holy crap. Clem is going to insist on kissing all these bruises better and that's going to take some time."

Cam pushed his broad shoulder into the door frame and she saw the heat in his eyes. She glanced down and, yep, there was that telltale bulge behind the buttons of his jeans. "I'd be more than happy to take over when she gets tired."

He would, too. He'd be gentle with her, kiss her slowly, investigate every inch of her battered skin and then he'd caress her in such a way that she'd not only forget that she'd been in an accident but her own name. If they started tasting and touching each other, everything else would fade.

Vivi pulled her eyes away, tipped her head back and

stared up at the ceiling. She couldn't go there, not with him. Their time to be lovers had passed. Now they had to find a new way of dealing with each other. A way that included Clem.

That was if Cam wanted to be part of Clem's life. She didn't even know. Right now, there were more important things to talk about, to figure out, than their crazy, combustible attraction.

Vivi gestured to her closet. "I'm going to get dressed and then maybe we can chat over a cup of coffee?"

Cam had the coffee ready when Vivi walked into her tiny, open-floor-plan living area ten minutes later. She'd changed into cutoff denims and flip-flops, pulling an open-neck, red-and-white-check shirt over her tank top and knotting it at the waist. Most of the bruises on her body were hidden and she'd toned down the ones on her face with some concealer. With her hair pulled back into a messy bun on the top of her head—her muscles ached too much to do anything more with the heavy mass—she felt 10 percent better and marginally human. She smiled her thanks at Cam as he pushed her coffee across the table.

"I left it black. That okay?"

"Sure."

Cam pulled out her chair and Vivi wasn't particularly surprised at his show of manners. Years ago, he'd opened doors for her, let her enter a room first. Held out chairs. Someone had drilled Southern manners into him somewhere along the way. Vivi watched as Cam took the chair opposite her, an unfamiliar laptop next to his elbow.

"That yours?" she asked, nodding to the state-of-the-art device.

A power cable snaked toward an electrical socket

and a glass of water sat off to the right, next to a pile of folders. He'd arranged her small fan so that the air blew on him as he worked. She could see that all the windows to her small house were open. He'd also, at some point, sat on one of her small sofas—her cushions had been pushed to one end and a couple were on the floor. Cam McNeal had made himself very much at home in her space while she slept.

"Yeah," Cam replied, lifting his cup to his lips. "I managed to get some work done while you were sleeping. Do you feel better?"

Vivi considered his question. "I'm sore but I'm not feeling so...emotional."

"A near drowning will do that to you."

As will waking up and seeing the father of your child next to your bed. It was time to address the elephant in the room. "We need to talk about Clementine, Cam."

"Yeah."

She suspected that only pride kept him from squirming. Oh, he looked so inscrutable, so calm, but in the tapping of his finger against his coffee mug and the slight shift in his chair, Vivi saw that he wasn't quite as insouciant as he wanted to be.

"Let me tell you about Clem." Vivi wondered where to start and decided that there was no point in pussyfooting around. "She's strong-willed, bossy, demanding and energetic. She's amazingly bright." Vivi saw his skepticism and held up her hand. "I know, I sound like a doting mommy, but she genuinely is bright, and she has a hell of a vocabulary for her age. She must get that from you because I didn't really start speaking until I was four."

Mostly because her parents subscribed to the adage that children should be seen and not heard.

"She is just old enough to be excited about the idea of having a daddy but she's also only two, so the novelty will wear off in about two seconds," Vivi continued. She pushed her coffee cup away, rested her arms on the table and leaned forward. "You need to take some time to think about what your intentions are with regard to being Clem's dad, Camden."

Cam's amazing eyes narrowed. "What do you mean?"

"I mean you can't come roaring into her life and play at being her dad and then decide, in a few days or a few weeks, that it's not your thing. You can't pick her up and discard her."

Vivi rubbed the back of her neck. "Look, if you want to walk away, pretend this never happened, I'm okay with that. I'm not going to ask you for child support or anything like that."

Cam didn't speak. He just listened, his eyes locked on hers. Vivi touched the top of her lip with her tongue and forced herself to continue. This was difficult, but it needed to be said. Her little girl's heart was more important to her than her own.

"However, if you do decide you want to get to know her, we can arrange supervised visits. If those visits work out, I might then be open to allowing you time with her on your own. We'll have to see how it goes."

"Good of you," Cam said, his voice bland.

She didn't care if he was feeling insulted or annoyed; she had to do this. Vivi glanced at the clock on her wall, conscious of the hour. "Okay, it's time for us to leave."

She pushed her chair back and stood up. Knowing that it was always a good idea to step back, consider the options, she looked at Cam.

"I'm not going to tell Clem that you are her dad, not

yet. Spend some time with her and then decide. But you should know that if you make a promise to her, or to me about her, you *will* follow through. I will make sure of it."

He looked a little amused at the thought of her pushing him around but he'd yet to realize that when it came to Clem, there wasn't a mountain she wouldn't climb, a creature she wouldn't fight, a country she'd not invade. She was more than a momma bear, she was the whole damn pack.

Point made, Vivi thought, turning away. But as she was about to step out of the kitchen, he felt Cam's gentle hand gripping her elbow. *Don't turn around, Viv, because if you do, you know exactly what's going to happen.*

She turned anyway and got a hit of blue, the suggestion of amusement and the curve of a mouth before his lips covered hers. He tasted like before, like a wonderful memory, but also like someone new, a deeper and darker and more intense version of the man he used to be. And God, he felt hard and tough and solid. She didn't mean to lean into him but he easily accepted her weight, his one arm banding around her back in a hold that was both strong and reassuring. His other hand held her jaw, his fingers tracing the outline of her ear just as gently as his lips were exploring hers. It was a tender kiss, one she didn't expect, a "hello, it's nice to taste you again" kiss. But it wasn't enough. She didn't need gentle from Cam, or tender. She needed hot and hard and fast. She needed him to remind her that she was alive, that she was breathing, that she was young and…here, dammit.

Vivi grabbed his hips and pushed her breasts into his hard pecs, dragging her nipples across his chest. She opened her mouth and pushed her tongue past his teeth, needing to taste him, to explore and delve, to dip and dive. Heat and lust ricocheted through her and she felt her knees crumble, her bones melt. She was alive, she was kissing a sexy man, she was safe...

Vivi was unaware of tears rolling down her cheeks until Cam eased away from her and he wiped them away with his thumbs. He placed gentle kisses on the side of her mouth, her cheekbones, her temple, her forehead. "It's okay, Viv, you're safe. It's all good."

Oh, God. Vivi closed her eyes as Cam rested his head on her temple, his strong arms cuddling her close. He felt amazing and she hated the fact that she missed this...this *thing* she'd never had. Not him, precisely, but what he represented: strength, support, someone in her corner.

But while it was nice, it wasn't something she could get used to, so Vivi tossed her head, stepped back and put a smile on her face and waved her hand in front of her face. "Sorry, delayed reaction to nearly dying."

"Understandable." Then Cam had the audacity to look amused. "But it could also be because you and I could still start a wildfire with the sparks we generate."

She was not going to encourage him, to respond to his sexy but smirky smile. "I nearly died. *That's* the only reason I kissed you."

Cam dropped his head and Vivi held her breath, waiting for his lips to meet hers again. She tipped her chin up and closed her eyes. Instead of his lips meeting hers, he murmured "BS" against her lips. Vivi jerked back and had to resist the urge to smack the smile off those sexy lips!

Gah!

And why was she still standing here, flip-flopping between smacking him senseless and kissing him stupid?

Cam pulled up to another house ten minutes from Vivi's and leaned across Vivi to open her door. His arm brushed her breast and he heard her intake of breath. Knowing that he couldn't look at her—if he did, he would crush his mouth to hers and nobody would be getting out of the car anytime soon—he pushed the door open and pulled back. She smelled incredible, of soap and shampoo and a scent that exuded her personality— forthright and clean, with a hint of spice.

Vivi released her seat belt and placed her hand on the door. She turned to face him, her eyes worried. "Maybe you should wait here. Charlie is a good friend, but I don't know if I'm up to explaining you just yet."

"If you had to, how would you explain me?"

Vivi released a laugh that was short on amusement. "I'd introduce you as the guy who seems to flip my world every time I run into him."

It was as good an explanation as any.

Cam watched Vivi walk up the path to the front door, hands in the back pockets of her cutoff denims. God, she was a spectacular-looking woman, but not in the rich- and-pampered way of the women he normally dated. Vivi was… What was the word he was looking for? She was *real*. Her hair was the same color it had been three years ago, a light brown with natural highlights. Her face was unpainted, those eyes lightening and darkening according to her mood. She was thinner than she'd been before, but all her curves were still there. And those legs, the ones that had gripped his hips as he slid into her, were still as jaw-droppingly shapely as ever.

His attraction to her burned brighter and hotter

than before. Three years ago, he'd liked her—obviously. She'd been fun, a way to pass a couple of hours, a human connection. But this woman, the mother of the child he'd never known he had, well, she intrigued him. She'd just shared a little of her past, and he realized that there was a lot more to her story than she'd told him. Rising up through the ranks of a restaurant like The Rollin' Smoke wasn't something that happened on a routine basis, so she had to have talent as a chef as well as business savvy. And the fact that she'd had this meteoric career rise while raising a child floored him.

His phone buzzed. Cam looked at his display and hit the button to answer.

"Camden."

He smiled as Ryder Currin's deep voice rolled through his car. Ryder, who was a curious combination of big brother, favorite uncle and best friend, was one of the very few people Cam allowed to call him by his full name.

If Cam did everything he could to be unlike his dad or grandfather or any of his useless male ancestors, then Ryder Currin was the man he *did* try to emulate. Ryder was tough but fair, strong with a solid sense of community. Like Cam, he'd pulled himself up all by himself, for himself, and was now the majority shareholder in Currin Oil, his massive company headquartered in downtown Houston.

Ryder was also how Cam had gotten his start. Cam had heard of a small company needing $50,000 to stake a claim on a piece of land they were convinced held natural gas. Convinced they were on the right track, he had been prepared to risk his savings to invest but didn't have the entire amount. Or even half that. Taking a chance, he'd approached his then boss Ryder Currin, who had loaned him the money, asking very few questions. Three months later, the company had announced that they'd found one of biggest natural gas deposits in the country, and the find blew up their bank accounts. Well, maybe not Ryder's, who was already rich, but Cam's had certainly detonated.

Without that loan, Cam would not be living in River Oaks, driving a fancy car or operating a billion-dollar company. He owed Ryder: for his no-questions-asked faith in him, his continued friendship and for the ear he continued to provide.

"Any news on your missing kid?" Ryder asked.

God, he'd forgotten about Rick Gaines. But that was understandable, since the mother of his child had nearly died when her car ended up in a fast-flowing ditch and he'd discovered he had a daughter.

"Hold on a sec," Cam told Ryder and quickly accessed his messaging app. Scanning his messages, he found the one he was looking for and released a long sigh. Rick was found at a shelter and Cam passed the news along to Ryder.

"Talking about the missing, has the body at the TCC construction site been identified yet?"

"No. And Sterling Perry isn't talking, and neither are his people." Ryder remained quiet for a few moments before continuing. "By the way, Perry has called an emergency meeting of the TCC."

"Can he do that? The club isn't official yet—it hasn't been constituted. There haven't been any elections of officials, and a board hasn't been chosen. Have I missed something?"

"You missed nothing," Ryder growled, obviously pissed. "I am furious that Perry pulled rank and called this meeting. And to make his boardroom the venue? That's unacceptable."

Cam knew a little of Ryder's history with Sterling Perry. Ryder had worked for Perry, who'd fired him for no cause. There were rumors that Ryder had an affair with Perry's wife, but Cam didn't believe that. Ryder wasn't the type to poach on another man's territory. What Cam knew for sure was that Ryder was left an oil-rich piece of land by Sterling's father-in-law and had built his massive empire on the oil he found on that land. Sterling, it was reported, had blown a gasket.

"So, are you going?" Cam asked. In the back of his mind he recalled an email about a TCC meeting but with the latest upheavals in his life—a daughter and her sexy, mind-blowing mother—TCC business had fallen way down on his list of priorities.

"I have no damn choice!" Ryder snapped back. "Everyone is going and I cannot afford to look petty. Especially since a representative from the state board of the TCC will be there."

"Must I be there to hold your hand?" Cam teased and grinned at Ryder's responding growl and muttered obscenity.

"I'm heading over there right now to give Sterling Perry a come-to-Jesus talk. In fact, I'm just pulling up to Perry Holdings now."

Crap. This wasn't going to end well. "Do you think that's a good idea?"

"Probably not," Ryder retorted. "But it will make me feel a lot better."

"Life is…complicated at the moment but I'll be at the meeting."

Ryder's voice dropped. "Are you okay, Cam?"

Cam hadn't intended to tell him, wasn't going to until

the words flew out of his mouth. "I will be if you can tell me how to deal with having a baby daughter I never knew drop into my life. And how I should handle being reunited with a woman I've never quite forgotten."

Ryder chuckled. "Holy crap, Camden. That's huge. And, on one level, hilarious."

Except it really wasn't. It was his damn life.

"Angela?"

At the soft rap on her open office door, Angela Perry looked up to see Perry Holdings' receptionist standing in the doorway to her office. Pulling her attention from the report she'd been trying to digest, she waited for Andrea to speak.

"Ryder Currin is here, wanting to talk to your father."

Angela cursed as her heart took flight at the sound of Ryder's name. Ridiculous, really. "My father is out of town."

"I told him that but then he said he was sure you could take a message."

Angela rolled her eyes. This had to be about the meeting her father had, rather high-handedly in her opinion, called, inviting TCC Houston members. Or potential members. Her father really had to stop acting like he was president of the world. So, in fact, did Ryder Currin.

Too many men, Angela thought, standing up. Not enough aspirin.

The public area at Perry Holdings was a room full of men, and a few women, but Angela immediately found Ryder Currin. It was as if she held the receiver to a homing device pinned to his shirt. Angela looked down at her blue-and-white-striped dress and wondered if the tangerine jacket was too much. Irritated with herself—she always second-guessed her outfits because she wasn't quite as stylish as her twin, Miranda, nor as flashy as her best friend, Tatiana—she cursed her slightly damp palms and her accelerated heart rate. She was a shade off forty, dammit, a grown woman. Surely she shouldn't be feeling fluttery when she laid eyes on him.

"Mr. Currin, this way, please," Angela stated, happy to hear her voice sounded normal.

Ryder half smiled as his big stride ate up the space between them and Angela wished that she could step into his arms, lift her mouth for a kiss. She wanted this man, craved him with a passion that would make her father pop a vein.

"Can I help you?" Angela said, holding her hand out for him to shake. Ryder surprised her when he took her hand and dropped a kiss on her cheek. She inhaled his soap-and-sex scent and her head swam.

Perfect.

Ryder pulled her into the quieter hallway and his big hand cupped the side of her jaw. "I wanted to talk to Sterling but thought I'd also check in on you. We had a pretty intense conversation about the past when we were together at the shelter."

Yeah, that conversation. The one where he told her that, contrary to what she'd always believed, he and her mother had never been anything but friends. Angela still wasn't sure whether she believed him or not. Oh, God, she wanted to, but a niggle of doubt remained. Okay, maybe more than a niggle.

"Why are you here, Ryder?" Angela asked, stepping back. "Oh, right, you want me to deliver a message to my father."

Ryder shook his head. "I'm more than capable of delivering my own messages to Sterling." He lifted a big shoulder and Angela wondered how his skin would feel, whether he'd taste as gorgeous as he looked. *Down, girl.*

"I just wanted to see you."

"There are these amazing things called phones and email." Angela pointed out, annoyed to hear that she was sounding breathless.

"Yeah, but that way I can't see you, smell you—" his voice turned rough, sexier "—kiss you."

Later she'd wonder what propelled her to act so out of character, to step up to him, to place her hands on his rough-with-stubble jaw and stand on her tiptoes to align her mouth with his. She felt his hands tighten on her biceps, and then his lips were under hers. Heat, lust and need shimmied over her and her tongue slipped between his open lips and into his mouth. God, he tasted like chocolate-covered sin. How had she lived for so long without kissing Ryder Currin?

She felt his hesitation, heard his silent "to hell with it" and then he took control of their kiss. His strong arm wound around her waist, pulling her up against his chest—and it was as hard as she'd imagined. He kissed her with assurance and confidence, like he knew exactly what she needed and how to give it to her. Angela teetered on her high heels but Ryder just tightened his grip on her.

"I've got you," he murmured against her open mouth. He hesitated, shrugged and dipped down again, and dialed the kiss up to hot and then to insane.

"Oops!"

Angela heard the feminine giggle and the masculine snort of laughter and yanked her mouth off Ryder's. She rested her forehead on his collarbone and tried to get her breathing under control. Dammit. The news that she'd kissed Ryder Currin—if such a tame word could be used to describe what they'd just done—would be all over the building in five minutes flat. God, she prayed that no one had the balls to tell her father.

Ryder's big hand skimmed down her back and rested on her hip. "I should go."

Angela nodded but didn't move. "Yeah."

Ryder's hand moved up and under her hair and he gripped the back of her neck. "This attraction between us is so damn unexpected."

Yeah. Unexpected and inconvenient. And messy. And liable to blow up in their faces.

But, Angela decided as she watched Ryder walk away from her, it was also the most excitement she'd had in *forever*.

TCC business and Ryder forgotten as he sat in his car, Cam banged his head against the headrest. He was attracted to Vivi's face and body, but he was also intrigued by her resilience, her strong spirit and her innate intelligence. Physical attraction was easy to ignore; mental attraction was hugely problematic. He didn't want to become emotionally entangled with Vivi. He couldn't afford the distraction. He needed to focus on his company, his career, on becoming the success he wanted to be.

You are already successful, he heard Ryder's voice say in his head. *How much money is enough? When are you going to be satisfied with how far you've come and finally be proud of your achievements?*

Cam didn't know. He just knew that he wasn't there yet.

He closed his eyes, remembering his father tossing out his newest plan, his latest scheme to make money.

None were legal, and none made money. Jack had no qualms about ripping off an elderly lady of her savings, stealing the social security checks of unemployed mothers and forging their signatures. Breaking into houses with his son to scoop up anything that he could flip for a profit.

Yet, despite their many scores, their standard of living had never changed. They still bounced from crappy apartments to squats to rented rooms; Cam still wore clothes that were too small and was constantly expected to miss school to pick pockets so he could feed himself and his father.

Would life have been better if his mother had stuck around? From what he'd heard about her, probably not. Fantastic genes he'd passed on to Clementine.

Cam gripped the steering wheel to anchor himself. How could he ever tell Vivi, and eventually Clementine, that his parents lived on the fringes of society, that they'd been criminals and cons? God, he should drive away, stay out of their lives.

He might have money and respect but it didn't change the fact that he was a product of the streets, the son of two people who had all the education and impulse control of a puppy. He didn't have a nurturing bone in his body because he'd never been nurtured. How could he be the father Clem deserved?

Terrified of being a dad and of Vivi finding out about his past, Cam touched the ignition button with his index finger. He was about to start the car when the front door of the house opened and Vivi stepped onto the porch, a little girl on her hip. Cam dropped his hands and stared, his heart bouncing off his rib cage.

God, she looked like him, a feminine version of the child he'd been. Her hair, held in two high pigtails, was the same color as his when he'd been a child, a lighter shade of brown than it was now. She had his nose, his chin and, yeah, his light blue eyes. She had Vivi's fine, dark eyebrows and long lashes and her mouth, but essentially she was a McNeal.

Cam was vaguely aware that Vivi was talking to her sitter, saw hugs and kisses being exchanged, but he couldn't keep his eyes off Clem. This was his kid. His DNA had helped formed her, his blood flowed in her veins. She was his.

Even if he wanted to, he couldn't walk away. Because how did one walk away from love at first sight?

Five

Please let him like her...
Please don't let this be weird...
Please let me do and say the right thing...

Conscious of Clem's chattering in her ear—something about Charlie and a cake—Vivi pulled in a deep breath and watched Cam exit his car and walk around the hood to meet them on the sidewalk. Vivi had always thought that Clem looked like Cam, but now she noticed how close the resemblance was. Vivi stopped a yard from him and met his eyes, suddenly tongue-tied. She wanted to hold Clem out to him, wanted to show her off like a toy. *Look what I made. See what I did. Don't you think I did a good job?*

Cam's eyes, deeper and more intense, bounced between her and Clem, and a small smile touched his lips. He jammed his hands into his pockets, and Vivi saw him swallow and heard him clear his throat. "She's—" he hesitated "—she's beautiful, Vivi."

Vivi turned her head to look into Clem's curious eyes, brushing the back of her hand across her cheek. "She really is."

Clem, suddenly noticing her mother's cuts and scrapes, placed both her hands on Vivi's cheeks and stared at her. "Owie, Mommy?"

"Not so bad, sweetheart," Vivi told her.

"Kiss better?" Clem asked.

"Absolutely."

Vivi closed her eyes as Clem's small lips gently kissed her cut, then her scrape and her bruise. Vivi thanked her and squeezed her, her love for this child threatening to drop her to her knees.

"Where Mommy car?" Clem asked, looking from Cam to his big car.

"My car isn't working," Vivi told her, hitching Clem's bag up higher on her shoulder. She smiled her thanks when Cam slid the bag off her shoulder and easily held it in one hand. Right, time to get this done. "Clem, this is Cam. He's going to take us home."

Clem sent Cam a frank look, tipping her head to one side and taking her time to decide whether to greet him or not. When she hid her face in Vivi's neck, Vivi knew that she was feeling uncharacteristically shy.

She patted Clem's back. "Honey, do you want to say hi to Cam?"

Cam shook his head. "Don't force it, Vivi. She'll say hello when she's ready."

Surprised by his sensitivity, Vivi thanked him as he opened the rear passenger door. She automatically turned to put Clem into her car seat and it took her a moment to realize that there *was* a car seat, in *his* car.

"You got a car seat. For Clem."

* * *

Cam shrugged. Well, yeah. Because she was a kid and kids needed to be protected. Work wasn't all he'd done while she was sleeping, he wanted to tell her.

"Uh, thank you?" Vivi said, obviously surprised.

Vivi's astonishment annoyed Cam. He could be considerate, capable of thinking of someone other than himself, and he would never do anything to harm a child.

Cam walked around the car, climbed inside and looked at the child sitting behind his passenger seat. She looked so much like him it was scary. Clem returned his frank assessment, and when a tiny smile touched her pretty mouth, he felt like she'd hit him with a two-by-four.

"Would you have ever told me about her?" he quietly asked when Vivi took her seat.

He felt Vivi tense. This was a question she didn't want to answer but...tough.

"Well?" he demanded when she didn't speak.

"Probably not," Vivi answered.

When she didn't expand, he turned his head and nailed her with a hard look. "Why not?"

"Because I like making decisions on my own, not having anyone to answer to. Involving you in her life would've made my life complicated and I don't do complicated. I like being independent and I like being on my own."

Truth coated every word she uttered and blazed from her eyes. Her warning—*I will never be controlled by you or anyone else*—could've been on a twenty-foot billboard and it still wouldn't be clearer than these quietly uttered words in his car.

Keep your distance, Cam.

Let me go back to my life, Cam.

Roll back the clock.

Cam rolled his head to look at her fully and their eyes connected, heat and want and desire arcing between them. He knew her brain wanted her to be sensible and distant but he also knew her body wanted what his did. To get naked as soon as possible. He wanted to taste those lips, explore her body, taste every inch of her creamy skin.

He also wanted to delve into that sharp brain, peek behind those walls she'd so carefully erected and reinforced.

He was looking for trouble. And couldn't wait to find it.

Vivi sighed when Cam parked his car in the driveway to her small red brick cottage. Fumbling with the clasp of her seat belt, she felt Cam's fingers on hers and silently cursed when lust skittered over her skin and flashed through her body. She'd had a hell of a day, so why was her battered body responding like this? Their earlier kisses she could put down to adrenaline and delayed reaction but she couldn't keep using those excuses. How could she, after a near-death experience, be feeling…well, horny? Sure, Cam was a great-looking guy with the ability to set female hormones on fire, but after everything that had happened today, shouldn't she be immune?

Vivi lifted her eyes to meet his and saw heat in the blue depths, heard his intake of breath, noticed the slight flush on his cheekbones. Dammit. He was feeling it as well.

Vivi pulled her bottom lip between her teeth and closed her eyes. She pulled her hand out from under his and the seat belt released with a soft snick. It was time to pull herself back to real life, to find some sort of stable ground. Yeah, she'd had a crap day, but it was over, and she needed a reset.

Except that she had a feeling Cam wasn't going to cooperate and allow her life to go back to normal. Vivi sighed and pushed her hair off her forehead. But after a day like today, how could anything be normal again?

Vivi felt Cam's thumb skate over her cheekbone. "Let's get you inside, sweetheart."

Vivi turned her head to look at him, her limbs feeling as heavy as steel girders. The soft, sweet-sounding word became deeper and sexier when he uttered it in his growly, deep voice. She liked hearing it…

But she had to remind herself that men like Cam— good-looking men who could be charming—knew how to turn it on. He was a Texan, and men like him knew how to use *sweetheart* and *darlin'* to maximum effect. It was practically part of the Southern boy's school curriculum.

"Let's get you and the half-pint inside," Cam said before leaving the car. Vivi waited for him to walk around his car to open her door—Texas manners again—and swung her legs around to place her feet on the footboard. Her body ached, her muscles moaned and the ground seemed like a long way down. She was sore, she was tired and all she wanted to do was to sleep.

Nearly dying had wiped away all her strength. Go figure.

Then Vivi felt Cam's hands on her waist, and with no effort at all, he lifted her up and out of the car, and lowered her gently. Keeping his arm around her waist, he tipped her chin up. She caught the concern in his face. And, yep, under the concern, desire flashed. "You okay?"

She wanted to tell him she was worried that if he let her go, her knees would buckle and, worse, she would burst into tears. She nearly told him she was exhausted, that she didn't think that tonight she was up to being the mommy Clem needed and deserved. That she needed, just this once, to have someone else's hands on the wheel.

Vivi dropped her eyes and sighed. She hauled back the words hovering on the tip of her tongue, swallowed them down. She would never, ever give anyone an inch of control. Because she knew that land surrendered could never be reclaimed. Her mom, her home, her church were all gone. She'd learned that lesson well.

"Thanks for the lift." Vivi stepped away from Cam, putting a whole bunch of space between them. "I'll just grab Clem and we'll get out of your hair."

His eyes moved from her face to Clem, who was still in her car seat, softly singing. When Cam looked back at Vivi, he shook his head before lifting his hand to encircle her neck. Vivi wanted to pull away, but because Cam's fingers were kneading the tension out of her muscles, she just sighed and released a small groan of pleasure.

Then Cam's head dipped down and he used his thumb to tip up her jaw. His breath was the only barrier between their lips and then there was nothing but his mouth on hers. Vivi felt her body sag, her knees buckle, and was grateful when Cam banded his arm around her back, taking her weight.

So good, Vivi thought, as his mouth moved over hers. Strong and masculine and assured and confident. Cam's tongue slipped between her lips, gently demanding entrance. She shouldn't, she really shouldn't, but her lips were suddenly operating independently of her brain.

She needed this, needed him to kiss her in the sunshine of a balmy, late afternoon. She'd take his kiss, suck up his strength, borrow some of his confidence and then she'd send him on his way.

She just needed this minute, and maybe one or two more.

Cam's hand slid down her back, his thumb tracing her spine. He then splayed his hand on her lower back, his fingers cupping her butt. He pulled her in and Vivi felt the ridge in his jeans as his erection pushed into her stomach. Pleasure, at both his response and at the fact that she could make this gorgeous man so hard, so quickly, rushed through her. Vivi gripped his shirt just above his belt, telling herself that she couldn't, shouldn't touch him, that she couldn't take him in hand.

They were outside her house, she had nosy neighbors, and her child was not a few feet from them.

Vivi twisted his shirt tighter, unable to stop herself from rocking into him, from winding her tongue around his, from moaning in the back of her throat. The heat he generated was insane; the need he dragged to the surface held the same power of the recent storm.

He was a perfect package of power and destruction in six foot something of sexiness.

But while climatic events were powerful and breathtaking, they were also destructive and damaging. They were, as she very well knew, to be avoided. So Vivi placed her hand flat against Cam's chest and pushed him away. He muttered a curse, reaching for her again, but Vivi quickly stepped back, shaking her head. No, it was time to be sensible, way past time to shut this down. After rubbing her hands over her face, she pushed past Cam to open the back door. Seeing Clem's face settled her, reminded her that she was a mommy first, a chef second, and that she had no time for kissing sexy men in the sunshine.

She had no business kissing Cam, her one-night stand.

And the father of her beautiful, smart kid.

Vivi flipped open the car seat clasp and winced when Clem tumbled into her jellylike arms. Grimacing, she settled Clem on her hip and reached for the bag Cam had placed on the floor below Clem's feet. Her back muscles screamed as she bent down, her fingertips brushing over the handle of the bag. Dammit, she was stiffening up. She reached for the bag again and this time she couldn't stop a low groan from leaving her mouth. She couldn't help looking at Cam, hoping that he hadn't heard. He was standing behind her, his arms crossed, his legs slightly apart. His head was cocked, and his expression inscrutable, but she recognized the frustration and annoyance in his eyes.

"Are you done being a stubborn ass?"

Vivi narrowed her eyes at him but swallowed down her hot retort. "Thanks for the lift. It was…" She hesitated, looking for the right word. Amazing? Great? Exciting? Knee-collapsing? "…interesting seeing you again," she finished.

Cam had the nerve to grin. "Do you really believe that I am just going to be a good boy and ride away?"

No, of course, she didn't. She wasn't that naive. Or stupid. "One could hope," Vivi muttered. She shifted Clem on her hip, wondering when her daughter had picked up another twenty pounds.

"Good try but…no." Cam lifted his hands and looked Clem in the eye, silently asking her whether he could carry her. Clem shocked her by leaning forward with a sunny grin. Two seconds later, she was perched on

Cam's thick forearm, two sets of identical blue eyes looking at her. Vivi stepped forward, wanting to take her back, needing to regain control of the situation. Then Clem dropped her head and rested her temple against Cam's collarbone, fully comfortable being held by this strange man.

Vivi couldn't blame her. Cam exuded capability and confidence, and babies were barometers. Cam made her and, apparently, her daughter feel secure, like he was the barrier that stood between them and an ugly world.

Vivi felt a burning sensation in her eyes and cursed the tears blurring her vision. That was her job; she'd been that person for Clem all her life! How could Cam stride into their lives and just take over? It wasn't right, and it wasn't fair!

But as she knew, so much about life wasn't fair.

Cam gently pushed her away from the door and reached down and snagged Clem's bag. He closed the back door and transferred the bright pink bag to his other hand. Then Vivi's hand was swallowed by his and she immediately felt calmer, as if the earth had stopped rocking beneath her feet. Like Clem, she couldn't help responding to his strength and his capability.

As they walked to the front door of her cottage, Vivi tried to convince herself to put her foot down, to tell him to leave. But she was utterly exhausted, and the words wouldn't come.

Pulling her house key out of the back pocket of her cutoffs she tried to open the door, silently cursing when she missed the lock. Cam didn't say anything but just took the key from her hand, jammed it in the lock and opened the door for her. And as Vivi stepped into her house—the home she'd made for her and her daughter—

she told herself that it was okay to lean, just for a half hour, maybe a little more.

She'd take a little time to gather her strength and her courage and then she'd send Cam on his way. She didn't need him.

She just needed her daughter.

Cam, with Clem still in his arms, stepped into the hallway of Vivi's small house, grateful for the cool, fragrant air. The house held that perfectly pleasant smell that only came with the presence of females—perfume and powder, sweet and sexy. Cam placed his hand on Clem's small back, his eyes moving from Vivi's face to his daughter's, thinking that his life had been woman free—casual sexual encounters couldn't be counted—and now he had two girls who'd dropped into his life.

And despite Vivi's not-so-subtle go-away attitude, he intended to keep them there. Being part of Clem's life was a no-brainer; he fully intended to be her dad, however bad he might be at it. But he could learn, he would learn. He had no intention of being the same waste-of-space parent his father had been.

He heard Clem's sigh and looked down to see her long eyelashes against her cheeks, her tiny hand on his chest. She suddenly felt a little heavier, her breathing a little deeper. She was, he realized, asleep. His mouth tipped up in a wry smile: at least someone in this house trusted him.

Vivi, who obviously had a finely tuned mom radar, lifted her head. Her expression softened as love, pure and incandescent, turned her dark eyes liquid. He'd never seen so much love in one expression, and his cold, hard heart rolled around his rib cage. His daughter was deeply loved, and Cam's throat clogged with gratitude.

He was pissed at Vivi's secretiveness, confused by her reluctance to contact him, discombobulated by her sudden and dramatic reappearance in her life and kicked off-kilter by his raging attraction to her.

But beside all that, he was fundamentally and completely grateful that she loved his daughter.

Not all mothers did.

Cam looked away from her, hoping she hadn't noticed his emotional reaction. He didn't know how to deal with these complicated feelings and he certainly couldn't discuss them.

"She normally goes down for a nap around about now," Vivi said. "I'll go put her down and then I'll walk you to your car."

Did she really think she'd get rid of him that easily? Vivi reached for Clem but Cam shook his head. "I've got her."

Vivi looked like she was wanted to argue, but instead she just shrugged and walked away. Cam followed her through the living room. Her house was nothing like his exquisitely decorated mansion in River Oaks; it could probably fit into one wing of his stupidly big residence. But every inch was warm and welcoming and personal. This was Vivi and Clem's space; they lived here. Unlike him, who just seemed to inhabit his house.

If the choice was between luxury and warmth, space and coziness, Vivi's house would win hands down. It was a home, while his place was just a richly decorated space.

Vivi opened the door to the small bedroom and gestured him inside. There were stuffed animals in Clem's bed, and the curtains were printed with tiny farm animals. A chest of drawers stood in the corner of the room and a battered bookcase held a wide variety of children's books.

Cam's attention was pulled from the room when Vivi bent over to toss the stuffed animals to the bottom of Clem's bed. God, she had a perfect ass. His eyes drifted down and Cam could easily imagine those long legs wrapped around his waist, her breasts in his hands, her sexy mouth on his. God, he wanted her. As much—no, far more than he had three years ago.

Vivi straightened and turned, and their eyes collided. Moments passed as electricity arced between them, and neither of them moved, each knowing that the other was remembering, wanting, craving. Memories of that night occasionally surfaced, along with mild regret, and he accepted that making love with Vivi was one of the best sexual experiences of his life. But Cam knew that if he made love to her now, tonight, nothing would ever be the same.

It was almost enough to make him walk away. If it weren't for Clem, he would.

Vivi wrenched her eyes away and gestured to the bed. "You can just lay her down. She won't wake up. She sleeps like the dead."

Cam stepped up to the bed and Vivi moved away, as if scared to touch him. He didn't blame her; they had the ability to go up in flames. He held Clem gently, releasing his breath when she was on the bed, her cheek on her pillow. Vivi, still taking care not to make contact, tugged her tiny shoes off her feet and then her socks, revealing perfect, perfect toes. Everything about Clem was perfect...

And Clem's mommy wasn't too bad, either.

Vivi placed the shoes and socks on top of the chest of drawers, crossed her arms and rocked on her heels.

"So, again, thanks for your help. But if you don't mind, I'd like you to leave."

He wasn't ready for go, not yet. He could stay here. This could be his place.

Cam closed his eyes and shook the fantasy away. *Just because you have a daughter doesn't mean you have a family. It doesn't work like that. Not now, not ever. You're projecting, fantasizing, McNeal. That isn't something you do, something you're allowed to do.*

You deal in facts, cold and hard.

Cam jammed his hands into his pockets, his eyes on Vivi's extraordinarily lovely face. *So, deal in the cold and the hard*, he told himself.

He wanted Vivi. Wanted her more than he wanted to take another breath.

He wanted to be part of Clem's life. He would be part of her life.

And that meant not allowing Vivianne to hustle him out of her house, her life. That meant sticking. And staying.

Cam tipped his head, considering a plan of action. He could seduce Vivi. It wouldn't be hard. She wanted him as much as he wanted her. Within a minute, maybe two, they would be swept away by lust and need and want, oblivious to anything but how they made each other feel. It would be easy, effective, efficient.

But sometimes easy and effective wasn't right, wasn't honorable. Vivi had had a hell of day and she looked wrung out. He knew that she was physically sore, bruised and battered, and she had to be as confused and wary about his reappearance in her life and Clem's as he was about her.

And he wanted Vivi willing and eager and hot and wild. He wanted her fully engaged, utterly focused on him and how he made her feel. He wanted all of her, every lovely mental and physical inch of her.

He should leave, give her some space, but he didn't want to. Not yet. But he didn't have a good enough reason to stay.

"It's been a crazy day, huh?"

Cam released a quick laugh at her understatement. "Crazy is one word for it," he admitted, pushing his hand through his hair. Suddenly noticing that his throat was dry, he gestured to the door. "Got anything to drink? I'm parched."

Vivi wrinkled her nose, as if trying to remember what was in her fridge. "I have some white wine... Maybe a beer?"

"Beer would be good," Cam replied. He sent Clem another look—God, he had a daughter!—and followed Vivi down the hallway and toward the kitchen. He leaned against the counter and crossed his legs at the ankles, watching as her head disappeared into the fridge, leaving him with a view of that ass and those legs again.

Cam rubbed his hand over his face and forced his thoughts out of the bedroom. God, he hadn't thought this much about sex and a woman's body since he was sixteen. *Time to get a grip, McNeal.* And maybe, dammit, it was time for him to go.

He could pick this up tomorrow, the day after... Maybe he should give himself, and Vivi, some time to come to terms with this turn-their-lives-upside-down day.

Vivi straightened and closed the fridge door before spreading apart her empty hands. "Sorry, no beer. And my wine is also finished."

Cam suspected that she was lying and that like him,

she'd had a bit of a talk to herself while her face was buried in the fridge. He didn't like lies—couldn't stand them, in fact—but he'd let this one slide. "No problem." He stood up straight and pulled his car keys from his back pocket. "Can I do anything else for you before I go?"

Surprise flashed across Vivi's face, suggesting that she wasn't used to offers of help. And that pissed him off. Where were her friends? Her family? "Do you want to use my phone to call anyone for you? Your mom, a friend?"

Distaste jumped in and out of her eyes and her expression cooled. "No, thank you. I'm perfectly fine on my own."

And he thought he was proud and self-sufficient. Miss Vivianne almost had him beat. "You sure?" he pushed.

"Very." Vivi snapped out the word.

Whoa, fierce. Cam lifted his hands, a little amused. His daughter's mom had fire in her veins and he liked that, liked that she wasn't a pushover, that she was independent and feisty. God help him when he got her back into bed. They'd both spontaneously combust.

Because that was exactly where they were going,

And if he didn't leave this house right now, that was going to happen sooner than later...

Cam heard the discreet beep from his phone and pulled the device from his back pocket. Like many other Houstonians, he'd set up a series of alerts on his phone to keep abreast with the flood situation. Now he was suddenly glad he had. He read the Tweet once, then again, just to make sure before releasing a quick, sharp curse.

Vivi snapped her head up, immediately realizing that something was very wrong. "What is it?"

"Water has spilled over the wall of the Addicks Reservoir, and the Barker Reservoir is very close to its limits. The Army Corps of Engineers are going to open the gates to the reservoirs. A mandatory evacuation order has been issued. You need to get out of here."

Vivi just stood there, her forehead wrinkling. "But those reservoirs are supposed to help with the flooding."

"I think they are in a 'damned if you do, damned if you don't' situation," Cam replied. "But we don't have time to argue about the pros and cons of the engineers' decisions, Viv. Your house could be flooded. I need to get you and Clem out of here. Let's go."

Vivi nodded and all but ran out of the room, Cam hot on her heels. "Can you grab Clem while I pack a bag?"

Cam grabbed her arm and spun her around. "We don't have time for you to grab anything, Viv, except Clem. We have to go now!"

"Some toiletries, a change of clothing," Vivi protested.

Because he understood how hard it was to walk away from everything you'd struggled to earn, he wanted to give her that time, but her life and Clem's were far more important than clothes and things. He forced himself to ignore her pleading eyes, her sad expression. "Clem. That's it."

He didn't give her a chance to answer, spinning on his heels to return to Clem's bedroom. Gathering her in his arms, he released a frustrated grunt when Vivi darted past him to pick up a stuffed monkey toy, well-loved and battered. He tasted panic in the back of his throat, not knowing how much time they had. Holding Clem against his shoulder, he grabbed Vivi's hand and tugged her through her house. He ushered Vivi into the front seat and took a moment to place Clem in her car seat, quickly figuring out the clasp that held her in place. She was still asleep, thank God. A screaming, crying child would make this situation that much worse.

Running around the hood of his car, he noticed that the neighborhood was suddenly alive with activity. A car farther up the street was pulling out, another on its tail.

This wasn't a drill, this was real life and it was as scary as hell. Would he be this worried if he was only worried about his own hide? Probably not. Being responsible for Vivi, and Clem, increased his anxiety by a thousand degrees.

He would not let anything happen to them…

Starting the SUV, Cam pulled out of the driveway. He stomped his foot on the accelerator as his eyes flicked between his rearview mirror, the road in front of him and his speedometer. He grimaced as he geared down, taking the corner on something that was close to two wheels.

Thank God that catching drivers speeding through a residential area was the last thing on the minds of cops this afternoon.

Six

She'd trashed her car, nearly drowned, been admitted into the ER unconscious and forced out of her house thanks to a dam overflowing. And Cam McNeal was back in her life. It was fair to say she'd had a hell of a day. So when Cam pulled into the super exclusive neighborhood of River Oaks and then into the circular driveway of a French-château-inspired home, Vivi didn't have any energy left to feel surprised.

She glanced into the back seat, saw that Clem was still asleep and looked past the house to the golf course that formed the back border to his house. She couldn't imagine Cam playing golf, schmoozing it up with his business buddies on the links. Despite his designer clothes and luxury car, Cam looked too wild for the preppy sport. With his height and build she could see him playing rugby or water polo, hard, intense sports that required strength and stamina, determination and aggression.

Following a small ball across acres of grass didn't seem his style.

But what did she know? She'd spent a night with the man three years ago; she'd barely scratched the surface of what made Cam tick. Vivi gestured to the golf course. "Do you play?" she asked, her curiosity demanding an answer.

Cam dropped his big hands from the wheel—long fingers, wide hands, hands that had caressed her with a skill she'd never known before or since—and released a short, sharp chuckle.

"Ryder Currin has pulled me onto the links more times than I'd like, and I hated every moment. He calls me a ham-handed philistine." Vivi caught the note of affection in his voice for Ryder. Ryder, as she'd read, had been Cam's first investor, and from their visits to The Rollin' Smoke, she knew they were good friends. But the admiration and respect she heard in Cam's voice, conveyed in only a few words, suggested he was more than Cam's good friend and that there was a bond between them that went deeper than she'd suspected. Vivi wanted to pry and probe but forced herself to pull the words. The world had shifted under her feet a few times today. She didn't need to complicate her life further by digging into Cam's fascinating inner world.

And dammit, every aspect of him was fascinating. He was rough and tough and acerbic and controlling, but underneath it all he was also kind and considerate and generous. She didn't know what to make of him. On her best day—and today was very far from being that—she'd find him challenging. He was still in top physical shape, but he felt harder, stronger, more capable than three years ago, more solid, like his feet were firmly anchored to the earth.

So were hers, Vivi admitted. They'd both come a long way in three years. They'd both worked their tails off, and while she wasn't as financially fluid as Cam— few people were—she was proud of how far she'd come.

She was also proud of her child's dad for what he'd accomplished. If only he still wasn't so damn sexy, if only he still didn't affect her. One look from him and she melted, envisioning him undressing her, those big hands skimming her body, his talented fingers finding her secret, long-neglected places, his mouth devouring hers. She still wanted him.

She really didn't want to want him.

Cam's gentle touch, his fingers brushing her hand, pulled her back to the present, and she realized that she'd been staring at him. Vivi felt her cheeks heat. "Are you okay?" Cam asked, his rough voice full of concern. How many times had he asked her that today? Far too many.

She had a damn good excuse for her inattention and she'd use it. After all it wasn't every day that one could claim to have cheated death. "It's been a long, tough day."

"That's an understatement."

And as much as she wanted to fall face-first into a bed, she had a child to look after, to feed and bathe, who needed love and attention. And she could do that someplace else. She couldn't stay here with Cam. It was all too much. "Can you take me to a hotel, Cam?"

Cam turned in his seat, rested his wrist on the steering wheel and sighed. "If I make you feel that uncomfortable, I'll drive you two blocks over and book you into one of the guest suites of the country club. At my cost."

"I can pay—" Then Vivi realized that she couldn't

actually pay for a damn thing. Her purse containing her identification and her bank cards was long gone.

"Look, why not just stay with me? I have guest bedrooms. My housekeeper will be in in the morning and since she routinely moonlights as a nanny to some of the neighborhood kids, she'll be more than happy to help me keep an eye on Clem if you want to sleep in or just take a break." Cam turned his eyes from her face to look at his enormous house. "You'll be safe here, and Clem will be safe here. Isn't that the most important thing right now?"

He used the one argument she didn't have a rebuttal for. Clem's safety would always be her top priority. Vivi ran her fingers across her forehead. She wanted to tell him she was scared, that she felt uncomfortable being here with him. She was terrified he would be too good to them, that she would find herself falling under his spell, swept away by the fantasy of playing a happy family with the wealthy, sexy father of her child. Cam was magnetic and her desire for him hadn't faded; she could easily imagine herself in this house, in his bed.

But Cam was a take-no-prisoners, my-way-or-the-highway type of guy, and she would never, ever allow him that amount of control over her or Clem. It was her life, and Clem was her daughter; she would sink or swim by her choices.

"I'm not asking you to marry me or to move in, Vivianne," Cam said, sounding impatient. "It'll just be for a few days, until you can return to your house."

Vivi narrowed her eyes at him. "So you aren't intending to seduce me, to find a place in my—Clem's life?"

Cam flashed her a quick, rakish smile. "Of course, I am. Our chemistry is off the charts. And Clem is my daughter, so of course, I want to get to know her.

But that doesn't necessarily translate into marriage and moving in. Besides, I'm not cut out for family life in suburbia."

Vivi looked from him to his big house with its elegant facade, sparkling windows and beautifully landscaped gardens. Raising both eyebrows, she said, "Then why the hell do you own this house in the trendiest suburb in Houston?"

Cam turned away from her, muttered something that sounded like "I have no damned idea" before tapping a button on his dashboard. The massive garage door opened and he drove his SUV into the garage. Vivi looked at the expensive super-bike, the powerful boat and a German-engineered, imported sports car and shook her head.

She'd come a long way in three years—from broke and pregnant to stable and successful—but Cam's success had been meteoric. Vivi looked behind her and smiled at her daughter's peaceful, beautiful face. Cam had the money but she had Clem.

She'd got the better deal, no doubt about it.

"Shh, Clem, Mommy might still be sleeping."

"I is hungry."

Vivi, half asleep, wanted to tell Cam that nobody came between Clem and her food, but her eyelids felt heavy and the words stuck in her throat. She sighed and pushed her head into the soft down pillow, allowing her body to sink into the super comfortable bed.

Vivi felt the tiny hand patting her face. "Mommeee! I's hungry!"

"I'm sure I have cereal, Clem. Let's leave Mom to sleep and see what we have."

Clem asked if he had a particularly sugary cereal that

wasn't standard fare in their household, and Vivi realized that sometime between yesterday and this morning, Clem had lost her shyness and was her normal
chatty self.

"Your teeth will fall out, Clementine, if you eat that
rubbish," Vivi mumbled, still unable to lift her heavy
lids.

Clem rested her lips on hers and Vivi smiled. Early-
morning kisses from Clem were just the best thing ever.
She opened her eyes and smiled. "Hey, baby girl. Did
you have a good sleep?"

Clem nodded enthusiastically. "I trieded to wake
you."

Bad Mommy. Vivi pushed away the surge of guilt
and stroked Clem's cheek. "Sorry, baby. Give me ten
minutes and we'll make a plan for breakfast."

"Am going to Charlie?"

Vivi forced herself to think. What was today? Friday? No, it was Saturday and that meant no day care.
And because she had Clem with her, that also meant she
couldn't go down to The Rollin' Smoke to help clean up
the restaurant. But maybe they could take a drive down
there and see if any progress had been made.

Then she remembered that she didn't have a vehicle.
Or a phone to arrange for one. Or identification.

"No, Clem, you're going to stay with me today."

Clem smiled and Vivi saw her dimple, the flash of
mischief in her smile. Her daughter was going to be a
handful when she was older and Vivi was going to have
to become a lot smarter. But not today. Today she just
wanted to go back to sleep. But she couldn't. She was a
single mom and single moms couldn't take the day off.

"I heard there was a little girl in the house. I wonder
if she likes pancakes."

Vivi frowned at the lilting Irish brogue and her eyes darted to Cam's, silently asking for an explanation. Having Cam see her sleepy, mussed and rumpled was one thing. Meeting a total stranger in one of Cam's T-shirts and with messy hair was not going to happen. She turned over to sit up and released a sharp hiss as her muscles protested, volubly reminding her that she'd tangled with a ravine and water and nearly lost.

"That's my housekeeper, Sally. She loves kids and she makes the best pancakes ever." Cam held out his hand to Clem and Clem immediately ran to him, sliding her hand into his, apparently without a second thought. They stepped into the hallway and Vivi listened as Cam introduced Clem to his housekeeper.

"You don't look like a girl who likes pancakes." Sally said.

"I does, I like them lots!" Clem immediately responded.

"How many can you eat?" Sally asked and Vivi liked the way she spoke to Clem.

"A hundred!" Clem proclaimed. Vivi rolled her eyes at her daughter's pronouncement. A hundred seemed like a good number to a two-year-old.

"Well, I've never made a hundred before but I'll be willing to give it a try. But I might need some help."

"I's can help!" Clem piped up.

"I'm sure you can. Let's go, then."

Clem ran back into the room and up to Vivi's bed, repeating the entire conversation word for word and ending with a rushed request for permission to go with Sally. Vivi looked toward Cam, who stood with his shoulder pressed into the door frame. He nodded his head, mouthing that Clem would be fine, and Vivi gave her consent. Clem ran out of the room again and Vivi heard her peppering Sally with questions as they moved down the hallway. Vivi fought the urge to call her back. Sally was a stranger. How could she let Clem go off with someone she hadn't vetted?

"Clem will be fine, Viv."

How did Cam know that she was worried? Had her expression said all that? If so, she really had to get her face under control. She could not allow Cam to discern how ridiculously attracted she was to him.

Vivi pulled her gaze off his tall frame, his messy hair. He was dressed in cargo shorts and a sleeveless shirt showing off his broad shoulders, big biceps and his smooth, golden skin. An overnight scruff covered his jaw and he wore flip-flops on his surprisingly elegant feet. She wanted to take a big bite out of him and then soothe the pain away with a long lick.

Vivi dropped her head back onto the pillow and placed her forearm against her eyes. Oh, God, she was in so much trouble.

Vivi felt the bed shift and inhaled Cam's fresh-from-the-shower scent, the heat from his body sliding over her. She felt his thigh against her hip and then his fingers gently pulled her arm from her face. Vivi reluctantly opened her eyes.

"Hello," Cam said, humor in his ridiculously pretty eyes.

Vivi felt her nipples puckering against her T-shirt—his T-shirt—and she licked her lips, noticing there was no moisture left in her mouth. He was too close, and this setting—a beautifully decorated bedroom containing a huge bed—was too intimate. She needed distance to regain some control. She couldn't, wouldn't let Camden affect her like this again.

Then Cam's mouth touched hers and she knew it was

too late. He did affect her, in every way. Her lips opened to his tongue, her back arched so that her nipple could find his hand and her legs fell open. She was putty in his hands, a morning mess of melted glue.

Unable to help herself, Vivi linked her arms around his neck, sighing as his thumb brushed her nipple, smiling when he yanked her shirt from under her butt so that his hand could find her skin. He brushed her hip, stopped when he realized that she wasn't wearing any panties and then carried on, his fingers skimming over her stomach and rib cage. As his tongue swirled around hers, sipping and sucking and rediscovering her, his hand found her breasts, giving both his attention.

Vivi allowed her hands to roam, exploring the hard muscles of his back, the width of those impressive shoulders, the taut muscles in his arms. He was so powerful, utterly and fundamentally masculine. Ignoring her aching body, Vivi wiggled closer, needing to have every inch of her body plastered against his.

Preferably naked and preferably immediately.

Cam wound his arm around her waist to haul her in and Vivi couldn't help the whimper of pain when his hand connected with a bruise on her back. Cam cursed and immediately lowered her to the bed. When he pulled back, Vivi saw the concern in his eyes and knew that the spell was broken.

Dammit.

Cam tugged her forward, pulled her shirt up her back and knelt on the bed to look over her shoulder. His mouth thinned and his eyes cooled; he looked thoroughly, utterly pissed off. Why?

Feeling self-conscious, Vivi pulled the shirt under her butt and the covers up to her waist. She pushed a hand through her messy hair and looked at a point past Cam's shoulder. They shouldn't be making out. That was part of their past, and it couldn't be part of her future. There couldn't, shouldn't be anything more between them but Clem, but desire—hot, fast and insistent—kept popping up and making its irritating presence known.

"You have a bruise the size of a dinner plate on your lower back and another on your shoulder blade," Cam said, his voice laced with frustration. That was when she realized that he wasn't pissed off at her but for her. He wasn't happy that she was hurt. And his obvious concern ignited a small fire in her stomach. When had anyone last cared how she was, how she felt? God, she couldn't remember. When she was a young teenager? A child? Maybe not even then. She was her mother's showpiece, her pet, her sense of self-worth. The one object Margaret Donner had control over.

"Any other bruises?"

Vivi thought about brushing his question off but quickly realized that if she didn't give Cam an answer that satisfied him—i.e. the truth—he'd pull up her shirt and find out for himself. Any other man would get a black eye if they were to be so bold. Cam, on the other hand, might just get lucky. Dammit.

Vivi pursed her lips before replying. "Top of my right thigh and on my knee."

Cam pulled back the covers and pushed up her shirt, whistling when he saw the livid purple and black bruises. His fingers brushed over her injuries, his touch too light to cause any pain, and his eyes met hers. "Sorry, honey."

Vivi shrugged. "I'm a bit stiff and a lot sore but I'll live."

Cam brushed his thumb over her cheekbone before

his fingers picked up a loose curl and tucked it behind her ear. The gesture was so sweet and tender, so
at odds with his big hands and hard-ass attitude, that
Vivi felt the sting of tears. Tenderness was such a for-
eign emotion.

"I'll bring up some pancakes and a dose of painkillers," Cam told her, his tone telling her that he'd not en-
tertain any arguments. "Then you can get some more
sleep."

"I need to be with Clem."

Cam looked past her to the window, his expression
tight and guarded. When he met her eyes again, his
held a range of emotions she couldn't identify. "I know
we haven't spent enough time together for you to trust
me, Vivi, but I wish you would. Please believe that I
would never, ever let anything happen to Clem. I might
only know her for a day but she's my daughter, my responsibility."

"Cam, I don't trust easily." Or at all. And she never,
ever let anyone take control. Of her or her daughter.

"I'm asking you to trust me for a few hours. We'll
stay in the house. And if we do go outside, we'll keep in
shouting distance of the house. I just want to give you
a chance to rest, to heal." His mouth quirked up into a
smile that she found hard to resist. "And I'd like to get
to know my daughter."

She was tired and sore, and she'd love to go back
to sleep. Could she release the reins for a couple of
hours and allow Cam this time? Vivi stared down at her
clenched hands, taking some time to think. By making
Cam her emergency contact person she'd created this
situation. Cam was now part of Clem's life. She'd have
to let them spend time together at some point, and if she
wanted Cam to be a good father to Clem, that meant

allowing them to spend time together alone. At some point she'd have to trust Cam. Why couldn't she start now? An experienced child-sitter was in the house if Cam ran into difficulties with Clem, and Vivi would be just a shout away. What could go wrong?

Nothing except that Clem might fall in love with Cam and she might fall in lust with Cam—oops, too late on that one—and the whole situation could blow up in her face.

God, she was so damn tired and so damn sore. She just wanted a few hours...

"Okay. Except that I will take the painkillers and skip the pancakes."

Vivi saw the relief in Cam's eyes and underneath, the determination. "Nope, you'll put a hole in your stomach if you take the meds like that. Pancakes, coffee and a full glass of water and then you can have the drugs."

He stood up and Vivi tipped her head up to scowl at him. "Did anyone ever tell you that you are as bossy as hell?"

Cam smiled down at her and her stomach flipped over once and then, because it could, did it again. "All the time." He dropped his head and brushed his lips across hers in a slow, gentle, supremely sexy kiss. When he lifted his mouth, he smiled at her. "Then again, like recognizes like, sweetheart."

Not so far away, Angela Perry heard the front door to her apartment opening and started a mental countdown.
Four.
Three.
Two.
One.

"You kissed Ryder Currin? In the hallway? At work?"

Angela lowered the bottle of water she'd been guzzling and arched her eyebrows at her best friend who'd just made liberal use of her just-for-emergencies key. Tatiana Havery was perfectly made up and immaculately dressed for eight thirty on a Saturday morning. Angela, makeup free and perspiring from a five-mile run, felt grubby and gross. "I'm going to shower. Can we discuss this later?"

Tatiana wrinkled her nose and waved her hand at her damp clothing. "Your shower can wait until we are done discussing the ludicrous rumor I'm hearing about you kissing the very hot Ryder Currin!"

The word "kiss" was too tame a word for what had happened yesterday. Inhaled? Devoured? Scarfed? Any might work but she certainly had not simply *kissed* Ryder.

"Why do you assume it's a rumor?" Angela asked, a little pissed because Tee made it sound like Ryder was so out of her league. "I did kiss him and it was amazing."

Tatiana's mouth fell open. "You did not!"

Angela couldn't help her small smirk. "I so did." The smirk morphed into a self-satisfied grin. "And it was freakin' amazing."

Tatiana lifted her eyebrows. "I can see that it was. Lucky you." Then a second later, "Or unlucky you."

Angela frowned at her friend. "And what do you mean by that?"

"Part of the job of being your best friend, honey, is keeping your feet firmly on the ground. So I'm reminding you that the man you just locked lips with allegedly had an affair with your mom. And there's also a chance that he blackmailed your grandfather into giving him land."

Tee's caustic statement blew away her warm and fuzzies. Dammit, she'd forgotten. How could she? But Ryder had told her that there was nothing more between her mom and him than friendship, and she believed him.

Didn't she?

"He explained that they were just friends."

"But you can't be sure, can you?"

She couldn't, dammit. She only had the word of a man she'd been taught not to trust.

"You know what your dad always says, Ange. Trust but verify."

"And who can I ask about the past who doesn't, to quote Dad again, have skin in the game?"

Tatiana considered her question. "Why don't you go back up to the ranch, find someone who has worked on the ranch, in the house, for a long time and ask what they remember? Servants know everything and someone will know if anything happened between your mom and Ryder."

It wasn't a bad suggestion, but Angela wondered whether it was worth the effort. "The thing is, Tee, I really do believe Ryder. While we haven't had much time to discuss the details, my gut tells me that he's telling the truth about the past."

But what if she was wrong? What if she simply wanted to believe Ryder? Was her desire for him confusing the issue?

"What should I do, Tee?"

Tatiana waited a beat before responding. "Like I said, go to the ranch and ask some hard questions. Because if something does develop between you and Ryder, you'll will always have this cloud of doubt hanging over you. Rather get it sorted now before you are in too deep."

It was sound advice, even if it was delivered in Tee's normal shoot-from-the-hip manner. Unfortunately, it was advice Angela really didn't want to hear. Or take.

Much later that Saturday, when Cam finally heard footsteps in the hall, it took all his willpower not to bound to his feet like a lovestruck puppy. It didn't matter that his heart was suddenly revving in the red zone or that his mouth was as dry as the Mojave Desert. He was a grown man—he should know better. Cam kept his eyes on the screen of his laptop and waited until he heard Vivi clear her throat before he slowly raised his head to look at her.

And instantly felt the sharp punch to his heart.

With her makeup-free face and hair pulled back, she looked like the young woman he'd seduced all those years ago. He'd sent Sally out to purchase some clothes for Vivi and Clem, and the denim shorts she'd bought made Vivi's legs look endless. The T-shirt boldly proclaiming "We the people like to party" skimmed her high breasts and her subtle curves. She was sunshine after a brutal storm, hot chocolate after shoveling snow, a breath of fresh air in an empty house.

She was both lightning and soft rain, strength and fragility, more beautiful than he remembered and more terrifying than he could've imagined.

God, he was in so much trouble. "Neck-deep, bleeding and swimming with alligators" kind of trouble.

Vivi pushed her hands into her back pockets and rocked on her bare feet. Sexy bare feet tipped with pale pink nails. "Hi. Where's Clem?"

It took Cam a moment to understand her question.

Clem? Right, her—his, their—daughter. "Uh, we gave her a sandwich and some juice, and she fell asleep while watching *Peppa Pig*. She's in the media room, two doors down."

Vivi frowned and stepped into his office and up to his desk, allowing her fingers to trail over the edge of his antique walnut desk. "I don't let her have a lot of TV time…for future reference."

"You don't?" Cam asked, surprised. "Why not?"

"I prefer for her to do puzzles or to look through a picture book. Too much TV numbs the brain," Vivi replied, sounding defensive.

Cam saw her mental retreat and silently cursed. "That wasn't criticism, Vivi, just a need to understand." He glanced down at the screen, wondering how to frame his next sentence, wondering if he should even verbalize his thoughts. But they needed to be said, and he needed to say them. "I spent the morning with Clem and she's…"

He should never have hesitated because it gave Vivi the chance to clench her fists and for fire to jump into her eyes. "Be careful what you say next, McNeal. I don't give a damn what you think about me, but don't you dare criticize my daughter."

Cam frowned, appalled that she would instinctively assume that he was about to pass judgment on her. He slowly stood up and folded his arms, wondering who had made this strong, vibrant woman assume that she'd be the victim of harsh criticism.

"I was going to say that I think Clem is a bright, happy child with a sharp mind and an extensive vocabulary. She's funny and interesting and sweet."

He would've been amused at her shocked expression if he hadn't been so angry on her behalf. Why did she expect reproof instead of praise? Why did she immediately brace herself for bad news?

"Judging by that amazing human tornado asleep on my couch, you must be an incredible mother," Cam said, holding her gaze and hoping she'd see that he meant every damn word. And more.

Vivi searched his face for any hint that he was lying, and when she finally seemed to accept that he wasn't, her shoulders fell and her cheeks flushed. He thought he saw a hint of tears in her brown eyes but she lowered her head too quickly. When she replied, her voice was husky with emotion.

"Thank you. But she makes it easy. She really is an incredible child." Vivi took a little time to lift her head, and when she did, her expression was inscrutable.

"I need you to know that I spent a lot of time thinking about how to tell you about her. About *whether* to tell you about her," she finally said.

A part of him wanted to be angry at her, to rail at her for denying him Clem's first months and years, but another part of him, a bigger part, wanted to understand her hesitation.

"I did some research on you and everything I read led me to believe that you wouldn't be interested in being tied down, in having a child."

Really, that was her excuse? She was a terrible liar. "You are old enough to know that you shouldn't believe everything that is written in the press, Vivianne."

Vivi wrinkled her nose and drew patterns on the Persian carpet with her toes.

"Why did you really not want me to know about Clem?"

Vivi looked him in the eye and shrugged. "I didn't

want you to think that I wanted your money. We do fine on our own."

Now that wasn't a lie, but it wasn't the complete truth, either. But he'd take the little she was prepared to give him. For now.

"Talking about money," Vivi said, looking ill at ease again, "I hate to do this but I need to get to the DMV on Monday to get a new license so I can get hold of some money. When I do that, Clem and I will find somewhere else to stay."

This again. He had a massive house, plenty of space and ample money. He could support two dozen families and consider it petty cash. He'd had many girlfriends who'd seen him as nothing more than a pretty face, a nice body and a healthy bank account. Yet Vivi wanted to prove, at every turn, how independent she was.

It shouldn't turn him on but it did. Hell, everything about her did—from her walk to her talk to her mouth and legs and voice and stubbornness and bravery.

"So, would that be possible? Or, if that's not something you want to do, could I get a loan to get there by cab?"

She made it sound like she was asking him to invest millions in a fly-by-night start-up instead of a loan of under a hundred dollars. "I'll drive you on Monday."

Then Vivi smiled at him and his heart ballooned and his pants tightened. Yeah, as he'd said before, he was neck-deep in trouble, all right. And was that an alligator snacking on his ass?

Seven

Vivi burst into tears when she walked through the doors of The Rollin' Smoke. The main seating area was still covered in an inch of water, but judging by the dark stains on the walls, the floodwater had swamped the leather-covered benches within the booths and knocked over chairs and tables. Her eyes immediately examined the rare photographs of long-ago Texas that hung on the walls, and she was relieved to see that most looked undamaged. The chairs and tables and the flooring could be replaced but the photographs couldn't.

Clem, who sat on Vivi's hip, patted her cheek. "No cry, Mommy."

Vivi felt Cam's broad hand on her back and turned her head to look up at him. "Yeah, don't cry, Mommy. It's all fixable."

Vivi bit her lower lip. "It's such a mess, Cam."

Cam's hand drew big circles on her back. "It's just stuff, Viv. Nobody got hurt, that's the main thing."

Vivi hauled in a deep breath, grateful for his succinct and pointed assessment of the situation. He was right—it was just stuff, and everybody who worked here was okay. It was, as he said, all fixable.

"Joe! Joe!"

Clem's piping, excited voice made Vivi turn. She saw Joe, her boss, friend and mentor, standing in the doorway to her kitchen, looking ten years older than before. This restaurant was his life's work, his baby. And his employees were his family. For him, this was like losing his home.

Vivi picked her way through the debris and walked straight into his arms, sighing when his big, brawny arms encircled her and her child. This man was her family, her sounding board, more than her own father had been. Vivi buried her face in his shirt and let the tears fall. She felt Joe taking Clem into his arms, and then his hand was rubbing her back and she felt his lips in her hair. "Shh, baby girl, it'll be okay."

After a few minutes Vivi raised her face and reached for the kitchen towel Joe always kept tucked into the waistband of his pants. She wiped her eyes, sniffed and sent a worried-looking Clem a shaky smile. "It's okay, baby, Mommy is just upset that the horrible flood made such a mess."

Clem pursed her lips. "So, no mac-cheese today?"

Vivi smiled and Joe laughed. Clem always ate Joe's specially-made-for-her pasta dish when she visited the restaurant.

Vivi looked around at the damage and forced the question from between clenched teeth. "So, how long are we going to be out of business?"

Joe ignored her to greet Cam, whom he'd met before. Vivi saw the speculation in his eyes, knew that he was wondering what was happening between Cam and her. She'd be getting a phone call later and demands for an explanation.

Joe led the way into the kitchen and placed Clem on the stainless-steel counter. Vivi smiled when Cam came to stand next to the table, one hand anchoring her small thigh so that she wouldn't tumble to the wet floor. He was already a protective dad. God help Clem when she was sixteen and wanting to date. Vivi boosted herself up onto the counter to sit next to her.

"Are you okay?" Joe demanded, cupping her face in his big hands, his eyes skimming her face. "You said that you had an accident and that you were fine, but I know you, Vivi. You treat an in inch-deep cut as a scratch."

Cam opened his mouth to speak and Vivi tossed him a don't-you-dare scowl. Joe didn't need to know how close she'd come to death; he had enough to deal with as it was. "I'm fine, Joe. I just have a couple of bruises." Wanting to change the subject, she looked around. "Where is everybody? I expected the staff to be here, cleaning up."

"It's Sunday and I sent them home," Joe said. "They are exhausted, and many needed to spend time at their own homes."

Vivi gripped the edge of the counter and asked again, "When do you think we can open?"

Devastation flashed in Joe's eye and Vivi's heart plummeted into free fall. When Joe dropped his gaze from hers, ice-cold panic skittered through her veins. "Joe, what's wrong? What's the matter?"

Joe placed his hands behind his head, sent Cam an uncertain look and lifted his shoulders in a small shrug. "I don't know if I can ever open again, Vivianne."

Jesus! What?

"Why?" Vivi demanded, the word almost sticking in her throat.

"I'm underinsured. Grossly underinsured," Joe admitted, pain and remorse coating every word. "I have some savings but I don't think I have enough to cover the cost of another renovation."

Vivi lifted her fist to her mouth. "God, Joe, no."

Joe took her hand. "I know how much you need a job, Viv. But I've been making some calls and I already have positions lined up for you, at some of the best restaurants in the city." He managed a small smile. "Some are even at better wages than what I offer you."

"But I don't want to work somewhere else. I want to work with you," Vivi said, disconsolate.

"I was going to pass this on to you, hand over the reins in a year or two, give you some shares." He kicked a plastic bottle floating at his feet. "Now I can give you nothing. I am so sorry."

Vivi saw the disgust on his face, the shame, and hopped off the counter to take his hands in hers. She waited for Joe to look at her. "Joe, you have already given me so much. You gave me a job when I was down to my last two dollars, without money to feed my baby or to buy diapers. You arranged for Charlie to look after Clem while I worked, and you looked after her when she couldn't. You taught me to cook, you gave me a way to support myself and my child. You gave me everything!" Vivi squeezed his hands. "Don't you dare apologize, not to me, not ever." She shook her head, determination coursing over her. "And I refuse to work for anyone else. We are going to resurrect this place."

Joe shook his head. "There's not enough money, Vivianne."

There was always a plan to be made, money to be found. Vivi had learned that years ago. When she was at her lowest, when she thought that she'd have to reach out to her mom for money to feed Clem, things had worked out right. The universe had yet to let her down and it wouldn't this time, either. She would find a way to reopen The Rollin' Smoke. It might not be as big, or employ as many people, but she'd reopen it, dammit. She just had to get creative and find a way.

"I'll do it, Joe. We'll do it," Vivi told him, her throat closing when she saw the relief in the older man's eyes. He wasn't alone and neither was she; they'd do it together.

They were a team, dammit.

Cam had wanted Vivi from the moment he saw her walking into that dingy bar in Tarrin, all long limbs and curly hair and wide, deep brown eyes. The sex between them had been explosive, and if he'd stuck around he would've been tempted to see her again.

Three years ago he'd sensed that she was still part girl, slightly naive and innocent, but she'd told him that she was up for a one-nighter and he'd taken her at her word. But that girl was a pale version of the woman Vivi had become. As a mother, friend, employee, she was dedicated and loyal and determined. And he wanted her with an intensity that threatened to knock him off his feet.

She was flippin' amazing.

But as much as he admired her, he was also a realist.

After putting Clem into her car seat and buckling her in, Cam climbed into the driver's seat and turned to look at Vivi as he started his car. "That was a hell of a promise you made Joe," he said, keeping his voice mild.

He knew how much it cost to set up a restaurant, having invested in one over a year ago, and he doubted Vivi had any idea of the reality of the promise she'd made.

Vivi met his gaze and lifted finely arched eyebrows. "You don't think I can do it?"

Careful, McNeal, you are wandering into a mine-field. "I'm coming to believe that you can do anything you set your mind to."

"But?"

"Putting Joe's place back on its feet will be a mammoth undertaking. It'll require guts and drive and determination." And money. So much money.

"You don't think I have those traits?" Vivi asked, her voice so devoid of emotion that he suspected he'd just detonated a mine. And that the explosion could only be heard in her head.

He was still trying to choose his words when she poked his arm with her index finger. He pulled his eyes off the road and caught the fury darkening her gaze and the annoyance thinning her lips. He could handle her anger, but the disappointment in her expression— at him—slew him.

Before he could speak, Vivi's low-pitched voice drifted over to him. "You have no idea what I can and can't do, McNeal. Yeah, you might have built this empire in three years but you didn't have to do it while you were pregnant or with a baby on your hip. I left home with a hundred dollars in my pocket, scared out of my head. I had no job prospects, no skills and no one to call since my mother banished me from my family and my town. Since all my friends were part of her church, I lost them, too. I slept in shelters, and one memorable night, on the streets. Do you have any idea how terrify-ing it is to know you have a child who's totally and utterly dependent on you for everything and to not know where you're going to sleep that night, how you're going to feed her or clothe her?"

Vivi pointed at the restaurant, her finger shaking. "That man in there gave me a chance and then a dozen more. He taught me to cook, to create. He was my salvation and my warm place to fall. He took me in when my mother and the world spit me out. I will part seas and move mountains for him—and I will rebuild The Rollin' Smoke—because he gave me a chance when no one else would."

The fierceness in her voice was a tangible force, as was the intensity in her expression. He felt like their combined effect was pressing against his chest, pushing him back into the seat. Not often at a loss for words, Cam opened his mouth to speak and closed it again, unsure where to start. He was pretty certain that Vivi hadn't meant to open the door revealing her past, but now that she had, he'd take the opportunity to look inside. He had so many questions.

"Your mom banished you?"

Vivi hauled in some air and closed her eyes. When they opened again and met his, he saw a mixture of emotions flash through them—determination and sadness tinged with anger. "Yeah. She insisted that I have an abortion, that my being unwed and pregnant would be a scandal she'd never recover from and that it would diminish her standing in her church."

Wait...what? That didn't make sense. "Aren't churches supposed to be against abortion?"

Vivi's smile held no amusement. "Apparently, it's an acceptable option when your position as the highest-ranking female, the moral authority, is threatened.

She made it very clear that I either leave or have an abortion."

"Did you call her out on her hypocrisy?"

Vivi shrugged. "Even if I had bothered to argue, nothing I said would've changed her mind. Besides, I'd been thinking of leaving for a while. Pregnancy forced me into action."

"Why the hell didn't you get in touch with me?" Cam demanded.

Vivi sent him a "get real" look. "I told you. I didn't have your surname or your cell number. And you'd told me you were leaving town but you didn't tell me where you were going. I didn't have the first clue how to get hold of you. I thought that you were a one-off encounter, so you can imagine my shock when I saw you at Joe's."

"I still don't understand why you didn't make contact then, why you chose not to tell me about Clem." Most women would've been all over him like a rash, demanding, at the very least, substantial child support. Even Emma now found him socially acceptable. She'd contacted him shortly after her divorce, wanting to re-ignite what they'd once had.

Money, it seemed, made a lot of wrongs right.

Vivi turned around, took a long look at Clem, who was half dozing in her car seat, and handed him a cool, pointed look. "I can give Clem everything she needs, Cam."

Sure, maybe she could. She could feed her and clothe her and send her to school. But she couldn't give Clem the one thing he'd needed the most growing up. "But you couldn't give her a father, Vivianne. So answer this—if you didn't nearly die yesterday, would you ever have reached out to me? Told me about her?"

Vivi's silence was all the answer he needed. Cam

looked away, annoyed and confused. He was angry, sure, but he also thought that, maybe, her instinct to keep Clem from him was right. What type of father was he going to be? He was a driven workaholic, someone determined to show the world that a McNeal could be successful, that a McNeal could hold on to a dollar for longer than a millisecond, that a McNeal could build a business, keep a job. He didn't know how to be a parent, to think about someone else, to put a child first. He'd spent most of his life looking after himself. He had no reference point, having come from a long line of messed-up, childish, irresponsible men.

Feeling sad, annoyed and totally at sea, Cam accelerated away. He had a child, he was a father and he was also totally in lust with Clem's mother. So where to go from here?

Back to River Oaks, he supposed, not that he would find any of the answers he needed there. It was just a house, not a home.

Vivi made it to Tuesday night without ripping Cam's clothes off and doing him against the nearest wall—which was not an easy feat. Also equally heroically, she managed not to put a pillow over his face when he was sleeping. Alternating between lust and annoyance, she felt like she was not only living her life in someone's else's house but also on a knife-edge. She was mentally exhausted; all she wanted was a break. From feeling horny and from insisting that Cam keep his credit card in his wallet.

"You cannot buy me a car, McNeal."

Cam, recently returned from dropping Clem off at Charlie's, looked up from buttering his toast and grinned. "How do you plan on stopping me, Donner?"

Semantics. "You can obviously buy me a car. I just don't want you to," Vivi responded, trying to hold on to her patience. "My insurance money should be in soon and if transporting Clem is a problem—"

"Which it's not."

Vivi ignored his interruption. "—I can take a taxi. But the point is, you cannot buy me a car." She pushed away the brochures he'd handed to her, knowing that if she looked at his suggestions, she might have a harder time saying no.

"No. A thousand times no. You cannot spend money on me."

"Why not? " Cam slapped jam on his toast, took a bite and chewed, his eyes dancing. He wasn't taking her seriously, dammit! "It's just money. I'm paying to have Clem's room turned into a nursery and you worked with the interior designer on Clem's room."

"Worked with" was overstating her involvement in the process. Yesterday, after visiting the DMV and her bank, she'd watched as a crew of men delivered a rocking chair, a bed and a chest of drawers to the room opposite the master bedroom, the one two doors down from her own. The interior designer—some bright-eyed blonde Vivi was convinced had shared sheet time with Cam—asked her whether Clem was a pink or neutral baby. Vivi told her that her daughter liked bright colors, but Clem's room was now a masterpiece in beige and cream. Clem didn't like her new room, which was why she still shared Vivi's big bed. Vivi was okay with that—if Clem slept with her, there was less chance of her inviting Cam to do the same.

"Clem doesn't seem to be particularly enthralled with her new room," Cam commented.

It's rich but it's as boring as hell. As dull as dishwa-

ter. But Cam was proud of what he'd done for Clem, so she couldn't hurt his feelings. "She's only two, Cam. And she likes the books."

There were lots of books in her new room, and Vivi was grateful to have new material to read to Clem at night.

"You could've saved yourself a fortune if you'd just spoken to me instead of going through your bland interior designer, but—"

Cam placed his piece of toast on his plate. "Bland? She decorated every room in this house."

"And it's beautiful," Vivi quickly responded. It was utterly gorgeous, but...

"But...? I can hear your *but*."

Vivi winced and decided that he was a big boy, he could handle the truth. "But it has absolutely no personality. There's nothing of you in this house."

Vivi thought she heard Cam murmur "exactly," but that didn't make any sense. Why wouldn't he want to live in a house that reflected who and what he was? His house should be filled with bold colors, interesting pieces of art, tactile accessories. Cam McNeal was anything but bland.

But how Cam decorated his house had nothing to do with her. She wasn't staying. In a few days—the authorities were asking residents to stay away for another week but Vivi was convinced they were being overly dramatic—she'd be back at her house, among her things, things that reflected her personality.

"The point is—"

Cam lifted a "hang on" finger when his phone rang. He picked up the device and after a couple of "yups" and a "that's fine" and a "look after yourself," placed the phone back on the table. "Sally isn't coming in today. She has a bad case of flu and she feels awful."

Oh…

Oh!

That meant that she and Cam were alone in the house. Wanting to keep Clem's routine as normal as possible she'd sent her to day care and, as a result there was no Clem to interrupt them or Sally to consider. Totally, utterly alone. Vivi knew the moment Cam realized the same thing, because his eyes deepened and focused on her mouth. His blatantly hungry stare sent a river of lust down her spine, pooling heat between her legs. She knew that if she moved, gave him the smallest sign of encouragement, they both could be naked and screaming in a heartbeat.

She really wanted to get naked. She might not scream but she'd definitely moan.

"Camden."

It was one word, small but potent, and he heard her unspoken demand. *Come over here and kiss me.*

Cam released a low growl and Vivi watched, fascinated, as he rocketed to his feet, the fast movement causing his kitchen chair to topple over. By the time the chair hit the floor, she was in his arms and his mouth was on hers, his tongue sliding past her teeth to take possession of her mouth. He tasted like strawberry jam and coffee, sweet and hot, and those sparks he mentioned morphed into a dozen fireballs.

Wanting to get closer, Vivi pushed her breasts into his hard chest, curling into his heat. She wanted more, needed to see him, taste him, have access to those gorgeous muscles. Vivi lifted her hands and attacked the buttons on his shirt, silently cursing when the buttons refused to cooperate. Cam solved that problem by push-

ing his hands between them, the backs of his hands
scraping over her nipples. He gripped the sides of his
shirt and ripped it apart. Buttons scattered and Vivi
quickly pushed his shirt off his shoulders, down his
arms. She needed to feel his skin, his heat. Standing
on her toes, she pushed her mouth against his, wanting
a harder kiss, and Cam obliged.

He tilted her head by holding the back of her head
while his other hand pulled her T-shirt up her back,
allowing cool air to touch her back. He was only her
second lover, and this was only the third time she was
doing this, but she didn't feel self-conscious or shy.
How could she when Cam interrupted his kisses with
compliments, telling her how hot she was, what he intended to do to her? She was inexperienced but that
didn't matter. Cam was in control.

Right now, in this instance, she let him be.

Vivi muttered her displeasure when he pulled his
mouth off hers so that he could do away with her shirt,
but a second later his hands covered her breasts, his
thumbs teasing her nipples and his mouth trailing down
the side of her neck.

Cam kissed her, finding all those long-neglected
places craving his touch and a few that she didn't know
existed before this moment. She was fire and heat and
need and want, a pulsing field of energy that started
and began with him. If she wasn't so desperate for this
to end in a big bang, Vivi would've been worried about
how precisely in tune with each other they were.

They were ice and cream, milk and honey, matches
and gas-soaked kindling. They *worked*, somehow bigger and better than before.

Vivi sucked in a breath as Cam pulled her nipple into
his mouth, sucking her through her bra. Frustrated by

the barrier, she reached behind her to unhook her bra and pulled the fabric down her arms, her breath catching at Cam's now blue-black eyes.

If the massive erection tenting his cargo shorts wasn't a clue, then his dark eyes would've been. He wanted her. Right here and right now. And having such a man—strong, virile, so experienced—desire her made her feel powerful and intensely feminine.

As Cam bent his knees to suck her nipple, Vivi locked her arms around his head, dropping kisses onto his wavy hair. She sighed as his teeth scraped her and whimpered when he moved his mouth across her breast to her sternum and licked his way down to her stomach. Cam hit his knees and his hands gripped her hips, his thumbs on her mound. Vivi couldn't help herself, she rotated her hips, silently telling him what she needed. Cam used one hand to flip open the button to her cotton shorts, and when the fabric fell to the floor, he gently inserted his finger into the V of her panties and ran his finger down her thin strip of hair.

"Is this what you want, Vivi?"

Vivi shook her head and couldn't get the words past her tongue. When she didn't answer, Cam sat back on his heels and stared up at her, his finger flirting on the edge of her clit. "Vivi, I need to know…can I carry on? *Should* I carry on?"

Vivi nodded and pressed his hand into her, lifting her hips so that he had better access to her secret places. She released a small cry of pleasure when his finger stroked her, skating over her folds and slipping into her wet channel.

"So wet. So hot," Cam murmured.

Vivi widened her legs and wrapped her arms around her waist, assaulted by the waves of pleasure. God, she was teetering on the edge of an orgasm. But she wanted him inside her, filling her, completing her.

"Come inside me, Cam. I need you."

"Protection."

Vivi shook her head. "I'm on the pill."

Cam surged to his feet, one hand fumbling at the band of his shorts. Vivi swatted his hand away and slipped the button from its hole, gently sliding his zipper down. Reaching under the band of his underwear, she freed him, wrapping her hand around his thick, pulsing cock. Vivi looked down and sucked in her breath. Like every other part of him, it was so beautiful, ferociously masculine.

Cam's compliments dried up and it was his turn to whimper. She stared down at him, her fist encircling him, her thumb sliding across his tip. Wanting to feel every part of him, she spread her fingers out so that she cupped his balls, gently massaging him. Cam jumped in her hand and she felt his shudder. Yeah, control wasn't anything either of them possessed anymore.

This time, this one time, control was severely overrated.

Vivi gasped when Cam wrapped an arm around her butt and lifted her up and into him, walking her to the breakfast table. She heard the crash of plates, the ping of cutlery hitting the tiled floor, and then she felt the cool wood beneath her back, her legs being pulled apart. Cam stood between her knees, his eyes glittering, his cheeks flushed. He removed her panties and then he was probing her entrance, thick and hard and wonderful. Vivi dug her heels into his hips and pulled him forward and Cam sank in an inch. He closed his eyes and she watched, fascinated as he fought for control, fought the urge to plunder and pound.

But she wanted both. Using her core muscles, she did a sit-up and wrapped her arms around his neck, pulling him down so that his mouth met hers.

Against his lips, sucking in his sweet breath, she murmured the words: "I need you. Now."

Cam's thumb skated over her cheekbone, across her lower lip, and he left his thumb there when his mouth enveloped hers. As his tongue slid inside her mouth, his erection pushed into her and she felt sensations she'd never felt before.

Overwhelmed. Taken. Fulfilled. Completed.

Vivi was on the verge of shattering when Cam's mouth turned tender. His kisses became more thoughtful and he slowed his hip action, taking her down an inch. Vivi murmured in protest and tried to insert a hand between their bodies but Cam pulled her hand away to place it on the table next to her hip. Pushing his hand under her butt, he lifted and tilted her and Vivi felt him scrape an area deep inside her. She didn't want to come, not yet, but she couldn't stop her free fall...

Exquisite sensation battered her and she willingly stepped into the ball of energy, allowing Cam to sweep her away. As she tumbled through space, through galaxies both familiar and undiscovered, she was vaguely aware of Cam's shout, his tense body, him pumping his seed into her. Then he joined her to dance on the stars.

Back on earth, her eyes flew open and she stared up into Cam's shocked face. "What the hell was that?" she muttered.

"God knows," Cam responded, his hands on her hips. Vivi dug a fork out from under her butt and tossed it to the floor. She stretched back against the table, arched her back and then realized that Cam, still inside her, was, astoundingly, still hard. She could've sworn that he'd come, too.

Cam pushed a strand of hair off her forehead and smiled softly. "I came, I saw, I was blinded in the process. But something about you, apparently, makes me recover superfast."

Vivi's eyes widened. "Uh, I, we…holy…" Cam covered her breasts with his big hands and played with her nipples and Vivi closed her eyes, loving the sensation. "That feels amazing."

Cam sank himself a little deeper and Vivi felt herself melting…straining for more. Cam smiled, dipped his finger between their linked bodies and found her clit, rubbing his thumb over her most sensitive spot.

Vivi climbed. And climbed. And within minutes, she was ready to fall apart again. Apparently he wasn't the only one who recovered fast.

Eight

Vivi stood in Joe's ruined kitchen, looking at the list of everything they'd lost in the fire. She lifted her head when she heard the front door open and the sound of masculine footsteps headed in her direction. Looking down at her grubby white T-shirt and filthy jeans, she hoped the representative from the insurance company wasn't an hour early—she'd hoped to clean up and change before meeting with him.

Vivi laid her clipboard on the steel table and raked her hair back from her face, securing her heavy ponytail with a band from her wrist. Picking through what was left of The Rollin' Smoke was hot, dirty and sweaty work and she was glad she'd sent Joe home to rest. Her old friend was not taking the loss of his restaurant well and whatever pain she could spare him, she would.

Vivi bit her lower lip, wishing she hadn't been so reckless with her promise to resurrect this place. After spending a few days among the detritus, she was starting to think that rebuilding Rollin' would be impossible. The insurance payout would barely cover the replacement costs of a third of the equipment they needed and none of the furniture. They was no provision for loss of trade and they had just enough money in the company account to pay the staff this month. It was clear that they'd have to release the staff and tell them to find new employment.

She had savings and job offers in her in-box, but she knew that most of her colleagues lived from paycheck to paycheck. Unlike her, they weren't living in a mansion with a billionaire who was determined to make up for years of not paying child support. She'd lost the battle on the new car—she was now, temporarily as she told him, driving a nifty new Jeep—and Cam had hired a personal shopper to restock their closets as her house was still off-limits.

There hadn't been any argument about her moving into his bed. Being with him, loving him and having him love her, was exactly where she wanted to be. She could handle playing house for another week or so. She'd enjoy his spectacular body, the fast, expensive car and living like a princess for the next week, and then she'd go back to real life.

"Hey."

Vivi saw Cam in the doorway of the kitchen and returned his smile. And man, he had a hell of a smile. It made her feel all gooey inside, like a perfectly cooked chocolate brownie. Vivi closed her eyes and shook her head. She was losing it, comparing Cam's smile to a brownie, his body to a work of art, his eyes to the color of the Mediterranean Sea…

"Enough, dammit."

"Sorry?"

Vivi did a mental eye roll. Now she was talking to herself? Cam McNeal should come with a danger warning.

"Nothing, ignore me." Vivi tipped her head to receive his kiss, a gesture that was becoming as natural to her as breathing. Which was a bad thing since she was leaving his daily life in a short time. "Hi."

"Hi back." Cam's thumb brushed against her cheek and he lifted one eyebrow. "You are a hot mess, Vivi."

At least he'd qualified the mess with *hot*. "I know. I've been trying to ascertain if anything in here can be salvaged."

Cam kept his hand on her back as he looked around the damaged kitchen. "And can you?"

Vivi shook her head. "Very little. The smoker, the industrial ovens and the electrical equipment were all soaked and the electrics fried. And even if they could be rewired, they are now a health risk. The crockery and cutlery have been washed and boxed but that's not worth a whole lot. The furniture in the restaurant all needs to be replaced and the entire building needs to be repainted. It's going to add up to tens of thousands of dollars, Cam."

Cam picked up her clipboard and flipped through her papers. When he grimaced, Vivi's stomach sank to her toes. "Basically, you're looking at setting up a new restaurant, Viv."

She nodded. "I know."

"Can Joe take out a loan, approach his bank?"

Vivi wrinkled her nose and placed her elbows on the table, holding her face in her hands. "I'd like him to, but he's close to retirement age, Cam. I'm asking him to take out a huge loan to rebuild a restaurant when it makes better sense for him to take the insurance money and invest it."

It was hard facing the truth but Vivi had experience in dealing with the reality of the situation, not the fantasy. Okay, she was living a fantasy life with Cam in his lovely house in the best area in town, but that would end. Real life wasn't housekeepers and fancy cars, a hot man in her bed, a full-time dad for Clem. Her future reality would be dropping Clem off with him for weekends, having him around for Clem's birthday parties, discussing their daughter's progress on the phone.

She could look at the future and see it clearly...and Rollin' didn't have much of a chance. In fact, if she gave Joe permission to retire—she knew he was only sticking around because of her—it would cease to exist. It was looking increasingly likely that she'd have to find a new job, in a new kitchen, run by people who neither knew her nor cared about her. She wouldn't be able to bring Clem to work, to take time off when she needed to, and wouldn't have the freedom of being her own boss.

"I think this is it, Cam."

Vivi felt his big arms surround her, felt the kiss he placed in her hair before he bent his head to place his cheek against her temple. "We'll find a way, Viv. Let me help."

She wanted to allow him to pick up her clipboard and wave a magic wand, throw some money at the problem and restore Rollin' to what it was. He was rich enough to do that, astute enough to make it work. But if he did that, if she allowed him to take over, it would just be another thing she lost control over, another part of her life that she'd have to share with Cam. Rollin', her job here and the people were *hers*. She'd washed every dish, learned every recipe, developed her own. She'd nagged and moaned and laughed with her staff, mentored them as Joe had mentored her. This kitchen was her domain, the one place she had complete hold over. If Cam became involved, because he wasn't the type to sit on the sidelines, she'd lose autonomy.

She might as well go and work for another restaurant.

"I can help you, Vivianne. Let me," Cam whispered in her ear.

But then it wouldn't be hers. It would be his because Vivi knew that he who held the cash exerted the control. She shook her head and patted the arm that was hooked around her waist. "Thank you but…no. Everything comes to an end, and this, I think, is the end of this journey."

She felt Cam stiffen and he jerked away from her. She slowly turned and saw the disappointment on his face and, worse, the hurt in his eyes. "Why won't you let me help you? I invest in companies, in case you've forgotten, and I'd like to invest in you."

If she wasn't sleeping with him, if she wasn't the mother of his child, would he still be making the same offer? If she came to him as a stranger, would he be jumping in as eagerly as he was now? She didn't think so. "It won't work, Cam."

"Why the hell not?"

Vivi folded her arms and made herself meet his eyes. "Because then it wouldn't be mine. It would be yours."

His sexy mouth thinned. "I don't understand."

"If you threw a vast amount of money into this place, you would then become my boss, and this wouldn't be my happy space anymore. While I don't own any shares in this business, Joe treated me like a partner, not an employee."

"And you don't think I can do that?" Cam demanded, irritation coating his words.

"I think you like your own way and you are not scared to demand it," Vivi said, carefully choosing her words.

"I have many interests in many businesses. I can be a silent partner."

"Could you be that with me?" Vivi demanded.

"I don't see why not." His frown deepened at the skepticism he saw on her face. "What? I can back off."

Yeah, sure. "Like how you backed down when I said I didn't need a new car? The way you listened to me when I told you I didn't need a personal shopper, or that Clem was too young for a professionally designed nursery? It's like you hear my words but they have no meaning."

"That's because you are stubborn!"

"No, it's because you are controlling." Vivi whipped back. She waved her hand around, trying to encompass the kitchen. "This has been my domain for three years. I know every inch, every piece of equipment. I know that the mixing machine sticks on three, that the oven is a half degree off, which pan makes the best sauce. This is my domain, Cam."

"And I'm trying to restore it to you!" Cam yelled, obviously frustrated. His anger didn't frighten her, so Vivi didn't react when his words bounced off the walls. "I want to give you what you want, what you need!"

And wasn't that the problem? She didn't need him to ride to her rescue. She could save herself. She'd done so three years ago, made something of herself without his help, and she could do it again. She *needed* to do it again. She couldn't allow herself to rely on him, to let him become her safety net, because she understood that people were fallible and frequently let you down at crucial moments, mostly when you needed them the most. No, it was better to rely on herself, only herself.

And if that meant giving up Rollin', then she would do exactly that. She'd just find a new spot, make a new home.

"You are stupidly, ridiculously, irrationally independent!" Cam stated.

"I worked damn hard for it, Cam. I won't give it up."

"But how much are you prepared to sacrifice in your bid to remain independent? Where's your red line?"

She didn't know.

Before she could answer him, not that she had an answer, Cam shook his head, obviously disappointed. "I'll see you at home, Viv."

Home, Viv thought, her thoughts immediately going to the house in River Oaks. Dammit, it might be his home but it wasn't hers. She was confusing fantasy with reality again.

She was not a lead character in a rom-com movie and Cam was not her happily-ever-after. Real life was hard, gritty, messy. It was best that she remembered that before life slapped her sideways again.

Ryder had thoroughly enjoyed this evening and the company of his friend Camden and Camden's new woman, Vivi, who cooked like a dream. He looked at the younger man who sat in the chair across from him, his daughter lying in his lap. Cam reminded him of his younger self, reckless, brave, so very convinced of his firm grip on life. Only now did Ryder realize how little he'd known then.

And after sharing a quiet family dinner with Cam, his brand-new daughter and the woman who was currently turning Cam's life upside down, Ryder realized how much he missed having a family, being part of one.

Yeah, his first marriage hadn't worked out, but he'd adored Elinah, his second wife, and she'd loved him back. He remembered many nights when Maya had fallen asleep in his arms, her sweet face tucked into his neck.

Looking at Camden's daughter, he recalled how fifteen years ago, Maya—the child of his heart but not his genes—had often been curled up like that, her mouth pursed. Now she was eighteen and demanding he tell her the exact details of her birth, about how she arrived at their house under circumstances that most people would term as suspicious. A tiny girl with medical issues...

How did he even start to explain? What words would he use to unravel the tangle that was Maya's birth? Hell, even Maya's biological mother didn't know that he was raising the daughter she'd given up nearly two decades ago. And he had no intention of her ever finding out that Maya was, originally and for a very brief period, hers.

Maya was his, and Elinah's. Why couldn't that be enough for his headstrong daughter?

Pushing those thoughts away, he glanced at Clementine again. God, he missed that, missed the time when his kids were young. Carrying them up to their rooms, then carrying Elinah to their bed.

Camden was—impatiently, he was sure—waiting for him to leave. Because Ryder knew it would annoy him, he accepted Vivi's offer of a second cup of coffee. His mouth twitched at his friend's scowl.

"Is the TCC meeting still on for tomorrow?" Cam asked.

Ryder nodded. "Yep."

"Then I'll see you there," Cam hinted. Ryder smiled and ignored his not-so-subtle jerk of his head in the direction of the door.

Cam scowled at him again before releasing a resigned sigh. "You never told me how your meeting with Sterling Perry went last week, Ry. Did you challenge him to pistols at dawn? Or swords at sunset?"

Cam loved taking the piss out of him. He was one of the very few people he'd allowed to do that. "Sterling wasn't available."

But Angela Perry had been...

Ryder shifted in his chair. Holy hell, he was fifty years old and it had been a long time since he'd been that turned on. Oh, he'd had several affairs since Elinah died—he wasn't a damned monk!—but those had always been about getting his rocks off. Kissing Angela had been...awesome. He'd have been happy to stand there and kiss her for another five, ten, fifty minutes. Since that kiss, his brain felt fried, and all he could think about was the way she stepped up and into him, laying those cool, pink lips on his. Her long, lean body with its subtle curves pressed into him made his head swim.

Dammit, he was utterly and completely attracted to Angela Perry—the daughter of his rival. What the hell was he going to do about it?

Cam noticed Ryder's expression change and wondered at the hint of panic he saw on his old friend's face. The bastard should've left a half hour ago and Cam knew, by the laughter dancing in his eyes, that he was hanging around purely to piss him off. But now the laughter was gone and worry turned his eyes a deeper shade of blue.

"Thank you, darlin'," Ryder said, taking a glass of whiskey from Vivi, who resumed her place in the corner of the overstuffed leather sofa.

Vivi asked Ryder about his kids and Cam looked down at his child. Clem, dressed in pale purple pj's with spotted dogs printed on them, was sprawled across his lap, legs and arms spread wide. Her eyelashes rested against her cheek, her perfect, rosebud mouth pursed. In sleep she looked like a porcelain doll, picture perfect. In real life, she was a walking, talking Energizer Bunny. The kid never, ever, stopped. Cam was an active guy, fit and strong, but Clem wore him out. Okay, she and her mother wore him out. The hours after Clem went to sleep were his and Vivi's and they didn't get to sleep until the wee hours of the morning.

It was as if they both realized that their time together was limited, that they had to take every moment given and enjoy every second. They were both acting like this couldn't last, like they were living on borrowed time.

Cam looked down at Clem and reminded himself that he'd soon run out of excuses to keep Vivi and his daughter with him. At some point, they'd return to their cottage in Briarhills and he would be left alone in this house. He looked around at his informal, tastefully decorated living room and realized that the only thing giving the space warmth was Vivi's presence.

Cam tuned out of their conversation, thinking about the way Vivi made him feel. He just had to look at her and his heart rate accelerated, his mouth dried up. He'd had lovers before but none, not even Emma, had made him feel so off balance. Sex had always been another basic function, something he enjoyed and forgot about. But sex with Vivi was different, wild and intoxicating. He couldn't get enough of her.

Whatever was between them was different from anything he'd ever experienced and he had no clue how to handle it. Before Vivi and Clem, he'd been content to live his life alone, but now he didn't know how he'd go back to that solitary life when they moved out.

He couldn't define what he and Vivi had but it wasn't meaningless. And he wasn't enthusiastic about rambling around this mausoleum on his own. He liked hearing Clem's high-pitched laughter, her tiny footsteps, her piping voice and her off-key singing. He liked coming home and seeing Vivi in his kitchen, sharing a glass of wine with her at the end of the day, watching her bathe their daughter. He wanted her to stick around and teach him how to be a dad, to let him share her bed and her body, have her explore his.

He liked this life with them in it.

But could he have it? Did he deserve it? He was, he reluctantly admitted, a controlling bastard. He liked calling the shots; of course, he did. He'd been a child without guidance, too much freedom and not enough discipline. He had run wild and free, with no sense of responsibility and no concept of accountability. Eventually he'd taken a path away from crime, but a part of him always thought that no matter how much money he made and how much he gave away to charity—anonymously, of course—he was stained by his past actions.

His daughter was pure goodness and Vivi was pure class. How could he possibly think he was good enough to be with them on even a semipermanent basis?

It would be so easy to lie to himself. To tell himself that he had a right to happiness, that he wasn't the same person. But he knew he was, deep inside. He'd translated his ability of reading people to scanning the business world with an eagle eye, looking for an opportunity to pounce. He was still the same person—hard, driven, wily and cunning. Except now he just operated in a field that was legal. He was still the boy with a chip on his shoulder, constantly wanting and needing more. He'd never been satisfied with much for long, always looking for something new, something he'd never had.

What if, in time, Vivi and Clem weren't enough, what if he wanted more? What then?

Cam was jerked out of his thoughts by Vivi's hand on his shoulder. He looked up into her lovely face and his heart bounced off his chest.

"I'll take Clem up to bed."

He nodded and Vivi scooped Clem up, easily holding her in her arms. Cam glanced at his watch, saw that it was getting late and asked if she was going to come back down.

Vivi shook her head. "You spend some time with Ryder." She turned to smile at the guest. "It was so nice to meet you, Ryder."

Ryder and Cam stood up, and Ryder's smile was easy. "I look forward to eating at your restaurant again soon, Vivi. I miss your ribs."

"That's kind of you to say." Vivi's smile held sadness and Cam reminded himself that he had to do something to convince her to allow him to bankroll the restaurant's resurrection. He'd find a way past her independence and stubbornness. Her dream deserved that.

"Please tell me that's she's going back to work," Ryder said once Vivi had left the room.

Ryder was so damn sharp, immediately picking up that something was off about Vivi's response. He trusted Ryder and told him the truth. "Joe was underinsured and wants to retire. Vivi isn't able to raise the cash needed to reopen."

Ryder sat down and placed his ankle on his knee, his whiskey glass nearly empty. He shook his head when Cam offered him more. "So, get a group of investors together and fund the renovation," Ryder said, frowning. "You've it done a hundred times before."

Like he hadn't considered that idea a thousand times. "She's won't let me. I've never come across anyone more independent or stubborn than Vivi Donner."

Ryder chuckled. "She doesn't want your money?"

"Neither my money nor my help," Cam admitted.

"That's hilarious."

It really wasn't. Cam poured himself another whiskey and frowned at his friend's amusement. "I want to give her what she needs but she won't take a damn thing," he grumbled.

Ryder dropped his foot, leaned forward and handed Cam a hard look. "Are you sure that money is what she most needs from you?"

Cam met his eyes. "Probably not, but I can't give her anything else, Ryder. She needs a good man, a man with no baggage, someone who isn't…me."

"Camden," Ryder sighed his name. "Please tell me this isn't about that horse crap Emma spouted so long ago."

Emma had just verbalized what Cam knew to be the truth. "I can't be the husband and father they need. I'm not—" He hesitated, unable to voice his deepest fear. He wasn't good enough for them.

"Jesus, Cam." Ryder pushed his hand through his thick hair. "Dammit, boy, when are you going to knock that chip off your shoulder? You're not that kid you were, the person you were. People can change, Camden."

"I'm terrified that I'll let them down, Ry."

"That's part of being a dad, Camden, part of love.

We all feel like that at one time or another. I felt like that with all my kids, and doubly so when Maya came along."

Cam cocked his head, interested. "I thought you would've felt more confident by then, having had Xander and Annabel already."

"I worried that I couldn't love Maya the same way I loved the kids of my blood, that I'd let her down, that I'd fail her."

"You adore Maya," Cam pointed out.

"Of course, I do. I love her with every fiber of my being," Ryder retorted. "She might not carry my DNA but she's my kid, every gorgeous inch of her."

Cam wondered whether he should ask and then shrugged. What the hell, Ryder would or wouldn't answer. "How did you come to adopt Maya? How did she come into your and Elinah's life?"

Ryder stared at him before looking away. A few seconds later, he spoke again.

"So what I'm trying to tell you is that every father has doubts, we are all scared. And anyone who isn't doesn't have the brains to realize how hard the job is," Ryder said, obviously choosing not to answer his question. Fair enough. It was Ryder's business after all.

Ryder stood up and placed his glass on the coffee table in front of him. Cam followed him to his feet and tried not to squirm when Ryder stared at him. "If you gave yourself the slightest chance, the smallest break, you'd realize that you'd be a great dad, Cam. Despite your past, you're as honest as the day is long, and your streak of integrity is a mile wide. You are not the boy you used to be. You'll be fine."

Cam released some tension and wished he could embrace Ryder's words, to trust himself as Ryder seemed to trust him. But he'd have to start doing that, if he was going to be the dad Clem needed him to be.

"You'd also make a really good husband." Ryder grinned at him. "Bad boys always do."

Ha-ha, funny.

Not.

Nine

Cam looked a little lost and very alone when he walked into his bedroom later that night. From the window where she stood, way on the other side of the room, Vivi watched him sit on the edge of his huge bed, his elbows on his knees, his fingers tunneled into his hair. His shoulders, usually so broad, were hunched and he stared at the hardwood floor beneath his feet as if it held all the secrets to the universe.

She'd suspected that he wouldn't come to her tonight, wouldn't make the first move for them to spend the night together. So, after putting Clem in her bed and showering, she'd slipped into Cam's room to wait for him. He'd been perfectly charming during dinner tonight, but as she laughed with Ryder and heard stories of Cam's past, she'd felt him retreat. His eyes had deepened, held more shadows, and he hadn't engaged in the conversation. Vivi knew he was mentally walking away from her and she wondered why.

"Hi."

Great opening line, Donner. Surely you can do better.

Vivi watched as Cam slowly turned around, his expression inscrutable. He tried to hide his feelings but his dark, beautiful eyes told her that he wanted her. It was in the way his gaze lingered on her legs, on her chest and her mouth before his eyes slammed into hers.

"You want me," Vivi stated, her voice stronger.

"You're a beautiful woman. I'd have to be dead not to," Cam replied, lifting his feet onto the bed and placing his hands behind his head. The big muscles in his arms bulged and she had to grip the drape to keep her feet in place. Because if she didn't anchor herself to something she'd be stretched out over him and reaching for that bulging zipper.

Concentrate, Vivi. "But you don't want to want me. You don't want the possibility of us."

For an instant Vivi thought he might deny her statement, but at the last minute he snapped his mouth closed and schooled his features, deliberately placing his hand over his erection. "It's late, Viv. Are we going to do it, or can I go to sleep?"

Vivi blew out her breath as she struggled to hold on to her temper. He was being a jerk and she wasn't going to let him get away with it. She told him as much.

His eyes widened at her statement and his hand fell from his groin to rest on the comforter next to him. Knowing that she couldn't allow him the opportunity to talk or walk away, she moved quickly and talked faster. "Let's talk about what's freaking you out, McNeal."

When he stayed silent, Vivi crawled onto the bed next to him, crossed her legs and placed her forearms on her knees. "My being here, Clem being here, is starting to feel less like playacting and more like real life, huh?"

His nonanswer was an answer in itself.

"Sometimes I feel like you want us to stay, other times I feel like you can't wait for us to leave."

Cam's fingers tapped the cotton comforter. "I enjoy spending time with Clem."

"But you're not enjoying me?"

Cam lifted his eyes and she saw his confusion. She understood it. So much had happened in such a short time that it was hard for him to wrap his head around it. But they had to, because this wasn't just about them. They had a daughter to consider. If Vivi was confused about what was happening between her and Cam, then Clem—bright as a button and an absolute barometer when it came to reading emotions—would start feeling confused, too.

"I love—" Cam hesitated and Vivi knew that he was picking his words carefully. He didn't want to hurt her but knew that he would anyway. "—this. The sex, it's awesome, Vivi."

It *was* awesome. "But?"

"But I can't be what you want, what you need."

Oh, this was going to be interesting. "What do you think I need, Camden?"

"I think you need and deserve it all, Vivianne." Cam lifted one big shoulder and let it drop. "I think you deserve the big house and the nifty car and not having to worry about cash ever again."

Whoa, hold on a second...

Before Vivi could tell him what he could do with his house and car, Cam spoke again. "You deserve a partner, Viv, someone who will be with you to celebrate the big and the small, to hold you when you are sad and pick you up when you are down. You deserve someone who will stand beside you, someone who thinks that

your happiness is more important than anything else."
Cam hauled in a deep breath. "I'm not that person, Viv."

She wasn't so sure. "What makes you say that?"

Cam shot to his feet and jammed his hands into
the pockets of his casual pants. By the way the fabric
bunched, she could see that his hands were clenched
into tight fists.

"I'm a selfish bastard, Vivi. I was raised to be like
that. My father and grandfather were the same. My entire life has been a fight for survival, to get ahead. I
don't think about other people. It's all about me."

What rubbish. A selfish person didn't offer his
money to help her rescue a failing restaurant, didn't
run to the bedside of a stranger when he found out he
was an emergency contact, didn't lavish time and attention on the daughter he'd just discovered was his own.
No, how Cam saw himself wasn't who he was.

"I see I've shocked you. Well, while I'm at it, let me
get this done." Cam's voice was pitched low but Vivi
saw his distress in his rigid neck, his thin lips, his taut
shoulder blades. "I was a childhood thief, Viv. I could
lift anything, anywhere, anytime. I could steal your
watch or your purse and you wouldn't even know it.
My father and grandfather were equally proficient in
the art of pickpocketing, grifting, conning. Crime, you
see, was so much easier than a day's work."

Now was not the time to speak, so Vivi just looked
at him, refusing to show any of the shock she felt. If
she did, she'd lose him.

"I grew bored with petty crime— Oh, that's the other
thing. I get bored really, really easily."

There was a subtext there and she was bright enough
to decode his sentence. *I'll get bored of you. I always
do.* She could challenge that statement, but it wasn't

time yet. Frustration passed over Cam's face, probably because she wasn't throwing up her hands and squealing like an offended teenager. She was stronger, smarter, than that.

Instead, Vivi just lifted her eyebrows in a silent "Is that all you've got?"

"I graduated to breaking into people's houses, even stealing into bedrooms while couples slept. You see, I'm not a good bet," he said, suddenly looking tired and defeated, washed out and embarrassed. "I've had a tough past and I'm a tough bastard and I doubt I'm going to be a good father...but I'm going to try." He shook his head. "But I can't be more than that, Vivianne."

She didn't respond to his last statement. Instead, she focused on his past. "Tell me, Cam. Tell me all of it."

Cam took a deep breath before shrugging. "It's not pretty."

"I don't want pretty. I want the truth."

"My mom left when I was two or three. My father said she couldn't handle it, couldn't handle me."

Even if his mother had been that much of a bitch, how dare his father repeat her words? Vivi pushed her fist into her sternum, immediately and intensely angry for the child Cam had been.

"Most people expect our parents to love us more than anything else in the whole world. I never did. I knew my mom left because she didn't love me and I knew I was nothing more than a burden to my father. When my grandfather came to live with us when I was five or so, he reinforced that idea. I was a drain on their resources, and if I was going to hang around, then I was going to earn my keep.

"I remember being five or six, and them teaching me to pick pockets, boosting me through small windows to pilfer items out of bedrooms and offices. Even then I knew what we were doing was wrong, but they told me that if I did this one thing, they would throw a ball with me, read me a story, buy me an ice cream. It was all about bribery, and they were masters at knowing exactly what I needed most at that time. They were damn good at manipulation."

Vivi wanted to throw something, to punch a wall, to go out and find his relatives so that she could strip skin off them. "Where are they now?" she asked, holding on to her temper.

"My dad is in jail, and will be for the next twenty years, and my grandfather died a few years back."

"Ah."

"Have you ever met a person who was never, ever at fault?" Now that the plug had been pulled from the dam, the river of words started to flow from Cam.

From his expression, Vivi suspected that it might be the first time he'd spoken about this, so she nodded, encouraging him to talk.

"They were always victims, you know? They always blamed someone else, frequently me, when something went wrong. They were Teflon coated. They never took ownership or responsibility for anything, ever. And they didn't teach me to do that, either.

"I spent my life analyzing my behavior, trying to be the person they wanted me to be. I was perpetually tired, drained, partially because I was constantly worried they'd be caught and I'd be shoved into the system. Turned out I was the one to be arrested first, and I was the one tossed into the system."

"You went to jail?"

Cam nodded. "Yeah. You've been sleeping with an ex-con, sweetheart."

"No, I slept with *you*," she was quick to correct him. "Why did you go to jail? And what happened inside that made you straighten out?"

"I went to juvie for burglary. My lookout, my father, ran when a silent alarm went off in a house. I got caught red-handed with my hand in a safe."

Vivi grimaced. How scared he must've been.

"And I was straightened out by a social worker who arranged for me to tour a prison, someplace I realized I didn't want to go. She told me that if I didn't shape up, some of those animals I met would be my new best friends." Cam shrugged. "I've never been stupid, so I shaped up. By the time I left juvie, Dad was incarcerated and I decided not to contact my grandfather again."

"That must've been hard."

When Cam shook his head, it finally hit Vivi how hard his life must've been. How alone he must've felt. "I'm sorry, Cam."

"I'm not a good bet, Vivi." Cam looked her in the eye. "I was exposed to stuff that no child should be exposed to. I did things no one is supposed to. My father and his father had screaming fights and frequently came to blows, so I never learned how to communicate in a healthy way. Can you understand why I'm so damn reluctant to settle down, have a family?"

"But you do have a family. You have Clem. And me."

"And I don't deserve either."

He uttered that sentence with such conviction that it tore into Vivi's heart. How could he still believe that? He'd come out of a dreadful situation to become an amazing man, a great human being. It was easy to be successful when you had the benefits of a supportive family and a good education. He'd had none of that, yet he'd been determined to better himself. She was

crazy about him—possibly in love with him—but she
also admired the hell out of him. And respected him
more than that.

"I can't fix my past, Viv."

"Nobody is asking you to do that." Vivi rested her
hands on his chest. "But you can focus on the positive
aspects of your past, the fact that you changed your life
around, that you had the guts to do that. Give Clem the
love and support you missed. Break the McNeal cycle."

"I don't know if I can."

Of course, he could, Vivi wanted to tell him. He already had. Why couldn't he see that? He was tough,
bold, wonderful. She didn't understand how he could
look at himself and see a failure. But didn't she do the
same? Didn't she refuse all offers of help, reject anything that threatened her independence because she was
still living in the past? Because she was still allowing
her mother to control her actions?

So, wow. Light-bulb moment.

But this wasn't about her right now. This was about
Camden. She could sit here and tell him he was being
unbelievably hard on himself, that she pretty much
thought the sun rose and set with him, that she wanted
to see where this went. But she knew that nothing she
said would make him change his mind.

But maybe she could show him.

Yeah, sometimes actions spoke so much louder than
words.

Vivi stood up and walked over to her badass billionaire and rested her hands on his hips, her forehead on
his chest. She felt the tension seep from him, just a little,
and she traced the hard ridges of his stomach. Nuzzling
her nose into the gap between his first and second button, she inhaled his spicy, masculine Cam smell. Want-

ing more, she pulled his shirt from the waistband of his pants and placed her hands on his hot skin, up over his ribs, his nipples and up to his powerful shoulders.

Needing more, she tugged his shirt up and over his head, sighing her pleasure when she had unrestricted access to his chest, his back, his stomach. After licking his flat, dusky nipple until it formed a tiny peak, she tracked her mouth over his shoulder and dipped her tongue into the deep groove between his muscled shoulder blades, then traced her lips over a scar on his back. She smiled when his hands came up to touch her thighs.

"I thought we were fighting," Cam said, his voice low and rough.

Vivi wrapped her hands around his erection, hard beneath the fabric of his chinos.

"You were trying to pick a fight with me, but I wouldn't let you," Vivi told him, keeping her voice soft. "You're not ready to believe anything I have to say. So I thought I'd try something different." Vivi dropped kisses on his spine, bending her knees to kiss the hollow of his back, just above the waistband of his pants held up by a thin leather belt.

She frowned and tugged at the offending object. "Crocodile, McNeal? Uh, no."

"What's wrong with the belt?" Cam demanded and she finally, finally, heard a note of amusement in his voice.

"It's a reptile! Ick." Vivi ducked around him and took off the belt. She dragged her thumb up his hard erection and smiled at his quiet shudder. After attacking the button, she pulled the zipper down and looked into Cam's beautiful, confused face. Good. Confusion was better than his relentless quest for control.

"You are so very beautiful, Camden McNeal."

Cam blushed, leaving Vivi to wonder if anyone had bothered to compliment him before. She cupped his face in her hands and stood on her tiptoes. "Your body is magnificent, your face is too sexy for words, but, man—" she tapped her fingers against his temple "this brain of yours slays me."

Vivi dropped back down to her toes and kissed his chest, somewhere in the region of his heart. "And your heart is as big as the Texas sky. You just don't want anyone to know that."

"Vivi," Cam pleaded, "*don't*."

Vivi shook her head. "Don't what? Tell you I want you, tell you that I'm not only attracted to your body but to the awesome person you are?"

Confusion was evident on his face. He opened his mouth, but no words came out.

Vivi smiled at him. "All you need to do right now is kiss me, Cam. Can you do that?"

Her quiet question seemed to jolt Cam out of his shock. His hands gripped her hips and he was lifting her up and onto him. Vivi wrapped her legs around his hips as his mouth took hers in a kiss that was a perfect mix of amazement and confusion, desire and tenderness. She sensed him trying to keep his passion under control, but when she sucked his tongue into her mouth, he utterly and finally lost control.

Oh, not of his strength or of the moment but of his need to hide, to run, retreat. It might not last but Vivi knew the exact moment that he surrendered to whatever this craziness was between them, fully embracing their madness.

Suddenly his hands were everywhere, kneading her breasts, cupping her butt, skimming her back. His mouth ravaged hers before he traced his tongue down the column of her neck, sucked the sensitive skin inside her collarbone. The buttons on her shirt popped and he lifted her up his chest so that he could tongue her nipple, sucking her lace-covered breast into his mouth.

Vivi cradled his head and sighed, knowing that here, in his arms, she was completely connected with the person he really was. The thought pushed hot liquid to her core and she felt her moisture soak her panties.

She wanted him buried deep inside her. Now. Immediately.

Unable to wait, Vivi whispered a dirty suggestion in his ear and Cam pulled his head back, blue-black eyes glittering.

"No."

Her suggestion had been explicit and, if she had to say so herself, damn hot. He should be tearing her clothes off, not staring at her like she was a tasty ice pop on a scorching day. Well, now, this could be interesting, she thought. She leaned back and rested her hands on his shoulders, confident that he could hold her. There was something so sexy about being held by a strong, hot, almost naked guy. The mere thought caused another mini flood down below. He was going to have to do something about that soon.

"What do you have in mind, McNeal?" she demanded in a haughty tone.

"This, for starters." Cam plumped up her breast and took her nipple into his mouth, his eyes still on hers. God, this was hot. Vivi felt her heart pounding, the beginning of an orgasm starting to build.

She really didn't want to go over the edge on her own. "Cam, seriously, I want to come, and I want you there with me."

Cam lowered her onto the bed and quickly, efficiently, stripped her of her clothing. Then he shucked his pants and underwear, his erection thick and hard.

"Faster or I'm going to handle my problem myself."

Cam had the audacity to grin at her. "Go for it, sweetheart. I'd love to watch you getting yourself off. And then I'll just take you back up again."

Such confidence. And absolute truth. Because he was still standing there, far too far away, Vivi narrowed her eyes at him. She wasn't confident enough to go that far…

And she needed his touch. "You do it so much better. Please, Cam?"

Cam's smile hit his eyes. "Are you begging me, Vivianne?"

"Asking nicely," Vivi countered.

"Sounded like groveling to me," Cam shot back as he dropped to his knees by the edge of the bed. Reaching for her, he draped her legs over his shoulders and slowly licked his way up her thigh.

Vivi squealed and released a curse.

"More dirty words, Donner?" Cam murmured, his breath tickling her feminine folds. "I like it."

"Cam, please," Vivi begged, lifting her hips to bring her core closer to his mouth.

Cam chuckled. "Definitely begging."

Vivi didn't bother to answer, not that she could. Every thought disappeared when Cam kissed her, gently sucking on her clit. She thought she'd reached the pinnacle of pleasure, that she couldn't take any more, and she shuddered, pushing herself against his hot, sexy mouth. But then Cam pushed one finger, then another into her and flicked at a spot deep inside her, and every cell in her body shattered. She shuddered, she screamed, her back arched, her skin flushed.

This was it—the best orgasm she'd ever had. Nothing would ever be as good as this. But Cam proved her wrong yet again when he pushed himself into her, pulling her legs up to accommodate him. He pounded into her, demanding that she come again—that she come with him—and those shattered cells disintegrated again.

Cam tensed, hesitated, and when he sank into her that last time, she felt his shudder and knew that he was there with her, fully in the moment, neither of them in control.

The next morning Vivi ran down the stairs, a broad grin on her face. She felt well rested, a little sore in all those good places that suggested that she'd been well loved—but happier than she'd been in a long, long time. She'd heard that sex was a gateway to the soul, but until earlier with Cam, she'd never experienced it. She'd never understood how powerful sex could be, how making love could open one's eyes and make one shift one's focus. Lying against Cam after the third time they'd made love was the most...*right* she'd ever felt. Vivi felt completely in tune with Cam and was convinced that they were better together than they were apart.

He was what she wanted, the person she and Clem needed. Not for his money or his position, though she deeply admired him pulling himself out of a situation that sounded horrible but because he was strong and protective and loving and flawed. For now, tomorrow, the next ten, twenty, forty, sixty years, she wanted to prove to him how worthy he was of love. He needed to understand that she knew him, that she saw him clearly, that he didn't need to hide who he was or what he'd done.

That no matter how uncomfortable, transparent and vulnerable he felt, she loved him and would continue to love him.

Rich, poor, she didn't care. They were stronger together than they were apart. And she thought Cam was finally starting to understand that. Thank God and all his angels and archangels.

Cam had kissed her goodbye much earlier, told her to sleep in and that he would dress Clem and take her to school. She remembered something about him saying he had a Texas Cattleman's Club meeting later that afternoon and that he might be late. It was Sally's day off and she had the big house to herself. Thinking that she would take another look at the offers of work she'd received, she walked into the kitchen and headed straight for the coffeepot.

Sitting down at the breakfast table, she stared out over Cam's landscaped garden, enjoying the bright blue sky and the lush vegetation. Pulling the laptop Cam loaned her toward her, she tapped her finger on the cover, unable to flip it open. She really needed to spend some time reading through, and understanding, the job offers she'd received. She didn't want to, she wanted to go back to what was familiar, what she knew and loved. Was she being stubborn in refusing to take Cam's offer to help resurrect the restaurant? Was she cutting off her nose to spite her face? Nobody was able to open a new restaurant without investors.

There was being independent and then there was being stupid. Was she being stupid or was she just allowing her new feelings—love and lust and hope and giddiness—to sway her?

She didn't know. But what she did know was that she was in love with Cam, that she probably had been since that night three years ago. He made her temper flare, her heart jump, her libido squeal. He frustrated her and turned her on, made her laugh and made her sigh. He certainly kept her on her toes.

And maybe that was a better reason than her independent streak to keep her from accepting his offer to fund the renovations. How she was feeling, how she thought *he* was feeling, was a good reason to keep their financial and work interests separate. Why add pressure they didn't need to such a fragile situation?

Everything had its season and maybe The Rollin' Smoke's had passed. And if she let go of her dream of renovating his restaurant, Joe could retire in peace and she could open her own place at some point down the line, when she'd cemented her reputation. Maybe then, she would feel comfortable asking Cam to invest. She'd have more experience, Clem would be older and their relationship would be better able to withstand the rigors of combining business with pleasure.

It was a plan she could live with. But she still needed a job. So Vivi opened the laptop and clicked on the message containing the first proposal.

Ten

Attending the Texas Cattleman's Club meeting was the last thing she wanted to do today but her father was insistent. Annoyed, Angela walked across the massive Perry Holdings boardroom, a room built to intimidate and impose, and glanced at the vast display of refreshments and the full bar. It was more than was needed for a late-afternoon meeting, but Sterling wanted to impress. And as usual, he had.

Ryder would be here, somewhere. They hadn't spoken since their lava-hot kiss last week and she was a nervous cat walking on a hot tin roof. How would he treat her? What would he say?

Too edgy to eat—thank God she rarely saw Ryder Currin or she'd waste away—she saw his dark blond head and, ignoring the swoosh in her stomach, decided to confront the sexy beast. She headed in his general direction, wondering how she could casually insert herself into the conversation he was engaged in. She looked at the man he was talking to and wrinkled her nose. She recognized Cam McNeal but she'd never met him. Oh, well, she'd just have to hold out her hand, smile graciously and welcome them to Perry Holdings. It would all be very civil…

If she could stop thinking about Ryder's big hand on her hip, his sexy mouth covering hers.

"Nice spread," Cam commented, his voice drifting over to her.

Ryder scowled at the food. "Perry always goes overboard."

"Hey, I'm not complaining," Cam replied, reaching for a plate and a small, elegant fish taco. After popping the delectable bite into his mouth, he nudged Ryder with his elbow. "God, Ry, lighten up. You look like you want to set someone on fire."

"Preferably Sterling Perry. Jesus, who does he think he is, calling a meeting of the TCC in his boardroom, in the headquarters of Perry Holdings? And especially given everything else that's happened."

He had to be talking about the discovery of the unidentified murder victim at the construction site. Angela, partially blocked by a screen just behind Ryder, stiffened.

"Look, this is a PR move by Perry, it has to be. He's just trying to curry favor with the powerful members of the TCC," Cam suggested.

"The *still-under-construction* TCC," Ryder snapped back before continuing. "Or maybe he's trying to distract and evade. Keep our attention on something else while he deals with the fallout of finding that body on his construction site. He might have something to hide."

Okay, she'd heard enough. Angela, her blood now

pumping with fury and not with lust—okay, a little lust but she'd ignore it—stepped into their space. They both winced and shame flashed in their eyes. Good. "Don't you think it's rude to malign my father while eating his food?"

Ryder looked like he was about to point out that he hadn't touched anything, but Angela narrowed her eyes at him and he got the message. Cam McNeal cleared his throat and she turned to look at him. He was even better looking up close. Tall (like Ryder), built (like Ryder), rough and ready and so very masculine, he exuded that bad-boy vibe. A woman would need a strong backbone to handle a man like him.

As one needed with Ryder. Right now hers was feeling a little jellylike.

"Ms. Perry, you are completely correct," Cam told her. "I sincerely apologize."

Angela nodded her appreciation and watched Camden walk away. When he disappeared into the crowd, she turned back to Ryder.

"Yeah, apologies," he murmured.

Half-assed, but it was better than nothing. Angela whipped a glass of wine off the tray carried by a waiter. Being this close to Ryder Currin, she either needed wine or a fire extinguisher. God, he was unfairly good looking. She'd always had a weakness for blue-eyed blonds. Because he made her feel off balance and fluttery, she channeled her inner ice goddess.

"May I remind you that Perry Construction has had to do major cleanup at the site due to the flood and we haven't been allowed access to certain parts of the site because it was designated a crime scene? Has everybody forgotten that a man lost his life? That he was shot? We don't know who he is, how he got there…"

"Have the police not asked anyone from your organization to help identify him?"

Angela shuddered. "Apparently his face came into contact with a slab of concrete and crushed his features."

Ryder's intelligent eyes sharpened. "Before or after the flood?"

Oh, he was quick. "They won't say. But if it was before, it would have to be a pretty strong and cold person to pick up and drop a concrete slab on his face."

"Not necessarily. You have forklifts on the site, don't you? It's not rocket science."

Angela grimaced and closed her eyes. Who could do that? And why? Man, people were sick. Her eyes flew open when she felt Ryder's big hand on her arm. And when he linked her fingers in his and pulled her behind the screen, she didn't protest. She needed his warmth, his strength, just for a moment.

Ryder rubbed her bare skin, from elbow to shoulder. Angela knew that he meant it to be a reassuring gesture but it had the unfortunate side effect of heating her panties. She wanted his mouth on hers, to feel her breast mashed against his hard chest, have his fingers mess up her hair.

"Let me try that again. I apologize if I was insensitive, Angela, and I do respect your views." Ryder sent her a wry smile. "It's no secret that your father and I have a history and that he rubs me wrong. And it annoys me that he won't accept that there was nothing between your mom and me but friendship."

She didn't want to think about any of that, not now. All she wanted was his mouth on hers.

He looked like he wanted the same thing. Ryder dipped his head and she could smell his sweet breath.

She lifted her heels to bring her mouth to his a fraction sooner. She genuinely could not wait for his kiss—touching him was that important.

Ryder's lips skimmed hers as a booming voice cut across the room.

"Ladies and gentlemen, if you can take your seats, please."

Ryder pulled back and they exchanged a long look containing enough energy to generate a nuclear power plant. She didn't want to talk about the Texas Cattleman's Club. She wanted to leave with Ryder and then not talk at all.

Ryder linked his fingers in hers and placed a gentle kiss on her temple. "This isn't over, darlin'."

God, she hoped not.

Across town, Vivi frowned when she heard the strident chime of the front door. She opened the front door to a woman in her midthirties, who looked perfectly cool despite the humid temperatures outside.

"Can I help you?"

The woman gave her a tight smile. She introduced herself and held out her hand. "I'm here about the nanny position."

The...*what?* Vivi shook her head and lifted her hands in confusion. "I'm sorry, what are you talking about?"

"Mr. McNeal contacted my agency first thing this morning and my supervisor set up this appointment. My current family is moving back to England, and as I'm one of the agency's longest and most experienced nannies, they immediately thought of me when Mr. McNeal said that he was looking to interview nannies for his daughter."

Vivi took a moment to process her statement. When

the woman started to speak again, she held up her hand for silence. So, shortly after leaving her this morning, after a night of mind-blowing, soul-touching sex, Camden's first impulse was to arrange for a nanny for Clem. What did that mean? What could it mean?

Vivi had no idea, but there was one thing she was sure of: she had no intention of taking Clem away from Charlie, and she most certainly didn't need a nanny. After sending the woman on her way, telling her that there had been a miscommunication, Vivi shut the front door and pulled out her phone. She tapped it against her thigh, debating whether she should call Cam and blast him for making decisions without talking to her first.

But maybe that was what he was expecting her to do and a good reason why she should bide her time and wait and see what else he'd had planned for her day.

Because she was pretty sure there was more to come.

Sterling Perry knew that Ryder Currin was mentally giving him the middle finger and he wished he could walk over to him and put him on his ass. He'd wanted to punch Currin's jaw for years now. Twenty-five years was a long time to keep his hatred under lock and key.

Ten minutes. Ten minutes was all he needed to show Currin who was boss.

Sterling stared down at the hands clutching the edges of the podium, ignoring the thought that his fists were no longer as big, his arms no longer as powerful as they had been a quarter century ago. But man, how he regretted not taking Ryder behind the barn and whipping the crap into him. Just seeing his insolent face, hearing his name hurtled him back to the past, to when he wasn't Sterling Perry the power broker but Harrington's lackey, the foreman of his ranch. Ryder reminded him of a time when his father-in-law's word was law, when he had no say in anything to do with his future or the ranch. He took orders back then, he didn't give them.

And he'd been the ranch cuckold, as useless as a steer. He'd never had a happy marriage to Tamara—they'd married to consolidate power and wealth—but he'd been proud of his beautiful wife. She was an exquisite woman but they'd never clicked, mentally or physically. He hadn't loved her but he couldn't allow her to be in love with anyone else, either, especially not Ryder Currin, a damned ranch hand. How dare he think he could lay a hand on a Perry, on any piece of his property? He still woke up from nightmares depicting Ryder and his wife rutting, hearing their laughter as they disparaged him. And the fact that Ryder had blackmailed Harrington into handing him land—oil-rich land that had made him a freakin' fortune—still burned like acid in his throat. He couldn't stand it then and he couldn't stand Ryder now. And if the rumors about Currin and Angela seeing each other turned out to be true, God help him...

Sterling heard a throat clear and came back to the present, looking out at the curious eyes trained on him. Dammit, the room would think he was a doddery old man, something he couldn't afford to happen. Once a thought like that took hold, the members of the TCC would start thinking that Currin was a better, younger, more energetic leader and they'd vote for him as president of the Houston TCC. That couldn't happen. He was Sterling Perry. Nobody would run this organization but him.

Sterling released his grip on the podium and cracked a joke. When he got the required laughs, he relaxed.

These were his people, his tribe. He knew exactly how to handle them.

"Thank you for giving up your valuable time to attend this first meeting of the Houston Texas Cattleman's Club."

"Can't be a meeting if there's no board yet, Sterling."

Shut up, Ryder. Sterling forced himself to smile at Currin's quip but chose not to address the interruption. If he ignored Ryder, maybe others would, too. "We do have TCC business to discuss, but before that happens, I'd like to take this opportunity to make a personal statement."

He saw the room come to attention, felt the tension increase. Good, he had them eating out of the palm of his hand. "I would like to make it clear to all—" he deliberately moved his eyes to look directly at Ryder "—potential board members and members of the soon-to-be-constituted TCC that neither myself nor any member of Perry Construction, or our holding company, had anything to do with the unfortunate murder at the construction site."

Sterling held up his hand to quiet the room when murmurs resounded. When he had their full attention once more, he spoke again. "I have also, with the full support of my family, decided that Perry Holdings will bear the cost of restoring the construction site to its pre-flood condition. We estimate it will cost a few million but we'll cover the bill."

His words, when they sank in, raised a roar of approval and thunderous applause. There was nothing Texans liked more than not having to put their hands into their own pockets. Sterling couldn't help his eyes drifting to Ryder Currin. He immediately noticed that Ryder's arms were still crossed against his chest. His expression asked what his lips did not: "What the hell are you up to?"

The applause lasted for a minute, maybe two, but Ryder didn't bother to put his hands together. The rat bastard.

Much later than he anticipated, Cam walked into his house, looked at his watch and winced. He'd missed Clem's bath time and she would be fast asleep by now. Dropping his phone and laptop bag in the hallway, he pulled down his tie and walked toward the kitchen, frowning when he saw it was in darkness. Only the small informal sitting room that he and Vivi usually retreated to after they put Clem to bed had light.

After only a week they had a routine, a favorite room and spectacular, soul-moving sex. It scared the hell out of him.

Cam swallowed, stared down the hallway and knew he was walking into a minefield. He'd made certain arrangements today and he knew his decisions would have consequences. Those consequences were still to be determined, but he knew, deep in his soul, that he was playing with fire.

Cam stared at the artwork on the wall opposite him—an expensive piece he didn't particularly like— and remembered the terror he'd felt when he left Vivi asleep in his bed earlier that day. She'd all but told him, through her actions and the way she'd made love to him, that she completely accepted him and that she might be in love with him. He hadn't slept, consumed with the idea of testing that theory. Did she really mean that? Or would she bolt at the first obstacle? His family had never managed to stay the course, had always found a reason to disappoint him, and he wanted to see if Vivi stuck or ran.

He'd expected Vivi's call by 9 a.m., shortly after the first nanny showed up at the front door. By noon—and after what should've been three appointments with three different nannies—there was still radio silence. He'd shrugged, thinking that she would definitely call when the local bank manager arrived, bearing papers already preapproving a massive loan to renovate The Rollin' Smoke. He was providing the guarantee to secure the loan but the loan would be in her name, her responsibility. He had no idea how that meeting had gone because, again, radio silence.

It had taken every ounce of willpower he had to not call her, to see if she was still here, to judge her mood and her reaction.

Would she stick or run? There was only one way to find out.

Cam took a couple of deep breaths and walked down the hallway. He hesitated at the half-open door, conscious of his dry mouth and pounding heart before pushing open the door with his foot. He stood in the doorway and looked around the room. He found Vivi sitting on a chair, her forearms on her thighs, her hands clasped and her head bowed.

He cleared his throat but Vivi didn't look up. Oh, God. She had to have heard him. Was she that upset? But good news, she was still here. That was a start.

He walked into the room and headed for the alcohol at the far end of the room. He dumped whiskey into two glasses, chased back the contents of one and refilled his glass before walking over to where she sat. He placed one glass on the coffee table in front of her and sat down on the sofa closest to her.

"Hi. Clem asleep?"

Vivi's face, when she finally looked at him, was blank and cool. "I presume so."

Cam felt a bolt of fear skitter along his skin. "She's not here? Where is she?"

"Charlie has her," Vivi answered him before picking up her glass and throwing the contents back. It seemed she needed the alcohol as much as he did. Not a good sign.

"Why is Clem staying the night at Charlie's, Viv?"

"She's not. I'm going to pick her up when I leave here tonight. Then we are going home, Cam. To our home, where we belong."

She was running. Why had he expected something different from her? God, he really didn't want her to leave.

"This is the point where you ask why we are going, Cam," Vivi pointed out, sitting back and rolling the glass tumbler between her palms.

Cam rubbed his hand over his face, thinking that Vivi looked far too controlled, far too calm for what he'd expected to be a humdinger of a fight. Had he read her wrong? Had he read too much into what happened last night? Why wasn't she railing at him, demanding to know what the hell he was thinking?

"What the hell were you thinking, Camden?"

Well, the question was right but there was no heat behind her words, no anger or emotion. He'd expected her to react in one of two ways—to leave immediately or to rail on him, tell him that he had no right to do what he'd done, that she wouldn't stand for it and never to do it again. And then she'd stay.

He never expected this quiet, still, intense response. What did it mean? Where was she going with this?

"You know that you had no right to arrange a nanny for Clem, that you had no right to organize a loan for me. You knew I wouldn't stand for any of it, but you did it anyway. I've been wondering why."

Cam slowly sipped his whiskey, desperately hoping that she'd put him out of his misery sometime soon. Mentally urging her to hurry the hell up, he forced himself to remain quiet, to see where she was going with this.

"So, the only conclusion I can come to is that today was a test. Last night something shifted between us and you were forced to face the fact that we have moved beyond being parents and bed buddies. That realization scared the hell out of you."

Well, yeah. Essentially.

"And you thought a reasonable response to that was to test me, my feelings?"

Cam winced when Vivi's voice rose and frustration and hurt leaked through that cool mask.

"I do want you to stay, Vivi." It was all he could say, the only words he could form. *"Please don't bail on me, please don't disappoint me"* were words he wanted to scream but refused to let pass over his lips.

"You have a damn stupid way of showing it, Mc-Neal," Vivi whipped back. "Why did you feel the need to test me?"

If he was less of a man, he could deny her charge, find a decent excuse for his actions. If she was going back to work, she'd need a decent nanny—Charlie was getting on in age and Joe wasn't going to be around to fill in the gaps—and she wanted her own restaurant. But he couldn't lie to her. She deserved the truth.

Before he could answer her, she lifted her hand to

stop him from speaking. "Don't bother answering. I've already worked it out."

He was interested to see if she came anywhere near the truth.

"You did to me what your father did to you. You did what you know." Okay, she was getting warm.

"Last night you told me that your father would test you, that he'd demand that you do something and then you'd be rewarded with his love. You never told me if it worked."

No, his father always reneged on his promise. Cam never received what he'd been promised.

"You expected me to disappoint you and then you'd have your excuse to push me away," Vivi said softly. "You set me up, knowing I'd never agree to your terms and that would give you the excuse to put the distance you needed between us. Because basically, you're terrified of being loved and even more scared of being disappointed."

Cam stared at her, utterly blindsided that she saw him so clearly, knew him so well.

"They say that in times of emotional stress we revert back to the child we were and you just showed me how true that is. Earlier I was tempted to tell you to take your controlling nature and shove it. It's my instinct to run at the slightest hint of controlling behavior because my mom controlled everything I did and said. And I so nearly did."

Cam gripped his glass tighter. "So why are you still here?"

Vivi's deep, dark, stunning eyes met his. "Because my love for you is stronger than my need to run from being controlled."

She loved him? *Still? How?*

"You love me?"

"That's pretty much the only reason I'm still here," Vivi said, not sounding happy about it at all.

Vivi leaned sideways and picked up her bag from the floor at her feet. She dug around inside, pulled out her phone and tapped the screen. After a minute, she dropped the phone back into her bag and met his eyes. "I just called for a ride and it will be here in five minutes. Just long enough to explain what's going to happen next."

What was going to happen next? He had no damn idea. He was still wandering through this minefield, blindfolded and confused.

"I love you, Cam, and I think, maybe, that you might love me a little, too. I think you want me, want the family we can be, but you're scared. That's okay, I'm scared, too."

Cam looked at her, hope blazing from his eyes. Maybe she'd stay…

"I'm not staying, Cam. I won't be controlled by anything, not you, not my mother and certainly not by your fear and your past. You've got to decide whether you can trust me, trust that I love you, trust that I'm not going to bail on you and you need to do all that without the need to test me, or my love.

"I need a partner who respects me as much as I respect him. Somebody who loves me without qualification, who can accept my love and love me back."

He couldn't let her leave, not without making some sort of effort to convince her to stay. Yet he knew that she might be asking for something he couldn't give. "I can try, Viv."

Viv tried to smile but didn't manage to pull it off. "This isn't about trying, Cam, I need action. There's no room for negotiation on this deal, McNeal. It's all or nothing."

He was still trying to make sense of her words, trying to wrap his head around the fact that she was leaving, when she dropped a kiss on his temple, her hand drifting across his hair. "You know where to find me, Cam. But make damn sure I am what, *who*, you want."

Eleven

It's late but I'm known for working longer and harder than many. But it's been many minutes since I looked at my monitor and gave any attention to the papers on my desk.

It's far more fun to remember every delicious detail of this afternoon's Texas Cattleman's Club drama. In the battle for control of the TCC, Sterling definitely won that round.

I've only ever allowed people to see what I allow them to, so I doubt anybody picked up how closely I observed the unfolding events. I noticed Ryder Currin's annoyance when he arrived at Perry headquarters, and as usual, Sterling got his back up when Ryder walked in. Two cocks fighting over the prize of the TCC, each thinking that the other is their greatest threat, completely oblivious that neither of them will win.

I will.

By the time I am done with them both, everything

*they value will be destroyed. I will make sure of that.
I've killed once. I'm not afraid to do it again.*

*People will remember that I was at the meeting, but
nobody will connect me with the demise of the two powerful families. Because I smile and pour on the charm. I
can do that as easily as I can manipulate, scheme, plot
and plan. The duality of my personality doesn't worry
me. I am what I am and nothing is more important than
seeing these two men taken down a peg or two.*

Or five hundred.

*I held many conversations with many people—all
boring—while keeping an eye on Sterling. Because I
pay close attention I immediately noticed the curl of
his lip when something displeased him. Because I know
him, I immediately noticed his stiff back, his clenched
fist. I followed his gaze across the room and yeah, there
was drama.*

*Ryder and Angela stood in the far corner, and since
their profiles were closer to me, I saw their tense exchange. Because I'm not a complete idiot, I quickly
clocked the sexual tension bouncing between them.
It was so obvious they want to see each other naked,
as soon as possible. I flipped my gaze to Sterling and
grinned. He'd also realized that Ryder and Angela
weren't having a conversation about the weather.*

*Sterling, never shy, headed their way to confront
this newest threat to the status quo and I couldn't help
laughing at the fact that a fox was in Sterling's henhouse
and, by God, he was determined to shoot it.*

The terrible twos should come with a box of aspirin
and a complimentary bottle of wine. A magical uni-
corn and a constant supply of chocolate wouldn't go
amiss, either.

Vivi looked down at Clem, now back in her own bed in their house in Briarhills and wondered if she dared leave the room. Clem looked asleep but the last three times she'd attempted to leave the room, Clem's eyes had popped open and high-pitched screaming had left her mouth.

Vivi was done. Physically, emotionally, mentally. She wanted a break.

Oh, who was she kidding? She wanted Cam. She wanted to hand her blaring daughter off to him and have him calm her down, because Vivi knew that the person Clem really wanted, the adult she missed at the end of the day, was her father. Her baby daughter, unable to articulate her frustration, was missing Cam. Vivi could relate because she was feeling the exact same way.

It had been nearly three days since she walked out of Cam's house. And while she remained convinced she'd done the right thing, she still wanted to fall asleep in his arms, wake up to his kisses, hear his deep voice laughing and talking with her and Clem. But as much as she wanted to drive her replacement car across town—the very basic sedan she'd rented on her own—she forced herself to stay put. She'd told Cam what she wanted. Now the ball was very much in his court.

Waiting to see if he would play it was killing her.

If he came, it wouldn't be easy. They weren't easy people. He'd try to boss her about, and she'd rebel. They'd fight but if they acknowledged that their pasts had left scars and recognized when they were acting from fear, they'd be okay. They just needed to love and laugh and negotiate their way through the hard times. She'd have to keep reminding herself that a partnership did mean relinquishing some control, and he had to believe that she wouldn't bail on him.

They could be amazing—if Cam decided that a family was what he wanted.

Vivi heard her phone beep and walked into her bedroom. She saw his name on her screen and wondered if her heart would ever stop lurching every time she saw his name. Probably not. Cam was her strong drink, her poison, her kryptonite. God, she wished she didn't love him so much.

She opened his message and read the words he'd typed seconds before.

Hey. I wanted to check on how Clem was. I haven't called her because I didn't know if it would upset her or not.

Vivi typed her reply.

She misses you like crazy. I miss you like crazy. She cried for half an hour and screamed for another fifteen minutes. How the hell do you think she is, we are?

She couldn't send that. If she did, he would rush over here, jumping on the excuse that she needed him, if only to help with Clem. No, that wasn't how she wanted him back. She erased that message, typed in a new response and hit Send.

She's good. We're good.

I'm not.

Vivi stared at his reply, confused. How was she supposed to answer him? Should she tell him he knew what to do? That all he had to do was to love them?

She was desperate to send some reply, anxious to end this stalemate between them. But in the end, even though her heart was breaking, even though it felt like her soul was weeping, she didn't reply.

Because nothing had changed. She wanted it all. She couldn't settle for anything else.

All three of them deserved more.

Sitting in the informal sitting room in his home, Cam stared at his phone, wishing that Vivi would respond, tell him what to do. Oh, he knew what she wanted—a family, him, her and Clem as a unit—but he still couldn't wrap his head around the concept. Neither could he stomach the thought of being away from her and his baby for much longer. God, why was this decision so hard to make? Why was he finding it so hard to act? He'd never been so indecisive.

Cam dropped his head against the back of his couch and idly rubbed the area of his heart. He missed them, more than he'd ever believed he would. His house, never the warmest place in the world, was now silent and cold, and his life was empty. Viv and Clem brought meaning and light and laughter and warmth into his world, yet he was sitting here, allowing his life to be dictated by the past.

Maybe he'd punished himself enough for being born a McNeal. Maybe it was time to let all that crap go and trust Vivi's version, instead of believing his version of his past—the one his father had taught him and Emma had reinforced. Maybe he should—

The insistent peal of the doorbell filled the house and Cam frowned. He sat up and looked at his watch. It was past ten, late for a social call. He rocketed to his feet and hurried to the front door, thinking that maybe, just maybe, Vivi was outside, that she'd come home to insist that they be together. He'd say yes, of course. Being with her and Clem was all he'd ever need.

But that wasn't possible. He knew that Vivi was her home in Briarhills. She shouldn't be. She should be here, with him.

There's only one person standing in the way of that happening and that's you, dumb ass.

Maybe it was time to stop being a dumb ass.

He made his way down the hall as his visitor leaned on the doorbell. Again he wondered who it was and how soon he could get rid of them.

Cam jerked the door open and frowned at Ryder, who had his finger raised to push the bell again. "Do it and die," Cam warned him.

"Still in a good mood, I see," Ryder said, pushing his way past Cam to enter his house.

"Not a good time, Ryder," Cam told him. He wanted to go to Vivi, to see if he could straighten out this mess.

"It's a very good time to talk some sense into you," Ryder said, ignoring the open door and walking down the hallway to the sitting room.

Cam cursed, closed the front door and followed Ryder into the room. Ryder poured himself a whiskey and pointed the glass in his direction.

"I'm sick of you not answering my calls, ignoring business. It's time to get your head on straight, Mc-Neal, and I'm the man to do it," Ryder said, lowering his brows in what Cam called his angry bison look.

"It's not necessary, Ryder."

Ryder was not in the mood to listen. "I've left three messages for you, a couple of emails, and you haven't replied to one."

He sounded like an irate teenage girl. "I didn't think

that your idea to host a Flood Relief Gala as the TCC Houston's first fund-raiser required an immediate response," Cam responded.

Some of the wind left Ryder's puffed-up sails. He stared into his now empty glass and Cam noticed his concerned expression. "I'm worried about you, Camden."

There was a lot of truth behind that statement and Cam felt his throat tighten. Ryder's genuine concern touched him. "I'm fine, Ryder, really."

"You might be fine in an 'I like being alone' way but you are not fine in an 'I'm in love' way," Ryder insisted.

Well, he could be if Ryder would just let him leave.

"I know what it's like to be in love, Cam, and I know how it feels to lose the woman you love. And I am so mad at you because I would've done anything to have more time with Elinah, anything at all! But it's your stubbornness that's standing in the way of your happiness and that just pisses me off."

"How do you know that Viv didn't dump me?"

"Because that woman is so in love with you she can hardly see straight. You're the one who has stomped on the brakes because you are scared of love."

"I know."

"Don't you argue with me!" Ryder retorted, obviously not hearing Cam's reply. "You haven't had a long-term relationship. You never even date the same girl twice! I've never seen you respond to anyone the way you do with Vivi. It's like she's switched on a light inside of you."

Exactly. "I know, Ryder," Cam said, trying to be patient.

"She's your Elinah, Cam. Why can't you see that and do something about it instead of hanging out in this god-awful house and moping?"

Okay, his house was quiet and a little cold but "god-awful" was pushing it. He needed to get Ryder to listen.

"Well, I'd really like to remedy that, Ryder, but instead I'm standing in my sitting room with an old man who seems intent on lecturing me about getting my head out of my ass. Just in case you're having a hard time keeping up, given your age and all that, I'd really like to go and win my woman back. So if you wouldn't mind leaving…?"

Ryder frowned, grinned as the words sank in, and frowned again. He picked up his dark brown Stetson, jammed it on his head and folded his arms. "Who are you calling old, boy?"

"You," Cam replied, unperturbed. He placed a hand on Ryder's back and pushed him in the direction of the front door. "And you called my house god-awful."

"It is," Ryder insisted, stepping into the hallway. "But maybe Vivi can sort it out for you."

"Vivi won't have time because she's going back to work," Cam told him, reaching around his friend to open the front door.

"She's got a new job?" Ryder asked as they left the house and walked in the direction of his massive truck. "Where is she working now?"

"Nowhere, as far as I know. No, she's going to re-open The Rollin' Smoke because that's what she really wants to do. I don't care if it takes fifty years to convince her, but she will resurrect that restaurant. It's her dream, Ryder. I want her to have it."

Ryder nodded and gripped Cam's shoulder. "Good man. But before you broach that subject, tell her you love her and because you love her, you'd do anything for her."

"Point taken."

Ryder surprised him by stepping up and giving him a quick, one-armed hug before slapping him on the back of his head.

Cam glared at him and rubbed the back of his head. "What the hell was that for?"

"For being an idiot." Then Ryder walked around his big truck to the driver's door. He frowned when Cam climbed into the passenger seat. "What the hell are you doing?"

"Hitching a ride." Cam smiled, pulling the door shut. "Vivi will find it difficult to toss me out on my ass when I don't have a car, any access to cash or a phone." Cam grinned. "Just hedging my bets."

Ryder rolled his eyes as he settled in behind the wheel. "I'm not a damn taxi service," he grumbled.

"I know." Cam looked Ryder in the eye. "I'm also relying on you to not let me chicken out at any point between here and her place."

Ryder started the pickup and the engine rumbled. "No problem. I'll just keep slapping some sense into you."

Tough love, Ryder style. Cam smiled, knowing that he wouldn't need it.

He only needed his lover, the love of his life, and his daughter.

Sleep evaded her. It seemed sleep was only something she'd done before her accident and before meeting up with Cam again. So she was awake when she heard pounding on her front door. It was way past ten. Who the hell would be banging on her door at this hour?

Vivi flung back the thin sheet covering her thighs and wondered if it might be another flood warning. Panic caught in her throat and she hurried through her small house to the front door, jerking it open without checking the peephole.

Cam, looking—oh, let's be honest here, simply wonderful—stood on her front porch.

"Check before you open, Viv. I could've been any random dude out to rob or rape you."

Okay, he looked great but his attitude could use some work. "Did you come over here at this crazy hour to harangue me about not taking safety precautions?"

"No, but it's an added bonus," Cam muttered. He pushed a hand through his hair and scowled at her. "Are you going to make me do this outside?"

"Do what?" Vivi asked, confused.

Cam answered her by placing his hands on her hips and pulling her into his hot, strong body, wrapping his arms around her and capturing her mouth in a searing kiss she felt right down to her toes. Her hands found their way to his face—the face she'd missed so much— and she groaned softly. It would be so easy to boost herself up his body, wrap her legs around his hips and allow him to carry her to her bedroom. Judging by his intense kiss and the hardness pushing against her stomach, he'd have no problem with that idea.

One more time, for old times' sake.

And then the pattern would be set. She'd push him away, he'd come back, they'd sleep together, and she'd realize it wasn't enough and she'd end it again. No, she had to be strong and stop this in its tracks.

She didn't want to be strong, though. She wanted to keep kissing Cam under her dull porch light.

Strangely, it was Cam who pulled away, Cam who stopped the craziness. He rested his forehead against hers and sighed. "I see you and my brain shuts down," he said.

Was that a good or bad thing? She had no idea.

"Can we please go inside?" Cam asked her, his sweet breath warm on her face.

Vivi nodded and stepped back into her house. Cam closed the door behind him and flipped the lock. Vivi shook her head; she lived in a safe neighborhood and she wasn't concerned about crime. But then she remembered that Cam had seen the darker side of life, had rubbed shoulders with some not very nice people, and remained silent.

"How's Clem?" Cam asked, rocking on his heels.

He'd asked her the same question earlier and nothing had changed since then. "She's asleep."

Cam whipped around and walked down her short hallway to Clem's room. Opening her door, Vivi watched as he walked inside to stare down at his daughter. She watched his face soften and his expression turn tender. His love for his daughter was indisputable and Clem was lucky to have such an amazing dad in her life. He'd protect her, love her, tease her and laugh with her. He'd be her first love, her shelter in any storm.

"She's so beautiful, Viv. So amazingly perfect," Cam said, running his finger down Clem's cheek.

She really was. Vivi couldn't help placing her hand on Cam's back and leaning her head against his shoulder. "We did good work," she agreed.

"I want her," Cam said, keeping his voice soft. Then he turned to her and his eyes blazed with conviction, determination sparking in those deep blue depths. "I want you, us. Together. All the time."

Vivi felt her knees soften and gripped the edge of Clem's cot to steady herself. She stared at Cam, not sure whether she'd imagined his softly spoken words. "Sorry?"

Cam's smile was soft and tender. "You heard me, Donner."

"I think I heard you, I'm just not sure I heard you correctly," Vivi replied, idly noticing that her words sounded breathless. Not a surprise, since she was sure that all the air in the room had disappeared.

"Well, let's get out of here and I can say it louder and with more emphasis. As much as I love our daughter, this next conversation is between her momma and me."

Vivi looked at the big hand Cam held out to her, felt her heart pumping and her stomach swooping, the rest of her organs abuzz. Could this be happening? Really? To her? There was only one way to find out. So Vivi placed her hand in his and followed him out of Clem's room. She expected him to turn left to go to her bedroom but instead he turned right and led her into the kitchen, pulling out a chair from under her small wooden dining table. "Sit."

Vivi, for the first time ever, obeyed his order and sat. Mostly because her legs were about to go on strike. Cam moved to stand by the counter, his hands gripping its edge with white fingers. Good, maybe she wasn't the only one who felt off-kilter.

"I'm going to stand here because I've got things that I need to say. It's far easier to kiss you than to talk, so I'm going to keep my hands off you for a few minutes, if that's okay?"

Not really, but if he was about to say what she thought he was about to say, she could live without him touching her, just for a little while. "Okay."

"I was as mad as hell with you for not telling me that I had a child, but I get it now, I do. I'm so glad you put me as your emergency contact, but most of all I'm grateful you didn't drown in that damn flood."

She did, too, but that went without saying.

"I've known you for two weeks and a day, if you count that night we spent together three years ago. My feelings for you should scare me because really, who falls in love in two weeks?"

He was in love with her? Her heart jumped and Vivi tried not to wiggle in her chair as he continued his speech.

"I didn't believe in love, not until you fell back into my life, wet, bedraggled and mud stained." Cam released the counter, flexed his fingers and resumed his hold. "I fought you. I fought what I'm feeling because it scares me stupid. You were right, I did arrange the nannies and the loan as a test. I wanted to prove to myself that you would run, that you are as unreliable as my parents, that you couldn't be trusted.

"I used your hot buttons—your independence and hatred of being controlled—to manipulate the situation to force you out of my life." Cam pulled his bottom lip between his teeth and shook his head. "It was a stupid move, Viv, and I'm so sorry. I will always regret it."

Vivi started to protest that he was being really hard on himself and she'd already forgiven him. But Cam held up his hand, asking for her patience. When she didn't speak, he nodded his thanks.

"But you called me on my BS," he said. "You saw right through me. I should've realized right then that you were right and I was wrong, but I can be a little stubborn."

She couldn't resist a comment. "A little?"

"A lot." His lips kicked up. "Just like you."

Fair.

"So, basically, I'm here to ask you, to beg you, to give me another chance. I can't promise to always agree with you, but I can promise that I will always listen to you. I can't promise to never make a decision on your behalf, but I promise to try and talk everything over with you. I can't promise to change overnight, but I promise to try. If I give you stuff it's to make your life easier, or because I think it'll make you happy, not to control you. I promise to be a better man, Viv, for you and our daughter. And I promise, with my hand on the Bible, that I will be a good dad to Clem."

Of course, he would. She didn't have any doubt about that. Vivi crossed her legs, rested her hands in her lap and cocked her head. She waited a beat and a tense silence filled the room. Cam stood up straighter and she knew that he was wondering whether he was going to be rejected again. She couldn't let him think that, but she had a few things she had to say first. She took a deep breath and tried to smile.

"You're not *that* controlling, Cam. I'm just ultrasensitive to it because I was controlled and bullied. Sorry to be the one to inform you of this, but I think you are pretty normal for an alpha male with a wide, protective streak. I'm not saying I won't rebel, but I'll try and tone down my instincts. I don't need your money or your gifts. Having you in my life is enough. I absolutely know you will be a good dad to Clem, and our other children, because you are already a good dad."

Was that a glint of moisture she saw in his eyes? Vivi felt her throat tighten and told herself that she couldn't cry. But one tear broke free and then another. She tossed her head and blinked, holding up her hand when Cam stepped her way. "Stay there. Not done."

She wiped away the tears with the balls of her hands, and when she looked at Cam again, she managed a wobbly smile. "One more thing…"

How was she going to say this without bawling? How could she tell him everything that was in her heart, share her deepest conviction? She just had to blurt it out.

"You don't have to be a better man, Cam, because you already are pretty damn spectacular. I am in awe of what you've done, how far you've come. I admire you and respect the hell out of you." Vivi released a wobbly laugh. "I'm so in love with you, McNeal."

"Aw, baby…"

Then Cam was in front of her, lifting her out of her chair and holding her to him. Somehow Vivi found herself in his lap, her fragile wooden chair creaking under their combined weight. The chair could break, the floor could open up and swallow them, and she wouldn't care. Cam was with her and her life finally made sense.

She didn't need him to say the words. He'd shown her that he loved her by opening up, by coming here, by exposing himself. The words would come.

Cam placed his hand on her cheek and tipped her face to look at him. She smiled as she stepped into the happiness that radiated from his eyes. They'd be okay, today, tomorrow, forever. She knew this. She did.

"Vivianne, I didn't want to fall in love or be with anyone. I didn't want to need anyone. I wanted to skim through life. Every rule I made for myself, every promise I made to keep myself apart and safe, I've broken. For you." Cam touched his lips to Vivi's cheek, held himself there. "I love you so damn much."

There. *Finally.* Vivi felt the last ice cube of resistance in her melt, felt herself sink into him. More tears slipped down her face and Cam kissed them away.

"Don't cry. I'm so sorry I hurt you."

Vivi shook her head and wrapped her arms around

his neck, burying her face in his strong, warm neck. "Hold me, Cam."

Cam's hands ran up and down her back. "I am. I will. You're pretty much stuck with me for the next sixty years or so."

Vivi sniffed and then laughed. She pulled her head back to see his tender smile, his soft eyes. "Does that comment come with a ring?"

"Maybe." He rolled his eyes and grinned. "God, who am I kidding? Of course it does, I can't wait to make you my wife." Cam's thumb drifted over her bottom lip. "Can I kiss you now? 'Cause I'm so much better at show than tell."

"I don't know about that. Your tell was pretty damn good. But sure," she said, placing her lips a fraction from his, "kiss away."

"Thank God," Cam muttered before doing exactly that.

And best of all, they got to do all of that and more. Much more. For the rest of the night. And for the rest of their lives.

* * * * *

MARRIAGE
AT ANY PRICE

LAUREN CANAN

One

It all happened in the blink of an eye.

There was a blur of motion to Seth Masters's right as a woman on a large thoroughbred came out of nowhere. She gave a cue, and the immense muscles in the animal's hind legs propelled the steed and its rider up and over the hood of Seth's low-slung sports car. He fought to bring the car to a screeching halt, narrowly missing one of the pines that grew on both sides of the country road. The rider stopped as well, turned the chestnut around and headed back to the car. She didn't look happy.

"You're an idiot!" she said as she brought the horse to a stop a few feet from the car. "Didn't you see the signs saying Slow Down, Bridle Path Ahead? Can't you read? You almost got us killed! Who goes eighty on a one-lane backwoods road?"

"I wasn't going eighty."

"Couldn't prove it by me!"

Seth was flooded with emotions: shock, relief that no one was hurt, an underlying sense of unease that he'd been driving too fast. But through all the self-recrimination, one thought stood out: the woman was magnificent. Rich auburn hair swirled about her almost angelic face, and though her green eyes sparkled with anger, they were stunning. Her slim, beautiful body seemed too slight to control the huge thoroughbred that tossed his head and pawed the ground, pulling air into its massive lungs. Obviously she was an expert rider, something Seth was enormously grateful for right now.

He opened the door and pushed out of the Ferrari. What could he say? He'd been so wrapped up in his own thoughts he hadn't paid any attention to the signs.

"I apologize. Sincerely. I hope you weren't hurt."

"Just slow down. The riding path crisscrosses the road several times over the next few miles. Needless to say, the next time you might not be so lucky."

Even in anger her voice was clear and attractive.

"Point taken."

She homed in on his face and tipped her head as a frown crossed her fine features.

"You're not from around here." It was a statement as much as a question.

"Los Angeles."

She opened her mouth as if she was about to say something else then must have thought better of it and shook her head.

"Could you tell me how far out I am from Calico Springs?"

"By the posted speed limit, about twenty minutes."

"Thanks," he replied, taking in her sexy-as-hell physique as she turned the stallion around and headed back in the direction they'd come, disappearing into the trees.

Seth returned to the car and started the engine. He hoped this wasn't a sign of what was in store this trip. He had to remember this wasn't LA—it was rural Texas, and things worked at a slower pace. Still not able to completely shake off the close encounter, he eased back out onto the narrow road and continued in the direction of Calico Springs.

Attorney Ben Rucker's office, an old Victorian house just off the town square, was easy to spot. It fit in perfectly with the other buildings along Main Street. Calico Springs was quaint. Innocent. Like a town out of the past. There were planters filled with flowers and wooden park benches in front of most of the stores and shops. After parking the car, he made his way inside the lawyer's air-conditioned office and gave his name to the receptionist.

"Of course, Mr. Masters. Mr. Rucker has been expecting you. I'll let him know you're here."

Minutes later Seth was seated across from the elderly attorney.

"It's a pleasure to meet you, Mr. Masters. I take it this is the first time you've been to Calico Springs?"

"Actually, I've been here several times. I met my half brothers and enjoyed the area when I was a young boy. I've been back a dozen or so times since then. The last time was about five years ago."

The attorney chuckled. "You certainly carry the family resemblance. You are most definitely a Masters."

"I wanted to come down early and see the ranch again. Do my brothers know I'm here?"

"I told them you were coming. Chance and Cole are in New York, and Wade and his wife are in London. They will all be back next week for the probate of the will."

Seth nodded. He'd been brought up the only child of a single mother. Then when he was six years old, his father had insisted he come to the ranch and meet his half brothers. Even at that age, he'd been nervous. But they had taken the news of his existence better than he'd hoped and welcomed him into the family. Those dozen or so summers he'd spent on the ranch were wonderful memories, and he looked forward to seeing everyone again.

"I must admit I'm curious about the will."

"I can understand." Mr. Rucker sat back in his leather chair. "Did you know your father very well?"

Seth shrugged. "About as much as anyone knew him, I guess. I saw him maybe a dozen times in my life. Mother wouldn't talk about him. I never saw or heard from him again after I entered Stanford, although I always suspected there was communication between him and my mother."

As he'd grown older, Seth had begun to realize that the home where he and his mother lived and the cars she drove were beyond the means of a single working mother who had no advanced degree. There had to be another source of funds. And though he'd been awarded a partial scholarship to attend Stanford, it hadn't nearly covered all the expenses. Yet when he needed money, it was always provided.

"From what little I know," Mr. Rucker said, "you would be right. Your father spoke highly of you when we were drafting the will. But he was never a man comfortable with family. Either of his families, as it turns out. His work always took priority. I guess he had his own reasons why he couldn't relate."

"I guess." Seth nodded. "The reason I mention the will is I sit on the boards of two regional hospitals, and a new research facility focusing on leukemia is on the table. The more funding we can get for it, the better. If I stand to inherit anything, it will certainly help me move things along."

The attorney nodded then seemed to hesitate. "Mr. Masters, you understand I cannot discuss the will without all heirs being present. But that said, I feel it only fair to ask if you're married."

"Married?" The question seemed odd. He'd come close once. It had ended badly. He'd given his heart to Gwen Jeffers, and she'd returned his love by having an affair with another man. He hadn't thought of getting married to anyone since. He liked life in the fast lane. Free of responsibility to anyone but himself and his companies. "No," he replied. "Not me. Why do you ask?"

"Well, there's a stipulation that needs to be met by the time we're in probate, so I'd better discuss this with you. One of the requirements of the will is that each of you boys be married. Mr. Masters never explained his reasoning. It may have had something to do with his own experiences in life. I'll never know for sure. But, of course, he had the right to set any conditions he wanted. If any of you aren't married by the day the will is probated, you'll be dropped from the will, and any financial assets or land holdings will revert to the other married sons or, in specific circumstances, to charity. As of now, you're the only one who doesn't meet the requirement.

"I tried to call to discuss this with you a few weeks ago, but you were out of the country. I left several messages with your office. I asked your brothers if they knew your marital status, but they couldn't say for sure—apparently you haven't been in touch recently."

"I see. Yeah, I have a boatload of calls I need to return. I regret not getting in touch sooner. This news is disappointing." And that was an understatement. "But—it is what it is. I look forward to seeing my brothers again and meeting their wives. It isn't every day I get to spend time with them."

"That's true." The lawyer chuckled. "It's too bad about the will. It sounds like the research center is a worthy cause."

"It is." Seth stood up from his chair and shook the lawyer's hand. "Well, thank you, Mr. Rucker. I appreciate you letting me know."

"Of course, Mr. Masters. You do have ten days or so. Perhaps you know someone who'd consider becoming your wife. There's still time."

"I don't think so, but again, thanks."

Seth stepped out of the lawyer's office with Mr. Rucker close behind him just as the front door opened and in walked none other than the horsewoman he'd met on the road. Her surprise at seeing Seth was immediate. But she quickly put it aside and turned toward Mr. Rucker.

"Did you get an appointment?"

"Ally, why don't you come back after lunch and we can discuss it in private."

"I have to go back to work. All I'm asking for is a yes or no."

"I'm sorry." He smiled at her and slowly shook his head. "I'm trying to get in touch with Wade or Cole, since they handle the company's finances. Wade is out of the country. Cole and Chance are in New York doing double duty while their brother is gone. Why don't we step inside my office for a moment?"

"I don't have time," she insisted. "You will excuse us, won't you?" she said looking at Seth, then turned back to Mr. Rucker.

The elderly gentleman held up his hands to Seth in a gesture of helplessness.

"It's okay," Seth said, grinning. "I'll be going."

"I managed to speak with Chance," Mr. Rucker said to the young woman, "and he said he knew nothing about it and we would have to wait until Wade returned."

"And when will that be?"

"When his business is finished, I gather. I believe he has an appointment here in the latter part of next week."

Seth heard her sigh behind him. Whatever they were talking about appeared to do nothing to improve her state of obvious frustration. She must be having a really bad day.

Still, Seth couldn't help but catch the names Mr. Rucker had tossed out. Wade, Cole and Chance were his half brothers. He was tempted to blurt out his relationship and see if he could help her but at the last second closed his mouth. It wasn't any of his business.

"Can you schedule an appointment for me then?"

"I'll see what I can do, Ally. You know I will, but..."

"You think it's pointless," she finished.

"I think," the attorney said, "that you have every right to talk with them. And to that end, I'll do the best I can."

"Thanks, Mr. Rucker."

As she turned to leave, her emerald eyes fell on Seth.

"I see you made it to town, presumably without mowing anyone else down."

"Miracles do happen. Actually, I did slow down after our encounter and enjoyed the countryside," Seth said. "Thanks for the tip."

"Any time."

He opened the door and she walked through it, turning right and continuing down the sidewalk. Seth couldn't help but watch as she seemed to glide down the street. She was still wearing the riding pants that outlined every detail of her slim figure. A leather belt emphasized her tiny waist, and her loose white shirt covered full breasts.

She had a small, impish nose and lips a man could enjoy for hours. He felt his body immediately react to her, something that frankly surprised him.

It was too bad he didn't pick up any vibes that she was the marrying kind. He just might be tempted.

"Mr. Rucker, could you recommend a good place to eat?" Seth said, turning back to look at the lawyer.

"Burdall's City Café, just one block up on the town square. As a matter of fact, I was about to head there myself. You're welcome to share my table."

"Thanks. I'd like that."

It was only a few minutes' walk to the café, and they just beat the lunchtime rush. Seth pulled out a chair and settled in across the table from Mr. Rucker. He grabbed the menu from between the salt, pepper and sugar canisters and looked it over. It had a pretty wide selection for a small hometown restaurant.

A waitress set tall glasses of ice water down next to them and said she'd be back in just a few minutes to take their orders. But before she could return, they had another visitor at their table.

"Hi." It was the redhead again. "Do you mind if I join you? There's a line and I have to get back to work."

"Of course," said Mr. Rucker without hesitation. "Ally, have you met Mr. Masters?"

She stilled. "No," she said, staring at Seth. "Not… formally, at least."

"This is Seth Masters. Seth, Ally Kincaid."

"Masters?" She frowned. Her eyes narrowed. "Are you any relation to Wade Masters?"

"Yes. As a matter of fact I am."

"I knew it. When you almost ran me down on the road. You look like a Masters." Her eyes rested on him, and she was silent for a few moments. Then, as though she thought better of saying what she had in mind, she changed the subject.

"You said you were from California, right? What do you do there?" she asked as she pulled out a chair and sat down.

"I own several companies, mostly electronics and pharmaceuticals."

"Huh. Who would have thought? I would have better believed you were a contender for the Indianapolis 500." She reached for a menu. "I'll bet your pharmacy comes in handy when you get behind the wheel."

"I'm just used to moving at a faster pace."

"Yeah, I'll bet you are. So, what are you doing in the sleepy little town of Calico Springs?"

"Just enjoying the view," he replied, looking straight at her.

Seth watched as a light blush ran up her neck and touched her face before he returned to the menu. Her very scent was exciting: a subtle blend of exotic herbs, strawberries and leather. It had his pheromones working overtime. He had never experienced such an immediate attraction to a woman.

"Is everyone ready to order?" The waitress flipped a page in her notebook and took pen in hand.

Ally ordered a ham and cheese sandwich while Mr. Rucker and Seth chose to have steak. Seth glanced at the older man and saw a twinkle in his eyes. He suspected Ben was attuned to the banter going on between him and Ally and maybe had a little subtle matchmaking in mind.

After they had given their orders Ally turned her focus to Mr. Rucker. "So, did you pencil me in?"

"I had my secretary send Wade a text to see when he's available. Once I hear back, consider yourself penciled."

"Good. Thank you. I just hope he's as reasonable as people say he is."

She wanted an appointment with Wade? Seth couldn't help but wonder as to the reason.

As though the question showed on his face, she set the menu aside and said flatly, "Wade Masters's father stole my ranch. And I want it back."

Two

"Ally," Mr. Rucker said in a cautioning tone, indicating she had spoken out of turn.

"What?" She shrugged her shoulders. "I don't care who hears. Half the town knows anyway." She turned her focus on the newcomer. "The old man was a crook. He stole my ranch. Claimed my father used it for a loan that Dad never paid back. My father wouldn't do something like that. Old man Masters took it all. Everything. Had me evicted after Dad died. I even had to fight to keep three mares and a stallion that were registered in *my* name. Talk about greed. You'd think someone with that much money wouldn't feel the need to swindle people out of their home."

"The horses, as I recall, were simply a misunderstanding," Mr. Rucker asserted.

"Yeah. How long would it have taken to straighten that out had I not caught it?"

When Ally turned away from Seth Masters, she could still feel his golden eyes watching her. Ben Rucker was probably right. She shouldn't be spouting off in front of strangers, although she found it hard to consider Seth Masters a stranger. He could almost be Wade Masters's brother, so alike were their looks. He had thick brown hair with a slight wave and gold highlights and a five o'clock shadow that covered a sharp jaw and prominent chin, complete with a sexy little cleft. High cheekbones complimented brown eyes with flecks of gold. His lips, too kissable to put into words, delivered a sexy grin showing perfect white teeth. In his white dress shirt and tie, he was the epitome of handsome.

"What about you, Ally? What do you do?" he asked.

"Rancher. Or I used to be before…" She grimaced and pressed her lips together. "Now I work at the Triple Bar Ranch east of town. I train horses."

"That must take a lot of skill and agility."

She'd never really thought about it. It was something she'd done most of her life. She shrugged. "Maybe."

The man nodded. "I would venture to say our jobs are equally challenging."

"Oh, you would, huh? Tell me, Mr. Masters, how many stalls have you mucked out? How many horses have you trained?" She couldn't help but laugh. The idea that she was anything like this rich hunk from California was absurd.

Ben Rucker snorted at her comment and fought not to choke on his coffee.

"It just so happens," Seth said, "that in my younger days, I mucked out plenty of stalls. Never trained a new horse, but logged plenty of hours exercising them. I spent most summers here in Calico Springs at the family ranch growing up. So I guess I have a good idea of what you do. Clearly you're accomplished. And that's worth saying."

"Thank you," she replied, feeling a blush coming on. "Still...my accomplishments probably don't measure up compared to yours."

"You don't accept compliments very well, do you?"

"Compliments I can handle. It's bullshit I'm not so good with."

"Then allow me to backtrack and just say you're a very skilled horsewoman."

"Damn good thing for you." She sat back as the waitress set her plate down in front of her. "It took me most of the ride back to the ranch to calm Monkey down."

"What happened to Monkey?" Ben asked.

"He had a fright this morning," she said, picking up half of her sandwich. "Some idiot nearly ran him down with his car."

"Good grief!"

"No grief. Just bad driving." She took a bite and picked up a napkin.

"Not that bad or I would have hit you. And it occurs to me that I wasn't the only one speeding."

"I take it you two have met each other before, then?" asked Ben.

"We almost had a collision on the country road leading to town this morning," Seth explained.

Ally dropped the sandwich back onto her plate, wiped her hands with the paper napkin and glared at him. "There's no speed limit posted on the bridle path. Most people with any common sense would appreciate the fact that it's the cars going down the road that are the hazard. Especially if they are trying to break the sound barrier."

"I say again, I was not going all that fast."

"That would depend on your definition of fast."

They held each other's gaze. After a few long seconds, she turned back to her plate. "You were in the wrong, and I really don't care to discuss it further."

She couldn't miss his pursed lips as he tried to hide a grin.

Hateful man. She didn't know what he was doing in Calico Springs. She hadn't missed how he'd sidestepped her question when she asked. And she hadn't appreciated that "enjoying the view" remark, even though it had been a long time since a man flirted with her. She didn't want any of the Masters men to say one word to her after what their father had done. She could only hope their paths would not cross again.

"I ordered fifty sacks of sweet feed and one hundred and twenty-five sacks of Nature's Best. What out of that says crimped oats? Does Colby have a hearing disorder now?"

She'd stopped by the feed store on her way home to pick up the order for the horses she was training. Instead of what she ordered, they had readied seventy-five sacks of oats. This day just seemed to keep going downhill.

"I'm sorry, Ally. If you can give me a few minutes, I'll fix your order. Are you in the farm truck?"

"Yeah. Thanks. I'll wait outside."

Despite the obstacles she'd overcome so far today, mostly set in her path by that Seth Masters, it was still a beautiful day with just enough fluffy white clouds overhead to keep the sun from turning up the heat. She wandered out to the gardening section and idly looked at the petunias and other bedding plants. Any other year, she would be picking up trays of assorted flowers to be planted in the beds around the large wraparound porch at her house. This year she had purchased one hanging basket that she placed at the edge of the small front porch of the cabin where she stayed, and that was all she would allow herself to have. No use spending money on stuff that would just die from neglect.

And they would be neglected. Her heart just wasn't in it. The cabin, provided by the ranch where she worked, sufficed, but it wasn't home. It would never be home. Why surround herself with tarnished memories of the things she used to love? She didn't need to be reminded of her home and the joy she'd known there. It was gone, and the sooner she accepted that fact, the better off she would be.

She would keep the appointment with Wade Masters once it was arranged, but down deep she knew she had little hope of convincing him to give back her ranch. Even if he agreed to sell it back to her, she didn't make enough money for monthly payments on a ranch that size. It would take time, at least another year, before she could start earning the kind of money she needed.

"It seems we keep bumping into each other." A deep voice came from behind her. Before she fully turned toward him, she knew it was Seth Masters.

"Are you following me, Masters?"

"On the contrary, I've been around back looking at the tractors. I didn't see you when I got here, so I would have to ask you the same question."

He smiled. She gritted her teeth and glared.

"So what are you going to do with a tractor?"

"Someday I might buy some land. And I've always been fascinated with tractors. The bedding plants look rich and healthy," he added, filling the intervals when she didn't respond. "Are you doing your flower beds in these?"

"I have no land. I have no house. Consequently, I have no flower beds. So no, I'm not buying any plants."

"I saw this store and had to stop. You don't often see old businesses like this still open and running. Most have been replaced by the newer franchises." He looked around at the large assortment of plants, hanging baskets and trees. "It's things like the old wood-burning stove inside and the sign on the back door. Have you seen it? 'This store is guarded by a double-barrel shotgun two nights a week. Pick your night.' You just don't find that kind of thing in the city. I think it's charming."

Charming? "You're kidding."

"No, not at all."

"How long are you in town?" She couldn't keep herself from asking. If he would be in and around the area, she needed to know it and be prepared for any more chance encounters.

"Just a few weeks this trip. I've been considering buying a small place with some land and a barn. I've always loved horses. Ridden most of my life." He shrugged. "This might be a great location."

"It's a little far from LA."

"Just a couple of hours by plane."

"It is a nice area. I'll give you that. And *most* of the people are friendly and aboveboard."

"Hey, Ally." She turned to see two feed store employees walking toward her, their shoulders laden with sacks of grain. "You in that black truck? We got your feed."

"Yeah. Make sure you have the right order this time."

"Yep. We got it. No crimped oats this trip?"

"That would be correct. Oh. Could you throw in two large mineral blocks, Jack?" She considered her mental list for a brief second to see if she could remember anything else she needed. "I think that will do it."

Soon the correct bags of feed and two mineral blocks were loaded into the back of the truck. As she walked to the driver's side, she again heard someone call her name.

"Ms. Kincaid?" Seth Masters stood at the back of the truck. "Would you like to have dinner with me tonight?"

The question was so unexpected, it took her a few seconds to realize he was waiting for an answer. "Ah... actually, I have prior commitments. I hope you find your tractor and whatever else you need."

She wasn't used to lying. It made her feel horrible. She didn't trust the man, but he hadn't really done anything to her—other than almost run her down. He was here alone and probably just wanted a little company. Still... he was a Masters.

"Thanks. I think I have. Well, good to see you again."

"Yeah," she mumbled as she climbed into the driver's seat and started the truck. The day did not exist that she would have dinner with a Masters. Today's lunch had been bad enough. Then, she hadn't known who he was. He may or may not be closely involved with the clan of thieves who'd stolen her family's land, but she wasn't about to take the chance. He'd said he was related. From his apparent age, and given that he looked exactly like Wade Masters, he could very well be their brother. But he hadn't grown up around here, otherwise she would have heard of him before. It made her wonder what he was up to.

As she backed out and headed for the main road, she noticed him still standing next to the fertilizer. He looked up and nodded as she passed. He seemed nice enough, but there was still the question of why he was here. Calico Springs was barely a dot on the map. It certainly wasn't the vacation capital of the world. Probably he was here visiting his family. But they were all out of town, according to Mr. Rucker. While it was none of her business, overall it was a bit suspicious. She didn't like suspicious. Especially when it involved the name Masters.

Seth decided time was on his side to do some house hunting. It was just over a week until his brothers were due back, according to Ben Rucker. It would give him a chance to find a local place to call home; he already had penthouses dotted around the US and the UK. Now that his business was well enough established that he could take some time off on occasion, having property in this area would afford him the chance to see more of his family.

"We have several ranches that fit your description, Mr. Masters. Shall we plan on a time to go and see a few of them?"

Seth sat across the desk from Kathy Chisum, the broker for Chisum Real Estate. Ben Rucker had recommended her as one of the better agents in the county representing the largest number of farms and ranches. He figured while he waited for Wade, Chance and Cole to return, he might as well look at some properties. He hadn't been lying when he'd told Ally Kincaid he was thinking of buying in this area. So far he liked what he'd seen. The quaint town sat in the center of rolling hills and far-reaching pastureland dotted with groves of pine and oak and a number of small lakes.

"That's fine. Any time. Any day," he replied. "I'll be here for a couple of weeks, and my schedule is pretty much open."

"What about right now? I've had a cancellation." Her voice was sweet and sincere.

"Works for me. Thanks, Ms. Chisum."

"Kathy." She smiled and rose from her chair. "Shall we take my truck?"

"Sure."

The first two properties they saw had most of the things he wanted in a ranch, but he found something wrong with both of them. He didn't want an old dairy farm. He didn't want a house with two bedrooms that would require major renovation. But the third ranch was almost perfect. White pipe fencing ran along both sides of the driveway. The house was a charmer. It was an example of antebellum architecture that was in remarkably good shape, although it could use a good paint job. Across the front and sides of the house, large white columns rose to the top of the second story, and a portico in the center drew the eye to the magnificent front door. Someone had cared a lot for the house and property. A deep porch surrounded the home on the first floor, and second-story balconies overlooked the pasture and hills on all four sides. Two chimneys peeked over the roof. Inside, a grand staircase led to the second floor, which contained four bedrooms and a larger room with a sitting area that he assumed was the master. The kitchen and baths had been completely remodeled with granite countertops that complemented the hardwood floors.

From the back porch, a path led to the barn. There were approximately twenty stalls, tack room, wash rack and a large open area where hay could be stored for the winter. The smell inside the wooden structure was amazing. He recognized alfalfa and the scent of leather. It brought Ally to mind.

"Kathy, would you happen to know who owns this farm?"

"Sure, let me look that up." She tapped something into

her phone. "Oh, wait. It's owned by the Masters family." She stepped back and eyed him closely. "Any relation?"

"Yeah, as a matter of fact."

"Then you know they have a large ranching operation on the west side of town, just over ninety thousand acres. This was a repossession and doesn't border their property, so they put it up for sale. But I guess you knew that."

"No, actually, I didn't. I'm not involved with the family business."

"The price they're asking is really good for this area. Well below market value. We've had a lot of interest. It won't be on the market very long." She turned to look at him. "I guess you want something away from the family compound?"

He nodded. "Would you happen to know who owned it before them?"

"Mmm. I'm afraid I don't know any of the history for sure. I could try and find out for you if you like."

"No. That won't be necessary. I like this place. I should talk to my brothers about it."

"Sure. If you're seriously considering it, don't wait too long."

He nodded. "I understand."

"It's getting late. If you have no plans, would you like to have dinner?"

"I'd like that." He smiled.

Kathy was a pretty, shapely brunette who appeared to like what she saw in him, and it wouldn't hurt to have a friendly meal with her. The problem was, he already had his mind wrapped around a certain perky redhead. And he was positive this last ranch had been Ally's.

On the way back to town, while Kathy chatted away, an idea began to form. Ally wanted her home back. He needed a wife. They both had a chance to get what they wanted with no strings attached. The ranch's low list price was certainly worth it if it ensured he would be included in the will where billions were at stake.

It was a crazy idea. He smiled to himself at the thought of her reaction. He suspected only the name Masters had prevented her from accepting his dinner invitation earlier. Would she dare dance with the devil and say yes to marriage? Become Mrs. Seth Masters? On the irony scale, that had to take the cake.

It would have to be a real marriage. One on paper for a few months. With the proper prenup, it shouldn't be a problem. He had developed a knack for reading people, and Ally did not fit the particulars of a gold digger. She had given no sign of wanting to know him better. In fact, she seemed to hate him, as much as someone could hate a person they didn't know. But she'd also impressed him as an honest person who only wanted what, in her mind, she was entitled to: her ranch.

When Ally got home the next day, Seth was waiting for her on the tiny front porch of her small cabin. It hadn't been hard to find; in fact, Ben Rucker had told him where she lived and provided directions. Seth had also confirmed since yesterday that the ranch Kathy had shown him used to belong to Ally's family. He'd been right about that.

She looked exhausted, surprised and anything but happy to see him. Admittedly not a reaction he was accustomed to.

She pulled up next to the convertible and hopped out of her old truck. "Did you get lost?" she asked as she approached where he sat. "'Cause I can tell you this isn't where you want to be."

"It's exactly where I want to be," he said. "I wanted to talk to you."

"Talk? Talk about what?"

"I think I found a place I want. I would like you to go with me tomorrow and look at it." She sighed and resolutely shook her head, so he jumped in before she could say no. "Look, I know we got off to a bad start. But I really do need your expertise. I've ridden horses off and on most of my life. But I've never had a ranch. I don't know the first thing about stocking a barn for the winter, so I can't know if there is adequate space. I know nothing about the equipment required. You said you grew up in this environment. I'm asking you to help me decide if this is the place I want to invest in."

"Why don't you ask your relatives?"

"They're out of town."

"What about Ben?"

"Rucker? I have a feeling he knows about as much as I do with regards to ranching. No. I assure you, I need *you*. Frankly, you're the only one who fits the bill." An understatement.

She was quiet a long time. Then, "Where is this place?"

"West of town. I can't remember the road names, but I'm sure I can take us there."

In the dim glow from the lamppost next to the driveway, he saw her lower her head. Was she thinking about her former home? Should he have just told her his plan here and now? He'd given it serious thought last night and decided that she might be more tempted to say yes if she were at her home when he hit her up with the idea. He could now see that might be taking unfair advantage. He drew in a breath, intending to explain, when she raised her head and looked at him.

"I guess I can do it. I have to work three horses in the morning, but I can skip the ones scheduled in the afternoon. How about one o'clock?"

"One o'clock is perfect. I'll pick you up here tomorrow?"

"In that?" She nodded toward the pricey sports car. "I wish you had a truck."

"Maybe I'll get one after I find a ranch."

"You'd better hurry. That's a rental unless I miss my guess. You'll tear out the undercarriage driving these rocky roads, not to mention the damage they will cause to the body and the paint job. You'll end up buying a trashed car." She stepped up onto the porch. "It's a shame. Nice car." She shook her head. "Okay, I guess I'll see you tomorrow."

"I'll be here. Thanks for doing this, Ally."

"No problem," she said as she walked to the front door.

"Good night."

She turned and looked at him as she opened the front door but didn't answer. Instead she disappeared inside the small house.

Seth followed the winding road from the Triple Bar Ranch with his spirits high, something he hadn't felt in a long time. Part of it was hope that this crazy idea would somehow come to pass. But another big factor was that he would get to spend some time with Ally Kincaid. He liked everything about her: the way she moved, the silky shoulder-length hair that swirled about the fine features of her face. He could get lost in the brilliance of her sparkling green eyes, the sensuous full mouth.

Best of all was her personality, even if she had given him a lot of grief. She knew who she was. She wasn't coy. She didn't try to cover her true nature with any kind of facade. Whether she liked him or not, that persnickety nature made him want to see more.

He caught the direction of where his mind was going and brought it to a stop. Even if she agreed to this crazy plan, it would be a marriage in name only. There would be no getting close to her, no hope of becoming more to her than a man who shared the same house. Unless…

He arrived at the hotel and fell onto the bed. There were some things he needed to do the next morning before he picked her up. Get a key to the house from Kathy, for one. Look at trucks, for another. Ally was right about the car and the gravel roads.

He stood up and pulled off his shirt and pants before heading for the shower. Tomorrow would be a turning point for the research center. His mother had died of leukemia, and he was as determined as he'd ever been about anything to help fund the center. He would still get it built—no doubts there—but the inheritance would speed up the process tenfold. He hoped a miracle happened and Ally said yes.

He knew he was putting a lot of trust in his gut reaction to her, but his gut had never let him down yet. He'd met more than a few self-serving society types who were willing to go so far as fake a pregnancy in order to marry a multimillionaire. He'd been played by the best and so far had kept his bachelor standing intact.

But it was hard to regard Ally as a money-grubber when she'd made it clear she didn't like him at all. Or any of his family. Ironically, that thought was comforting.

Three

Ally was sitting on the small front porch of her cabin when Seth Masters drove up the next afternoon. It was another beautiful day, and he had the top down on the car. She climbed in, fastened her seat belt and they were off.

She leaned back and looked at the sky, eventually putting her hands above her head, feeling the wind whip through her fingers like a child on her first outing on a merry-go-round. Even though she still didn't trust this man, riding in a car like this on such a perfect day made her feel free.

But as they traveled farther west of Calico Springs, she grew tense. He couldn't possibly be taking her where she thought he was taking her. Could he?

When he turned the car into the long drive between the rows of white fences, she had her answer.

He stopped the car in front of the house and killed the motor. Ally felt his eyes on her, but she sat frozen, staring at her childhood home. Seth exited the car and walked around and opened her door. She accepted his hand as she got out.

"You knew, didn't you?" she said after a long silence.

"I guessed. I saw three ranches yesterday. This was the last one. I liked it a lot and ask who the sellers were. That pretty much gave me the answer." He held up the key. "I thought you might like to see it again."

Ally turned to the house. Her heart was beating out of her chest, and elation battled overwhelming grief in her stomach. She came to a stop at the front steps, not sure if she should go any farther. As though sensing what she was feeling, Seth walked past her and unlocked the door then pushed it open. Stepping inside, she paused and looked around. Everything was as it had been, except several pieces of furniture were gone. Step by step, room by room, she made her way through the house, stopping on occasion to touch an object or the mantel of the fireplace that meant something special to her.

"My mother used to always have a fire in the fireplace here in the kitchen when she cooked on a winter's day. It made the room seem especially warm and cheery."

"It's something not found in many kitchens today."

She turned to face him, her arms wrapped around her chest. "I can tell you unequivocally that this ranch has everything a person would need to be successful in any horse venture. Whether you're looking to breed, train and raise or merely have a few horses to enjoy, you won't go wrong. From the house to the barn to the foaling paddock to the land…it's all here." She swallowed back the tears and tried to talk through her throat that wanted to close. "Are you serious about buying it?"

"I am."

"I guess I'm a little confused. Being part of the Masters family, don't you already own it?"

"In a manner of speaking. It's owned by the family conglomerate, Masters International, LLC. If I decide I want it as my own personal property, I contact my brothers, usually Cole because he handles all property management, and put in a request. He'll pull it from the market and transfer the deed to my name. He's done it for me one other time. Of course, if I do nothing, it can and probably will be sold to someone else outside the family."

She didn't know if that idea made her happy or sad. It would still belong to a Masters, but maybe he was different. It was the best she could hope for. Seeing her home again drew the heartache into a large black mass inside her chest. The pain returned as sure and quick as the day she'd received the notice of foreclosure. But she refused to cry even though the tears filled her eyes. She wouldn't let them fall. It was pointless. She didn't want Seth Masters to think she was using a ruse or poor-little-me syndrome to get her house from him. If it was meant to be hers, she would find a way to get it back without relying on sympathy.

"It really depends on you."

She frowned at the absurd comment. "What? How could you buying this ranch have anything to do with me?"

He hesitated before walking over to lean against the kitchen cabinet then looked at her deeply.

"First of all, you were right in suspecting I was kin to Wade, Cole and Chance. They are my half brothers."

"I knew there was a relation." At least he was admitting it. Finally.

"What you don't know is about a month ago my brothers and I were notified of the probate of our father's will."

"I still don't see what any of that has to do with me."

"I have the plans ready to start building a research

facility in California. The money I get from the estate could put me well ahead of the game. The center is badly needed. The research will primarily focus on finding a cure for leukemia." He paused. "My problem is, according to Mr. Rucker, any of the heirs who aren't married by the time the will is probated won't receive an inheritance."

"So…let me get this straight. You need someone to pose as your wife long enough to obtain money." She thought she saw him grimace.

"Put that way, it sounds underhanded and conniving. But most of what I inherit will go to the center. You can see the plans if you have any doubt of that. Or I can put you in touch with my partners, who are doing their part to get this building up and running." He paused, giving that time to soak in. "And it wouldn't be just pretending to be my wife. It must be a legal marriage."

"Surely you know someone who would agree to marry you."

"No. Because of my schedule, there's no time or place for a woman in my life on a permanent basis. I don't know of anyone I would trust to say 'I do' then walk away a few months later, not expecting anything more than what was stipulated in our original agreement."

"But you think you can trust me?" she said, picking up on his idea. "You don't even know me, Masters."

He shrugged. "Call it a gut feeling. When I realized this was your home, I felt it worthy of asking just how badly you want your ranch back. And if you'd be willing to marry me for a few months in order to get it. It would fulfill the terms of my inheritance, and you would have your ranch."

"It's preposterous."

"It's a crazy idea," he agreed. Silence settled over

them before he continued. "So, will you marry me, Ally Kincaid?"

That took the breath from her lungs. The man really was crazy. Like she would ever marry a stranger. The very idea was ludicrous. Insane.

"Of course," he began, "it would be temporary. I figure about three months should do it. I'll need to check with Mr. Rucker on that. But when it's over, I head back to LA with some money to go toward my research center, and you have a clear deed to your ranch in your name. We both win."

"I thought you wanted a ranch or a small farm for yourself."

He shrugged. "I do. But I can always find another one."

He made it sound so simple. She looked at Seth Masters for a long time. "How do I know I can trust you? How do I know if I agree you will give me my ranch when you get your money? How do I know if you're a decent, honorable man? You could up and walk out and leave me with nothing. Hell, I would be worse off than I am now."

"Mr. Rucker," he stated. "He can attest to who I am. And I can fly my legal staff in to prepare the document. Exactly like a prenuptial agreement, in writing and completely aboveboard. You won't lose this time, Ally."

"What about you? What if we do this and it ends up that you don't receive any money from the estate? I mean, do you know for sure you'll get any funding?"

"It's a gamble. But I'm willing to risk it."

"That research center is really important to you, huh?" She frowned, only now realizing what Seth was willing to put on the line.

"It's become my life. It's worth taking the risk."

She looked around the familiar room, the walls calling to her. "How soon would you want to do this?"

"As soon as documents can be prepared. Kathy Chisum, the real estate agent, said they have already had quite a lot of interest. If we don't make a decision—correction, if *you* don't make a decision—pretty quick, the ranch might be sold to someone else and we both lose. The probate hearing is on the eleventh, which is eight days from now."

She thought about his offer. Without it, she knew realistically she had little to no chance she would ever come home again. Was thinking his plan might work merely a measure of desperation?

"No," she said finally. "Thanks for the offer, I guess. But no. I'll have to pass."

For the longest time, there was silence in the room.

"Then, if you're ready, I guess we should head back."

Why did she feel as though the breath had been knocked from her lungs? As they made their way to the front door, the walls seemed to call to her. She remembered the last time she'd walked out of this house, fearing she would never see it again, leaving behind cherished childhood memories. Memories of her father. Her mother. Even her first horse. And now she had the chance to come home permanently and she'd turned it down.

It still wasn't too late. She could have it…if she believed in Seth Masters. If she trusted him. Something she had no reason to do. *He is a Masters*, she reminded herself. *You're making the right decision.*

Why, then, did it feel so wrong?

He dropped her at her little house without mentioning it again. There was no attempt to convince her to go along with his plan, no telling her she was making a huge mistake, no pleading with her to change her mind or give it additional thought. He bade her good-night, thanked her for her time and disappeared back down the driveway through the trees.

It occurred to her she didn't know how to find him. But why would she want to find him? She wouldn't let herself dwell on the answer to that question. She'd made the right decision. It was a scheme formulated by a member of the Masters family, and she was correct in turning it down flat. Was this what had happened to her father? Had Reginald Masters offered him something that meant so much to her dad that he'd gambled everything on an outcome that Mr. Masters knew would never happen? If so, in the end it had cost them everything. The ranch was taken, and her father died of a massive heart attack knowing he'd lost it all. She couldn't go through it again. She couldn't. Parting from the ranch a second time was more than she could deal with.

Trust had to be earned. Seth Masters had done nothing to prove himself. If he was setting her up and if she went for it, it would only confirm she was as big a fool as her father. Masters would laugh all the way back to LA.

She dropped down on her small, well-worn sofa. It was either the cruelest thing she'd ever experienced or the chance of a lifetime. Either way, it was done. She had to let it go. But why would he do such a thing if he wasn't serious? It was a very expensive joke. She couldn't figure out the catch, but there had to be one.

Grabbing her cell, she punched in Ben Rucker's phone number.

"Ben," she said when he came on the phone. "This is Ally Kincaid. What can you tell me about Seth Masters?"

All Ben would say was that Seth was an entrepreneur and sat on the boards of two large regional hospitals in

Los Angeles. He couldn't attest to the man's nature, but he'd made a positive impression.

What did that mean? *Positive.* So he was a good liar?

By the end of the next day, Ally was exhausted. On the ranch, she'd made all sorts of stupid, thoughtless mistakes, and when you were working with twelve-hundred-pound horses, stupid mistakes could turn deadly in a heartbeat. But that was what happened when she didn't get any sleep. The night before, she'd lain in bed, tossing and turning, picturing herself in her home, in her own barn. She remembered the silence of the evenings when a cooling summer breeze swept over the land. She remembered the sound of the horses eating their grain with an occasional low nicker, the smells of sweet alfalfa and leather. Those same sounds and smells were here, too, but they were somehow different. It just wasn't the same. It never would be. She remembered the pride she'd known when a client or a buyer came to pick up their new future champion, one that she'd bred and trained.

Once back in her cabin for the night, she forced herself to eat a sandwich. Then, stepping into the shower, she relaxed under the warm spray. She had to let it go. The whole idea of marrying a stranger was unconscionable. What if he was abusive? Or had any number of undesirable qualities?

What if he didn't?

Then she asked herself another question. What if he'd found someone else to marry? He was certainly attractive enough. Most women would probably jump into his arms and hope they stopped by a bedroom on the way to the altar. All he would have to do was show them that grin.

Just as she stepped from the shower, the lights flickered, and a long, low rumble of thunder passed overhead. Usually she loved the rain. Not tonight. It made her aware of how lonely she was. She looked at her bed then glanced around to her closet. Was it go to bed for another sleepless night or grab a fresh pair of jeans and a shirt and see if she could track down Seth Masters? There were only three hotels in Calico Springs…

An hour later the rain pelted her as she entered the front lobby of the Calico Springs Hotel and Suites. Soon she was standing in front of room 214. Without allowing herself a chance to back out, she raised her hand and knocked.

A couple of minutes later, Seth Masters pulled open the door. Bare to his waist, dressed only in formfitting jeans, he leaned one muscled arm against the door frame and looked surprised to see her.

"Ms. Kincaid?" He opened the door wider.

"Yes." Ally swallowed hard. "And yes. I will marry you, Mr. Masters," she said, "as long as that document conveys what you told me."

"It will."

"So what do we do now?"

He backed up to let her in, that sexy grin on his face. "First, let's get you dry."

"And then?"

"And then…tomorrow I'll have my attorney fly in, and while you provide the information for the legal agreement, I'll arrange to buy the property."

"Just like that. You're going to buy the ranch."

"Just like that."

Ally had never believed in fairy tales, but if this proposition was real and not some cruel joke, she was living in one.

Seth's attorney, James Buchanan, and his legal assistant arrived by two o'clock the following day, ready to get to work. The fact that Seth let Ally set the conditions gave her added confidence in what she had agreed to do. Ally had no problem with clauses that precluded her from any claim on Seth's current holdings. Fair was fair. The only thing she wanted was her ranch.

At some point during the afternoon, it finally hit her: she was getting married. Married to a man she didn't know. At twenty-four years old, she'd honestly never thought about getting married. While her friends in school planned and daydreamed about that special day, Ally's thoughts had been of horses and taking the winning trophy at quarter horse competitions. All that changed in seconds when she agreed to say "I do."

The following day Seth picked her up and drove to the county clerk's office, where they applied for the wedding license. In two days' time, she'd become Ally Masters.

It was an unbelievable situation, one that would have her father rolling over in his grave if he knew. She put it out of her mind and kept telling herself that Seth wasn't a real Masters. He was from Los Angeles and not in cahoots with the local members of the family. Sometimes it worked for a few minutes. Then at other times she would look at Seth and see shades of his father and the truth came screaming back at her of how closely Seth was related to the Masters patriarch who had betrayed them, the man who'd taken them for all they had and left her alone struggling to survive.

What was she doing?

Two days later the civil ceremony was a short, no-frills affair. Mr. Buchanan and his legal assistant served as the witnesses. The surprise came when Seth extracted a black velvet box from his pocket that contained a beautiful diamond-encrusted wedding ring and slipped it onto

Ally's finger. Then he handed her a solid gold band to be placed on his hand, and with a few words from the county judge, they were pronounced husband and wife.

When Seth took her into his arms, their eyes met and the world tipped a little. Ever so slowly Seth lowered his lips to hers. His kiss was gentle, almost soothing. Reassuring. Ally became lost in his touch, in his strong arms. The kiss felt like something more meaningful than a token kiss at a fake wedding ceremony.

Seth lost no time in taking it to the next level, his mouth closing over hers, his tongue entering and tasting, letting her taste him. When they finally drew apart, she glanced up at his face as he released her and caught a twinkle in his amber eyes. Her heart thumped a few hard beats. She hoped she saw merriment in his eyes, that the twinkle didn't represent the dreaded *gotcha*.

Either way, it was done. Because land acquisitions and sales were handled by a special department in Masters International, LLC., it was not necessary for any of the Masters brothers to be present for the transfer of the deed. Seth had received a phone call that morning from Cole, welcoming him to the neighborhood. There were three days until the purchase of the ranch was finalized. Another few days until the probate hearing. A few months until he would return to his life in LA. *You can handle a few months.* What would happen between now and then was anyone's guess. The only thing she was assured of was that the ranch would be hers. Nothing else mattered.

Returning the waves from Mr. Buchanan and his legal assistant, she let Seth escort her out to his car.

"Are you hungry?" he asked. "It's almost five o'clock. Care to grab a bite to eat?"

"Sure. Whatever you'd like to do."

She saw him purse his lips to subdue a grin.

Soon they were seated across from each other at a small table in Burdall's café. Ally couldn't help but remember the last time they were here. Then, she didn't even know his name. Now, his last name was hers. *Masters.* She eyed the glittering diamonds on her left hand.

"You went to a lot of unnecessary expense," she commented. "The ring is beautiful."

Seth shrugged. "I guess I'm a bit old-fashioned. I couldn't see not giving my bride a ring for the ceremony."

My bride.

"Well, I'll certainly return it to you before you leave."

"I'm not worried about it." He sat back while the waitress placed glasses of ice water on the table and took their order. "So…where are we going to spend the night?"

"Excuse me?"

"Your place or mine?"

"Ah… I thought we would each go back to our own previous living arrangements. You at your hotel and me at the cabin."

"Not really indicative of a newlywed couple. Remember, this has got to look as real as it is on paper. For all intents and purpose, as far as anyone knows we are in love. Any doubts someone might raise as to the legality of our union might challenge my rights to be considered in the will. In which case, all bets are off."

Ally could feel the irritation like a slow burn inside. Regardless of what she'd agreed to on paper, she'd never given thought to having to spend the night…nights… with this man. "You never said anything about sleeping together."

He looked at her, dumbfounded. "I didn't think it necessary. We are, in fact, legally married. Why bother to tie the knot if you live on one side of town and I stay on the other?"

"Did you or did you not tell me we had to put up a good front when we're out in public? That does not hold true behind closed doors."

"Why?"

She leaned over the table toward him. "You know why," she shot back.

"Do most married couples not stay together? Share living arrangements?"

The waitress set their plates down on the table. The steak appeared cooked to perfection, but she knew if she tried to eat at this moment, she would choke. Her throat was closing until she could barely breathe.

"Yes," she hissed. "But we are not most couples!"

"Ally, you're getting upset over nothing. Just because we share a home doesn't mean something will necessarily happen between us. Don't get me wrong—" he began to cut his steak "—I'm on board if it does. You're a very beautiful woman. But it's your call."

"Share a home? You mean you intend to move into the house on the ranch?"

Seth looked at her as though she'd told a really bad joke.

"Fine. We can go to my cabin. It has a twin-size bed and a sofa." He had to be at least six foot two, with broad shoulders. There was little doubt that if he tried to sleep on either the bed or couch, his head would hang off one end and his feet the other. "You can take your pick."

"When do you have to be out of the cabin?"

"I have it as long as I keep my job, which I intend to do."

"That doesn't make any sense."

"What do you expect me to do? Live in a tree?"

"I expect you to give your resignation and move to your ranch. Isn't that what you wanted?"

"I can't move to the ranch until you close on the property."

"Which is the day after tomorrow."

"Regardless, in the meantime I need someplace to live. Plus, I need my salary. Jobs in this area are not plentiful."

"You don't need a job. I can supply anything you need. Which reminds me, we are going to need some furniture for the house. In the meantime, we'll stay at the hotel. Or, if you prefer, we can go on a short honeymoon."

"That's ludicrous."

"It's expected."

"Not by me!"

The simmer was back. He expected her to act like the blushing bride and go off to some strange place with him? Not happening.

"Look, Masters." She quickly looked around them to ensure they weren't being overheard then lowered her voice. "I'll play this game only so far. I have zero intentions of getting into bed with a man I've known less than a week. You flatter yourself if you think I can be coerced into such a thing. If that's what you believe, you picked the wrong woman."

"Mrs. Masters, I never said anything about sharing a bed. That was your own idea. One I'm not opposed to but not one I suggested. We will, however, share accommodations. If you want to explain to your friends and cohorts why we spent our wedding night in a cabin that's barely large enough for one person, so be it."

"I had no intention of telling anyone about this sham marriage. That's your thing, not mine."

"I don't care if you spread the news or not, but this is a small town. Sooner or later someone will recognize you and ask about the man you're with. What are you going to say then?"

Why hadn't she considered all of this before she signed that stupid contract? Suddenly the ranch didn't seem all that important. A fleeting picture flashed in her mind of her lying on a feather-soft bed with Seth's strong arms around her. Of snuggling there, warm and protected. A flare of heat bloomed in her lower region, and she crossed her legs to fight off the sensation. It didn't help.

"Fine. Have it your way. We can go to your hotel and I'll take the couch or the floor."

He smiled and put a bite of steak in his mouth. "It's not a very big couch."

"I don't care." She sprinkled some salt over her baked potato and began to eat.

"You might after a few nights."

"I'll be fine. Don't worry about me. Just keep to your side of the room and do not come into mine."

At that he smiled then pursed his lips as though to keep from grinning outright.

"Whatever you say, Mrs. Masters."

Four

Seth recalled a time from his childhood when he'd been scratched by a neighbor's cat. He had a strange feeling he'd just taken on one again, only this time the feline was taller and its claws twice as sharp. Still, he loved a challenge. He had no intention of making any moves on her, but she kept bringing up the subject. Maybe he should give making love to the fiery redhead a bit more thought. She was a beautiful woman, and the idea was tantalizing.

"Do you want to go and look at some furniture tomorrow?" Seth asked, changing the subject. "How about we check out some furniture stores in the afternoon?"

"Okay," she replied. "The mattresses at the house are old. We're gonna need places to sleep."

"And a refrigerator. Stove. Kitchen table. You might want to look for a sofa or a couple of easy chairs to go in the den as well."

She laid her fork down and met his gaze. "Why are you doing this?"

"Because I don't happen to like sleeping on the floor. However, if you do I'll simply purchase a couple of air mattresses and call it done."

"No," she said after a time. "A bed would be nice. As would a stove and refrigerator. I just don't know how long it will be until I can pay you back."

"I don't recall saying you had to pay me back. Anyway, don't sweat the small stuff. We'll figure it out."

After dinner Ally agreed to show him around the area. It was prime land, with beef cows and horses dotting the horizon. Pine and oak trees towered at the edges of the vast pastureland. A river wound its way through the hills and close to the small town at the center of it all.

"Were you born here?"

"Yeah. I spent a few years in College Station northeast of Austin while I was in school, but that's about it. What about you? Born and raised in Los Angeles?"

He nodded. "But I've always craved the country. A place you can see forever and take a deep breath."

"Why didn't you leave or move farther out of the city?"

"I would have liked to. California has some of the most beautiful places to live in the United States. But there wasn't time to think about it. Generally I'm on call 24-7. Many times I have to fly out on a minute's notice."

"That's gotta be rough. You must really like what you do."

Seth nodded. "I especially like the fact that it gives me the opportunity to work on projects like the research center. A friend of mine is a hematologist. Another is an oncologist. We are combining efforts toward our goals. They are so close to developing a cure for a lot of diseases. I want to help push that research forward." He was quiet for a moment, unsure of how much to tell her about his past. "My mother died of leukemia. I promised her I would help find a cure."

He caught Ally's gaze; her eyes shimmered with understanding. "I'm sorry."

"It was a few years back. But thank you."

When they turned back toward the ranch where she worked, it was already growing dark. Seth helped her out of the car in front of the small cabin that was nestled in the trees within the borders of the ranch.

"I just have to grab a few things," she told him as she got out of the car. "I won't be long."

Seth watched her disappear inside then followed. As he looked around, he was a bit surprised at what he saw. The single room was even smaller than it looked from the outside. There was a sink, a commode and a tiny shower stall in one corner, and a closet without any doors in the other. In the center of the room was a single bed, along with a tiny moth-eaten sofa and one straight chair against the wall. Having seen the house where she'd grown up, it was a shock to him that she now had to make do with such poor accommodations.

She looked up from packing and saw him standing inside the door. "I don't have a suitcase. Pillowcases will have to do. Tomorrow if I need anything else, I can probably find a box."

Seth nodded and kept his thoughts to himself. She would not be coming back to this place no matter what he had to do to prevent it. She needed clothes and a good bed and enough space to turn around. From her strong attitude, he would never have guessed she was living in such deplorable conditions. He walked over and picked up the first pillowcase she'd filled.

"I'll take this to the car. Take your time."

When they arrived at the hotel, Seth helped her carry two filled pillowcases inside. The suite wasn't a big room by his standards but three times the size of her cabin. But there was only one bed. A quick phone call to the hotel office confirmed what he feared: they were fully booked. It was Friday night. No two-bed rooms available.

"There are hangers in the closet, extra pillows in that cabinet." He pointed to a closet door. "And extra blankets, I think." He couldn't keep from glancing over to the small, curved sofa. He should be a gentleman and offer to sleep there, but at the same time, he saw no reason they couldn't share the California king. If she insisted on using the little sofa, that was her decision.

Ally stood in the center of the room looking lost, as though she didn't know what to do next. He found her timidity charming. According to her driver's license, which he'd seen when they applied for the marriage certificate, she was twenty-four. Most of the women he knew wouldn't think twice about stripping down and crawling into the bed. It made him curious what her previous life had been like. Married and divorced? Engaged? Maybe a few boyfriends here and there but nothing serious? As beautiful as she was, he found that hard to believe.

A glance at his watch told him it was almost midnight. It had been a long day. He suspected it had been a long and emotional one for Ally. Walking into the bedroom, he pulled back the covers with one hand while he loosened his tie with the other.

"You're welcome to first shot at the bathroom. There are extra towels and bathrobes in the small pantry in the dressing room."

"Thanks," she said and turned in that direction, disappearing behind the closed door. The bath had a large whirlpool bathtub. He hoped she would partake and let some of the tension ease out of her body. He couldn't help but smile when he heard her turn on the tap.

Sometime later she emerged wearing an old T-shirt that hung a few inches above her knees. Her hair had been washed and dried and fell in feather-soft layers around her head. He grew hard despite the control he tried for. Her full lips were closed tight; not even a hint of a smile touched her features. She pulled a blanket and pillow from the closet and set about making up the tiny sofa. By the time Seth was finished in the bathroom, she was perched on the makeshift bed in the main room, looking as though she was in deep thought.

Curled under her blanket, she looked miserable.

"Are you sure you don't want to share the bed?"

"I'm fine."

With a sigh Seth turned off the light next to the bed. Short of picking her up and physically putting her on the bed, there wasn't a lot more he could do. He had a feeling the little feline would show her claws big-time if he tried it. He loosened the string on his sweatpants and closed the adjoining door.

The next morning Seth woke up to an empty room. Then he found the note on the nightstand next to where he slept. *Gone to work. Back at six.* He grabbed his cell and looked at the time. It was barely seven in the morning. Ally worked twelve-hour days?

He showered, got dressed and headed to the ranch where Ally worked, stopping along the way for a to-go breakfast and coffee. When he arrived at the Triple Bar Ranch, he found her at the back of the main barn lunging a chestnut yearling in one of the exercise pens. He stepped over and held out a sausage biscuit and a cup of coffee.

She walked over to where he stood against the corral fence and took the coffee and biscuit. "Thanks."

"No problem. Are you going to talk to your boss today about leaving?"

"No," she told him hesitantly. "I'll quit only after you can tell me the house is yours. Or mine." She shook her head. "You know what I mean."

"You can trust me, Ally."

"Time will tell."

"How about this afternoon we head to Calico Springs and see if we can decide on some furniture?"

"I have to work."

"I close on the property tomorrow. What are you going to sleep on if we don't get some beds?"

"I was reconsidering, thinking I'll just stay here."

Seth sighed. "Why purchase the farm if you don't want to be there? Was I mistaken to think you wanted your ranch?"

"No. But—"

"No buts. If you don't want your ranch, tell me now."

He knew what she was thinking: she wanted her ranch, but without him.

"I'll be ready at noon. Thanks for breakfast."

Seth nodded. "I'll call my assistant in LA and have her arrange for some housekeepers. Setting up that house is going to be a big undertaking."

"How much help is needed to tell the delivery people where to put two beds and a stove and refrigerator?"

"I had in mind a little more than that."

The filly began to paw, anxious to return to the barn or pasture. Ally broke off a small piece of the biscuit and fed it to the young horse, which seemed to soothe its impatience somewhat. Dropping the remains of the biscuit into the sack, she took another sip of the coffee and handed the cup and bag back to Seth.

"How did you know I liked cream in my coffee?"

"Just a guess," he answered as he took the empty sack. "I'll pick you up about noon."

Ally watched him walk away from the corral, his long strides carrying him down the graveled road to his car.

He was a strange man. She didn't as yet have him figured out. His looks were what she'd always pictured someone from California would look like: tanned and muscled with blond highlights in his hair where the sun hit it. His face was strikingly handsome, with laugh lines around the edges of his mouth and dimples when he smiled. His wealth should have made him arrogant, but she still hadn't seen any sign of that. He almost blended in with the locals, people she'd known most of her life. Strange. The other Masters brothers had grown up in Calico Springs. Someone who didn't know him would assume Seth had as well.

He came back at noon, and they went shopping. The first stop was to a car dealership, where Seth picked out a new pickup truck. Then they went to shop for furniture and some household necessities.

"Don't you want to try out the mattress before you make your decision?" Seth asked Ally, standing next to a row of floor models.

"I'm sure whatever you select will be fine."

"At least sit on it. Ultimately you will be the one who keeps and sleeps on the mattress when you take over the house. You might as well pick out what you like."

Humor him, she thought, *and move on.* She sat down on the closest display model and immediately didn't like it. She moved to a second then a third. By the time she found one she liked, they were at the opposite end of the large showroom.

"That's it?" Seth asked. "That's the one?"

"Yeah."

"Send out two, both king," he said to the sales associate. "Now let's find bedroom suites to go with them."

"How do you know you'll like the mattress I picked out?"

He looked around the huge showroom, which was on the third floor of the shop, and at all the mattresses she'd tried out. "I doubt I could do better. Come on."

Together they went to the second floor, where they purchased two bedroom suites, a living room suite, a kitchen table and chairs, and loungers for the den.

"I'll have the list of items we bought sent to Karen, my assistant, and tell her to fill in the rest. Anything she misses we can get later," Seth said as he gave Ally a ride back to work.

When they got back to Triple Bar Ranch, he told her he'd pick her up at seven, take her back to the hotel to change and they'd go out to dinner.

Head spinning, all Ally could think was, *What have I gotten myself into?*

"So tomorrow you're a ranch owner," Ally said as the waitress set her dinner plate in front of her. She put her napkin in her lap and picked up the fork.

"Tomorrow the deed will be transferred to my name. I don't have to be there. It's all handled internally within the company." He took a sip of his coffee.

A rush of goose bumps covered her skin. What must it be like to be able to obtain a ranch with no more concern for the cost than she would have buying a can of beans at the grocery store? Granted, Seth didn't write a check for the purchase price but he could have had it been necessary. She hadn't been raised in poverty—far from it. But this was new to her.

"A can of beans."

"Excuse me?" Seth asked.

"You buy a five-hundred-acre ranch as easily as I would buy a can of beans."

He grinned. "Firstly, I didn't actually buy it. No money changed hands. The company has over one hundred thousand acres in Texas alone so this wasn't a big deal. And secondly, isn't that what families do for each other?"

She opened her mouth but no words would come out. Then, "Okay. Sure. You've got me there. The next time I need a cup of sugar I'll know who to call."

Seth's baritone laughter rang out over the restaurant.

Seth had chosen a new restaurant located along the banks of the Calico River. They'd been given a table next to the wall of glass overlooking the water, which shimmered with a silver glow from the lights along the banks. A small candle in a glass chimney spread its ambient light across their table. Looking up at Seth, she was once again drawn in by the handsome planes of his face. The deep laugh lines on either side of his mouth added to the overall integrity of his features. His dark brows seem to bring out the golden flecks in his brown eyes. As her gaze dropped to his generous lips, she realized they were pursed in an effort to hold back a smile.

She immediately focused on her plate and the perfectly prepared steak.

"By this weekend you should be able to start getting the barn ready for the transfer of your horses. I'm sure they'll be glad to be home again. How long has it been?"

"Just over a year."

"You're gonna need someone to help you out, at least

at first. Unless you know someone, why don't you stop by the employment office tomorrow and arrange for some cowboys to come to work?"

"I can do anything that needs to be done."

"You can't do it all—check the fences on that much land, repair the barns, do whatever it is you have to do to the stalls, clean out the feed bins, fill up the water tanks—and that's just the parts I know about—besides horses to train. There's probably a lot more to it than I've mentioned. If you need more than three ranch hands, get them."

Ally sat back in her chair and placed her fork by the side of her plate. "Why are you doing this? The agreement was you buy the farm in exchange for me marrying you for three months. There was no furniture involved. Certainly no ranch hands. Right now I barely have the money to buy feed for the horses."

"Then get whatever you need."

"That isn't what I meant. You didn't answer my question," she said, exasperated. "Do you not understand that I don't have the money to repay you for all of this? Marrying you for ninety days hardly gives me carte blanche to your bank account. And right now I have no clue how I'm going to pay you back for what you've already provided."

Seth put his silverware down and folded his hands in front of him, his elbows on the table. "What you're doing for me means a lot, Ally. I don't expect either of us to stay in a practically empty house for three months. The rest is just common sense. I wish you would see it that way. You're paying me by allowing me to be a part of the probate. And before you say it, if my part of the estate turns out to be nothing, you're giving me a chance to try. My mother died from leukemia. I promised her I would find a way to fight it. The research center depends a great deal on the money from the will. Without you there would be no money and no chance for obtaining any."

Ally knew there were a dozen women she could name right off the bat who would jump at the chance to marry Seth Masters. Ironic he would choose the one least interested. She consciously relaxed. She had a document, signed and notarized, that would ensure his agreement was honored. He had the same. All she had to do was get through three months. As to the household furnishings, she'd explained she couldn't afford what he seemed intent on buying. She had no choice but to let him buy what he wanted and hope they could settle in the end.

He was a man's man. A rugged, self-assured, no-nonsense kind of guy who looked every bit of his million dollars. Maybe billion dollars.

"Okay. I'll say no more about it."

"Good. How is your steak?"

"It's good."

By the time they arrived back at the hotel, she was exhausted, more from emotional stress than physical exertion. Dropping her purse on the small sofa, she grabbed a clean T-shirt and headed straight for the shower. They had accomplished a lot. Tomorrow Seth would close on the ranch. Then, in a few days, he'd deal with the probate of the will. Understanding his need for additional funding for the research center made her look at him in a different light. For the first time she began to see him as someone who cared, not just a millionaire who wanted more. His mother's death must have been devastating. She could relate after losing her dad and having no one. No siblings, no family. He had his brothers, but how close had they been at the time of her death? She hoped the probate went well for him.

After a quick shower, she dressed in the oversize T-shirt and returned to the main living area. Making her small bed on the sofa took no time. She lay down and wiggled, trying to find a comfortable spot, plumped her pillow and closed her eyes. Sleep when it came was not restful. She tossed and turned. And it was cold. She tugged the blanket around her, but it did little to help in the cool room. A thought drifted across her mind that she should get up and adjust the thermostat, but instead she lapsed into a troubled sleep.

The warmth that surrounded her was heavenly. A heavy weight rested over her waist, while delicious heat met her back and legs. The feel of silken sheets beneath her stirred her to consciousness. A hard mound pressed against her lower back. Slowly she opened her eyes and immediately knew where she was. On the bed. In Seth's arms. His erection pressed against her. How she got there wasn't clear. She heard his deep, even breathing and tried to slow her speeding heart. Hoping not to disturb him, she lifted the covers from over her and slowly moved his arm from around her waist. Before she could slip to the edge of the bed, his arm was back wrapped around her as his large body nestled her closely, his hot breath against her neck. Good grief. He must think she was a pillow. This was not good. She didn't want to be in his arms when he woke up. She didn't want to be in his arms, period. While her mind raced to figure out what to do, she heard his breathing change.

"Good morning." His deep voice caused goose pimples to flash down her spine.

Ally immediately sat up, threw the covers back and slipped out from under his arms. The room had a slight chill, and for an instant she wanted to go back to the warm nest they'd formed during the night. Instead she walked into the main room where her jeans lay on the sofa, grabbing them and her shirt.

"Good morning," she replied, looking at him suspiciously. He was still lying on his side in the bed, his arm propped on top on the pillow, his head resting on his hand. His hair was tousled. The five o'clock shadow gave him a devilish look that was highlighted by his eyes. His full lips were open, showing strong white teeth. It looked as though he'd found a tasty morsel in his lair and wanted to devour her piece by piece. She watched as his eyes roamed over her.

She swallowed hard as her body blossomed with heat that sizzled from her lips all the way down to her core. This was not a man who would be happy to be her new best friend. He knew a woman's body, and he wouldn't hesitate to show her just how well he knew her if she gave him the least bit of enticement. Which she did not intend to do.

"Do I need to ask how I came to be in your bed?" She seriously doubted she had made her way there in her sleep, and she darned sure didn't do it on purpose.

"I found you on the floor. You'd lost your blanket. You were cold. Rather than go through the hassle of getting you stuffed back onto that tiny couch, it just seemed logical to pick you up and put you in bed. I made sure you were warm and went back to sleep."

"Well. Thank you for that. I think. Excuse me," she said as she turned and marched to the bathroom, still clutching her clean clothes.

How was she going to make it through three months of this?

Two days later excitement overtook her common sense when it came to her job. Why train horses for someone else when all she wanted to do was be in her childhood home and get her own ranch up and running again? After Seth gave her his assurances, she tendered her resignation at the Triple Bar Ranch. Then they were on their way to the farm. Her farm. Seth's farm. She wouldn't be honest with herself if she didn't admit to having misgivings that she'd come to rely on Seth a little too much. She was putting her future in the hands of a man she really didn't know, trusting him when he told her everything would be okay. Trusting him when his father had brought all of her hardship to bear. Knowing her heart was becoming involved scared her the most.

The cleaning ladies arrived around ten o'clock, and after receiving instructions from Ally, they set to work.

By two o'clock, the furniture arrived. And at the end of the day, Ally put aside her own cleaning implements, feeling a sense of accomplishment for the first time in a very long time.

"It all looks good," Seth said as he entered the kitchen where she was unpacking a box of dishes his personal assistant had bought online and arranged to have shipped. They'd also received linens, cookware and three other large boxes of miscellaneous items.

"It's getting there," Ally agreed. "The new furniture will fit in the house perfectly. I still need to finish unpacking and buy some groceries."

"You can do that tomorrow while I'm at Ben's office."

"Oh! I'd forgotten. Tomorrow is the reading of the will. I hope it goes well for you. Do you know your half brothers very well?"

He nodded. "Well enough, I suppose. I've been coming here every summer since I was six. Spent a couple of Christmas holidays with them. That pretty much stopped when I went to college, but we've kept in touch."

"I've never had any direct dealings with them," Ally said. "When I lost my ranch, it was handled by corporate attorneys and your father. I never met any of your brothers. I hope they are not as bloodthirsty as your father. I'm sorry, but that's what he was to me."

"I understand. I had a different impression of him, though under different circumstances, I could see how he'd be somewhat cold." Seth said. "But I've never found my brothers to be anything like that."

"Good. Seth? Try not to worry about tomorrow. I know how important it is for you, but believe it will go as planned. No reason why it shouldn't, right?"

"You never know. I hope you're right." He looked at her as if he'd seen a whole new side of her. But maybe she was just being ridiculous. "Thanks for the encouragement."

"Of course," she responded. For a long moment their gazes caught, and neither moved to break the eye contact. "Well, I need to go to the barn and check on the progress out there."

Ally strove to make her heartbeat slow down. Seth was just standing there, his thumbs hanging from his jeans pockets, the long-sleeved shirt rolled to just below his elbows, and those eyes so brown, the flakes of gold glinting. He had her pulse hammering. He was so male. Extra stamina was needed to avoid falling for this guy. Still, she couldn't help but ask, "Want to come with me?"

"Sure."

Together they walked toward the large, sprawling barn, and for the second time in as many days, Ally wondered what she'd gotten herself into.

Five

The town square was brimming with activity when Seth arrived for the meeting at Ben Rucker's office the next day. He had just found a parking spot when he heard his name being called in a deep voice like his own.

"Seth!" He turned to see Wade and Cole walking down the sidewalk toward him.

"How in the hell are you doing?" Cole said as he gave Seth a quick hug and solid pat on the back. Wade held his hand out to him and shook it warmly, followed by a friendly pat on his shoulder.

"It's been a long time," said Wade, smiling broadly.

"It has," Seth answered. "It's good to see you both again. Where's Chance?"

"He's on his way. Had a mare unexpectedly go into labor and said he needed to make sure all was okay. He called a few minutes ago and said he was en route."

"Good. It will be good to see him."

"So, how have you been? I was sorry to hear about your mother."

"Thanks. Yeah, she fought a brave battle, but…"

"So now you're building a cancer research center?"

"That's the plan." He should have been surprised that Wade and Cole knew about his project, but Wade tended to keep abreast of everything that touched the family.

"I hope it goes well for you today," Wade told him just as a white pickup truck slid up next to the curb. A tall, lanky man got out, a smile of welcome clearly etched on his face.

"I know you… I think we've met before," Chance teased as he reached Seth.

"Could be," Seth returned. "How have you been?" He extended his hand.

"Couldn't ask for better, brother. And you?"

"Doing good."

"We should all get together with the wives before you leave," Cole suggested. "How long are you here?"

"I'd planned on it just being a couple of weeks, but that's changing. I got a ranch. A small repo you guys were sitting on. Went through the LLC. Cole said it was fine. We're setting up house. I wanted a place closer to my family."

"Well all right," Chance said, giving his approval. "It's about time."

"I appreciate that. My wife had her heart set on this place west of town," Seth said. "At least being in the county will afford me the opportunity to see more of you guys when we all happen to be in town."

"And speaking of wives, when are we all going to get to meet her? And I don't think you've met my Laurel. We need to get together while we are all here," Wade said, and everyone agreed.

They talked for a few more minutes until it was time to go inside Ben Rucker's office. When they were all seated in the small conference room, Mr. Rucker began to go over the terms of the will. Seth was made a full partner in Masters International Inc., plus awarded a substantial cash endowment. He fought to keep the tears of happiness from clouding his eyes. It was better than he'd hoped.

Their father had divided the bulk of the estate among the four brothers, less bequests to charities and personal contributions to a smattering of individuals Seth didn't know. In short, he was now a billionaire. Their business would envelop his own companies, and he would work through the conglomerate company on his own endeavors plus take on some of the responsibilities of Masters International Inc. The main thing was the research clinic would now be fully funded, something he felt overwhelmingly grateful for.

"Seth," Wade said as they exited Ben Rucker's office. "We were thinking about getting together Saturday night. It's rare we're all here at the same time. We would love to meet your wife. And I don't think you've met my wife, Laurel. Are you free?"

"I would like to say yes, but let me check with Ally. Can I give you a call?"

"Absolutely. Hopefully we will see you both then."

"It's nothing fancy," Chance added. "Just some burgers and steaks out on the veranda. Jeans and T-shirts will be fine."

They all shook hands and got into their separate cars. Seth drove to his new ranch, hoping Ally was there.

When he got back to the ranch, he met a delivery truck leaving just before he reached the driveway. He parked and headed for the door. Letting himself in, he immediately noticed that the painters had done an excellent job. The draperies had been freshened. The old furniture they'd chosen to keep had been cleaned, and some of the new furniture was already in place.

"Anybody home? Ally?" he called from just inside the foyer.

"She's out at the barn." A middle-aged woman with a kind smile came out from the kitchen down the hall and greeted him. "I'm Pauline Haddock, your new house-keeper. I live in Calico Springs." She offered her hand, which Seth accepted. "That wife of yours loves her horses."

Seth grinned. "Yes, she does. Nice to meet you, Pauline." And he turned toward the back door, eager to find his bride.

"Where do you want these old planks?" Stony Oster-man asked. He was one of four ranch hands Seth had hired to help get the barn and land ready for livestock.

"Ya know what?" Ally mused. "Let's make a debris pile outside the barn area where it will be safe to have a fire. We'll just burn the lot as well as the tree trimmings."

"That sounds like a good plan," Stony agreed. He immediately tossed his load of old, worn pine lumber on a spot that didn't have grass and was far away from any buildings and trees.

"Might as well add the old shavings to the pile," Ally said before he could turn away.

"Yes, ma'am," he said before heading to the barn. She could hear his voice as he conveyed the orders to the other three. In just a few minutes, she heard Seth's new tractor start up as it scraped up the pine shavings from the main hall of the barn, carrying them out to the burn site.

"Is this trash day?" Seth asked, smiling as he walked up behind her.

"Yep." Ally couldn't help but smile back. "Thanks to the ranch hands and your tractor, we should have the barn ready for the horses by the end of the week. I never realized so much decay could happen in just over a year."

"Looks like you're going to need some more lumber. Get whatever you need. I'll have my assistant set up an account with the local lumberyard. Are the hands working out?"

Ally nodded. "They're great. All hard workers. No grumblers. We did good."

There was an unmistakable twinkle in Seth's eyes.

"I thought we could just stack the old shavings and lumber out here and have a fire. There's currently no burn ban. If we keep it small, it should burn nicely."

Seth nodded.

"How did the probate go? Do you get to build your research center?"

She was anxious on Seth's behalf. He had already spent so much money on the house and land, and gone to so much trouble to marry her, all in the hope of being part of his father's will.

Seth drew a deep breath. "Good, as I'd hoped. I spoke with Ben Rucker just before the others arrived. He was pleased I'd found a wife. Surprised but tickled to learn it was you."

"Good. Congratulations." Ally smiled.

"This means we can commence building the research center in a couple months. Probably midsummer."

"So…you're a billionaire now?"

"Yeah." He frowned and looked at her questioningly. "Primarily it's tied up in the family corporation, where I'm now a partner, but yeah. I suppose you could say that. Why?"

"I've never known one before. Are you going to get snooty?"

Seth grinned and fought to keep from laughing. "I'll do my best not to. But tell you what. If you see me start to get snooty, I expect you to put me in my place, okay?"

She watched him intently as though not knowing if he was teasing. Then she said, "You can count on it. So, you'll be leaving to oversee construction at your research center."

"Maybe in a week or so," he answered, watching her face. "Most of the plans have been drawn up, and the rest can be handled with Matthew Rundles and John Sizemore, my partners in the center, during a conference call. We have a general contractor, so unless an issue comes up, which I'm always expecting, he will handle everything. I may have to make a couple of trips back to LA over the next few weeks, but that's about it." He tipped his head. "Are you okay with that?"

Ally shrugged. "Sure. No problem here. I mean, it's your business. It's your ranch."

He held her gaze as though he was expecting a different answer but then changed the subject. "Speaking of the ranch, I'm going to need a horse. Could I get your help in finding a good one?"

"Of course, although you're welcome to ride one of mine. They're all very well trained, and I trust you to be gentle with them."

"I'm always gentle. At least when I need to be."

"Yeah, well. With these girls, you have to be. They are very responsive to the lightest touch."

"Like master, like student?"

Ally chanced a look at Seth, and the sparkle in his eyes caused a blush to run up her neck and over her face. She turned away. "I want to show you the house. Are you busy?"

"After you."

Between what was left of the old furniture and the new items they had purchased, the house felt warm and welcoming. He especially liked the den. The sofa and two recliners fit perfectly around the fireplace. It would be a good place to spend a wintry evening.

"Your bed is set up in the master bedroom. Mine is down the hall." She walked toward the stairs, intent on showing him the second floor.

"Why didn't you just have your bed put in the master bedroom?" Seth asked, following behind her. "It will eventually be your house."

Ally shrugged. "It just didn't seem to be the right thing to do."

"Of course, we could always share the same bedroom. That would solve the problem."

"There isn't a problem," she returned and continued up the stairs.

When he caught up, she was in the midst of making the bed in one of the bedrooms. She walked to the edge and grabbed the comforter.

"We have staff to do that. You don't have to make the bed."

She shrugged. "The hands are handling the barn stuff. I didn't have anything else to do."

"Of course not. Just oversee a housekeeper and a barn full of cowboys."

She shrugged. "I wanted to get this bed ready. Mine is down the hall, and Pauline is working in there. The kitchen, den and living room are set up. The stove, new dishwasher and refrigerator are being installed as we speak, and I have a carpenter downstairs making room for a microwave. Hope that was okay. We're going to need a few more pots and pans, but otherwise, it's all set."

"Karen took care of that. Another delivery should arrive tomorrow."

Ally sighed and gave him a rare smile.

"It all looks good. You've done a great job," he said.

She pushed a pillow into a fresh new pillowcase. "Still a lot to do."

He shook his head and smiled. Leave it to him to marry a perfectionist.

"By the way, are you free Saturday evening?"

Ally frowned and shrugged. "I don't know. Why?"

"My brothers want to get together with the wives over dinner—"

"No. No, I can't," she interrupted and hastily made for the door. "Pauline? Could you finish making this bed?"

"Sure thing, Mrs. Masters."

Turning at the upper landing, Ally quickly made her way down the stairs.

"Ally, wait." He hurried after her.

"Gotta go to the barn," she said over her shoulder as she hurried through the kitchen and toward the back door.

"Ally—"

She seemed to quicken her pace and was out the door and halfway across the yard before he could catch her.

"Ally, what's wrong?"

"Nothing. Look, I really have things I need to see to in the barn. The hired hands will need—"

"Whatever they need can wait. I want to know what the sudden flight down the stairs is all about. Is this something to do with the dinner Saturday night?"

Ally stood in front of him, lips drawn into a thin line.

"Do you still hold it against them for what our father did regarding your ranch? Is that it?"

She looked down at her boots. "No. How can I when you've given it back?" She bit her lower lip, a gesture that made him crazy. He wanted to be the one to suckle on those full lips.

"Then what is it?"

She shrugged, peering up at his face, then away. "Look, I'm just a common person. I don't exactly hang out with billionaires. I wouldn't know what to say, and I'm very sure I have nothing to wear. God…" Her face began to grow pink. "I can't even imagine consorting with your family. No. Not gonna happen. Give them my apologies."

"Ha!" Seth laughed. "You're a snob!"

That brought her head up. She glared at him.

"You are."

"I am not," she argued indignantly.

"Yes, you are. Snobbery goes both ways. You think you're too good to eat a simple meal with my family. In my book, that's a snob."

"That's not at all what I said! You're turning it around."

"So prove me wrong. It's going to be a barbecue at the ranch. Jeans and boots. Probably finger foods. If you're not too good for that, then prove it by coming."

She looked at him then, her eyes filled with unshed tears.

"Seth, you know what I'm saying. I would be a laughingstock."

He reached out and took her gently by the shoulders, turning her to face him. "No, you wouldn't. If you'll just meet them, I think you'll find they are a laid-back, fun-loving bunch who will treat you with complete respect.

I guarantee within fifteen minutes, you'll feel like part of the family."

"And why would I want to do that?" she asked, shrugging out of his arms. "How am I supposed to sit and make conversation with these people knowing all the time I'm a fraud? Knowing all the time they're the sons of the man who caused me to lose my farm. Maybe that doesn't bother you, but it bothers the hell out of me."

"First of all, I don't believe my brothers had anything to do with taking your ranch. Secondly, you're not a fraud. We are married. The marriage certificate is on file at the courthouse, and the ring is on your finger."

"Yeah, but for how long?"

"How long does anyone have, Ally?" he shot back. "There is no guarantee in this life."

"You're twisting my words again."

"No, I'm not. Dammit, Ally." He pulled her to him, and his lips came down over hers.

At her resistance, he immediately loosened his hold, but when she didn't move away, he continued the kiss, his arms going around her. One hand moved up to her head as he held her to him. "Open your lips for me," he growled against her mouth. When she complied, he covered her lips with his, his tongue going deep, searching and discovering her hidden secrets. He heard a soft moan, and his body surged to full attention. He felt her hands slide up his chest and over his shoulders.

He broke the kiss and nuzzled her ear, inhaling the natural sweet perfume of her body. He looked down into her face. She was standing with her eyes closed, her lips open and waiting for him to return. Sexual urges raced through his body, and he took her mouth again, this time not so gently. He was on fire, and he wanted her in the worst way.

He felt her hands against his chest, gently pushing him back. Reluctantly he lifted his head and stepped back.

"I... I'm sorry," she whispered. "I can't do this."

She turned and walked to the barn. This time he let her go.

Six

That evening Ally accompanied Seth back to the hotel, where they gathered their things and Seth checked out. This was it. The day she'd dreaded. She and Seth would live together under the same roof. It had seemed different living at the hotel. But this…moving into the house… was very real.

She had been an idiot to let him kiss her. Not that she could have done anything to prevent it. Down deep where no one would see, she had wanted his lips on hers since that first day they'd met at the crossing of the road and the bridle path. Then with each successive encounter, her desire for him had grown. If she were honest, part of the reason she so dreaded him living with her in this house was because he was the kind of man who could undermine her defenses. No woman was immune to those eyes…those lips. He had an aura about him that worked like a magnet, drawing a woman into his web.

But she had to be strong. This was a temporary situation, and in a few months, he would be gone. She didn't intend to be left with a broken heart when she saw him off, but if she wasn't careful, Seth was just the man who could do it.

It had bothered her when Wayne Burris left a year ago, more than she cared to admit. She knew when they began a relationship that Wayne was biding his time until he put some money together to get back on the rodeo circuit. That was his life. Anything or anyone he met along his journey eventually became a forgotten memory. Like a fool she thought she would be different; she would be the one he couldn't leave. She would be the love of his life and he'd want to stay and make a home together. It had hurt when she found the note on her pillow. By the time she awoke and read it, Wayne was long gone, never to be heard from again.

Seth was the same way. She didn't have any proof but she knew. He was a billionaire, a jet-setter who traveled places she would never see. The women in his life were fun times along the way, there temporarily but soon to be forgotten. She wouldn't let herself be a fool this time. The marriage certificate changed nothing. And she didn't intend to go through abandonment again. Seth was pure temptation. But there was always a price to pay for indulging in the kind of temptation he represented.

That evening as Ally dressed for bed, she couldn't stop thinking about Seth. It felt both strange and oddly comforting to have him here with her. She got in bed determined to stop thinking of the handsome man. She could hear him moving around in the room next door, the old floor creaking with every step he took. She heard the shower come on. A few minutes later, he turned it off.

She heard him as he walked to his bed and got in. Apparently they didn't believe in insulation in these old houses. She was surprised she didn't remember hearing sounds when she lived here before. But then, her dad had stayed in the extra room downstairs, unable to easily navigate the stairs. Maybe that was why.

The old house popped and squeaked, and it seemed the darker the night became, the more sounds she could hear. Finally she drifted into a restless sleep.

The sound that woke her came from downstairs. She immediately sat up in the bed. Not moving, she listened closely for another crash. She was sure that's what had woken her up. What could have fallen? It sounded like someone was in the house, prowling around the kitchen. She inhaled deeply.

You're being ridiculous.

The only way to know for sure was to get up and go down there. She swung her feet to the floor and stood from the bed. About the time she opened her bedroom door, another crash came from downstairs. Maybe it was Seth getting a glass of water. But he would turn on a light. Wouldn't he?

Her heart was beating hard in her chest as she turned in the direction of the stairs. Seth's bedroom door opened, and she heard him call her name. She ran back to where he stood in the doorway of his bedroom. He was shirtless, and his hair was in disarray. The moonlight highlighted the muscles in his arms and stomach.

"Ally? What is it?"

"There…there was a crash downstairs. Twice. Were you just downstairs getting a glass of water?"

"No." The door opened wider, and he pulled her into his room. He quickly put on a pair of jeans and, opening a bedside drawer, picked up a large-caliber handgun.

After checking the load, he slipped it into the back of his jeans. "Stay in here."

He walked through the open doorway, and Ally was right behind him.

Seth stopped, and she bumped into his back.

"Ally." He kept his voice low. "Stay in the bedroom."

"Not happening! What if someone is down there?"

"Then I'll take care of it. I don't need to worry about you getting in between us."

He turned her around and gave a light push toward his bedroom before he disappeared into the deep shadows of the hallway. She reached his door, but before she could step over the threshold, she heard another sound coming from downstairs. The temptation to follow Seth was strong. But instead she backed up and closed the door. Making her way to his bed, she sat down on the edge and clasped her hands tightly together.

Maybe she should call the police? No, she decided. She had lived here her entire life and had never experienced any sort of break-in. The very idea was preposterous.

Time seemed to crawl by. About the time she'd reached the end of her patience, Seth walked back into the bedroom.

"We had a break-in," he told her, his voice conveying annoyance. "Someone was looking for something and apparently tripped over the boxes that were still on the kitchen floor. About the time I turned on the lights, the back door slammed behind him. I got to the door immediately, but he was already gone, disappeared into the night."

"We should call the police," she said as she headed for the door.

"I already have," he responded as she bolted toward the door. "Where are you going?"

"Downstairs. I want to see what damage they did. How dare anyone break into this house!"

"Ally, I didn't see any damage. Wait until the sheriff gets here."

"You wait if you want to," she retorted as she rushed from the room, Seth right on her heels.

The kitchen was a mangled mess of open cabinet doors and drawers pulled out and dumped on the floor. The few remaining boxes were scattered around as though someone had kicked them out of their way.

A few minutes later, they heard a siren getting closer. Seth answered the knock on the front door and led the deputy into the kitchen, where together they made a full report. Mason Crawley, the deputy sheriff, painstakingly wrote down all the facts, but without a description of the man, there was little he could do. He would put out the word and send extra patrols throughout the night.

As soon as he was gone, Ally set about closing all the cabinet doors and putting back the drawers. After restacking the boxes with Seth's help, she rubbed her arms and looked for something else to do.

"Come on, Ally," he said stepping up behind her, crossing his arms over her shoulders and around her neck, holding her close. "Let's see if we can get some sleep. There's nothing more we can do in here tonight. I doubt if the burglar will be back. I'll arrange to have some security here tomorrow."

She solemnly nodded her head, and together they walked up the stairs.

"I want you to sleep in my room."

"No, I'll be fine."

"I'm not willing to take the chance," he countered and guided her to the master bedroom.

She let him help her into bed before he went around

to the other side and placed the gun on the nightstand. He slipped in between the sheets and turned off the light.

"Who would break into the house?" she had to ask, still sitting up. "They must have seen the cars and known someone was living here."

"I'm guessing somebody was squatting in the house during the months it sat vacant. They probably left something important and are desperate to get it back. I suggest we go through the house thoroughly tomorrow and see if we can find anything you don't recognize."

"Absolutely. Seth?"

"What, sweetheart?"

"I'm glad you were here." She felt a shiver go down her spine. She would have gone downstairs herself and encountered no telling what kind of situation.

"Come here," he said as his arm went beneath her and he pulled her close.

"I just wish I knew who it was."

"Let it go for tonight, Ally. Maybe the sheriff's office will find who did it."

"Or maybe they will come back."

"You're safe, Ally." He pressed her head down onto his shoulder. "Try and go to sleep."

"I'm not worried about my safety. I want to catch the creeps. Ugh! I feel so violated. How dare anybody break into this house! If you're right about it being a squatter then they will be back. But we haven't found anything unusual in all the cleaning that's been done recently. Still, I intend to go over every inch of the house tomorrow."

"And I'll help you. But for tonight you really do need to let it go. Get some rest."

She shrugged. "You're right. It's just that I've never experienced a break-in before."

"I left the downstairs lights on for tonight."

"You don't think he'll come back, do you?"

"Doubtful. Between me catching him inside and the police coming I seriously doubt if he'll try anything else. At least not tonight."

Ally willed herself to relax. It felt good to have Seth's warmness surrounding her. Being held tight and feeling protected wasn't something she was accustomed to, but she couldn't deny the comfort it gave her. Tomorrow... tomorrow she intended to go over this house until she discovered what would draw someone into the house even knowing someone was at home. With one last sigh of determination, she turned into Seth's neck and, breathing in his essence, closed her eyes.

After dressing the next morning, she went downstairs. Seth was sitting at the new kitchen table, sipping a mug of coffee and reading the local newspaper. She helped herself to a cup and sat down across from him.

"How'd you sleep?" he asked without lowering the paper.

"Good. You?"

"Like a rock. There's something about this country air that just intensifies everything." He put down the paper and looked at her. "The breeze is cooler, the air crisper, the scents of the clover and wildflowers more fragrant. And this old house...you can sense the culture, like it's steeped in tradition. And that's saying nothing about my sleeping partner." He looked at her and grinned. "Yep. Definitely slept like a rock."

"I guess." She shrugged, ignoring his sexual jibe. "It was an old house when Dad bought it. He had a lot of updates done but insisted on honoring the integrity of the original." She stretched and stifled a yawn. "Well, I'm headed to the barn. The stalls are mostly cleaned, but some other things need to be done. Then I'm coming back and with the household staff I'm going to turn over every nook and cranny in this house."

"I'll walk with you."

He stood and poured the remains of his coffee into the sink. Then together they walked the path to the stable area. Once inside, she grabbed a rake and began mucking out one of the stalls that still needed some cleaning, trying her best to ignore Seth. Every time he came near her, she felt herself heat up. It soon proved difficult to focus.

"Explain to me why you won't have dinner at my brothers' ranch."

"I already did."

"They're nice, laid-back people, Ally. Chance is a rancher, same as you."

"Somehow I doubt that." She cast a skeptical look in Seth's direction.

"Maybe he has a bigger spread, but he is a rancher. Other than a stint in the navy, it's all he's ever wanted to do. His wife, Holly, is a veterinarian. Her clinic is across the road from the ranch. You remind me of her in a lot of ways. Cole is the businessman of the bunch. Has an office in Dallas, but they choose to live on the ranch. He commutes into Dallas a couple of times a week. His wife is an archaeologist."

"An archaeologist?"

"That's right. In fact, they met when she obtained a court order to search a section of the ranch for artifacts. They originally hit it off like oil and water but eventually got together and have been in love ever since. Wade is the newest married, besides us. He used to spend most of his time in Europe, but since he met Laurel, he has pretty much delegated the work to someone else. I've never met her, but I understand she is an accomplished artist. Other than some stray cousins, that's the family. And they all want to meet you."

Ally kept sweeping at the debris in the stall. She didn't know how to answer him. Here stood the man responsible for getting her ranch back wanting to introduce her to the men arguably responsible for taking it away. To Seth this was a small thing he was asking of her. She supposed she owed him this much. But how she could feign being a happily married bride for an entire evening, answering questions and making small talk? Especially with the entire clan of Masters brothers and their wives?

She sighed. "All right. I'll go. But I have to go to town and find something to wear."

"Not a problem. We'll go tomorrow."

She stopped raking. "No. *I* will go. I'm quite capable of buying my own clothes." She looked at Seth and saw him nod. She needed some new clothes anyway. She might as well take advantage of this excuse and take the time to buy some. She'd use the money she'd been saving for breeding fees and hope she could earn it back before it was needed. She wasn't about to appear at a barbecue at the home of a Masters in worn out jeans and a raggedy T-shirt.

By Saturday all of the repairs on the barn had been completed. The last of the supplies for the house had been delivered, and her horses were scheduled to come back to her stable on Monday. Everything should be in order, but the evening's festivities still loomed. Ally didn't want to go to the Masters ranch and visit with Seth's brothers and their wives. Still, she'd promised Seth she would go.

At least she had plenty of outfit options after her shopping trip the other day. She'd bought a whimsical pale green blouse and denim skirt with wedges to match, plus two other dresses just in case. It had felt good to be out on a full-blown shopping excursion. She hadn't done that since Wayne Burris had dumped her for the rodeo circuit, leaving a note that said he hoped she would understand. Oh, she'd understood, all right. Macho males seemed destined to sweep in, make a woman feel special then in the blink of an eye disappear again, never to return. Wayne had been popular with the ladies and knew how he affected them. He'd expected Ally to understand that, too.

She went inside the house in search of Seth. She found him in an extra bedroom with one of the ranch hands, arranging a new desk, chairs and filing cabinets. He'd decided he needed a home office, and she couldn't think of a reason to deny him.

The ranch hand immediately nodded and excused himself.

"So what gives?"

"My new office. Do you like it?"

"Oh, yeah. It's…an office."

"I've made arrangements to fly in two of my security detail."

"You have a security detail?"

"Yes. A necessary evil, I'm afraid. Anyway, they will stay a couple of weeks and help the sheriff's office find the person who broke in. Once they arrive, they'll have rotating shifts overnight. I don't want any more surprises. I doubt you do, either."

Ally shook her head. "Pauline and I looked everywhere and found nothing that could belong to a squatter."

"Maybe there's nothing to find," Seth said.

"I intend to keep looking. Your office does look good, though," Ally said, changing the subject. "Where will your assistant sit?"

"Hopefully I won't need one locally. I guess I'll cross that bridge when I get to it."

The day passed quickly. Too soon it was time to get ready for the evening outing. After a hot soak in the tub, she dried her hair and donned the new blouse and skirt she'd purchased. With a light touch of makeup and some lipstick, she was ready to go.

Seth stood waiting for her at the front door when she came down the stairs.

"Very nice."

"Thanks. Let's get this over with."

She didn't miss the grin that sprang to his lips. She wished she was as calm as he appeared. He opened the door. "After you."

She walked to the truck, where Seth helped her inside then they were on their way.

Seven

It was a twenty-minute drive to the ranch, and Seth felt Ally's anxiety the entire way. But he knew once she really got to know his brothers and their wives, she would be at ease. He wished she didn't have such preconceived concepts of his brothers, but he could understand where they came from after her history with the Masters family, particularly his father.

She looked incredibly beautiful, the pale green blouse accentuating the deep auburn highlights of her hair and the emerald green of her eyes. A touch of pink lipstick made her full lips irresistible. Kissing. They needed kissing.

Seth turned off the main road and drove under the metal Masters Ranch sign arching over the wide drive. They passed the original house on the left. The sprawling stone-and-log structure was a vision set against the backdrop of the deep pine woods. They continued along the drive, past the main barn capable of housing one hundred horses. Its white columns and dark green facade spoke to the quality of the Masters breeding program that had long been heralded by local ranchers. They then turned off to the west. The road curved around rock formations and deep blue pools then went up a rise until Chance's house came into view. Similar to the original house though not as large, it was still breathtaking. Seth felt Ally's uneasiness heighten.

"This is it," he said. "This is where Chance and Holly live."

He parked the truck behind another and helped her out.

His brothers were awaiting their arrival in the front yard. They each embraced Seth, and he proceeded to introduce them to Ally.

"Glad you could come," Chance said. "Come around to the backyard and make yourselves at home. We're eating outside tonight."

"Welcome! It's so nice to meet you," said a beautiful blonde woman as Ally rounded the corner of the large house. She came forward and hugged Ally. "I'm Holly. This is Laurel and Tallie," she added, pointing out the two women who now joined them. They each grinned and welcomed Ally to the group. "Dinner is almost ready. Burgers and steaks. Hope you like pecan pie and home-made ice cream. Martha is our cook. She's making her mother's recipe for dessert."

Soon everyone was seated around the large table on the stone patio. The area was edged by a rail fence that looked out over the grasslands nestled between the higher elevations with the river running like a ribbon through it all.

As the time passed, Seth watched Ally begin to engage in the banter with the other wives. That she was ill at ease was clear, but eventually the other wives worked their magic and Ally began to respond. Soon she was laughing at the stories of how each couple got together.

"What about you?" Tallie asked.

"Seth almost ran me down with his car. Had to jump the hood to keep from becoming roadkill."

"Oh my gosh! What is it about these Masters men?" Laurel shook her head.

"Hey, now." Wade spoke up. "It isn't entirely our fault."

"Nope. It sure isn't," Cole chimed in. "We're the ones caught off guard. It's the women who cause all the friction."

"Friction?" Laurel and Holly both repeated.

"I'll remember that, bud." Tallie glared playfully at her husband, her eyes sparkling in challenge.

"I want to propose a toast." Holly spoke up, raising her glass. "Here's to our husbands. May they all reap what they sow."

"Hear, hear," said Tallie. The others raised their glasses.

Ally joined in the toast, but Seth caught her glance as she did. Underneath the smile was sadness. He was sure of it. She hid it well, but in that instant he had seen through her bravado. Was it knowing theirs was only a marriage of convenience, and of short duration at that? He frowned. She'd assured him she didn't want any long-term commitment when he first approached her about this arrangement, so it must be something else.

When it was time to leave, the group saw them out to the truck. On the way home, Ally was quiet.

"So, what do you think of my family?"

"They're all great," she replied. "I really enjoyed tonight, Seth. Thank you."

"My pleasure."

"You were right. They weren't the awful people I had imagined. I still don't understand what really went on between my father and yours, but I accept your brothers had nothing to do with it."

"I honestly can't see Wade or Cole or Chance doing something like that. I'm sorry if my father caused you unnecessary pain."

Out of the corner of his eye, he saw her shrug.

"It's a beautiful night," he continued.

"Yes, it is. I loved the view from the terrace where we ate dinner. You said all your brothers have homes at the ranch?"

"Yes, they do. Wade and Cole have to make trips into Dallas periodically, but they told me they're all happier at the ranch."

"I can understand that. I wouldn't want to be anywhere else. I mean, if it were a choice between the city and the country."

"I never minded the city, although I grew up there and didn't know any better. I must admit, the country is starting to grow on me." He couldn't help grinning. "I want a horse."

"I'll put the word out that you're looking. Do you want a specific breed?"

"Whatever you recommend."

"You might also call Chance. He could probably fix you up with the perfect mount. The Masters Ranch carries some of the best bloodlines in the country. If I'm remembering correctly, they have several different breeds."

"Why don't I arrange a day for us to go and see some? Have you ever been inside their barn?"

"No, and I would love to see it."

He glanced over and saw her smile. "Then consider it done."

Soon they pulled into the long driveway going to the house. Seth walked around to her side of the truck and helped her out. As her feet touched the ground, he held her just a moment longer than he probably should, but she made no move to walk away. The moonlight glistened on the strands of her hair, turning them to a burnished gold. His hands moved from her shoulders to cup her face, and without giving it a second thought he lowered his lips to hers.

He heard her inhale deeply before she opened her lips to his. His arms came around her and pulled her tight against his body. The taste of her made his hunger increase, and like a starving man, he fed. Her mouth was a deep well of temptation, and he couldn't get enough. He heard her moan, and his erection throbbed inside his jeans.

"Let's go inside." His voice was rough even to his own ears.

Suddenly Ally pushed against his shoulders and stepped away from him. "I... I can't do this. I'm sorry, Seth."

"What's wrong?"

"You're bored and I'm here. I've played that game before, and I won't do it again."

She hurried to the front steps. He looked up at the dark sky then rubbed the back of his neck. Maybe she was right. It wouldn't last. She knew that and so did he. His only excuse was that she was impossibly tempting.

He followed her inside the house and to the kitchen. She was there, taking a glass from the cabinet. A glass of water sounded good.

"Do you mind handing me one?"

"Sure," she replied, giving him a glass and walking to the faucet.

"Did someone hurt you?" he couldn't help but ask.

She took a sip of her water and was quiet for a long moment. He didn't think she was going to answer. But then she said, "His name was Wayne. Wayne Burris. We were together a few months. Long enough for him to make promises. Plenty of time for me to fall for him and believe what he said. The next thing I knew, I found a note on my pillow. He said he hoped I would understand. No problem there. It was never his intention to stay around, but I let my hopes get the best of me. I was a fool. But I'm not about to put myself in that situation again. God, I hate that man. He goes through his life not caring who he hurts, not giving a second thought to the people he interacts with. The world revolves around Wayne."

"It doesn't have to be like that."

"No? Then how would you imagine this will end? Eventually you'll leave to go back to California and that will be that."

"I'll be back, Ally."

"You can't say that, Seth. If there's one thing I've learned, it's that the future is never set. You want an affair, and I'm saying no."

"I can't promise anything more right now. Why don't we take it one step at a time and see where this goes? I think you're attracted to me a lot more than you want to admit."

"You're crazy." She turned away and headed for the den. He caught up in four long strides, stopping her forward progress and turning her back to him. His hands cupped her face.

"Don't judge every man by one man's bad behavior."

"I'm not. I—I'm not."

"Yes, you are."

With lips set in determination, she pulled free and continued her flight to the stairs.

Ally finished off the last of her eggs, took a bite of toast and walked to the sink, rinsing the crumbs down the drain. The morning was overcast, dark clouds on the horizon telling of rain in the distance. She hoped the rain would hold off. While they needed a good downpour, there were too many things to be done that required dry weather.

Seth started a fresh pot of coffee. It smelled like a lifeline, and she eagerly grabbed a mug from the cabinet and poured her second cup.

"So, what time do your horses arrive?" he asked.

"All I know is before noon. Mac Dempsey, the manager over at the Triple Bar Ranch, is bringing them himself this morning. He said he would try to be here by noon."

"Good deal. I'm happy for you."

She looked over at Seth. "You know what? I think I'll take my coffee to the barn. I need to get out there early." She walked to the kitchen door and stepped out onto the covered porch where she'd left her boots. Pulling them on, she slipped outside without a backward glance.

An hour later the van arrived holding Ally's three mares and her stallion, Monkey.

The ranch hands were there to assist in unloading them from the trailer and into their stalls. Hay was provided and plenty of fresh water.

When they were all settled and happily munching on their hay, Ally turned to Mac.

"I can never thank you enough."

"Glad to do it. They're beautiful, quality mares. I'm glad they could come home again. It's where they belong."

Ally hugged the older man, tears forming in her eyes at the remembrance of all he had done for her after she lost the ranch. "Thank you so much."

She stepped back just as Seth entered the barn.

"Mac, this is my husband, Seth. Seth, this is Mac Dempsey."

The two men shook hands. "You two have a fine place here," Mac said, putting his hat back on. "I guess I don't have to tell you, but you're married to one of the best trainers in the state. I'm glad she's home, but we're sure going to miss her."

"I understand," Seth replied. He looked at Ally and grinned. "She's pretty special, all right."

Together they walked Mac out to his rig and saw him off. Then Ally hurried back inside the barn. Stopping at the first stall, she sprang the latch and stepped inside, pouring the morning grain into the feeding trough. Seth came in and stood in the entrance to the stall.

"This is Lady Mary, a thoroughbred out of Nimbus Cloud Rising," she said as she ran her hands over the horse's chest and down her legs. "She has produced some of the finest foals around. I'm going to try to save up and breed her to Standing Tall Vision, a stallion out at the East Fork Ranch."

"Why not mate her with your own stallion?"

"He's her son out of Jault Amar. Standing Tall Vision is currently a high-stakes winner in the major races. Don't know if I can do it by next year, but I intend to try. His stud fee is several thousand dollars, but a colt out of the two of them would be unprecedented."

She patted the mare's shoulder and backed out of the stall, closing the latch behind her.

"This is Sassy Lady," Ally said, dipping up another measure of feed and going into the next stall. "She's a quarter horse." The mare was a bay with one white foot and a blaze face. Slowly Ally approached the mare and ran her hands over the legs and back.

"Is she in your breeding program, too?" Seth asked.

"Yeah, but I'd rather wait and make Lady Mary the priority. I can't afford the breeding fee on them all, and the foal Mary produces will sell for enough to pay the breeding expenses for both of the others and then some."

She fed the third mare, a chestnut with three white socks, then stepped across the wide hall to where her stallion stood, patiently munching his hay.

"This is my Monkey man, also known as Jupiter's Rising Star." She ran her hands over the horse's glistening black coat after pouring the mixture of grain into his feeder.

"He's a fine-looking stallion," Seth commented.

"He's a thoroughbred. He's produced four colts, and they all did great on the racetrack. I've had quite a few inquiries about him already, but Mac didn't have the room to set up a separate area for breeding. That and his barn is full, so no way to board any mares." As she talked the stallion turned to her, searching her jeans pockets for a treat.

"Hey, there, Monkey. I've got your carrot right here."

She pulled two carrots from her back jeans pocket, and he eagerly snapped them up.

"Why do you call him Monkey?"

"When he was a yearling, he was into everything. His antics almost took him out more than once. But the crowning glory was when, at two years old, he became enamored with two mares a couple of runs down. Mr. Monkey here decided he would just jump the fence. And he did. He went sailing over a six-foot-high expanse of pipe fencing. But while his front feet cleared the top rail, unfortunately his hind feet didn't follow and he hung himself on the top rail. His front feet were swinging about an inch above the ground and his hind legs were straight up in the air. Quite the sight. Mac was over visiting Dad and he came running. He sized up the situation and pushed Monkey's hind legs up and over the top rail. Monkey landed in a heap, bruised but thankfully otherwise unharmed. Mac called him a crazy monkey, and the name kinda stuck."

Seth laughed. It was the first time she had heard such a bellow of laughter from him. She grinned.

"He loves carrots but won't touch apple slices or corn. Most horses love all of them. Monkey spits out a piece of apple as quick as it goes into his mouth."

She turned to Seth. "Thank you for making this happen, for allowing me the opportunity to bring them all home."

"Not a problem. Glad to do it. Don't forget, this ranch was only part of the arrangement. You made funding for the research center possible."

"Well, I'd better get back to the house. I want to do a full search. See if I can find whatever that thief was looking for."

"My two security staff should be arriving this afternoon. I need to have a meeting with them," Seth said. "I would help you, but I have no idea what I'm looking for."

"That's okay. Neither do I, really. But I think I'll know it if I see it."

They returned to the house together, then Seth got in his truck to drive to the local airport to pick up the men.

Ally went to the kitchen to try her search again. She pulled out each drawer and went through the contents and examined the bottom. When she finished with that room, she headed to the living room then on to the den. Pauline joined her in the search for a while, then went back to cleaning upstairs.

By the time Seth returned from the airport, Ally had nothing to show for her efforts except a list of grocery items she needed to pick up at the store. It was a long list. And if she knew Seth at all, he would insist on going with her. She'd never been around anyone who wanted to protect her like he did. He was a special man. She just had to be sure to protect her heart as well. It was becoming more difficult every day.

"Guys, this is my wife, Ally," Seth said when he found her in the den. He stepped aside so his security men could enter the room.

"Nice to meet you," she replied and shook their hands.

"Frank, I want you to stay around the back and cover the west end of the house tonight. Bryan, you take the front and the east side."

The men nodded.

"I don't know what to tell you to look for. I don't have a clue what the guy was doing inside this house. But if he comes back, I want him caught. There are two spare bedrooms on the left side of the hall upstairs. Make yourselves comfortable. T-shirt and jeans will work here and help you blend in with the ranch hands. You're welcome to roam around the property and get your bearings. I suggest if you run into any of the ranch hands, you introduce yourselves as friends of mine here visiting for a few days.

Word travels fast around here, and I don't want news of a security team getting back to the culprit. And try to get some sleep. You're on duty at ten o'clock."

"Yes, sir," both said in unison.

"I'll show you to your rooms," Ally offered and walked toward the stairs. The housekeeper stood at the top of the stairs.

"Pauline, these are friends of my husband, Frank and Bryan. This is Pauline, our housekeeper." Ally led them to the upstairs hallway and continued on to the guest rooms. "I think you'll be comfortable. If you need extra blankets, check the closet. Anything else, Seth and I will be around, or if we aren't, Pauline should be able to help you."

"This is great," said Bryan, stepping inside one of the rooms. "Thanks, Mrs. Masters."

Seth stepped up behind where the small group stood. "Any questions?"

"Is there any outside security?"

Seth shook his head. "No, not yet. I prefer to wait and see if he tries something else before we go full-scale surveillance. That could draw attention and scare him off. I want this creep caught."

"We're on it," Frank advised.

Seth turned toward Ally. "I'll drive you to town if you need to go to the store."

She gave him a tight smile and headed for the stairs.

In the kitchen they faced off in the argument he knew was coming.

"I'm fully capable of driving myself to town," she said, her hands on her hips.

"I know that. But what I don't know is who broke into this house last night—or why. He could have been after you."

"What? That's ludicrous."

"Maybe. But I'm not willing to take a chance. You're welcome to go with one of the security team instead of me, but I'd prefer you not go into town alone."

"Fine. Let's go. This time. And Seth?"

"Yeah?"

"Don't do this again."

Eight

Seth drove the seven miles into town and parked in the lot of MacKenzie's grocery store. Ally was out of the truck and hurrying toward the front entrance by the time he rounded the vehicle. She grabbed a shopping cart and headed for the vegetable aisle. She picked up some lettuce and potatoes before walking around the corner to the next aisle. When Seth arrived she was talking to a tall man who was reaching out for her. Ally's body language said she was anything but pleased to see him. Each time he reached out to her, she backed away. Seth stepped up next to her, and she seemed to relax at his presence.

"Seth, meet Wayne Burris," she said, stepping closer to Seth. "Wayne, my husband, Seth Masters."

"Masters?" he repeated, showing his surprise. "Well you did real good for yourself, darlin'." He offered his hand to Seth, who reluctantly shook it. If his memory served, this was the man who'd walked out on Ally, leaving her to face her father's death and the loss of the ranch alone.

"So, how long have you been married?"

"A few weeks," Seth answered. He brought his arm up around Ally's shoulders and kissed her on the cheek.

"Newlyweds. Well, all right." Wayne scratched his jaw, looking thoughtful. "You guys living out at the Masters Ranch?"

"It's been nice to meet you, but we've got to get going," Seth told the man, ignoring his question and leading Ally away toward the meat counter.

"Yeah, you too."

Ally was visibly shaken. It must have been a shock to see her ex again, seemingly out of the blue. Had there ever been love between them? Did she still have feelings for the man?

She finished her shopping without saying a word and headed to the checkout. Seth paid the bill and accompanied her back to the truck. She didn't wait for the store employee to finish loading the groceries into the back before she opened the door and got in. Seth climbed in after her.

"Are you okay?" he asked before starting the engine.

"Yes, I'm fine. I just never expected to see him again."

"Ally, is that the guy you were telling me about?"

"Yes."

"Are you in love with him?" he asked quietly.

"No," she immediately responded. "I question if I ever was. How can you love someone when he's never around? He hit on half the women in this town before I found out about it."

Seth started the truck and backed out of the parking space. He was glad he'd insisted on coming along with Ally. There was just something about the man he didn't like, other than the obvious.

"Again, thank you for being there, Seth."

"Not a problem."

Ally was quiet on the drive home. The housekeeper bustled out and helped bring in the groceries. Ally looked lost. Clearly it had something to do with meeting Wayne Burris.

Suddenly she turned toward Seth. "Are you up for a ride this afternoon?"

"I would be if I had something to ride."

"You have three very well-trained mares to choose from. I'd like to see the property and double-check the fences. Thought it might a good outing."

Seth grinned. "Sounds like a plan."

By two o'clock Ally had saddled the chestnut and bay mares and they were on their way. Seth was impressed by his horse's training. They let themselves through the large back gate and headed north. The recent snow had melted and the trees were showing their tiny buds of spring. Though still early in the year, the sun was shining down and the sky was a clear blue.

They rode through open pastureland then followed a trail into the trees until they eventually came to a small lake surrounded by large boulders. Ally dismounted and led her mount to the edge, where it splashed in the water. Seth followed, and they let the horses drink. Ally took a canteen from her saddle and offered it to Seth.

"How many acres do you have here?" he asked, handing the canteen back to Ally.

"Almost five hundred, but as you can see, not all of it is suitable for grazing. There's a lot of timber. Still, it's enough. I prefer to do hands-on with the horses I get in for training so I never have more than a dozen here at any one time."

"They do training at my family's ranch, too."

"As I understand it, the Masters Ranch has several trainers and a manager that oversees their breeding program. Then there are the cattle. It's a magnificent operation."

"It's big," Seth added. "As kids we never thought about the size and all that went on. We had chores, but once those were done, we were off searching for some adventure that most likely would land us in trouble." He chuckled. "Good memories."

Ally tied her reins to a nearby tree limb and climbed to the top of a boulder that overlooked a spot where the river flowed into the small lake. Seth followed suit.

"This used to be my favorite place. Dad always knew if he couldn't find me around the barn or house, this is where I'd be."

"Your thinking place."

"Yeah. When I was little, nothing seemed as bad up here. Problems had a way of disappearing for a while."

"Speaking of problems," Seth ventured. "I'm going to need to go back to LA for a couple of days. Something has come up with the research center sooner than I expected. I want you to come with me. I have a place right on the beach. I think you'll enjoy it."

"I don't know… There are so many things I need to do here. I'm barely moved in and—"

"And it will still be here when we get back. You have a housekeeper to oversee the house and four good cowboys to take care of the horses and any other ranching issues that may come up. Past that, there are now two security men to keep an eye on things. Frankly, security or not, I don't want to leave you here until they find whoever tried to break into your house. Granted, my security team is good, but there is always room for mistakes. I don't want to take the chance."

"What would I do in California?"

"What can't you do in California?" he countered and grinned. "It's only for a couple of days. Come with me. Let me take you out to my favorite restaurants, show you the places that are special to me like this place is to you."

Ally looked again at Seth. He seemed to hold the world in his hands. So strong and capable. It had been years since she'd taken any time off. Doubt and worry had plagued her ever since her father had gotten sick and died and the ranch had gone into foreclosure. Having a few days to cast her worries aside sounded almost too good to be true. If she had any sense at all, she would just thank Seth and accept his generous offer without questioning if there was an ulterior motive. Seth was not Wayne. And although it was hard to let go of the grip of caution she'd always carried, she wanted to trust Seth.

"Okay. I'll go," she told him. "Thanks for the invitation."

"You're welcome. If you have nothing in particular keeping you here, we'll head out in the morning. My plane is fueled and standing by at the local airport."

He had a plane? Oh, of course he had a plane. Probably more than one.

"Do you like what you do?" It was a question that begged asking. She loved working with the horses, but Seth was on a completely different playing field. If she made a mistake, it might mean a sprained wrist or loss of a week's work. If Seth made a mistake, it could cost millions, and that pain would have to be a good deal worse.

"Yes," he answered. "My businesses are diversified enough that it isn't the same thing week after week. I get to meet new and interesting people, go interesting places. And I'll probably be doing even more traveling once everything is in place and I officially join Masters International as a working partner. I'll have not only my own companies to oversee but new assignments with the family corporation as well."

"It's not going to leave you much downtime."

Seth's intense brown eyes held hers for a moment. "No, it's not."

He'd be here one day, gone the next, with no end in sight. At least he wouldn't have to worry about leaving a family behind. He and Wayne were alike in that way. Always anxious to see what lay around the next bend or just over the far hill. Relying on quick wit and skill to achieve their goals. Risk takers. Full speed ahead.

The thought made her sad.

They climbed back in the saddle and veered east, following the fence line. Over the next rise, they saw where a large tree had fallen, landing on top of the fence. Ally made note of the location and they continued on. Eventually the sun began to set and they turned toward home. The cowboys were waiting on them to return and kindly took the reins. Each horse would receive a good brush down and their nightly feeding. And she and Seth would return to their own rooms. Another day would have passed. Then a new assignment would take Seth away. Tomorrow, it would be Burbank. After that, the world.

The private jet was ready for takeoff when they arrived at the airport at seven the next morning. Ally couldn't believe how luxurious the main cabin was as she took her seat next to Seth and buckled her seat belt. Within a matter of minutes, she was watching the world grow smaller as the plane shot into the cloudy sky. Breakfast was served by a flight attendant, and in under two hours they were circling the airport in Burbank, ready to land.

A limo was waiting to pick them up in front of a small avionics hanger near the private landing strip. Everywhere Ally looked, there were palm trees and flowers. The sky was bright blue, dotted here and there with wispy white clouds. It was as different as you could get from the still brown landscape of home.

Once their luggage had been transferred and they'd settled into the back seat of the limo—which was larger than her cottage on the Triple Bar—they were off, turning onto a busy road with more palm trees, flowers and blooming hedges edging the highway.

"It's beautiful here," she said, staring out her window. Before Seth could answer, his cell began to ring. He spent the rest of the trip in conversation with one person or another. Eventually the limo pulled up under a large portico, and the driver walked around the car and opened the door. Ally stood up and waited for Seth. He ended his call and accompanied her past the building's security and into a waiting elevator. At the top floor, a soft ding announced they had arrived, and the doors silently swooshed open. They stepped out into a foyer decorated with a mixture of potted plants and ferns.

"Good morning, Mr. Masters," said a uniformed servant. "Welcome home."

"Good morning, Brewster." Turning to Ally, he added, "this is my wife, Ally."

"Of course." Brewster smiled.

With fluid precision, the houseman opened another door and stepped aside to let Ally and Seth enter. It was a world she'd only seen in magazine articles about the wealthiest people in the world. The main living area was open, the room as big as her entire barn, with a view of the Pacific Ocean framed by floor-to-ceiling glass panels.

"Put Mrs. Masters's luggage in my suite," Seth instructed, watching Ally for a reaction. "Ally, I have to go downtown for a short meeting. Make yourself at home. The kitchen is through there. If you don't find what you want, ask Brewster. Order anything you want. Feel free to wander. I'll be back as soon as I can. Promise."

He stepped up to her and slowly pressed his lips to hers. "I'm sorry to drop you off and leave. I'll make it up to you tomorrow."

"I'll be fine. Don't hurry on my account."

He kissed her once again, this time with more passion. Too soon he broke it off.

"Derrick?" he called out.

"I'm here, Seth," a tall, imposing man replied as he stepped into the room.

"Derrick, I'd like you to meet my wife, Ally. Ally, this is my head of security, Derrick Johnson. He'll accompany you wherever you want to go. The car is available if you'd like to see the local sights or do some shopping. The beach is just a few steps from here. Just tell Derrick and he will make sure to set up anything you need."

"Oh, well… I'll be fine here until you get back…" she said and swallowed hard. "Sweetheart," she added, not knowing how to address Seth in front of other people. It seemed to tickle Seth. With one last kiss, he walked out the door, closing it behind him.

Derrick handed her a cell. "This is a phone with a pager. Just push the red button and I'll be here as quickly as possible."

"Okay, and please, call me Ally."

"Let me know if you need anything, Ally." And with a polite nod he disappeared into the foyer.

Holy crap. She couldn't get her head around this. She walked to the far side of the room and opened the sliding glass doors to the large balcony. The ocean was a blend of dark blues and turquoise. A few beachcombers walked along the edge of the incoming waves. Colorful umbrellas dotted the sand as far as she could see. It was as different from the pasturelands of Texas as one could get. Still, as beautiful as it was, a longing for home surged through her.

Seth was back by seven o'clock that evening and seemed happy to see her. She was definitely glad to see him. He was her link to home and despite her denial she was ready to head back. She met him at the door with a hug, which seemed to surprise them both.

"What did you do with your day?" he asked, removing his tie and jacket.

"I sunbathed out on your balcony and watched the ocean. It was nice."

"Good. You need some downtime."

"Well, I sure got some today. I almost fell asleep," she grinned at him.

Seth smiled back. "Ally, the good folks who are involved in the research center want to have a gathering tomorrow night at one of the local hotels. Nothing big, just cocktails and hors d'oeuvres. I really want you to go and meet the people. I've arranged for Karen to take you shopping tomorrow while I'm at the office. I thought you might like a new dress for the occasion. She knows the stores and said she would be delighted."

"That's very nice but I don't need to go shopping." She didn't know what to say. She didn't have the money for an expensive dress she would only wear once. Panic began to work its way up her spine.

Seth must have noticed her reaction. He came over to her and cupped her face in his hands.

"Ally, if it's about money, please don't worry about it. I want to do this. I want you at the party. I want to introduce you to everyone there. I don't care if you wear jeans, but I thought you would feel more comfortable wearing a cocktail dress. That's usually what the other ladies wear to these things."

She took a step back and his hands fell to his sides. "Introduce me as what? An old friend from Texas? A casual acquaintance? An associate? You surely can't introduce me as your wife."

"Why not? That's what you are."

"That's ridiculous."

Seth bit on his lower lip, then continued. "Ally, it would mean a lot to me if you would attend…as my wife. No one has to know our marriage is temporary or the reason for it. I can always explain that it didn't work out at the end of the three months."

Hearing him say those words made her sad. It shouldn't have, but it did. Seth approached her again, this time lowering his lips to hers.

"You are a very beautiful woman," he murmured against her lips. "Go shopping with Karen. You'll like her. Have a good time. See some of the sights that I won't have time to show you. Buy a dress. Buy ten."

"Attending a special event was not part of our bargain."

"It's part of being my wife. We have to keep up appearances here as well as in Texas. Because of the center, there will be reporters asking questions and taking pictures. I guess you should prepare yourself for that, too."

"But—"

"I want to kiss you." He saw her eyes fall to his lips and he couldn't stop from placing his mouth against hers.

It started as an innocent kiss but immediately the tenderness and warmth turned it into something more. Seth raised his head and looked at her expression. Her eyes were closed, her face upturned toward his. He kissed her again, and this time she couldn't help but respond. Feeling that response, Seth immediately deepened the kiss. She felt his arms go around her as his lips moved to her ear then down her neck. "Or if you don't want to go shopping, I can think of something else a husband and wife could do."

He raised his head and watched her as confusion filled her. At times like this it was as though Seth was treating her like a real wife, like theirs was a real marriage. She didn't know what to make of it. Or how to respond.

"All right. I'll go. But your bank account will be sorry, and I make no promises to repay you."

He laughed. "None needed. What shall we do for dinner?"

Nine

"Do you like Italian food? Or seafood? What's your favorite?"

"I rarely get great seafood."

"Okay." Seth grinned. "There's a new seafood restaurant in Malibu I have yet to try. It's getting rave reviews. Does that sound like something you might like?"

"Sure," she said, looking down at her jeans and boots. "Can I have a minute to change?"

"It's casual." Seth indicated his own attire. "But, of course, take all the time you need."

She ventured down the hall where she'd seen Brewster take their luggage earlier. At the end were double doors to what must be the master suite. When she stepped inside, her jaw dropped. The high ceilings and painted-linen walls gave the room an airy, spacious feeling. Three arches led out to another terrace that provided exquisite views of the sea. And she couldn't help but notice the bed, fit for the master. With its brown, blue and off-white bedding, it was masculine yet very luxurious.

Ally roamed through the massive expanse until she came to another set of double doors. They opened to a walk-in closet filled with suits and shirts and casual clothes. In a smaller section to the right, someone had hung the dresses and blouses she'd brought with her. She stepped forward and selected a navy blue dress and matching sandals.

Through still another door was the powder room and bathroom with floor-to-ceiling mirrors and a hot tub that would easily hold six. Across the room a rain-forest shower with ferns and an assortment of foliage tempted her. But the shower would have to wait. The small bit of makeup she'd brought was laid out by the sink along with her hairbrush and other toiletries. She quickly brushed her teeth, freshened her mascara and lipstick, and declared herself ready to go.

Soon they were on their way to the Sand and Sea. The restaurant was repurposed from an old distillery perched on the edge of a cliff that overlooked a lighthouse and the ocean below. Seagulls flew overhead, occasionally dipping low toward the water. The scents of salt water and cedar filled the air around them.

A tall man with a ready grin pushed open the rustic door and welcomed Ally and Seth. "Mr. and Mrs. Masters, your table is ready," he said and led the way across the room to a table by the window looking out on the water. The soft illumination of a single candle added an enticing glow to the darkness around them.

"How does he know who we are?" she whispered to Seth.

"Does it really matter? He might have seen my face

before, and I told him our name when I made the reservations."

"You mean he's seen you on the news or in the papers, don't you?" To be recognized in public like that must mean Seth had quite a high profile.

"Come on, Ally. I've heard the lobster here is truly delicious."

"I don't care for lobster," she snapped.

Seth gave her that grin that would no doubt melt any female heart. But not hers. She felt slammed into this unreal world, off balance and totally unprepared for what might come next. When Seth had asked her to accompany him to California, she'd thought...well, she *hadn't* thought it would be like this, and she was not prepared for such luxury, such opulence. She didn't like feeling off-kilter, and to make it worse, Seth knew it and was laughing at her although he tried to hide it.

"So, how did your meeting go?" Ally asked after they had placed their orders.

"Good." He smiled. "Groundbreaking is set for early June. How was your afternoon?"

"Okay. I found a spot out on your balcony and watched the boats and the people. I especially loved the surfers. What must it be like to have your back door open out onto the ocean? Do you go jogging in the mornings?"

"Actually, I did for a while. Then the business started to really grow and there was less time every day. Then I was spending fewer days here in the States, which made it even harder."

"You really should make time for jogging again. The mornings are the best. You can lose yourself. Clear your head and make plans for the coming day."

"Is that what you do?" He draped his linen napkin over his lap.

"When I go riding? Yes. I usually take one of the horses on a brisk ride just as the sun is coming up. They seem to like it as well."

"So that's what you were doing the day we...met."

"Yep." She picked up her glass of ice water. "And you cratered my whole day."

Seth reared back and gave a husky laugh. "Now I understand why you were so upset."

"Well, yeah. Almost being run down."

"Seth!" A woman's voice came from behind her. "I thought that was you!"

As the woman approached their table, Ally looked into her laughing blue eyes. She was a tall brunette, model thin, who made no effort to disguise she was enamored with Seth.

"Gayle." Seth acknowledged her and stood from his seat.

She stepped into his arms and kissed him on the cheek then looked up into his eyes as if expecting him to do or say something more. *Hello? Don't mind me*, Ally thought.

While Ally knew she had no right to be jealous, she couldn't stop the sensations of anger and resentment that began gnawing at her stomach. Before she could take another breath, Seth set the woman away from him.

"I want you to meet my wife."

The woman's head shot around, and she looked at Ally in surprise.

"Ally, this is Gayle Honeycutt. Her father and I have done a lot of business together. Gayle, my wife, Ally."

"You're married?" the woman gasped. She looked as though she'd just been slapped. But she gathered her wits quickly and produced a smile that would challenge anyone who would accuse her of not being happy for the new couple.

"Congratulations," she breathed. "Oh my gosh. You didn't let us know you were getting married." She turned toward Ally. "Are you from this area?"

"Texas."

"Texas? Really. Well, he certainly kept you hidden."

"Hidden from what?" Ally managed to give the woman a blank stare.

"All the ladies whose hearts will now be broken." She eyed Ally with suspicion. "I would love to know how you reeled this one in. We've been trying for years."

"Gayle." There was a warning in Seth's tone.

That seemed to bring her polite facade back up. "I'm just saying. Well, nice meeting you, Ally, and good luck. Seth, take care."

"You too."

She disappeared as quickly as she'd appeared, into the darkness of the low-lit restaurant.

"Sorry about that." Seth returned to his seat.

"Oh, no. No apology needed. This is your hometown, and it would surprise me more if you didn't have women clamoring over you. I'm just sorry you had to share our secret."

"You mean our marriage?"

"Yeah. It's going to cause a rift in your social life when you come back after the three months are over."

"Don't worry about it." He flexed his jaw as if he were agitated.

The appetizers were served, and for a while the conversation stilled, but it wasn't an uncomfortable silence. The shrimp cocktail was delicious, as were the salad and homemade bread. The wine he'd ordered tasted incredible with the food. Ally forgot her nervousness and let herself enjoy the dinner. She had just laid down her fork after a delicious main course when the waitress came back to check and make sure everything had been okay. When dessert was offered, she turned it down. She couldn't hold another bite. She and Seth ordered coffee to finish out the meal.

"This was delicious. Thank you, Seth."

"My pleasure. I enjoyed it as well. We'll have to come back again sometime."

Ally smiled. Seth might come back, but it wouldn't be with her. In two days they were due to return home. Ally was ready. This break in her daily routine was nice, but her place was in Texas. It was where she fit. What she knew.

"Seth Masters, you sneaky thing!" Another woman approached the table. Seth muttered something foul and politely stood up.

"Rachael," he said.

"I just ran into Gayle Honeycutt…this is your wife?"

"Ah, yes. This is Ally. Ally, meet Rachael Larson."

"Nice to meet you."

"I can't believe you're married," this new woman said, turning back to Seth. "You never let on you were seeing someone seriously."

"Now you know," Seth told her and returned to his seat.

"I guess so." She eyed Ally then returned her gaze to Seth. "Well, good luck to you both."

"Thanks, Rachael."

He looked at Ally. "Are you ready to go?"

"Yes."

Without another word, he stood from the table and reached for her hand to help her up. They headed for the door.

Seth couldn't believe his luck. Two women he'd once dated showing up at his table within an hour of each other was unbelievable. He could only imagine the impact it had on Ally. But then again, why should it? They weren't in love. They had not married under normal circumstances, so why should he worry about the effect this had on her? He helped her into the car and walked to the other side and got in.

"I'm really sorry about that, Ally."

"About what?"

"Gayle and Rachael showing up like that."

She shrugged. "It doesn't matter to me. Why should it? We're not really married, plus I never assumed you'd been a monk."

"Good."

Ally turned her head and looked at him, one eyebrow going up.

"I mean it's good you weren't bothered by them showing up."

"Not at all. So, we leave the day after tomorrow?"

"Two more days. Think you can stand it?"

"It'll be good to be home again."

Seth was still grimacing as they walked through the door to his condo. He'd asked Ally to accompany him to California to show her a bit of his world. But that didn't mean she'd sleep with him in his bed. She'd no doubt have major objections to sleeping in his suite. With him. And he couldn't blame her. While he was majorly attracted to Ally, he sensed her pulling away from him.

"Would you care to take a late-night stroll on the beach?" he asked as they crossed the threshold. "It's a full moon, and usually on nights like this there's plenty of light."

She stood still, contemplating her answer. "I'd like that."

Moments later they were standing at the condo's private entrance to the beach. Ally slipped off her shoes. Seth did the same.

"It's been a long time since I did this, visited the ocean. Especially at night. My work has become increasingly hectic. When I'm home, I rarely notice the ocean anymore. Even the view."

"That's too bad. You need to find some time to enjoy this. Especially living seaside. You must love the beach to want to live here."

"Yeah, you're right," he answered as they stepped out onto the sand. It felt both flour-soft and crisp at the same time. Somewhere in the night, the seagulls called to one another away from the sound of the waves rolling onto the shore. The moon cast its light down over the water, highlighting the spray of each wave. A soft breeze filled the air.

"It's beautiful," Ally commented. "I can smell the sea."

He watched as she ran to the edge of the water and laughed as the waves rolled over her bare feet. "It's warm! Come on, Seth. Be daring." She laughed and held out her hand to him.

He approached her and took her hand. Together they began to stroll down the beach.

"We have beaches in Texas, but the sand isn't this soft. I used to go with some friends back when I was in school. I loved the ocean," Ally said.

"We have that in common. Growing up I used to walk along the shore and look for things the tide had brought up. I had a whole treasure trove of driftwood and dried starfish. My mother finally threw up her hands at me bringing so much trash, as she called it, into the house. But I thought it was special."

"Do you still have your collection?"

"Nah. After she died I sold the house, and my treasures had to go."

"That's too bad. I would have liked to see some pieces."

He'd never told anyone about his love of beachcombing. People would probably laugh it off as a childhood phase. It suddenly hit him that he hadn't hesitated in telling Ally. Somehow he knew she would understand.

"What did you like doing as a kid? Any childhood fascinations?"

"Antiquing. The land on the ranch is riddled with artifacts from both the Native American culture and the Civil War era. I once found a set of eyeglasses and a small metal powder flask used by a soldier. I've found clay pots and arrowheads and a piece of jewelry. I still have most of my finds, but for me, the fun was in the looking."

Seth grinned to himself. "Definitely."

Ally stopped and bent down, retrieving something from the sand.

"What did you find?"

"Just a piece of shell. I would think it would be fascinating to walk along this beach during the daytime."

"It is. Especially early in the morning when the tide is going out. You can find lots of shells and all sorts of stuff. We will have to make time to do just that the next trip in. This is a private stretch of beach, so not a lot of people get to the treasures."

Ally was quiet for a long time. As they continued their walk, he had to wonder what she was thinking.

"What's the matter, Ally?"

"Not a thing. Just that this has been a great mini vacation. I haven't once worried about the horses or break-ins or anything that might be going on at the ranch. I owe you a huge amount of gratitude for taking me away from all the worries for a while."

"Not a problem. We will have to do it again."

"You know that isn't going to happen. You have your life and I have mine. Even if you didn't mind carrying around the extra baggage, I have responsibilities. Anyway, by the time you need to return to California, our time together will probably be over."

"It doesn't have to be," he said, stopping in his tracks, pulling her to a halt.

"Yes, it does."

"Why? Tell me why."

He didn't wait for her answer. He pulled her into his arms and found her lips with his. She was soft and welcoming, her scent standing out as pure, luscious desire against the aroma of the sea. He heard her moan, and his desire doubled. He pulled her body firmly against his, wanting to show her what she did to him. Her arms climbed up and over his shoulders, and she ran her fingers through the short hair at his nape. She was so responsive, so sensual, he knew the possibility existed that this would get out of hand fast and he would take her right here on the beach.

Pulling back, he cupped her face with his hand while bestowing kisses on her cheek and ear.

"I want you," he said. "There's something between us. I know you can feel it, too. Let's go back to the condo."

She studied his face in the moonlight. Finally she nodded in agreement, and his excitement surged. He had to kiss her one more time. It started in gentleness like the soothing waves that crept up on the shore: calming, relaxing, providing a glimpse of what deeper waters held in store. But the underlying power of a storm that pulled an ocean to the brink of fury settled between them, and he knew there was only one way to silence the turbulence.

He released her face and took her hand and began the trek back to his penthouse. The warm waves rolled over their feet but he hardly noticed; he felt like the air had been torn from his lungs. All he knew was Ally. All he wanted was Ally. It wasn't supposed to be like this. He never intended their marriage to be consummated. But there was something about her he hadn't known with any other woman. There was no comparison. There was no right or wrong. There were no second guesses. He would have her.

Ten

He pulled her into his arms again as soon as the elevator doors closed. She was hot and trembling and oh so decadent. He pushed her into the corner, lost in the moment, his mind leaving his body to be replaced by pure animal instinct.

The doors opened, and they were inside his condo. Her shoes fell to the floor as he swung her up and into his arms and walked purposefully toward the master bedroom. There, next to the bed, he set her on her feet and began taking off her dress.

Again his lips found hers in the inky blackness of the night. He knew the passion that lay between them was only a breath away. She could deny it all she wanted, but he could taste it, feel it. Smell the arousal on her skin. She wanted him as much as he wanted her. He couldn't promise her forever. He couldn't promise anyone that. But he could give her now.

For long moments she kissed him with raw, honest

emotion, giving back each kiss, each stroke of the tongue. Her hands moved to his chest, and he wanted her touch on his skin. Ripping open his shirt, he placed her hands against him. Cupping her hips he pulled her to him, pressing his erection against her belly. He felt her shudder. He pushed her hair back from her face and kissed her jaw and neck and nuzzled her ear before moving to the other side. He heard her moan and felt her hands go around his back, pulling him closer.

Ally felt as though she was in a dream. She knew what was coming. It both excited and terrified her. She didn't want to have feelings for this man. But he was under her skin, and she knew tonight she wouldn't say no again. She stood watching him silently as he undressed her; the soft blue dress fell silently to the floor, followed by her bra. His mouth formed a thin, tight line as he concentrated on what he was doing. She reached out to his belt, unhooking it, then found the button on his jeans.

"Let me help you, sweetheart." His voice was raspy, deep. Her heart beat a fast rhythm in her chest as he quickly unzipped his jeans.

Then he again picked her up, laid her softly on the bed and followed her down. She had never made love with a man she had known less than three weeks, but that thought didn't linger. Seth had shown up in her life and turned her world upside down. He wasn't like any other man she had ever known or would ever know.

She cupped his face in her hands, feeling the texture of his five o'clock shadow. Her thumb played against his full lips, and she felt the grooves on either side of his mouth. The world grew more intense. He smelled like the robust cologne he wore mixed with his own unique manly scent. His body was hot, aroused. It served to bring her own body to a highly awakened state. With gentle kisses he sent adrenaline zipping down her spine. He nibbled at her neck, and she threw back her head to allow him more access. His hands played with and molded her breasts, then his lips trailed down and he licked in circles around each nipple. She moaned with need.

"What is it, Ally?" he whispered in a deep, masculine voice. "What do you need?"

"Please," she whispered.

"This?" he asked playfully, running his tongue over her pink nubs.

"Yes," she said and arched her back.

"Or how about this?" he murmured, taking one bud between his lips and sucking gently.

She was on fire. She strove to breathe as she clutched the hair at his nape.

"I need to be inside you," he said, taking her other nipple in his mouth and giving it the same treatment. "Are you ready for me?"

She felt him reach down between their bodies and test the wetness between her legs. Two fingers probed the opening then pushed gently inside. Her body naturally squeezed, increasing the need she had for him as her legs spread wide. He pushed her gently back on the bed, removing her bikini panties as he hovered over her, sliding them down her long legs.

He straddled her on the bed, one leg on either side, holding himself above her with his arms. She felt his erection at the entrance to her womb. Raising her knees, she moved to where she needed him to be. He entered her then, slowly, then withdrew before entering her once again. Deeper this time until she felt his rhythm and sought to hold on and move with him.

"God, Ally," he rasped. Then with one hard push, he

was fully inside. She inhaled deeply, sharply, at the full penetration.

"Easy, sweetheart," he said in her ear. "Just take it slow. God, you feel amazing."

Ally couldn't speak, couldn't think. She was lifted off the bed by pure sensation that wrapped her from her head to her toes. She thought it couldn't get better. Then Seth began to move again. Slowly at first, drawing back and pushing increasingly deeper with every thrust. She found herself on the edge of a great precipice, and only Seth could determine whether she shot to the heavens or rode the wave that seemed to go on forever.

She sensed his forearms on either side of the pillow, his hands under her head as his lips again found hers. His tongue entered her mouth and filled her before withdrawing. He emitted a low growl, biting at her lips and throat. Pushing into her. It was raw sex. Unlike anything she had ever experienced.

He slid his fingers through her hair and held her head as he feasted on her lips, her mouth. Then he was biting her ear, sucking her lobe, his breathing hot and rapid. His hands again cupped her breasts, pinching the swollen buds, and a current shot from her chest to between her legs. He pushed in deep, his hips rotating. The world stood still.

"Come for me, Ally." It was a hot demand, his voice rough and guttural.

Her body complied. Without warning, she was caught up in the whirlwind Seth had created, soaring toward the stars and feeling as though she would never come down. Her breath surged from her lungs, and she didn't care if it ever came back. She felt him push hard over and over, deep into her, before calling out her name as he joined her in their shared ecstasy.

Seth fell to one side and hugged her close to his body. Breathing hard, he pressed fevered kisses against her brow, her cheek, her lips.

"Are you okay?" he asked, his voice still low, still winded.

She nodded. "Yes." In fact, she was better than she'd been in a long time. For these few remarkable minutes, the burden she carried dissolved into nothingness. She snuggled into his strong arms and inhaled his arousing scent. She felt safe and protected, and even though her conscious mind knew it was just for the moment, she let herself enjoy the sensation. Sleep overtook her as she settled into his arms.

The next morning Ally stretched and yawned. Drawing in a deep breath, she opened her eyes. Something was off. This was not her room. She sensed warmth next to her, and immediately the events of the previous night flooded her mind. Turning her head, she came face-to-face with Seth's twinkling eyes.

"Good morning," he murmured sleepily. "Sleep well?" He grinned, leaned over and kissed her.

"I did. Too well." She stretched and felt unfamiliar discomfort between her legs.

"Did I hurt you?" he asked, looking deep into her eyes.

She felt a blush run up her neck. "No."

Seth had made love to her again during the night, and as stupid as it was, she hadn't denied him. She knew she was asking for trouble down the line. The day would come when she got used to being with him. And fast on the heels of that would be the day he said goodbye. It was inevitable. He was a globe-trotting executive who had no intention of settling down.

What had she done? She'd made love to Seth Masters,

that's what. And she had never been loved as deeply and as thoroughly as she had last night. She'd been right. Seth Masters was amazing in bed. So much so that she didn't regret one instant. The ecstasy had overwhelmed her so completely it took away any regrets she might have otherwise felt this morning.

But she wouldn't fall in love with him. She absolutely wouldn't. She wouldn't be that foolish. Again. Making love with Seth so far overwhelmed anything she'd felt with Wayne, it wasn't even a contest. Who was this stranger who had dropped into her world and turned it inside out and upside down?

She stretched again, slipped out of the bed and headed to the shower. The soothing spray was exactly what she needed. For a few minutes, she claimed the right to indulge in its heavenly warmth. Eventually, her hands getting pruny, she stepped out of the shower. After drying off, she wrapped a towel around herself and returned to the suite to get dressed.

Seth wasn't there. She supposed he was using another shower in the apartment. She toweled her hair dry and combed it out before getting dressed. When she was done putting on her makeup, she stepped out into the hallway.

"Good morning," Seth said from behind her. She turned around. He was looking way too sexy in a white bathrobe as he strolled into the main room. He walked over to her and lifted her chin with his finger. Bending over, he placed his lips against hers, and Ally felt the sizzle of temptation run throughout her body. "The coffee should be ready, and there are fresh pastries on the counter," he said against her lips. "Make yourself at home while I get dressed."

She grabbed a cup of coffee and a croissant and went outside, finding a seat on the terrace. The morning activity made the beach a different place than it was last night. People were talking and laughing, and there was music playing somewhere in the distance. It wasn't long before Seth joined her, walking just past where she sat to stand at the balcony railing.

He turned to look at her. "I have a conference call today, around ten, and I have to be at my office for that. Karen should be here about the same time to pick you up."

"Then I'd better go get dressed."

Karen Silverton arrived at exactly ten o'clock. A perky blonde, she was not at all what Ally had expected. Welcoming and warm, she introduced herself, and they were off. Karen was a genuinely nice person who gave Ally the lowdown on what to expect at the types of dinner parties and social events Seth attended. Ally didn't bother to tell her this was a one-shot affair.

Over the next couple hours, they went to innumerable shops, and the dresses Ally tried on were elegant and stylish and made her feel like she'd just won the lottery. Whether red or black or gray, each fit her to perfection. She especially liked one of three-toned brown, starting with gold at the neck, with the layers of fabric getting darker as they fell to her knees. It felt elegant and took away any hint someone might have that she was a cowgirl.

They had lunch at a small restaurant in Hollywood. Karen was easy to talk to and commented several times on how much she enjoyed working for Seth.

"He's a real guy," Karen said. "No arrogance, no games. Just straightforward and honest. In the seven years I've known him, he's always maintained that he would never get married. Imagine my surprise when he told me he'd done just that. You are one lucky lady, if you don't mind me saying so. Of course, Seth is lucky, too. I'll bet you made a beautiful bride."

Ally smiled and swallowed hard. Only she and Seth knew there was no bride, no engagement. Just a sham marriage of convenience. She realized she was in over her head with this arrangement. For the first time since accepting Seth's business proposal, she wished she'd said no. She'd imagined a wedding, of course, but then the two of them would pretty much go their separate ways. The very last thing she'd thought would happen was that she'd be sharing a house with him and becoming part of his life. Now she was lying to his administrative assistant. And Seth, the honorable man Karen thought him to be, was lying, too. Somehow Ally felt as if the entire charade was her fault.

"The clothes will be delivered in the morning," Karen explained as they got in the car to head back to the condo. "Saves us carrying all those bags."

Ally felt bad about spending so much money on clothes. At least she would happily wear them. They wouldn't sit idle in her closet. It was the first truthful thing she'd done since marrying Seth and it felt good.

Ally spent the afternoon getting ready for the research center reception. She had chosen to wear a dark violet cocktail dress with tiny sequins sewn into the material. It set off her hair and her slim figure. She looked amazing. Beautiful. She'd had a manicure, and her make-up set off her high cheekbones and the delicate features of her face.

The limo was there on time, and they were off.

When she and Seth walked through the door to the hotel restaurant, all eyes turned to them. Rather, to Ally. Cameras flashed as several partygoers came forward to

greet Seth and introduce themselves to Ally. Her grin
ever at the ready, she shook their hands and returned
their compliments as though she'd been doing it her entire life. She seemed perfectly at ease and was immediately accepted by various people in the group.

"It's certainly nice to meet you, Mr. Smothers. And
is this your beautiful wife?"

"It is. Ally, meet Gretchen," the older man replied, and
his wife stepped forward to shake Ally's hand.

"Your dress is lovely," Mrs. Smothers said. "It goes
so beautifully with your hair."

"Well, thank you. That's very kind of you to say." Her
southern accent stole the show. "And thank you for your
kind contribution to the treatment center."

Seth watched as Ally made her way around the room,
talking to the people, laughing, accepting a drink from
one man, compliments from several. He felt pride as he
watched her work the crowd. He tried to keep up but was
pulled aside by a few attendees who didn't realize this
was supposed to be a celebration, not a business meeting.

Later Seth caught up with her at the punch bowl.

"My feet are killing me," she said through a smile.
"How much longer are we expected to stay?"

"Not much longer. You've handled this beautifully,
by the way."

"The people are nice. It's easy to be nice back. But
you'd better watch Larry Buddress. I thought I was going
to have to kick his leg. He latched on and wouldn't leave
me alone."

"He came on to you?" Seth was horrified.

"No, but he flattered me to no end. Only because I'm
your wife. He's a climber. Wants to get to the top of your
group and figured buttering me up was the way to get it
done faster. I just really hate people like that. Oh. Look

out. The man himself is headed this way. This time he's all yours. I've gotta find a ladies' room. Later."

Seth turned to find Larry approaching them, his hand out.

"Larry, good to see you. Thanks for coming," Seth said.

While the man went on about all the things he could do for the project, Seth saw Ally turn down a hallway and walk out of sight. Just before she turned the corner, he saw her take off her shoes and couldn't help but laugh.

The music started, and he walked over to where Ally had disappeared. Soon she came back down the hallway, still holding her shoes.

"Put your shoes on and dance with me," Seth said, humor lacing his words.

"Ugh."

When she put them on, he took her hand and led her to the dance floor. The small orchestra was playing a slow song, and he pulled her into his arms. It felt good to hold her. She fit his body perfectly, and they swayed to the music, his arms locked around her, pulling her close. Her head lay against his shoulder.

The music changed to another slow tune, and they continued to hold each other as they swayed to the beat. Ally didn't say anything and neither did he. Being close was enough. No one tried to cut in. It was as if they knew she was his and interruptions would not be tolerated.

The evening was winding down. When the music ended, Seth led Ally back through the crowd, and they began saying their goodbyes. As they made their way toward the door, several men stepped forward and patted Seth on the back, congratulating him on marrying such a fine wife.

Seth felt good about the research center. So many people had come forward pledging their help and making donations. Within two years they should be close to opening. He wouldn't have been this close to making it happen if it weren't for Ally. He wished he could tell everyone about what she had done to help the project along, but of course he couldn't. As far as everyone knew, they were a happily married couple.

Until their three months were over.

"Are you asleep?" he asked, looking at her as she lay back against the leather seat of the limo, her eyes closed.

"No. Just thinking back over the party. The people were so nice. Are they all going to contribute to your project?"

"Most already have, and others have made pledges."

"I'm so happy for you. Your dream is going to come true."

"Yep. Thanks to you."

"I've done very little. You're the one who made it happen."

"On the contrary, the building itself will cost several million dollars. The proceeds from my father's will are going to cover most of that. There would be no inheritance were it not for you."

"You're sweet to say that."

"I imagine you're ready to get back to the ranch."

"What time will we leave tomorrow?"

"I have another meeting in the morning. I should be back by noon then we'll go. You can sleep in."

"It's been great, Seth. The entire trip. You live in a very beautiful part of the world."

He smiled. "So do you." And he meant it. He hoped she would return here someday, but there was no use inviting her to come back. They both knew that probably wouldn't happen. She had her life in Texas, and he had his in LA. Maybe a visit was possible if life didn't get in the way. But he was about to start his role in the family business in addition to maintaining his own companies and working on the research center. There was no use kidding himself.

When this was over, it was over.

Eleven

Ally didn't want to leave LA. For perhaps the first time in her life, she didn't miss the ranch. Being here with Seth had been a wonderful experience. Last night had been so much more than she'd ever dreamed. Dancing in his strong arms, feeling his body sway to the music, alternately pushing against her then stepping away. By the time they'd left the party, she was so hot she'd practically attacked him as soon as they made it through the door of his condo. Then they'd fallen into each other's arms and the evening had exploded into pure ecstasy.

She'd better lock it away in her memory book, because it wouldn't happen again. It couldn't.

Now it was time to go home. Seth was back from his meeting by one o'clock, and they were on their way back to Texas. The flight was quick by comparison to their trip out to California, when she'd been on pins and needles. Seth hadn't mentioned anything last night to indicate any change in his feelings, but he looked at her in a different way—a twinkle in his eyes and a look of possession on his face. Like she was his.

It wasn't true. It never would be. But just for the moment, she let herself believe it was. Just for the moment, they were husband and wife and the life they led was real. A warm feeling began to grow as she remembered all he'd done for her. He didn't have to. He'd gone over and above, and she'd begun to see him as someone special. The chemistry between them came alive whenever she was with him, and now it was strengthened by the love that had started growing in her heart.

She shook her head to remember none of it was true. None of it was real. She could savor being in Seth's arms for now. But when the plane touched down, all fantasies were off.

Ally had been quiet this morning, and Seth didn't try to encourage her to speak, deciding to let her work through it in her own way. He wished, however, he knew what she was thinking. Had he taken advantage of her? She'd given no indication she regretted last night. So all he could do was assume it had been as incredible for her as it had for him.

The small town of Calico Springs came into view as the plane circled for final landing. Seth looked over at Ally, surprised to find her dozing lightly. He couldn't resist leaning over and placing a kiss on her succulent lips.

"Mmm," she murmured, opening her eyes.

"We're here. Time to wake up."

She blinked as though recalling where she was. "Okay." She smiled up at him, and his body surged with want. God, she was a beauty. Her crystal-green eyes sparkled, while her full lips parted in a smile, showing perfect white teeth. Framing her delicate features was that dark red hair laced with strands of burnished gold from the sun. Her small turned-up nose completed the effect.

He looked forward to being at the ranch once again. Enjoying some alone time with Ally. First thing on his to-do list was to find a horse of his own. He'd call Chance and see if they could come out and look at any he had for sale. Then they could go exploring and share a day.

"Did you ever hear anything from your security team about the break-in?" Ally asked, sitting up in her seat and straightening her clothes.

"Nothing. All was quiet while we were away."

"Good. I'd hoped they would catch him, but quiet is good, too."

"If the person thought the house was empty, he no doubt had quite the surprise. It might take him a while to get up the nerve to try again. But we're ready for him."

"Good."

"Ally, how about I call Chance and see if they have any horses for sale?"

"Great idea."

"Or maybe we could borrow a couple of their horses and make a day of it on my family's ranch?"

"I would like that. I've heard it has some of the greatest views of anywhere around. And you can ride for days."

"I'll call Chance tomorrow morning."

Once they landed, they made the trip from the airport to the ranch in silence. Entering the house, Seth noted it felt as though he was returning home. In the few weeks he'd lived here, he had come to regard it as home away from home. Bryan from his security detail met them at the door.

While Seth stopped to talk with Bryan, Ally continued up the stairs to her room. He hoped her interludes of silence weren't indicative of something wrong.

It was good to be home again. The days spent in California had been good, especially the time spent with Seth, but home was nice, too.

As Ally stepped inside her bedroom, she noted the room felt out of sync. Everything was the same but felt different. She set her luggage on the bed and sat down next to it.

What would happen now that they were back? Recent events had changed everything. Could they return to the way things were? She felt a kind of panic at the thought. It would be no use pretending that they hadn't made love. But how did they go forward from here? She was trying hard to keep barriers in place that would prevent her from falling in love with Seth, and he probably had barriers equally strong that kept him free and able to live his single lifestyle, unburdened by any relationship that would tie him down. Where did he see their immediate future? She knew he was as determined to maintain his freedom long-term as she was to maintain hers.

She never should have made love to Seth. But she had, and while she didn't regret it, she was in the dark about where it put them going forward. Did she talk to him about it? Or just keep quiet and play it by ear?

That seemed to be the best alternative. The only trouble was she wanted to make love to him again. That didn't mean she had to fall in love with him. It didn't mean he would lose his freedom. Did it?

She stood and opened her suitcase. Taking her clothes out of the bag and hanging them in the closet kept her hands busy but couldn't stop her mind from wandering. She was glad he'd gotten his inheritance. She was thrilled she got her ranch. She should just stick to thinking about that and leave the relationship alone. Trouble was, it was easier said than done.

She changed into her jeans and a loose shirt and headed to the barn. It was late, but she wanted to check on the horses. As soon as she stepped inside, the familiar scents of alfalfa, molasses and leather filled her nostrils.

"I had a feeling I would find you here," Seth said from behind her. He put his hands on her shoulders, turning her around to face him. "Is everything all right?"

"Yeah, it appears to be." She looked over at the stalls. The horses had finished their grain and moved on to munching on their hay. They looked contented and happy.

"Good. I have to make some phone calls. It will keep me tied up for a while, in case you wondered where I was."

"Okay. Thanks for letting me know. I guess I'll see you in the morning."

"No. You'll see me later." He gave her a devilish grin before he turned and walked out of the barn.

Ally fiddled with the horses for a while then, realizing she was tired, turned off the lights and walked toward the house. Seth hadn't said anything about their trip to LA. She should have felt relieved, but she didn't. He probably wasn't giving it two thoughts, which only made her yearn for the closeness they'd discovered. Apparently it meant a lot more to her then it did to him.

When she got back to the house, she decided to get ready for bed. The shower felt good. It reminded her of the rain-forest shower at Seth's home. She got into bed and turned off the bedside light. She needed to put this past weekend out of her mind. Stop dwelling on it. The house grew quiet, and she finally drifted off into a restless sleep.

In a fog, she felt lips against hers, reminding her of Seth's kisses. As sleep receded, she became aware that it was Seth kissing her. She couldn't stop her moan of welcome. The kiss deepened, and his arms came to rest on both sides of her, cradling her face, playing with the strands of her hair.

"Did you finish your phone calls?" she asked when he raised his head.

"All finished." He nuzzled her neck, making shivers go down her spine.

"That didn't take too long."

"Mmm. It's two o'clock, Ally. You've been asleep for hours."

"Does your work always require so much of your time?"

"Yes. Unfortunately."

And his job would always come first. Yet another reason why she must maintain a friendship and not fall in love with Seth Masters. Even if he cut back on his work, which wasn't likely, there was no future with him. She would not again fall for a handsome man knowing only too well all the future held was another note on her pillow.

"I want to make love to you." His deep, throaty voice threatened to overcome her determination to put some space between them. Her body reacted to his words as if she had no control at all. A rush of pure fire ran down her spine, and she fought to hold still and not press herself against him.

"I… I don't think that's a good idea."

"Oh? Ally—"

She pushed him back and struggled to sit up.

"I let it get out of hand in California. We shouldn't have made love. We've taken our relationship to the next level. This can only end badly."

"It doesn't have to."

"But it always does."

Seth was quiet for a long time. Long enough that Ally began to regret her words. Yet she couldn't take them back. They were true. And if this relationship grew deeper, she would be the one who suffered when he said goodbye.

"Okay," he said finally. "I'll see you tomorrow. Sleep well."

She doubted she'd be able to do that.

He stood from the bed and walked to the door. "Good night, Ally." He looked back at her one more time before closing the door behind him.

What was she doing? Was she crazy? Apparently Seth wanted her as much as she wanted him, and she'd just rejected him. He probably thought she was some kind of tease.

With that unsettling thought, she rolled onto her stomach and bunched the pillow under her head. It was going to be a long night.

By five o'clock she was no closer to a sound sleep than when she'd first lain down. The covers were oppressive, but when she kicked out from under them the room was too cold. Memories of being with Seth filled her mind. The walk on the beach. The restaurant. Kissing him at the water's edge with the sound of ocean all around them. Making love…

Those women.

This wasn't going to work. There would be no more sleep tonight. All her body wanted was to be touched by him again. To feel his big hands roaming over her, squeezing her breasts, to feel the nips on her neck causing electric currents to race over her body.

Frustrated, Ally sat up in the bed. Seth was next door.

Did she dare wake him up? No. That would only increase her need for him. She moaned to herself and punched the pillow. It was, indeed, going to be a long night.

The sun had yet to reach the horizon when Seth dressed and headed downstairs. He paused in the kitchen to make a pot of coffee before going outside to find Bryan. The night had been quiet—too quiet, in more ways than one. But the intruder hadn't come back. It had been two weeks, and there hadn't been any more incidents. He would talk to Ally later when she woke up and see what she thought about sending his security guys back to California. He didn't want to make the decision without her input. Perhaps she still needed the extra assurance right now.

After talking with Bryan, he headed back to the house. The eastern sky was a soft pink as the sun began to crest over the horizon. As he entered the kitchen, he was surprised to find Ally helping herself to the coffee. She looked tired, worn-out, not her usual perky self. He had to wonder if her night had been as restless as his. It couldn't be. At least not for the same reason. He had tossed and turned through the night, wanting her so badly it hurt.

"I thought I would call Chance and see if he had some time today to show us some horses."

She nodded, looking at her coffee instead of his face. "Sounds like a good plan. And yeah, I'm all in. They have some of the best bloodlines in Texas. I'd be curious to see a few myself."

Seth took out his cell and noted the time: seven o'clock. Chance should be up by now. He pushed a button, and the phone began to ring.

"Seth? Hey, what's going on?" his brother answered.

"I'm looking for a horse. Do you have any that might be for sale?"

"For you? You bet. Why don't you come over about ten o'clock? Let me get a few things out of the way and I'll be glad to show you some."

"Sounds like a plan. Thanks, Chance."

"See ya later."

The Masters Ranch was immense. They drove past buildings containing offices, an on-site veterinary clinic and corrals and finally arrived at the main barn. The gabled building had enormous white columns set against green walls and a door large enough for cars and trailers to go inside. Next to the main barn door were smaller glass doors that opened into a lobby. Carpeted in dark green, there were several chairs and sofas. Across one wall was a display cabinet holding a slew of trophies. Down the hall to the right were offices. To the left and straight ahead were stalls, tack rooms and rooms for feed storage.

"This is unbelievable," Ally commented.

"It's big," Seth agreed. "The main structure was built before I was born. Over the years they added on as needed. Go straight down the main aisle and you'll find an indoor riding arena. Come on." He led her to an office several feet from the lobby. Chance was just getting off the phone. He looked up and immediately smiled.

Standing, Chance walked around his formidable desk and came toward them, his hand held out. Dressed in worn jeans and a long-sleeved shirt, he looked like your everyday cowboy.

"Seth, Ally," he said, shaking their hands. "Welcome."

"Thanks for doing this, Chance."

"It's my pleasure. So, what kind of horse are we looking for?"

Seth paused a minute. "I was thinking maybe a quarter horse."

"Good choice. We have quite a few you can choose from. Let's go take a look."

They followed Chance to a section of stalls just down from the indoor arena. Seth noticed Ally had become very quiet, but her eyes were alert and she seemed to be taking in her surroundings. She walked close to Seth, her hair gleaming under the neon lights.

"These are magnificent horses," she said.

"Thanks," Chance replied. "Most of our bloodlines go back quite a few years. My grandfather started breeding our quarter horses before I was born. He took real pride in the results eventually produced. Seth, I want to show you a couple that have been trained to ride but as yet haven't gone through cutting training. These horses can turn on a dime, sometimes when you don't expect them to. You'll find yourself on the ground in a heartbeat."

"I appreciate that," Seth laughed. "My goal is purely pleasure and that means staying in the saddle. I've seen what these highly trained quarter horses can do."

Chance stopped in front of a stall on the left. Inside was a large bay quarter horse with four black socks and a white star on his face. His coat glistened under the fluorescent lighting. A truly magnificent animal. Chance grabbed the halter hanging on the door, quickly put it on the horse and led him outside the stall into the wide hallway.

"This is Cajun's Creed. He's sixteen hands tall and smooth to ride, a quality not always found in quarter horses. He handles real nice. Would you like me to throw a saddle on him?"

"That would be great."

Chance led the horse down the hall, stopping in front of a tack room. Soon Cajun was saddled and ready to go.

"Let's go to the indoor arena. It's kept partially opened this time of year, and it's the closest. Here ya go."

Chance handed Seth the reins, and they walked to the arena.

Seth swung up into the saddle with no problem. The horse held perfectly still until Seth was seated and ready to go. After a few rounds in walk, trot and canter, Seth drew the horse up to the entrance.

"He's nice," Seth said. "Ally, what do you think?"

"Me?" She seemed surprised he would ask her opinion. "He's definitely a keeper."

"I think I agree."

They tried out three more horses and came back to the first one.

"So, Cajun is going to be your choice?" Chance asked as he lifted the saddle from the horse's back and placed it back in the tack room.

"I think he's perfect."

"Well, all right then. He'll be ready to go anytime you want to come and get him."

"Would tomorrow be okay?"

"That's fine. I'm supposed to go to Oklahoma City in the morning, but I'll let the section manager know you're coming to pick him up."

Seth shook his brother's hand, and together the three of them walked toward the front of the building. Seth helped Ally inside the truck and they were off.

"That horse is fantastic, Seth. You're going to have a lot of enjoyment riding him."

"I think so, too."

"We can go and pick him up any time tomorrow."

Seth smiled. "How about we go home and discuss it?"

"Home, huh?"

"Yeah. I want your full attention."

"My full attention? On what?"

"Me." He looked at her and grinned.

Twelve

"I'm thinking of sending the security detail back to California," Seth said over breakfast a few days later. "It's been over three weeks, and nothing else has happened."

"I think that's a good idea," she replied. "Besides, I can handle the intruder myself if he comes back."

Seth's eyes twinkled as he struggled to contain a grin.

"I don't care what you think. I have a perfectly good baseball bat sitting in the closet begging to be swung. Hard," Ally argued.

"You're too feisty for your own good."

"Call it what you want, but I want a chance to confront this guy."

"And what if he has a gun?"

She shrugged. "So do you."

Seth shook his head. "What am I going to do with you, Mrs. Masters?"

She shrugged. She refused to be drawn into that conversation.

"So, how are you and Cajun getting along?"

"Good. He's a great horse. Thanks for letting him stay in your barn."

How could she have said no under the circumstances, even if she'd wanted to? The horse was not a problem and got along with her horses very well. That made it possible for him to go out to pasture with the others rather than being kept in a stall. She believed in pasturing horses whenever possible and felt sorry for any that were stalled for long periods of time.

Seth was a good rider and seemed to love his horse. Where Cajun was going to go when Seth returned to LA, she didn't know. They hadn't talked about it. Seth was welcome to leave him with her, but he might have other ideas.

"I spoke with Chance the other day, and he said we could bring our horses over and trail ride all we wanted. How about this afternoon?"

"I'm getting in two horses to train this weekend, so this afternoon or tomorrow would be great."

"All right then. Let's go after lunch. I have some calls I need to make, but I should be finished by lunchtime."

By one o'clock they'd put one of Ally's horses and Cajun in the trailer and were headed for the Masters compound. Passing through the north gate, they ventured into the largest section of the ranch. They followed an old cow trail that took them over hills, through trees and down into canyons, where they discovered a lake at the bottom.

"Can we stop?" Ally asked. "This is so beautiful."

"Sure. How about over there next to that gray boulder?"

"Perfect."

Stepping down from the saddle, Ally tied her horse to a small pine tree. Seth followed suit. Together they climbed to the summit of the large rock and found a flat spot to sit down. Ally could see the river below them as it cut its way through the flatlands that seemed to go on forever.

"This is great," she said. "I'm amazed at how far you can see."

"As boys we used to trail ride all through this area. At the time, we were about ten or twelve. We didn't notice the picturesque quality, we just wanted to see what was around the next bend or over the far hill. There are a lot of stories about outlaws who camped in this area after robbing a bank or the general store in Calico Springs. We found old trapper cabins, one supposedly used by Jesse James and his gang. Wade once found an old revolver up in the attic of one of the cabins. That was a day I don't think any of us will forget. As boys, we thought we'd struck gold." Seth laughed, and his chuckle sounded deep and sexy.

"For me it was searching for pieces of pottery and spoils from the Civil War," Ally said. "I've found a pair of eyeglasses, a canteen and several tin cups. Knives, old razors used for shaving and once an old rifle that was inside the trunk of a tree. The soldier apparently set it down, leaning against the oak tree, and left it there. Over the years the tree grew around it. I can't imagine why anyone would leave their weapon like that. But it's still there. I didn't have the heart to cut it out."

"That's wild. So…we experienced many of the same things growing up."

"I guess we did. I never pictured you here, in the Texas countryside. You looked like a businessman from the city when we first met."

"I am a businessman from the city," he replied with a laugh.

"Speaking of life in the big city, how are things going with the research center?"

"The blueprints have been finalized. And the official groundbreaking is still on track for the month of June, which is when I return to California."

"I see." And she did. Apparently Seth was counting the days until he could return to LA. She was counting down, too, only not with the excitement he was apparently feeling. She was going to miss him.

She shook her head to clear the tears that welled in her eyes. Seth had gone from being an arrogant stranger to a trusted friend. More than that, a lover and partner, helping her over the bad bumps in her life and standing beside her through the rough times.

"I wish you could be there, Ally."

"You'll have so many things to oversee, you won't want me getting in the way."

"That's not true. You're always welcome. Anytime. We may have started off on the wrong foot, but I'm glad for the opportunity to get to know you."

Seth looked at her with a serious expression. She felt her heart speed up as a delicious heat began to envelop her. Slowly he lowered himself toward her. She closed her eyes as they kissed. His lips were moist and succulent, and she was unable to stop the desire that sprang to life inside her.

She felt him cup her face in his big hands, and she melted a little bit more. He adjusted his position and lay down on his back, pulling her on top of him. Her head rested in his hands, his knee separating her legs.

"I want you, Ally," he whispered against her mouth. One hand moved to cup her breast, and with a squeeze she knew she was lost to this man. She wanted him, right or wrong, here and now.

Her hands came up and over his wide shoulders as she kissed him back, silently giving him the answer he sought. There was no holding out. No foreplay. No teasing. It wasn't necessary, she was so hot for him. There was something about Seth that tore down all barriers. Her body succumbed to his touch, his rugged scent, to the sparkle in his brownish-gold eyes. His deep voice sent chills through her and left her hot and wanting.

He slid off her boots then found the zipper on her jeans and quickly slid it open. "Lift yourself up for me, Ally."

As she did he pulled her jeans and panties down her legs and off her feet. For a second the soft wind touched her, and she felt bare and open. Seth rubbed his hand against her bottom, and she felt her body grow warmer still. She pressed against his hand, and he answered her need, pushing first one finger then two into her. The blood rushed to her head, and she felt encompassed in a soft cocoon.

Seth adjusted his position until she was covering him, legs parted, and slowly he pushed inside. Ally struggled to accept him.

"Take me inside, Ally," he encouraged.

Again his words caused a heady sensation to capture her body. She was drowning in Seth's possession and loving each second. When he was all the way in, Seth sat up and perched Ally on his lap. He filled her, and she succumbed to the mind-blowing sensitivity of her body fused with his. Then Seth began to move. He held her hips as he lifted her up and down, making her shiver with reckless abandon. Far below she could hear the sound of running water as the river surged into the lake, creating a small waterfall.

Ally was lost in sensation. She looked down into Seth's eyes, and her heartbeat doubled. Her breathing became fast as she saw her passion reflected in his eyes. She threw her head back. His motions grew faster and faster. She knew she was on the brink. Suddenly the dam broke, and she felt herself suspended between earth and sky, a thousand lights sparking around her.

As if sensing her climax, Seth wasn't far behind. He gripped her tight as he slammed into her, his hips lifting her off the ground. She heard him call out her name as he too reached his orgasm.

Ally fell forward, sprawling on top of him, momentarily too weak to sit up. He wrapped his arms around her and held her close, kissing her head and cheek. She heard his heart beating in his chest, his deep breathing as he strove to catch his breath. It had never been this way with anyone else. Not even close. But she wouldn't give in to her emotions and end up heartbroken when he went away. Seth had made it clear from the beginning that he was not a family man. He wanted no part of a wife and children, instead choosing to live his life as he always had: as a carefree bachelor. Not pinned down by anything or anyone. And the time until he would return to LA was growing ever shorter.

She'd had a glimpse of his life and knew she could never be a part of it. Not only for the reasons that Seth didn't want her there, but it was so far removed from the life she had always known. It had been especially nice walking along the beach with Seth, but she could tell it was something he rarely did. What would they do together? He had his clique of friends, his work, his routine, and she didn't fit into any of it. If he ever did decide to marry for real, she had no doubt he'd choose a woman like those they'd met at the restaurant in Malibu. And she had a ranch to run. She couldn't do that from LA.

"Ally? You're quiet. Are you okay?"

Summoning all her resolve, she pushed up and smiled at him. She was lucky to have known such a man. "Yeah, I'm good."

"I think we should probably head back. It's getting late."

"Okay."

She rolled onto her back, grabbed her jeans and began to dress.

Seth knew something had changed in Ally. He could feel it in the air. He could sense it in Ally. It wasn't because they'd made love. It went deeper than that. It had started when they were talking about the research center and him returning to LA. It wasn't anything new, nothing he hadn't said before, but this time was different because he was talking about leaving Texas. Maybe permanently. His intention was to come back and visit both his brothers and Ally, but he hadn't reached the age of thirty-five without learning that the best intentions sometimes didn't pan out. He wanted to see her again. Hell, he didn't want to leave her to begin with. No matter how he tried to picture it, he couldn't imagine being in a long-distance relationship with Ally.

He'd been single for many years, not accountable to anyone or anything other than his business. Running his company and trying to get the research center started didn't leave any time for personal relationships. And with taking on the additional responsibilities of Masters International, his free time would be even more limited. Any thought of making this a steady relationship, let alone continuing the marriage, was ridiculous. That's just the way it was, and he'd better accept it. Ally understood. Why couldn't he get it through his head that this was one relationship that just would not work out?

Two of the Masterses' ranch hands were waiting for them when they approached the main barn. With smooth efficiency the horses were unsaddled and loaded into the trailer, and as the sun set beneath the horizon, they were on their way home.

"It was a good day," Ally said. Her delicate features were barely visible in the ambient glow of the dashboard lights.

He reached out and found her hand. "Yes, it was a very good day." He kissed the back of her hand.

"That ranch is everything I've always heard it would be. The farther you go on the land, the more beautiful it is."

"Don't sell your ranch short. The Rockin' H has merits all its own. It has two lakes, hills, and the pine and oak forest is beautiful. Plenty of rich, good pastureland. And, from what I've been told, some of the best horses in the county."

She smiled at him. "Yeah. You're right. But still, there is one particular spot on the Masters compound I will always think of fondly."

"Maybe we will just have to find a special place on the Rockin' H."

"Maybe."

All too soon they were turning into the long driveway of her ranch. Seth pulled around beside the barn, and together they unloaded the horses and put them in their stalls. One of their ranch hands walked in and offered to see that the horses were brushed down and fed. For once Ally didn't argue that she would do it herself. Maybe she was finally understanding and accepting that some things could be done for her. No matter where he went, regardless of what he did in life, he would make sure she always had the help she needed. Her days would soon be filled with training new horses and no telling what else. She needed to be able to delegate some of her responsibilities.

And his life would be in California. At least for the foreseeable future once he left Texas. It was fact, and he'd better stop daydreaming of Ally and get back to reality. She was such a temptation, and he wanted all of her he could have.

Today had been unexpected and amazing. Making love in the great outdoors had been a first for him. He'd never been with a woman who was so responsive, so perfectly in tune with his own needs and feelings. He knew when he left to return home, she would close the door she'd opened to him. He hated the very idea. But, he reminded himself, he never intended to be a family man, never wanted to be married. He liked the freedom his lifestyle allowed. Still, for the first time in his life, he was tempted to give a permanent relationship a try.

Ally went to the barn to check on her brood and found two new horses eating their oats.

"They were delivered this afternoon," said Stony, one of the cowboys. "Didn't know for sure where you wanted them, so we put them in a stall. They seem content."

"You did good," Seth commented, looking at the grin on Ally's face.

"Yes, you did. These guys weren't expected until tomorrow."

"That's what the owner said," Stony explained. "The one on the left is a two-year-old named Denim. The other is three, and they call him Scout. Mr. Deevers said you would know what to do with them."

Ally nodded. She opened the first stall door and approached the horse.

"Good boy," she cooed. She ran her hands over the smooth glistening coat, checked the legs and moved to the head, where she checked the teeth. "He looks good. We'll find out how good in the morning."

She left that stall and approached the other horse. This was the two-year-old that wasn't quite as willing to meet a strange human. Eventually Ally won him over and managed to do a cursory examination. "We're gonna have fun, aren't we, Denim." She patted his shoulder and eased out of the stall.

"Have a good evening, Stony," she said and walked toward the main barn door.

"You too, Mrs. Masters."

Seth was beside her as they returned to the house.

He wanted her again in the worst way, but it was her decision. At the top of the stairs, she said good night and he had no choice but to continue on to his room.

It was midnight, thirty minutes past the last time he'd last checked the clock, when he heard a soft knock at the door. Before he could respond, the door opened and Ally stood in the doorway. Without pausing she padded softly to his bed and leaned over him. She lowered her head to his, her lips soft and warm as she kissed him. Seth responded immediately, his arms around her shoulders as he pulled her down beside him. Then he was kneeling over her, kissing her deeply, wanting her more than he rightfully should.

"Seth, I…"

"Shh," he told her as he put a finger against her moist lips. Then he kissed her again, and passion flared between them. He didn't know what had brought her here, and he didn't care what the future would bring. There was only now: this moment. Whatever this was between them demanded his full attention, and he would gladly give it. He tugged her T-shirt over her shoulders, and when she lay back against the pillow, her full breasts were there for him to love. Scooting down in the bed, he held them in his hands and gently squeezed as he put his mouth and teeth into action. As his tongue played with the rosy tips, first licking then sucking, she arched toward him, letting out a small moan.

He moved up her body to kiss her lips, hunger driving him on. He felt her fingers play in the hair at the back of his head. His body was hard now; he was ready to take her. He wanted to taste her in the worst way. Leaving her lips he kissed his way down her body to the apex of her thighs.

"Spread your legs for me, Ally," he told her in a jagged voice. When she complied he thought he would lose it right then.

He moved to her most sensitive flesh, loving the taste and feel of her. She drew herself up, lifting her hips toward him, and he fed. Her breathing grew fast, and she clutched the back of his head, holding him to her.

"Seth," she moaned, and her body grew still. Then spasms rippled through her as she climaxed, her hips bucking under his mouth.

When her tension began to ease, he moved slowly back to kiss her face. His entire body was tense and hard. If he didn't get release soon, he would explode. Using his hand he positioned his erection against her opening and pushed inside. She raised her legs to take all of him, and he pushed deep.

She was tight, and she moaned as he entered. He stopped, allowing her body to accept him. When he felt her push against him, he began to move.

With others he'd always held back, but with Ally his restraint all but vanished. He felt wild, as though nature itself were consuming him. The rhythm grew more frantic, passion overtaking all other emotions. When she came, Seth couldn't hold out any longer. It went on and on until both of them collapsed back on the bed.

He fell to her side, not wanting to crush her. He held her close to him, their bodies fused in moisture and the need for contact. He left a trail of kisses down her neck, loving the taste of her.

Eventually Ally fell asleep. Seth pulled the covers over her and stared at the shadowy ceiling. She turned onto her left side, and Seth caressed her smooth back and shoulder. He didn't want to give her up. Just the idea of another man making love to her filled him with anger. So what in the hell was he going to do?

Thirteen

Ally slipped out from between the covers, leaving Seth to sleep. Quietly she tiptoed from the room. Grabbing some clean clothes from her room, she headed to the shower. Seth's scent was on her skin, and she didn't want to wash it away. She hadn't wanted to get up but instead lay in the bed nestled next to him. What was wrong with her? She was close to falling in love with him, and she would pay for it one day if she weren't careful. A day not so far away.

She stepped into the shower and let the steam work its magic. Today she had two new horses to train. She would concentrate on them and try to forget last night—and yesterday afternoon—with Seth. Try to forget how caring he was, how he made her feel wanted and protected. She'd been on her own for over a year, and she'd done well enough. If her ranch hadn't been stolen from her, she would have done better. Still, she didn't need a man in her life, and that included Seth Masters. She would make herself believe that.

She dressed quickly and headed to the barn. She wanted to get an early start on the new horses. Placing the halter on the three-year-old, Ally led him out of the stall to the round pen and started him off in a trot. The horse obeyed her voice commands and went around the ring perfectly, not requiring a pull on the lunge line to control him. After a few times around, she pulled him up and turned him in the opposite direction. He went around the ring less willingly, stopping several times to try to turn around. Whoever provided his basic training had apparently let him get away with going the way he wanted. Not happening under Ally's watch. The horse had to learn to take and accept directions, and that included going to both the left and the right on a lounge line.

She became so intent on working with the colt, she didn't see Seth approach.

"It looks like you have him trained already," Seth said from behind her.

She pulled the horse to a halt, giving verbal commands to reinforce the training. "He's already had the basics. That's one step ahead for both of us."

Seth stood next to the pipe railing, a mug of coffee in one hand. He was dressed in well-worn jeans that hugged his trim physique and a pullover sweater. He looked devastatingly handsome. His golden-brown eyes sparkled, and his full lips were tantalizing. A wisp of hair, bleached by the sun, fell over his forehead. He was wearing a gold watch on his left wrist. And on his third finger, his gold wedding band.

"Did you send your security home?"

"Yeah, I did. I can have them back here in a couple of hours if need be."

"I think it will be fine. The break-in was probably a onetime thing. I doubt if the intruder will come back."

"We'll be ready for him if he tries again."

"You've got that right!"

Seth shook his head, a smile on his lips. "You know, one of these days you're going to get yourself in trouble with that attitude."

"Why, Mr. Masters, I don't know what you mean."

"Hey, folks," their ranch hand Thomas Thurman said as he approached the corral.

"Morning, Tom."

"Stony and one of the other hands finished a perimeter check on all the fencing. They found three tree limbs down on the fence that needed to be cut away and a gate on the far side that looks like it's been forced open. We're going to repair that and put new locks on it. It looks like tire prints going through the opening and heading in this direction. None of us has been that route. Thought you'd want to know."

Ally felt Seth stiffen. "We do. Thanks, Tom."

"You betcha. Say, is Pauline in? I'd like to say hello."

Ally smiled. She'd seen Pauline coming from the barn and Thomas visiting in the house on occasion. She'd wondered if something was up between them. "She's right inside. Go ahead."

He tipped his hat and walked to the back door.

"Isn't that sweet?" Ally couldn't help saying.

"Oh, absolutely. Sweet," Seth said, his eyes twinkling. "How much longer are you planning to work your new horses?"

"I'm about finished with this one for the day. Maybe three hours on Denim. Why?"

"I've got to make some calls. I'll probably be tied up for a few hours."

"Go ahead. I'll be perfectly fine."

As Seth winked and walked away, Ally's heart pounded in her chest. There was something about that man that called to her. She didn't need his touch for her to turn to mush inside, just a wink from those incredible brown eyes. And that grin. And his deep voice. With a sigh she turned back to the colt. It was time to keep her mind on the business at hand.

Three hours later Ally returned to the house. Pauline greeted her with a shy smile and a blush.

"Tom said you wouldn't mind him stopping in," she told Ally.

"Not at all. Are you two now a couple?"

"Oh, I don't know if I would say that, but we're going out Friday night." She beamed. "He sure is a handsome dude."

"Yes, he is. Well, I hope you have a good time."

"Thanks, Mrs. Masters. I put on a pot roast for dinner. I hope that's okay with you."

Ally nodded and smiled. "That sounds perfect."

"It should be ready about seven o'clock. I'm also making a batch of my grandmother's corn bread rolls. I hope you and Mr. Masters like them."

"I'm sure we will. And Pauline, call me Ally."

Pauline nodded enthusiastically. "Sure will. Thanks Mrs.—Ally."

Still smiling, Ally headed up stairs to find Seth. He was in his makeshift office, still on the phone. He had a file in front of him, and from what she could tell he was having an argument. He switched lines and talked to someone else then switched back. There would be no lunch for him today.

She returned to the kitchen and grabbed an apple. She wanted to talk with Ben Rucker and figured while she was in town she'd stop by the sheriff's office to see if anything new had surfaced regarding the break-in. Holding the apple between her teeth, she hopped inside the truck and backed out of the parking place.

Ben had someone in his office, but Ally decided to wait when his secretary assured her that he shouldn't be long. But two minutes soon turned into twenty, and Ally decided to come back another time. She'd only wanted to assure him her dispute with the Masters brothers had been resolved. She was now certain they hadn't taken her ranch. Seth might have already spoken to him, which was fine.

Her next stop was the county sheriff's office. The officer who had come out to the ranch was not in, but she was assured they considered the case open even though nothing new had come to light. Thanking them, she next headed for the feed store to order grain for the new horses. The owner had left a list of what they were accustomed to. She never liked to switch their feed immediately. If she didn't like what they'd been given, she would change to another supplement slowly, over several weeks.

"I figured I would find you here eventually," said a voice behind her as she left the feed store.

"Wayne." The very last person she wanted to run into.

"How ya doing, sweetheart?" His smile of greeting had a cruel edge to it.

Ally brushed past him and headed for her truck. She had nothing to say to this man.

"Aw, come on. Don't be mad. I had to leave. I left a note." He was following her.

"I have nothing to say to you. I don't want to see you again. Leave me alone."

"That rich guy is gonna drop you. Then where will you be?"

Ally kept walking, refusing to be drawn into any kind of conversation with the man.

"Dammit, listen to me." He grabbed her arm, and she yanked it away, finally turning around to face him.

"Don't touch me," she spat out.

"Look, I'm sorry I left. I had some important things I needed to see to."

"No, you didn't. You snuck out of the house in the middle of the night. But you know what? It's in the past. Leaving was the best thing you could have done for me. I'm glad you left. Don't bother me again." She continued to walk toward her truck.

"What about what we had? You and me?"

She ignored him and unlocked the truck.

"Did you hear me?"

"Save your bull for someone else. Whatever you think you left behind has long since died out. Now back off and leave me alone."

She got into the truck and tried to slam the door, but Wayne grabbed the handle and refused to let go. "You're going to give me what I want, sweetheart. You can make it easy on yourself, or we can do this the hard way."

Ally turned to him and glared. "There's nothing between us, Wayne. I want nothing from you. And there is nothing I have to give. Release the door or I'll call the police."

"Aw, baby, can't we at least be friends?"

"Stay away from me."

His cold stare should have frightened her but instead served to make her furious. She grabbed her phone from her purse and quickly dialed 911.

"You bitch," he snarled. "You haven't seen the last of me. You can try hiding behind that rich bastard, but if you do, just remember accidents happen. Either way, you're mine." He slammed the door shut and walked off.

"Nine one one, what's your emergency?"

"I'm sorry, I called by mistake," Ally said, locking her doors.

After another five minutes of assuring the operator there was no longer an emergency, she terminated the call and dropped the phone back in her purse. She put the truck in Reverse and backed out of her parking spot. She drove straight home, not bothering to stop back by Ben Rucker's office.

The encounter with Wayne had taken her by surprise and left her more than a little shaken. She tried to shrug it off on her way back to the ranch but hadn't completely stopped shaking from pure rage by the time she pulled into the driveway.

She remembered how Wayne used to love to fight. Had he been serious when he threatened to do harm to Seth? She couldn't let that happen. Seth was a different kind of person. Refined. Intelligent. He fought with words, not his fists. And while Seth might carry a gun, Wayne was a crack shot.

He'd changed since he left over a year ago. His actions and crazy talk reminded her of someone who was afraid of something. She knew behind all that bravado there lurked a coward. What she'd ever seen in that man she would never know.

There was only one person who could tell her what was really going on: her neighbor, Sam Shepherd. He'd been Wayne's friend for the two years Wayne had lived here. Without considering her actions, she backed out of the driveway and turned to the north and the Big Spur Ranch. She would find Sam. He would know what was going on.

She found him moving cattle on horseback. He closed the gate just as Ally drove up. He took off his cowboy hat and wiped his brow on his long-sleeved shirt, giving her a long, hard stare. He muttered something under his breath and walked toward her truck.

"Ally," he greeted her. "Long time no see. What's going on?"

"Wayne. Why is he here?" She got straight to the point. "What does he want?"

For a long moment, she didn't think Sam would say anything. He looked back over his herd like he was about to ignore her questions. But he didn't.

"Wayne's bad news. He's up to no good. You need to stay away from him, Ally. If he shows up at your house, don't answer the door. Call the police if you have to."

"Why?"

Sam spit tobacco off to the side. "Because he got himself into some trouble with the wrong sort, and he's running scared. I heard he's into them for some fifty grand. These are not people who extend payment terms. If he don't pay, they will take him out of the game permanently."

"What does he want with me?"

Again Sam hesitated. "He's looking for two gold and silver belt buckles he won at Nationals. He stashed them somewhere around your place. Figures they're worth a few thousand."

"There are no buckles at my house. I don't know anything about that."

If Wayne thought she had them, he was probably the one who'd broken into the house that night.

"I don't know what to tell you, Ally. If you don't have those buckles, he must think you already found them or you've got money. Or access to it. He was by here last week. Said you'd gotten married to one of the Masters brothers. He figured fifty grand would be nothing to you or your husband. Past that, I couldn't tell you what he's up to. I told him he'd better get ideas like that out of his damn head, but he just laughed and walked out. Haven't seen him since."

Sam spat again, and his eyes narrowed in serious contemplation. "You and your husband need to clear out of here for a while, Ally. Wayne's desperate. He got him a gun, and there's no telling what he'll try. He spent some time in prison for theft and found him a whole new set of friends. It changed him. That's all I know to tell you. You need to leave here for a while as soon as possible. The police have him on their radar but haven't found him yet."

Her first thoughts were of Seth. She had to convince him it was time to leave. Wayne was an arrogant man who could become mean with little coaxing. And he now had an agenda. Who knew when he would come back and try again? She brushed away the tears at the idea of Seth leaving, but he had to be safe. That was all that mattered.

She thanked Sam and turned her truck toward home. She couldn't let Seth be dragged into this situation. No matter how badly she wanted him to stay, she had to make him leave. She knew if any of Wayne's threats got back to Seth, Seth would not back down. She had to prevent that from happening.

Would Seth be hurt when she asked him to leave? Maybe. Or perhaps he wouldn't care. Would he ever come back? He had his brothers here. Maybe he would come back to see them but stay clear of her. Or would he walk in and want to pick up where he'd left off? Would he expect to be forever friends after what they'd shared? Probably not after she asked him to leave.

Her heart was beating hard in her chest. She needed

to bring the police up to date. She turned her truck toward town and the county sheriff's office. When she got there, she explained who she was and what she wanted. The deputy who came to the front counter was aware of the break-in at her ranch and quickly put two and two together. He confirmed there was a warrant out for Wayne's arrest but no one had seen him as yet. Ally was asked what felt like a hundred questions but nothing seemed to help. The deputy finally urged her to return home assuring her they would put extra patrols in her area.

This was a nightmare. It was making an already bad situation into something much, much worse. It was already going to be hard to say goodbye, only now she had to find a way to make Seth leave to try to save his life.

As soon as she walked through the front door, she could hear Seth upstairs talking on the phone. From the sound of his voice, he was not happy with something the person on the other end was saying. Then his voice dropped low and she couldn't understand his words, but clearly he was talking about the research center project.

She went into the kitchen, stopped to grab a soda and made her way out the door to the barn. She'd let her guard down with Seth. She'd fallen in love with him. She knew that now. And now she was about to pay for it. Wayne returning only made the situation worse. Time and events changed a person. Wayne proved that. Once Seth was gone, would they ever see each other again? Probably not. She crossed her fingers that the police would capture Wayne before anyone was hurt. Especially Seth.

And Wayne... She wasn't sure how seriously he took her demands that he leave her alone, but he'd better figure it out. She didn't handle threats well, and Wayne had clearly threatened her this afternoon. Worse, he'd threatened Seth. She had nothing of Wayne's and she wanted nothing from him. She wasn't afraid of him. Maybe she should be, but she wasn't. What could he take? Only one thing made any sense: Seth really had to leave.

Entering the barn, she grabbed a brush and unlocked Denim's stall, closing the gate behind her. She'd forgotten to bring carrots, but he stood still for her as she began to brush his shiny coat. As much as she'd told herself not to fall in love with Seth Masters, she'd done exactly that. He must never know. He would soon be off on his next adventure as if nothing between them had ever happened, and that's the way it had to be. And once again she would be left to pick up the pieces of a broken heart.

Seth found Ally out back working one of the horses in the circle arena. If she saw him, she gave no sign. He approached the fence and stood watching her. Finally she pulled the colt to a stop and gathered the lunge line.

"Pauline left something that smells great on the stove. Are you about ready to eat?"

"No. You go ahead." She didn't turn to face him.

"I'll wait for you. It's only six o'clock on the West Coast. I still have some calls I can make."

She didn't respond as she ran her hand over the silky neck of the horse.

Something was clearly wrong. He didn't have a guess what it could be. He was due to leave in a couple of weeks, but they hadn't talked about it. He wanted to come back and see her every opportunity he got. Maybe that's what she didn't want.

He returned to the house and went straight to his office. He sat down in his desk chair and stared blindly out the window. They needed to talk. Their temporary situation had turned out a lot differently than he'd ever thought it would. He hadn't expected to grow so close to her. Have feelings for her that were a lot more than friendship.

Still, what could he offer her? He didn't believe in marriage—or at least real marriage. He'd come close one time. He'd even proposed, only to discover his fiancée was seeing another man and together they were plotting to get the money he'd worked hard his whole life for. It had been a close call. Too close. And he'd vowed right then never to trust a woman. Never get married. Never have kids, because kids were the ones hurt by it all. He knew that firsthand, too. He'd been raised by a single mother who loved a man who wouldn't marry her. He hadn't seen his father very often growing up. There was no love. There was no affection. There was money if they needed it, but that was all his father ever offered until the day he died.

Not that he believed Ally was like the women he dated back in California. Or like the woman he'd almost married. Ally was as honest as they came. He believed she had every intention of paying him back for the small amount he'd spent on furniture and lumber for the barn. At least she would try, but he wouldn't accept the money, because it was a gift. She had never given any indication she expected any more from him. She understood from the beginning that this was a marriage of convenience, and she knew it was drawing close to the time for him to go.

Suddenly he wasn't hungry. He would wait for her to come back to the house and they would talk. If she was ready for him to leave, he could go immediately, as if business required it. When the time was up, she could file for the divorce and it would be over. He planned to be generous and leave her a healthy trust fund to ensure her future would be good. He was determined she would never want for anything. It was the least he could do.

It was almost ten o'clock when he heard the back door slam. It had to be Ally. He finished his call and hurried down the stairs. She was there, drinking a glass of water.

"Looks like we will need to warm the stew," he said. "The rolls as well."

"You go ahead. I'm not really hungry."

"Ally, what's wrong? You know you can talk to me."

"I don't need to talk to anybody. And nothing is wrong. Good night."

She brushed past him, and he listened to her footsteps as she headed upstairs. *What in the hell is going on?* He released a sigh. He would give her the night to cool off and maybe she would talk with him tomorrow. He hoped it was nothing he'd done. He hoped it was not about him leaving.

Because he had no choice.

Seth awoke the next day to find Ally already gone. Pauline didn't know where she was, just that she'd said she had some errands to run and would be back later. He pulled out his cell and speed-dialed her number. No answer. He hung up without leaving a message, not sure what to say. He poured a mug of coffee and sat down at the kitchen table. This was getting stranger and stranger. First she had seemed angry last night and wouldn't talk to him, and now this morning she was gone, no one knew where, and wouldn't answer her phone.

The house phone rang, and Pauline answered it.

"Mr. Masters," she said. "It's the feed store in town. They're calling for Mrs. Masters."

"I'll take it." Seth stood and walked over to where the phone hung on the wall.

"This is Seth Masters. Ally isn't here right now. Can I help you?"

"Ally was in the store late yesterday," said the shop employee. "She placed an order then left before we could get it to the truck. I need to know what she wanted us to do with it."

"Grain?" Seth asked.

"Yes, sir. Ten bags."

"I'll be there in a few minutes and pick it up. Thanks for calling."

Seth hung up the phone and poured the remains of his coffee in the sink. "I guess you heard, Pauline? I'm going to the feed store. If Ally gets back, tell her to please wait here for me."

Once he got to the store, the grain was loaded in the back of his truck in no time. Ally still hadn't been there. The owner said it was strange the way she left after ordering the feed.

"There was a man standing near the truck. I saw them talking. Then she got in her truck and drove off."

"Do you know who it was?"

"He looked vaguely familiar. If I had to give a name, I would swear it was Wayne Burris, but he's been gone a while now. Ally looked upset. If it was Wayne, I can understand why. He's no good."

Fourteen

Seth got back in his truck. Why would she have been talking to Burris? Did they go somewhere together? Did they arrange to meet someplace? He didn't have a clue where to look. He turned the truck toward the Masters Ranch. Maybe she'd gone over there to talk with Chance about his breeding program. It was a far-fetched idea, but the only one he had.

Ally wasn't there. Chance hadn't seen her since the day Seth had picked his horse. Chance's daughter had been sick for the past week, and he'd been preoccupied with taking care of her.

Seth thanked him and started back toward Ally's ranch. Should he be worried? Could something have happened to her? He recalled the break-in. Surely that had nothing to do with Ally going missing.

He tried once again to call her. Still no answer. He drove around the area hoping to catch a glimpse of her truck. Finally out of options, he headed for the ranch house.

As he pulled up, he immediately spotted her truck. She was standing in the yard. He jumped out of his truck, slamming the door behind him, and rushed over to her with long, angry strides.

"Where in the hell have you been? I've been looking for you all day. Are you okay?"

"I'm fine."

"Want to tell me where you've been?"

"Not really." She shrugged. "Visiting some friends."

"Why didn't you answer your phone?"

"Didn't feel like it."

"Look, Ally, if I've done something to offend you…"

"No. You haven't. I just feel as though I've been wasting the past few weeks and I need to get back to business. People to see. Things to do."

"If this is your way of telling me to leave, just come right out and say it. I'm a big boy. I think I can take it."

"Any time you want to go…just leave. You've only got a few weeks left anyway."

Seth watched her and nodded his head. He'd been right. The impending deadline was looming, and this was obviously her way of getting it over with. Maybe she'd made up with her ex-boyfriend, which didn't sit well at all.

"Fine. I had hoped we would separate on better terms, but okay. If this is what you want, give me a couple of hours and I'll be out of your hair."

Ally chose to remain silent. Finally Seth turned and went upstairs, where he pulled his suitcase from the closet and began packing. She was afraid. He could see it in her eyes. Was his leaving making her this way?

He'd promised her he would come back. And he'd intended to try.

Why worry about it now? She was effectively throwing him out of her home with the least amount of effort. So he would leave. What else could he do?

With a curse, he opened the bedroom door and went back downstairs. He found her in the kitchen, sitting in a chair and gazing out over the pastureland.

"I thought we had something between us," he said quietly. "I thought you shared my feelings. I care for you, Ally."

He thought he saw her shudder, but then she shook her hair back from her face and looked at him like she was already bored with this conversation.

"Ah, but caring doesn't win the big prize, does it? I've realized I don't want to settle for a few romps in the hay. I want it all. Failing that, you might as well leave so I can get on with my life. Frankly, you're holding me back. But don't worry about the marriage thing. I'll still uphold my end of the bargain. Just file for divorce when the appropriate time has passed and I'll agree to whatever."

Her words hit him like a brick in the face. Something was going on. This wasn't like Ally. He stared at her trying to see a glimpse of the Ally he knew. Nothing. This Ally was cold, indifferent, calculating and appeared completely resolute in what she was saying.

He nodded. "Well, you certainly cleared that up. I'll leave tonight." He went back upstairs to resume his packing.

An hour later he was headed for the small municipal airport to board his flight home. There had been no sign of Ally when he walked out the door for the last time. He would have Karen call her to make arrangements for his horse. Maybe Chance would take Cajun for a while until he'd had an opportunity to work this through.

He was gone. Seth Masters, who had come into her life so suddenly, had left just as fast. There had been no goodbye kisses or hugs. How could there be when she'd thrown him out? But he was gone. That was the important thing. He'd gone back to California, where thugs like Wayne couldn't touch him. Seth would be safe, walking on his beach, working with his friends, maybe even dating some woman who was clearly on his social level. He would be safe and happy. That's all that mattered. Still, the pain deep inside wouldn't leave.

She gazed out over the pastureland. She owed him so much. She wouldn't have her ranch were it not for him. He'd given her reason to smile again. She couldn't help but recall those moments she'd spent in his arms. She'd felt loved and protected and so cherished. No doubt he made every woman feel that way. She was nothing special. At least not to Seth, who could have about any woman he wanted. The real kicker was, he didn't want any. At least not on a permanent basis.

She walked over to Seth's horse. Cajun nickered softly. She opened the stall door and approached him. What would become of Cajun? Seth would probably arrange for Chance to pick him up. She smoothed her hand over the horse's shiny coat and put her arms around his neck. Suddenly the tears she'd held back wouldn't be held any longer. She held on to the horse as the sobs racked her body. She loved Seth so much. She'd gone and done what she'd pledged not to do. She'd fallen in love with Seth Masters. This was not like the love she thought she'd had for Wayne. This love was real. It was deep and pure and all-consuming. And she was going to hurt for a very long time.

When her sobs began to subside, she patted Cajun and exited the stall.

The house was quiet when she stepped into the kitchen. She poured a glass of water, wishing it was something stronger. Her mind drifted to Sam and what he had said about Wayne and those two belt buckles.

She looked around the kitchen. They had combed the house and found nothing like that. Her eyes came to rest on the fireplace on the south wall. Ally walked over to it and looked up into the chimney. Nothing to be seen but black soot. When she reached up and touched it, soot began to fall down on the hearth. Could something be hidden in the chimney? It was one place they hadn't looked. She stretched, moving her hand deeper inside the chimney. Suddenly her fingers encountered a piece of fabric. It felt like some kind of bag. Her heart began to race as she nudged it from its resting place. Then it was free and in her hand. She quickly untied the small bag. Inside were two shiny gold and silver buckles. Wayne's. It was Wayne who had broken into the house. And he would be back for them.

If she knew how to reach him, she would call and tell him to come and get them. But no one knew where he was. She didn't have his phone number. Sam. Sam might know. She grabbed her purse and fished out the phone. She was relieved when Sam answered on the first ring.

"Sam, this is Ally. I found Wayne's belt buckles. Do you know how to reach him?"

"No. I don't. I haven't seen him again since we spoke yesterday."

"Well, if you do run into him, tell him I found them and he can come and get them."

"Ally, you don't want him in your house. The man is deranged. Take them to the sheriff's office and let them handle it."

Why didn't she think of that? "Okay."

She thanked Sam and headed for the truck, buckles in tow. She made it to the sheriff's office in record time and asked for Mason Crawley, the deputy sheriff who had come out to the house the night of the break-in. Luckily he was in.

Ally explained the situation, including the recent confrontation with Wayne Burris. The deputy came to the same conclusion that it was possibly Wayne who broke into the house. The deputy took possession of the buckles and advised her to not have any contact with Wayne if at all possible. He also issued a caution to not let the man in the house and to call 911 immediately if he showed up.

Ally left the office feeling somewhat better about the entire situation. But—Wayne was still here in Calico Springs and Seth was gone. How could that be anything but bad? Tears welled in her eyes at the thought that she could have had a few more weeks with Seth were it not for Wayne. But Seth was safe, and that's what mattered the most.

Seth sat in the private aircraft and stared blankly at the clouds that passed below. He couldn't get it out of his head that something wasn't right. It just wasn't Ally's way to come off like a gold digger, like a woman who needed him out of the way so she could find someone else. Someone wealthier. Dammit, he couldn't figure it out, but something had happened. And he had a feeling it wasn't good.

She'd been seen talking to Wayne Burris, someone she professed to hate. Ally was very strong in her convictions, and she wouldn't have been talking to him through any choice of her own. And she wouldn't have gone from making love to Seth, letting her emotions and her love for him show freely, to abruptly telling him to leave the way she had. The entire thing just didn't make any sense.

His cell started to ring, and he fished it out of his pocket. He didn't recognize the number.

"Hello?"

"Mr. Masters?"

"Yes."

"We have a bad connection. I apologize."

He obviously didn't know Seth was at twenty thousand feet in the air.

"This is Deputy Crawley with the Calico Springs County Sheriff's Department. I wanted to give you an update on the break-in. Thanks to your wife, as you probably know, we think our man is Wayne Burris. He was after two gold and silver rodeo belt buckles he'd hidden in the kitchen chimney. Mrs. Masters found them and brought them in this afternoon. She told us Wayne had approached her a couple of times trying to gain admission into the house. We know about the threats on your life. We have a warrant out for his arrest, but no sign of him yet. He's also wanted for grand theft in another county. It's good that you and your wife are leaving town for a few days. We spoke at length to your neighbor Sam Shepherd, and he confirmed Wayne has acquired a gun. Wayne Burris is out of prison on probation, and that's a violation. He's considered armed and dangerous."

"Wait, Deputy Crawley. Ally isn't with me. She's still at the house."

A knot of fear like he'd never experienced before tightened in Seth's gut. Suddenly Ally's actions before he left all made sense. She was trying to get him out of the house if Wayne Burris should come back. For God's sake, she was trying to protect him.

"Mr. Masters, we're in our final approach. Landing estimated in five minutes," the captain said over the intercom.

"Is there anything else, Deputy Crawley?" Seth said into the phone.

"No, sir. But I suggest you get Mrs. Masters to another location as soon as possible. We have every reason to believe Burris will go back to the house. I tried to reach her on her cell, but there was no answer. We have cars patrolling the area. But it's best to get her to a safe location as soon as possible."

Sweat broke out on Seth's brow. He thanked the deputy and terminated the call. Immediately he dialed Ally's number. No answer. He hung up and dialed again. No answer.

Seth unbuckled his seat belt and hurried to the cockpit.

"Gene, as soon as we land, be prepared to leave again. We'll be headed back to Texas as fast as this plane can go. I'm calling my security to meet us. As soon as they're aboard, we take off. Understood?"

"Yes, sir."

Back in his seat, Seth contacted his head of security and made arrangements for Frank and Bryan and one other staff member to meet him at the small regional airport as soon as possible.

He rubbed the back of his neck, just one thought circling over and over in his head.

Please let us make it back to the ranch in time.

Ally finished checking the locks on the windows both upstairs and down. The front and back doors were locked. With one last sigh, she turned off the lights in the kitchen and made her way into the den. Her baseball bat was next to the chair in the back corner. She pulled her phone from her jeans pocket, glancing to make sure it had reception. Just two bars, and the second was flickering. And there were five messages that apparently had not come through earlier due to the poor reception in the area. One from the sheriff's office. Four from Seth. She didn't have time to check them now. Placing the phone on the table next to the chair, she knelt down and waited.

She'd spotted the police cruisers driving up and down the road in front of her house a couple of times. While somewhat reassuring, she knew Wayne, if he came tonight, would sneak in through the back. No one on the road would know anything was happening. She was as ready as she could be. Maybe when she told him that his buckles were with the sheriff and Seth was gone, he would finally give up and leave.

She didn't know for sure how long she sat there. The old pendulum clock ticked by the minutes ever so slowly. Suddenly she heard the knob to the kitchen door jiggle. That was followed by what sounded like kicks to the door. It could only be Wayne.

She picked up the bat and scampered behind the chair just as the kitchen door crashed open. She heard footsteps on the kitchen floor—followed by two voices. One was Wayne's. Someone was yelling at him to get out of the house. Wayne shouted a curse, and seconds later, a gunshot rang out. *Oh my God.* What was happening?

She grabbed her cell and quickly dialed 911.

"Nine-one-one. What is your emergency?"

"This is Ally Masters. Please tell Deputy Crawley that Wayne Burris is here. At my house. He's just broken in, and someone has been shot." Her voice wavered when she said the last sentence. *Please don't let it be Seth.*

"Ally! Where the hell are you?" Wayne shouted out through the stillness.

"He's coming for me," Ally desperately whispered into the phone. "Please hurry!"

She terminated the call, placed the phone on the floor and double-fisted the bat.

"I know you're in the house, darlin'." She could hear him kick over a piece of furniture in the other room.

"I don't want to hurt you, Ally. I just need my buckles and some money."

Ally heard him stop in front of the door to the den.

"Come on out. I won't hurt you."

Slowly she stood up from behind the chair, the bat held at her side.

"I found your belt buckles this afternoon. They are at the sheriff's office. Had you told me what you needed instead of making ugly threats, I would have given them to you."

Wayne cursed. "Never mind the buckles. Cash will do fine."

"I don't have any cash."

"Lady, you're married to one of the wealthiest men in the country. Don't even go there."

She swallowed hard. "Seth is gone. We...we had a fight. He's gone back to California and will file for divorce. I don't even know how to reach him. He said his attorneys will contact me."

"You're lying," he accused as he came into the room. Ally saw the gun in his hand through the ambient lighting of the back porch.

"Have you ever known me to lie?" she said, looking straight into his eyes. They were cold. Calculating.

That seemed to slow him down. She'd always been completely honest with Wayne. He knew that.

"Then you'll have to do. Your soon-to-be ex-husband will get to pay dearly for your safe return or it's on his hands. You're coming with me."

"Where?"

"Don't worry about it. Come on. The cops will be here soon."

"I'm not going anywhere with you. I told you before, leave me alone!"

"Dammit, Ally. You always did have to do things the hard way."

He stuffed his revolver into the back of his pants and came for her. When he bent over to move the chair, Ally brought the bat into play. One hard *thunk* with all her might against the side of his head and he went down hard. He was moaning, and she knew she hadn't knocked him out completely. She had to get out. She quickly stepped around the chair, pulled his gun from out of his pants and ran for the kitchen.

Just as she threw the gun out into the darkness as hard as she could, someone grabbed her. She felt a very strong arm circle her waist and a large hand over her mouth. She cried out and fought for all she was worth.

"Ally. Ally," a voice said in her ear. "It's me, Seth. You're all right."

Breathing hard, she ceased her struggles. He removed his hand from her mouth as three large men hurried past them and into the house, guns drawn. "Seth?"

"It's all right, Ally. You're fine. We're both fine."

In the distance she heard the sound of sirens. She turned into Seth's arms and couldn't get close enough to the man she loved. The tears flowed as he held her. She couldn't stop trembling. His hand cupped the back of her head as he pulled her close.

"You silly woman," he said softly. "Sometime you're

going to explain to me what in the hell you thought you were doing trying to take on somebody like Burris by yourself."

"He…this…it had nothing to do with you. It was my own bad judgment to become involved with him in the first place. I… I thought I could talk to him, make him see he needed to leave us alone and—"

Just then, Wayne Burris stumbled out the back door, in handcuffs, escorted by Seth's security team. The sirens screamed from the front of the house. Doors slammed, and the sheriff's deputies hurried to take control of the prisoner.

"Mrs. Masters, are you all right?" asked Deputy Crawley.

"Yes," she said, as Seth still held her close. "But I heard a shot. I'm afraid one of the ranch hands may have been hurt."

"You two go toward the barn and check to make sure no one was hurt," the deputy told his officers. They soon returned to report that one of the cowboys had been shot in the arm and the ambulance was on the way.

"You both will need to come down and give a statement," he said, "but it can wait until the morning."

"We will be there," Seth answered. "Thanks, Deputy Crawley."

The officer tipped his hat and disappeared inside the house.

"What am I going to do with you?" Seth said against Ally's temple. She turned in his arms.

"Just hold me," she said, and Seth's arms came around her, holding her close.

Fifteen

The police left with Wayne in the back seat of Deputy Crawley's car, throwing out threats to any and all. Then the ambulance with the wounded cowboy took off for the hospital. Throughout all this, Ally still stood with her arms around Seth. Every breath she felt him take was a small miracle. She loved him so much. She still couldn't believe he'd come all the way back here to save her.

"How about we go to a hotel tonight?" Seth asked. "Then, after we give our statements in the morning, we will head to California."

Ally was too emotionally exhausted to argue. But this was her home. Good or bad, it was where she needed to be. The house would need repairs, the cowboys deserved an explanation and she wouldn't leave until all was seen to. But for tonight, a hotel sounded like heaven.

"Let's go." She smiled up at Seth, and together they walked to his truck. His three security personnel would stay at the house in case Wayne had any associates.

When they arrived at the hotel, Seth went inside to secure a room then returned to help Ally out of the truck. The room was just like the first one they had shared before they were married. Once they were settled, Ally headed for the shower, and to her surprise, Seth followed her in.

"Hand me the shampoo," he said, standing behind her. He took the small bottle and began to wash her hair, massaging her scalp, then moving his hands down over her shoulders. Ally bent her head as Seth worked the tight muscles in her neck and shoulders. At some point he poured soap in his hands and began to lather her arms and back then reached around to her breasts. She leaned against him as he massaged lower, between her legs. Shivers shot through her body. She turned around and took the soap from him.

Pouring some in her hand, she began to lather his broad chest and arms. She turned him around and went to work on his back, loving the feel of his muscles as her hands slid over his hot skin. He turned toward her and guided her hands lower, to his erection. He was rock-hard. She rubbed the soap over his silken shaft, loving the feel of him.

Seth pulled her to him under the spray of the shower and rinsed the soap from her hair and body. Ally stepped out, grabbing a towel while Seth finished washing himself off. Then he took her towel and helped her dry off.

Before she could say anything, his mouth came down over hers. He tasted of spice and pure raw male. His hands cupped her face, and the kiss grew from compassionate to intensely compelling. He shifted his body so his bare chest was against her breasts, his erection pushing against her belly. His arms came around her waist. He slid his hands up her rib cage and massaged her breasts before finally giving due attention to the tips with his hot mouth. She couldn't suppress a moan as her nipples hardened under his attention. She ran her arms up over his broad shoulders and raked her fingers through his thick, damp hair.

She tipped back her head, allowing him to push her mouth farther open, giving him full access. They were now in their own private world. She met the intensity of his kiss with passion of her own, her nipples tightening with desire as she arched toward him. Flashes of pure heat coursed through her lower abdomen as she pulled him close.

Seth scooped her into his arms and walked to the bed. With one tug he threw back the covers and placed her gently on the bed, following her down.

"I'm so angry with you," he whispered as his long, muscled leg covered hers. He kissed her neck, taking nips along the way to her breasts. "You did a very stupid thing." He placed his mouth over one breast and gently began to suck. With his hand he cupped her other breast and began to massage her.

"No, I didn't," she responded between kisses. "Removing you from a situation that had nothing to do with you and could have gotten you killed was not a stupid thing to do."

Seth moved so his body was fully on top of her, his erection finding the core of her desire.

"Trying to take on a violent felon single-handed was." His lips again took hers. "You're a wild lady, Ally Masters," he said against her lips. His voice was so deep and sexy.

She didn't want to talk any more. She wanted Seth. Every glorious inch of him. She wanted to love him and rejoice in the knowledge that he was here with her.

Maybe not for much longer, but she wouldn't think about that now.

Then he pushed inside her and the world outside the sphere of magic that surrounded them ceased to exist.

The next morning, once they'd made their statements to the police, it was time to return to Ally's ranch and figure out what their next step would be. As they drove up to the house, they saw three of the ranch hands out front waiting for them to arrive. While Ally went inside to assess the damage from last night, Seth approached the group of men to see if there were any updates on the hand who'd been shot.

"It was just a flesh wound," Tom said. "He was lucky. We found the gun Wayne used in the shooting and turned it over to the police."

"That's great news. I'd wager Wayne Burris is going back to prison for a long time. But I can't apologize enough that you had to become involved with this."

"Heck, no problem here. Had we known what was coming down, we might have been able to help. We're glad you and Mrs. Ally are okay."

"Thanks again, guys." Seth offered his hand to each one. "I'd better get to the house."

He found Ally in the kitchen, muttering over the broken back door. Then she started straightening the chairs Wayne had kicked over. Seth followed her into the den, where he helped her set up the chairs there.

He was still amazed that this tiny woman had taken on someone like Wayne Burris and gotten the better of him.

"The cowboys found the gun out by the barn. I assume you threw it out there?"

"I didn't want him to find it and use it on anyone else. I had the chance to grab it when he was knocked out, so

I took it." She shrugged like it was no big deal. "Seth, all of this was my fault. I am so sorry I got you involved."

"It isn't your fault, Ally. How can you possibly say that?"

"Because it's true. I made the wrong decision to ever let Wayne into my life. Granted, I never intended to get you involved, but nonetheless, I did." She walked back to the kitchen. "This is going to require a new door. I'll call a friend of mine and see if he has time to pick one up at the hardware store." She stared at the opening. "I guess, now that things have settled, you'll be on your way back to California."

Seth didn't move. He didn't want to go back. He wanted to stay right here with Ally but she seemed to be pushing him away again. Was that what she wanted—for him to leave for good this time?

"Ally, I need to know if you want me to leave, like permanently. And I need to know why."

She drew in a deep breath and turned to him with tears in her eyes. "This is my world. Cows and cowboys. Horses, rodeos and people who talk funny. We don't do social events, wear evening gowns, or know the meaning of words like posh. We don't travel in jets or live in penthouses."

"Ally—"

"You would be bored. And embarrassed to present me to your friends. We are from two different cultures that weren't meant to mix. And if someday we had kids, what then? We just wouldn't work."

"I see your point," he said finally. "And I think it's a load of bull. I love you, Ally. I don't know what that means to you but it means a hell of a lot to me. We would work by taking it one step at a time. By fighting for what we want. By showing our determination to be together."

"You don't understand," she cried.

"I understand more than you know. I wish to hell you did." He paused and rubbed his forehead in frustration. "I guess I'd better head to the airport. Are you sure you're going to be okay?"

"I'll be fine. This door is the only thing that needs repair. Plus, I have two new horses in for training with more expected, so I'll stay busy." Her eyes welled with tears, and she quickly turned away.

"Ally, come with me."

"I can't." She brushed the tears from her eyes and faced him. "You have your world and I have mine. We knew from the beginning this marriage or whatever it was wouldn't last. It turned out well for both of us. I really do appreciate getting my ranch back, and I'm enormously happy for you. That research center will save a lot of lives. We both know we live in two different worlds. I'm not a socialite by any means, and while you're pretty good with a horse, you're a city dude. You always will be."

Seth pulled her into his arms and kissed her. He could taste the salt of her tears. Ally would never admit she was wrong about him. Their worlds weren't so different that they couldn't bridge the gap. She might trust him, but she would never tear down that wall. He slowly backed away. Her eyes were closed, her face raised to his. Her refined features had never looked more beautiful. One tear slipped down her cheek. He brushed it away with his thumb.

It was an impossible situation.

"Take care of yourself," he said.

"You too." She forced a smile.

Knowing there was nothing else to say, Seth turned away and walked toward the front door and the truck that waited outside. He pulled out onto the white rock road and turned toward the airport.

Less than a mile down the road, he stopped the truck. Dammit, he didn't want to leave. Specifically, he didn't want to leave Ally. He had been shown what it meant to have a wife that was honest and loyal. Being here these past few months with Ally, and getting to know his brothers and their wives and children, had shown him the truth about caring for someone and knowing they care for you. He was a part of something, a family, for the first time in his life, and he wanted it desperately. His work and all he'd accomplished in the past seemed insignificant in comparison. He'd always been a loner, never spending very much time in the same place, but suddenly, he needed a home and, even more, someone to share it. There was only one person who could make it happen. He had to make her listen. He had to convince her.

He turned the truck around and headed back to the ranch. When he hurried into the house, Ally was nowhere to be found. He raced for the barn. She was there, sitting on a bale of hay, crying.

"Hey, you're going to ruin that hay with all those tears."

Surprised, she took a deep breath and brushed the tears from her face as she stood from the bale.

"What are you doing here?" Her voice was hoarse.

"I live here. That is, if you'll let me."

Ally opened her mouth as if to say something but instead shook her head.

Seth approached her, placing his hands on her shoulders.

"Things that might have once seemed impossible can happen, Ally. I'm in love with you," he said, lifting one hand to stroke her hair from her face. "I didn't expect it to happen, but it did. I want you to marry me for real and have my babies and be with me the rest of my life. I don't care if it's here or in California or anywhere else in this world as long as you're there. You are my home. You are my world. If you'll give me a chance, I know we can make it work."

He stepped back and raised her face to his. "How about it? Are you up for a challenge?"

"Are you sure, Seth? Are you sure I'm what you want?"

"I've never been more sure of anything in my life."

Her tears began to roll down her face. "Then, yes," she whispered. "Oh, yes." He held her close while he kissed her, over and over, cupping her face, unable to get close enough.

"I love you, Seth Masters," she murmured against his fevered lips. Then she whispered, "Welcome home."

* * * * *

COMING SOON!

We really hope you enjoyed reading this book. If you're looking for more romance, be sure to head to the shops when new books are available on

Thursday 16th May

To see which titles are coming soon, please visit

millsandboon.co.uk/nextmonth

Want even more
ROMANCE?

Join our bookclub today!

'Mills & Boon books, the perfect way to escape for an hour or so.'

Miss W. Dyer

'Excellent service, promptly delivered and very good subscription choices.'

Miss A. Pearson

'You get fantastic special offers and the chance to get books before they hit the shops'

Mrs V. Hall

Visit millsandbook.co.uk/Bookclub and save on brand new books.

MILLS & BOON